THE CASTLE OF OTRANTO

and

THE MYSTERIOUS MOTHER

D1073301

THE CASTLE OF OTRANTO
A GOTHIC STORY

and

THE MYSTERIOUS MOTHER
A TRAGEDY

Horace Walpole

edited by Frederick S. Frank

broadview literary texts

National Library of Canada Cataloguing in Publication

Walpole, Horace, 1717-1797
 The castle of Otranto: a gothic story, and, The mysterious mother: a tragedy / Horace
Walpole; edited by Frederick S. Frank.

(Broadview literary texts)
Includes bibliographical references.
ISBN 1-55111-304-X

I. Frank, Frederick S. II. Title. III. Series. IV. Title: The mysterious mother.
PR3757.W2C3 2002   828´.609   C2002-905134-7

Broadview Press Ltd. is an independent, international publishing house, incorporated in
1985. Broadview believes in shared ownership, both with its employees and with the general public; since the year 2000 Broadview shares have traded publicly on the Toronto
Venture Exchange under the symbol BDP.

We welcome comments and suggestions regarding any aspect of our publications–please
feel free to contact us at the addresses below or at broadview@broadviewpress.com.

North America
PO Box 1243, Peterborough, Ontario, Canada K9J 7H5
3576 California Road, Orchard Park, NY, USA 14127
Tel: (705) 743-8990; Fax: (705) 743-8353
email: customerservice@broadviewpress.com

UK, Ireland, and continental Europe
Thomas Lyster Ltd., Units 3 & 4a, Old Boundary Way
Burscough Road, Ormskirk
Lancashire, L39 2YW
Tel: (01695) 575112; Fax: (01695) 570120
email: books@tlyster.co.uk

Australia and New Zealand
UNIREPS, University of New South Wales
Sydney, NSW, 2052
Tel: 61 2 9664 0999; Fax: 61 2 9664 5420
email: info.press@unsw.edu.au

www.broadviewpress.com

Broadview Press Ltd. gratefully acknowledges the financial support of the Government of
Canada through the Book Publishing Industry Development Program for our publishing
activities.
This book is printed on acid-free paper containing 30% post-consumer fibre.

Series editor: Professor L.W. Conolly
Advisory editor for this volume: Colleen Franklin
Text design and composition: George Kirkpatrick

PRINTED IN CANADA

EcoLogo Certified, 30% Post.

Horace Walpole, 1759

Contents

Acknowledgements

I wish to express my gratitude to several people and institutions for their assistance and guidance in the preparation of this book. Thanks to Professor Julie Hayes of the University of Richmond for putting me in touch with important critical material on *The Mysterious Mother* at an early stage of the project. Thanks to Professor Douglass H. Thomson of Georgia Southern University and Professor James C. Bulman of Allegheny College for their generous erudition and support. I am deeply indebted to Professor Jean-Paul Carton of Georgia Southern University for contributing expert English translations of all of the French passages from Walpole's correspondence and other writings. The staffs of several libraries also responded magnanimously to my numerous requests for information. I thank the Rare Book Department of the Alderman Library, University of Virginia, and its curator, Kathryn Morgan; the Lewis Walpole Library of Yale University, Farmington, Connecticut, and its curator, Margaret Powell; and the entire staff of the Pelletier Library of Allegheny College, Meadville, Pennsylvania for their many services and favors. I must also recognize the patience and expertise of three Broadview Press editors, Barbara Conolly, Leonard Conolly, and the vigilant copy editor, Colleen Franklin. As always, my wife Nancy Frank has helped my work in infinite ways that can never fully be repaid.

List of Illustrations

Introduction

"That Long Labyrinth of Darkness": *The Castle of Otranto*

The first Gothic novel and the first Gothic drama were the inventions of Horace Walpole, dilettante, socialite, and patron of the medieval revival that permeated the arts of architecture and literature in the 1750s. While the novel enjoyed an immediate success following its publication at Walpole's private press at Strawberry Hill and quickly established itself as the prototype for the Gothic novel, the play fell into scandalous obscurity, was never acted, and was printed only in limited editions during Walpole's lifetime. *The Castle of Otranto* has never been out of print while *The Mysterious Mother*, as a comparative study of the publication history of these two pivotal Gothic texts will reveal, "has remained oddly secret long after political or gender-based criticism might have been expected to recover it."[1] This edition marks only the third printing of the play in the twentieth and twenty-first centuries, a strange oversight given the excess of Gothic studies and general interest in the revival of obscure and neglected Gothics since the 1950s.

Both the novel and the play expressed the new Romantic impulse to reclaim the strange, the exotic, the savage, the improbable, the mysterious, and the supernatural as legitimate zones of artistic pleasure. These corridors to a forbidden sublime were made accessible again by a speculative Gothic that opened the door to an alternative universe of pleasing horror and of psychic and social disorder whose very existence had been denied or consigned to a dead past by Augustan value systems. By elevating feeling over thought, *The Castle of Otranto* and *The Mysterious Mother* gratified the timeless human need for inhuman and superhuman things, a need that had been ignored or suppressed by the decorous standards of the Enlightenment. The poetry of the

---

1 Paul Baines, "'This Theatre of Monstrous Guilt': Horace Walpole and the Drama of Incest." *Studies in Eighteenth-Century Culture* 28 (1999): 287. The curious absence of modern editions of *The Mysterious Mother* has been redressed by the inclusion of the play edited by Baines in *Five Romantic Plays, 1768-1821* (Oxford & New York: Oxford UP, 2000).

Graveyard Group, the novels of Samuel Richardson, Henry Mackenzie, and Laurence Sterne, and the aesthetic theories of Edmund Burke and Bishop Richard Hurd as well as the eccentric architectural extravaganzas of the Gothic Revivalists directly addressed this need.

Both the novel and the drama were natural projections of Walpole's clever promotion of private notions of Gothic architecture with its hyperbolic tendencies, odd and wild ornamentation, rude irregularity and deliberate disharmony, and infinite opportunities for self-indulgence and self-dramatization. The movement away from classical symmetry toward a flamboyant display of disparate parts manifested itself in Walpole's conversion of an ordinary Georgian house into a Gothic fantasy villa and sham castle at Strawberry Hill on the upper Thames. Replete with disproportionate towers, absurd plaster battlements, cloistered interiors and a plethora of pointed arches, the Strawberry Hill project represented the first fullfillment of the Gothic imagination in artificial stone a decade well in advance of the composition of the novel and play. Thus, both the novel and the drama were, in a sense, imaginatively composed before the fact in Walpole's architectural fantasizing throughout the 1750s as his little castle became one of the prime curiosities of the Gothic Revival. Walpole's purpose in both his architectural and literary Gothicizing was to secure freedom from the ennui and malaise engendered by neoclassic order and form. "When life is fierce and uncertain," Sir Kenneth Clark explains in *The Gothic Revival*, "the imagination craves for classical repose. But as society becomes tranquil, the imagination is starved of action and the immensely secure society of the eighteenth century indulged in daydreams of incredible violence."[1] Walpole's statement in the Preface to the second edition of the novel that "The great resources of fancy have been dammed up by strict adherence to common life," seems to expose just such a frustration with the normal and the natural that led him to try out the Gothic style, first in the reconstruction of Strawberry Hill and

---

1   Sir Kenneth Clark. "Ruins and Rococo: Strawberry Hill," in *The Gothic Revival: An Essay in the History of Taste*, 1928 (Harmondsworth, UK:.Penguin, 1962), 36. Clark refers to Walpole's castle as "dramatized decay."

then in the writing of *The Castle of Otranto* and *The Mysterious Mother* where he realized his monstrous daydreams, transposing architectural fantasies of "gloomth" into the literary reality of the first Gothic novel and Gothic play. (The word "gloomth" was used by Walpole in his letters to express pleasure in the gloomy aspects of medieval buildings, "the gloomth of abbeys and cathedrals." For a discussion of "gloomth," see David D. McKinney, *The Imprints of Gloomth*, 1765-1830. Charlottesville, VA: Alderman Library, 1988.)

Corresponding with his fellow antiquarian on the motives underlying his urge to Gothicize, Walpole told Sir Horace Mann precisely what his reasons were for superimposing a medieval building style and a vocabulary of "gloomth" on the dull regularities of modern life: "I perceive you have no idea what Gothic is; you have lived too long amidst true taste, to understand venerable barbarism. You say, 'you suppose my garden is to be Gothic too.' That can't be; Gothic is merely architecture; and as one has a satisfaction of imprinting the gloomth of abbeys and cathedrals on one's house, so one's garden on the contrary is to be nothing but riant, and the gaiety of nature."[1] Quite clearly at this stage, Walpole equated Gothicism with exhibitionism. By the time he came to write *The Castle of Otranto*, his Gothicizing was no longer "merely architecture" but an attitude of discontent reflecting the subconscious fears and desires of an age grown too fond of reason and beginning to question its own empirical assumptions. Appealing as it did to the "venerable barbarism" of one of the most civilized men of letters of the eighteenth century, the Gothic asserted itself as the literature of collapsing structures, malign enclosures, dark passions, and supernatural chaos. The foundations of *The Castle of Otranto* were laid from the moment when Walpole, with the assistance and encouragement of his friends Richard Bentley and John Chute, began to redesign Strawberry Hill into a fullblown medieval fortress that became the catalyst for the bizarre tale of aviating helmets, mobile portraits, subterranean flights and pursuits and supernatural alarms and diversions. While

---

1   Horace Walpole, Letter to Sir Horace Mann, 27 April 1753. *Horace Walpole's Correspondence*, Ed. Wilmarth S. Lewis (New Haven: Yale UP, 1937-83), Vol. 20: 372.

musing over his architectural bauble, Walpole experienced a nightmare in which he dreamt he saw a gigantic hand in armor above the bannister of a staircase within an ancient castle. The iron hand became the surreal inspiration for the novel. Walpole recounted in a letter to his friend William Cole just how his eerie dream had been transmuted almost automatically into a "Gothic story":

> I had time to write but a short note with *The Castle of Otranto*, as your messenger called on me at four o'clock as I was going to dine abroad. Your partiality to me and Strawberry have I hope inclined you to excuse the wildness of the story. You will even have found some traits to put you in mind of this place. When you read of the picture quitting its panel, did you recollect the portrait of Lord Falkland all in white in my gallery? Shall I even confess to you what was the origin of this romance? I waked one morning in the beginning of last June from a dream, of which all I could recover was, that I had thought myself in an ancient castle (a very natural dream for a head filled like mine with Gothic story) and that on the uppermost bannister of a great staircase I saw a gigantic hand in armour. In the evening I sat down and began to write, without knowing in the least what I intended to say or relate. The work grew on my hands, and I grew fond of it—add that I was very glad to think of anything rather than politics—In short I was so engrossed with my tale, which I completed in less than two months, that one evening I wrote from the time I had drunk my tea, about six o'clock, till half an hour after one in the morning, when my hand and fingers were so weary, that I could not hold the pen to finish the sentence, but left Matilda and Isabella talking, in the middle of a paragraph.[1]

The vision of the huge hand crystallized Walpole's desire to reconfigure his passion for Gothic architecture into the narrative

---

[1] Horace Walpole, Letter to William Cole, 9 March 1765. *Horace Walpole's Correspondence*, Vol. 1: 88.

excitement of a new kind of romance that would combine the ancient with the modern. The power of the originating night-mare also had a strong basis in the various theories and philosophical justifications of a new aesthetic of the sublime based on the paradoxical connection between fear and pleasure. Such a Gothic aesthetic had been propounded by Edmund Burke and had been elaborated by the discourse of Bishop Hurd on the value of Gothic romance. In *Letters on Chivalry and Romance*, Hurd had asked: "May there not be something in Gothic romance peculiarly suited to the views of a genius, and to the ends of poetry? And may not the philosophic moderns have gone too far, in their perpetual ridicule and contempt of it?" (Letter I, 317). Although Walpole never mentions by name Edmund Burke's treatise on the aesthetics of horror, *A Philosophical Enquiry into the Origin of Our Ideas of the Sublime and Beautiful* (1757), *The Castle of Otranto* and *The Mysterious Mother* demonstrate an application of Burke's theories of the pleasing power of fear and the sublimity of terror. Optimal pleasure in the horrid, Burke had posited, arose out of a confrontation with objects and events with which the mind could not rationally cope. Elsewhere, he argued for the sublime's power in neutralizing the reasoning faculties while intensifying a sensory appreciation of awesome objects that overwhelmed the observer. "The mind is so entirely filled with its object that it cannot entertain any other, nor by consequence reason on that object which employs it. Hence arises the great power of the sublime that hurries us on by an irresistible force."[1] The first Gothic novel and drama abound in situations that place the characters in confrontations with Burkean objects designed to displace or diminish reason. Confronted by portraits that come alive and walk, statues that bleed, walls that seem tumescent with some gigantic body seeking egress, the characters are given repeated opportunities to test Burke's idea that dreadful astonishment could be a necessary aspect of an object's beautiful qualities, and furthermore, that such sublimity was often heightened and intensified by its very gruesomeness and fearfulness.

---

1 Edmund Burke, *A Philosophical Enquiry into the Origin of Our Ideas of the Sublime and Beautiful*, 1757 (Notre Dame, IN & London: Notre Dame P, 1968), Part II, Section 1, 57.

When *The Castle of Otranto* was published at his private print-ing press (the Officina Arbuteana) at Strawberry Hill on Christ-mas Eve 1764, Walpole self-consciously concealed his authorship behind two antithethical pseudonyms. Uneasy over the novel's public reception, Walpole counterfeited his authorship in the Preface to the first edition, in which readers were told that the book had been recovered from an Italian manuscript set down by the monastic chronicler, Onuphrio Muralto, Canon of the Church of St. Nicholas at Otranto, and later rendered into Eng-lish by that scholarly gentleman, William Marshal, whose anti-quarian zeal to recover the Gothic past closely resembled Horace Walpole's own exuberance for "venerable barbarism." Thus we have in the two names William Marshal and Onuphrio Muralto Walpole's two alter-egos, the polite gentleman-scholar of the Age of Reason and the medieval man of the dark ages. In the Preface to the second edition, Walpole abandoned these poses, declared his authorship, and cited invulnerable examples from Shake-speare's plays to justify his methods of characterization and tragi-comic mixture of styles. He also affixed the capitalized adjective "Gothic" to the subtitle of the novel, perhaps recalling Bishop Hurd's earlier use of the phrase "Gothic romance." Because of its disgraceful connotations for the eighteenth-century mind, Wal-pole's description of his novel as a "Gothic Story" was a bold choice, for it both enticed the curious reader and captured the essence of the form in a single word, later proving itself to be one of the most durable literary labels ever attached to a particular kind of fiction. The bogus authorship of the first edition was a favorite game of eighteenth-century writers, but in Walpole's case, the double pseudonym was protective as well as diverting. By giving free vent to the Gothic impulse in the composition of his novel, Walpole had risked his reputation as a man of taste, refinement, and social standing. Reassured by the success of the hoaxing first edition, Walpole emerged from behind the medieval and modern pen-names to announce his authorship and take his bows. The denotations and connotations of the adjective "Goth-ic" were changing as the aesthetic *Zeitgeist* itself changed, and Walpole, keenly aware of the word's heightened value, cleverly exploited it as a thrilling descriptor. Gothic implied not just something medieval, barbarous, and ignorantly superstitious, but something mysterious and strangely attractive, a password to an alternative universe to which entry had been forestalled by the neoclassic outlook. The word "Gothic" would later become the catch-all signifier for the horror tale, its current usage evincing the brilliance of Walpole's choice. Adhering closely to Walpole's master plan, Gothic spaces would contain claustrophobic victimization within "a vault totally dark." An outrageous new first law of motion (or more accurately, commotion) replaced Newtonian laws of motion as seen in the arrival of the Brobdingnagian helmet; this law states that the deader or more inanimate an object is supposed to be, the more likely it is to move, to feel, to think, and to exert its own peculiar supernatural jurisdiction over events and people in the natural world. In fact, it is the unnatural or supernatural sentience of space and place, the total inorganic hyperactivity and material ghostliness of the haunted castle and its chambers of horror, that very nearly *is* the Gothic at this point in its development.

From the descent of the enormous helmet atop the hapless Conrad, the novel's initial supernatural jolt, to the shattering of the castle walls by the immense and reinvigorated anatomy of Alfonso, Walpole crafted his Gothic so as to achieve a dismantling of reason within dark enclosures, where readers might feel as lost and disoriented as the entrapped characters, but also find pleasure in such sequestration and helplessness. Referring to terror as the "principal engine" or driving force of his story, Walpole designed a plot consisting of an inlaid system of macabre contraptions, weird acoustics, and mobile spectral props installed throughout a Gothic castle where normal laws of gravity gave way to the occupancy of "extraordinary positions" (*Otranto*, Preface to the Second Edition, 65) that were soon to become the hallmarks of the Gothic experience. The enclosure of the characters also extended to their circumvention by "a constant vicissitude of interesting passions" (*Otranto*, Preface to the First Edition, 60).

The Prefaces to the first two editions of *The Castle of Otranto* stand as manifestos of the technology and psychology of future tales of terror. Both Prefaces offer criteria for the future construction of catastrophic narrative. In an aptly chosen metaphor, Walpole's reference to terror as "the author's principal engine" (*Otranto*, Preface to the First Edition, 60) anticipates the mechanistic format of the Gothic plot, the gearworks of supernatural devices that would come to characterize Gothic action. The operation of the castle's infernal machinery ensured the level of terror needed to locate the inmates of the castle in "extraordinary positions" such as the predicament of the mangled and crushed Conrad beneath the fallen helmet on the first page of the novel. Walpole did not provide specific examples of "extraordinary positions," just as he did not state precisely what he meant by "interesting passions," but clearly at the top of the list of such positions and passions is the characters' sexual consternation. As the Gothic grew from Walpole's prototype, an "extraordinary position" for a castle prisoner might be either physical or psychological or both. Conrad's spectacular death in the lethal landing zone of an enormous helmet is entirely physical, but later "extraordinary positions" might be both physical and psychological such as that of the victim in Poe's "The Pit and the Pendulum" where both mind and body are menaced *in extremis*.

The falling (or more accurately, descending) helmet disrupts all natural law and introduces a cosmic disorder that cannot be redressed. In the absence of a cogent, deistic God, Otranto's prime mover is a huge but empty headpiece grotesquely alive and disturbingly mobile. Manfred's reaction to the absurd execution of his son and heir by the flying helmet illustrates the process of desacralization that will occur regularly throughout the novel whereby a deific icon—in this case, the god's head—is transformed into an atheistic icon—a headless void in armor—while retaining and even increasing its previous godlike force. The crushing of Conrad is not the righteous intervention of God but some odd revenge from the godless void. Manfred takes "the miracle of the helmet" as a portent of some savage and meaningless power. Rather than contemplating the meaning behind the event, Manfred is obsessed with the ghostly materiality of the helmet itself exactly in the manner of an overawed Burkean observer:

He beheld his child dashed to pieces, and almost buried under an enormous helmet, an hundred times more large than any casque ever made for human being, and shaded with a proportionable quantity of black feathers. The horror of the spectacle, the ignorance of all around how this misfortune happened, and above all, the tremendous phænomenon before him, took away the prince's speech. Yet his silence lasted longer than even grief could occasion. He fixed his eyes on what he wished in vain to believe a vision; and seemed less attentive to his loss, than buried in meditation on the stupendous object that had occasioned it. He touched, he examined the fatal casque; nor could even the bleeding mangled remains of the young prince divert the eyes of Manfred from the portent before him. All who had known his partial fondness for young Conrad, were as much surprised at their prince's insensibility, as thunderstuck themselves at the miracle of the helmet. They conveyed the disfigured corpse into the hall, without receiving the least direction from Manfred (*Otranto*, 74-75).

Although the castle is not in ruins at the outset of the story as is the case with many Gothic works to follow, its stability is illusory, just as its legitimate ownership is in doubt. Marked for a fall, Walpole's castle would become Gothic literature's first unstable and unsafe world in which irrational forces are in control. The novel's resolution in favor of the supernatural presents the colossal specter of Alfonso the Good bursting through the castle's foundations, and in so doing, obliterating the rational defenses of the reader. The first Gothic ruin created by coalescent supernatural forces suggests the shift from reason to feeling, from unity to fragmentation, from stability to collapse, from classical stasis to romantic kinesis, and from natural to supernatural that marked the period and defined the goals of the early Gothicists as deistic equipoise gave way to romantic agitation. Reflecting this shift in values is the castle itself, the most potent personality in the cast of the novel. More than simply a dark stage set for the villain's persecution of the maiden, the biologized castle has a body and a mind of its own. It responds to Manfred's erotic villainy and concealment of paternal crime with all the vigor of a revitalized corpse stirring to life. The intricate stratification of the castle with its own heaven and hell and its interior networked with secret corridors spiraling inward and downward to secret compartments are features that suggest the mysterious structure of the mind. Commenting on the imagery of the haunted castle, Elizabeth MacAndrew draws an analogy between the interior of the castle and the interior of the mind under stress: "A dire and threatening place, it remains more than a dwelling. It starts out as a stone representation of the dark, tortured windings in the mind of those eminently civilized, and therefore unnatural vices, ambition and cruelty; it bears the whole weight of the ages of man's drift away from an ideal state; and it becomes a lasting representation of the torments of the subconscious pressing upon the conscious mind and making a prison of the self."[1] Once the goal of grail knights as well as the sanctum of high religious mystery, the castle now becomes a place of supernatural danger no longer associated with refuge and redemption but a type of hell where "nobody is entirely safe; nothing is secure."[2] The subterranean compartments of the castle equate symbolically with the subconscious aspects of the self, and loss of way with loss of mind. The primary function of the characters is just that— to lose their way, their misdirection imaged by their entrapment within the castle maze. The gropings of the hero-villain and heroine deep within the hell of the castle suggest spiritual perplexity and disenchantment as the Gothicist's vision involves a repudiation of all norms, ontological, epistemological, ethical, and aesthetic. The maze of dark, twisting passageways underlying the Castle refers iconographically to the terminal "amazement" of the characters. To the idea of the castle as symbolic of the imprisoned self can be added the historical implications of the castle's fragility, for like the bastions of reason erected by the Enlightenment, it is a doomed social structure, seemingly solid but decaying within and about to explode. Rich in symbolic possibilities as well as the power to astonish and amaze, the Castle of Otranto's basement becomes the Gothic novel's recurrent bad place for the staging of Gothic terror:

1   Elizabeth MacAndrew, *The Gothic Tradition in Fiction* (New York: Columbia UP, 1979), 48-49.
2   Ann B. Tracy, *The Gothic Novel 1790-1830: Plot Summaries and Index to Motifs* (Lexington: UP of Kentucky, 1981), 3.

The lower part of the castle was hollowed into several intricate cloisters; and it was not easy for one under so much anxiety to find the door that opened into the cavern. An awful silence reigned throughout those subterraneous regions, except now and then some blasts of wind that shook the doors she had passed, and which grating on the rusty hinges were re-echoed through that long labyrinth of darkness (*Otranto*, 82).

Next in importance to the personality of the castle in Walpole's Gothic cast is the very human superman, Manfred, a Gothic hero with no face as yet described at this stage in the character's development. A figure of great potential virtue, he has a certain magnificence and heroic stature warped by dark passions and twisted by dark motives. His lust for power and perverted moral energy are similar to Milton's Satan, while his domestic savagery carries reminders of many of the sexually-driven hero-villains of the Elizabethan and Jacobean blood tragedies, especially Shakespeare's Macbeth, a castle tyrant also driven by "black and deep desires."[1] Never totally degenerate, Manfred has been tainted by a corrupt family line, and his maliciousness seems to be a result of a divided nature continually at war with itself; he is, like Goethe's Faust, a tormented man within whom "two souls in one breast contend."[2] Although Manfred lacks the contorted brow and evil eye of later Gothic villains, he exhibits most of the mental traits of the Gothic's half-evil protagonists. Walpole endeavored to give his tormented tormentor some morally ambivalent qualities when he described Manfred as a man who was "naturally humane when his passions did not obscure his reason" (*Otranto*, 87). Throughout the story, Manfred is driven by base passions, making him the ancestor of the Byronic hero,[3] whose vices are often his virtues in reverse and whose defiance of fate and commitment to evil has heroic overtones. When Manfred calls himself as "a man of many

---

1 William Shakespeare, *Macbeth*. I. iv. 52.
2 Johann Wolfgang von Goethe, *Faust: A Tragedy*, trans. Bayard Taylor (New York: Modern Library, 1950). The Taylor translation reads: "Two souls, alas! reside within my breast, / And each withdraws from, and repels its brother (Part I, Scene II, 39)."
3 For a study of the Gothic villain as forerunner of the Byronic hero, see: Peter Thorslev, Jr., *The Byronic Hero: Types and Prototypes*, Minneapolis: U of Minnesota P, 1962).

sorrows," (*Otranto*, 121) he forecasts the *Weltschmerz* and meta-physical exasperation later to be seen in the half-evil heroes of the Romantic period. Never completely delighting in his evil, Manfred is the progenitor of Gothic literature's strangely fascinating race of fallen creatures whose bondage to a mouldering feudal building signifies both their devastated inner condition and their enslavement to exhausted ideals of power. Although Manfred may appear to possess the Kingdom of Otranto and to control its interior affairs, it is Otranto that possesses and torments him.

Manfred's villainy is directed against the two Gothic maidens condemned to reside in perpetual suspense in the gloomy chambers of Otranto. Isabella and Matilda are the forerunners of the menaced maidens of countless Gothic thrillers who spend most of their lives in subterranean distress in the Gothic underworld. One of the two, Manfred's daughter, Matilda, is Gothic literature's first victim of a homicidal father. The other persecuted maiden, Isabella, is little more than a focal point for Manfred's erotic urges and despotic scheming, her principal function being to give Manfred the opportunity to fulfill his legacy of evil by pursuing the maiden through "that long labyrinth of darkness." Flight and pursuit in an underground setting is a repeated pattern of emergency for Isabella, but the rhetoric used in describing her Gothic panics sometimes spills over into a sardonic sense of the ridiculous. As she descends through a series of trapdoors and screams on cue, Isabella's hysterics during her flight from Manfred sometimes turn from crisis into comedy as in this stroke of witty doubletakes: "'Oh, heavens!' cried Isabella, 'it is the voice of Manfred! Make haste, or we are ruined! And shut the trap-door after you'" (*Otranto*, 85). Yet, this scene becomes mandatory in what will later be called "the female Gothic." To Walpole must go the credit for first staging the collision of villain and maiden, while Isabella's desperation as she seeks an exit from the hell of the castle to a domestic Eden outside its walls remains the formula for success of the Gothic romance throughout the history of the form. Isabella's rescuer, the virtuous Theodore, like other good young men in Gothic fiction, hardly matters and is ineffectual although necessary to the plot's genealogical dénouement.

Like so much Romantic art, *The Castle of Otranto* is also an intense personal expression of the artist's buried emotional life, an ersatz journal of secret sexual tensions and anxieties. Some recent readings of *The Castle of Otranto* and *The Mysterious Mother* explain Walpole's compulsion to Gothicize as a way of confronting his homosexuality, masculine inadequacies, and lifelong sublimated fear of the father, Sir Robert Walpole, the most powerful politician in England. The novel has been scrutinized as a psychoanalytic dossier by Betsy Perteit Harfst[1] while other Freudian critics have found it to reveal "a psychobiographic record of parricidal guilts and fears, homosexual longings and drives, castration phobias, and Œdipal desires. Manfred's sexual frenzy and violent self-assertion are in some significant ways connected to Walpole's own suppressed or misdirected anger and contempt."[2] The stunning contrast of the novel's various Gothic parts, for example, the sexual puniness of the crushed son and heir, Conrad, juxtaposed to the huge and overwhelming form of Alfonso, and the peculiar affection of Manfred for the male child (Conrad) as against his indifference to the female (Matilda), are among the data that invite such readings, raising as they do, issues of potency and sexual worthiness.

Without denying the psychological validity of the subtexts in *The Castle of Otranto*, it is its hardware of horror that remains Walpole's most enduring achievement and contribution. The durability of such hardware can be seen in Walpole's mastery of those type-scenes that recur throughout the Gothic tradition. One such type-scene is Frederic of Vicenza's encounter with the hooded monk in Isabella's chapel. The scene demonstrates the transition from terror to horror or from faith to doubt when a character is moved from something dreaded to the appalling realization that the dreadful thing that confronts him is real. While investigating the chambers of Otranto in search of the missing Hippolita, Frederic comes upon a robed figure kneeling before an altar. The meeting that follows becomes a regular event in Gothic fiction when the figure slowly turns to reveal a skeletal face. A

---

1 Betsy Perteit Harfst, *Horace Walpole and the Unconscious: An Experiment in Freudian Analysis* (New York: Arno P, 1980).

2 George Haggerty, "Literature and Homosexuality in the Late Eighteenth Century: Walpole, Beckford, and Lewis." *Studies in the Novel* 18 (1986): 342. Reprinted in *Homosexual Themes in Literary Studies*. Eds. Wayne R. Dynes, Stephen Donaldson. New York: Garland, 1992: 167-178.

famous cinematic version of this terrible turn occurs in *The Phantom of the Opera* (1925) with the unmasking of the Phantom at the organ. Perhaps Walpole's introduction of this jolt-scene lacks the horrific effect it would attain in later adaptations. Yet the scene itself is fully installed and ready for future use as an inverted conversion episode during which a believer is forced to abandon his beliefs and is compelled to religious doubt by the icon of the grinning skull. When Frederic gazes directly into the hollow sockets of the death's head he is forced to accept the cynical substantiality of a man of God now become the first of Gothic literature's animated skeletons. Like Manfred when faced with the monstrous void of the headless helmet, Frederic's confrontation with an icon of appalling nothingness whose most horrifying aspect is its hollowness gruesomely mocks the anticipated religious ideal:

> The marquis was about to return, when the figure rising, stood some moments fixed in meditation, without regarding him. The marquis, expecting the holy person to come forth, and meaning to excuse his uncivil interruption, said, "Reverend Father, I sought the Lady Hippolita." —"Hippolita!" replied a hollow voice, "camest thou to this castle to seek Hippolita?" And then the figure, turning slowly round, discovered to Frederic the fleshless jaws and empty sockets of a skeleton, wrapt in a hermit's cowl (*Otranto*, 156-157).

Fitted out with effective contraptions of this sort, it is plain to see why *The Castle of Otranto* became the convenient dynamo to which later Gothic writers found it convenient to connect their own trappings of terror. From its inception, enthusiasm for the Gothic would derive in no small part from its audiovisual gadgetry of shock and horror. From its survival in the Gothics of Radcliffe, Lewis, Maturin, Mary Shelley, Poe, and Hawthorne to its abiding presence in H. P. Lovecraft, Stephen King, and Joyce Carol Oates in the twentieth century, Walpole's model remains a steady source of Gothic energy. H. P. Lovecraft, who pronounced *The Castle of Otranto* "flat, stilted, and altogether devoid of true cosmic horror," did not dismiss Walpole's accomplishments. "All this paraphernalia appears with amusing sameness, yet sometimes with tremendous effect, throughout the history of the Gothic novel; and is by no means extinct even today, though subtler technique now forces it to assume a less naive and obvious form."[1]

By replacing the rationalist's dream of bliss with Gothicist's nightmare, Walpole had dared "to disturb the universe" by raising a terrifying new hypothesis about existence itself that can be stated in the form of a question: what if all traditional norms of reality,— psychic, social, cultural, and spiritual, turned out to be illusory and self-deceiving, mere flickering horror images on the walls of the Platonic cave? Such a tormented scepticism coupled with the startled awareness of a contrarian cosmos becomes the basis for much of the terror and horror of later Gothic fiction. In the fall of the House of Otranto at the climax and the rise of the massive figure of Alfonso "dilated to an immense magnitude ... in the centre of the ruins" (*Otranto*, 162) there can be felt the reverberations of what a later and greater master of the Gothic, Edgar Allan Poe, would call the "terrors of the soul."[2] Subsequently, the deepening Gothic of *The Mysterious Mother* would surpass *The Castle of Otranto* by drying the tears of the rationalists with hellfire and damnation.

"Hear, hell, and tremble!—thou didst clasp thy mother!": *The Mysterious Mother*

Written four years after *The Castle of Otranto*, *The Mysterious Mother* was published in 1768 in a limited edition of fifty copies at Walpole's Strawberry Hill Press. Because its subject was incest, Walpole chose his audience carefully by circulating the play only among close friends, never permitting it to be performed except as a closet drama or private theatricale. "The subject is so horrid,"

---

1   H.P. Lovecraft, *Supernatural Horror in Literature*,1927 (New York: Dover, 1966), 26.

2   Edgar Allan Poe, "Preface to Tales of the Grotesque and Arabesque," in *Collected Works of Edgar Allan Poe*, eds. Thomas Ollive Mabbott, Eleanor D. Kewer, Maureen C. Mabbott, (Cambridge: Belknap P of Harvard U, 1969), I, 362. Poe's exact statement is: "If in many of my productions terror has been the thesis, I maintain that terror is not of Germany, but of the soul,—that I have deduced this terror only from its legitimate sources, and urged it only to its legitimate results." By "Terror ... of Germany," Poe refers to *Schauerromane* or "Shudder novels."

he wrote in the play's Postscript, "that I thought it would shock, rather than give satisfaction to an audience," (*Mysterious Mother*, 251) but this disclaimer is somewhat misleading since it is obvious from Walpole's letters that he did not regard his play as morally unfit for the stage, telling George Montagu of his "wish to see it acted." It was fear of being accused of indelicacy, not the repellent theme of incest, that prohibited Walpole from putting *The Mysterious Mother* on public display in the same way that he had exhibited his Gothic in his home at Strawberry Hill and his novel. As he declared in the Postscript, the play's moral content was legitimate even if it violated the stage standards of his own age: "The moral resulting from the calamities attendant on an unbounded passion, even to the destruction of the criminal person's race, was obviously suited to the purpose and object of tragedy" (*Mysterious Mother*, 251). By placing natural characters in unnatural circumstances, Walpole generated psychological tension through intense pictures of familial victimization and secret guilt, thus creating the paradigmatic Gothic drama of internecine family conflict and sexual depravity.

Walpole was aware that he was working within a well-established theatrical tradition in choosing incest as the subject. Numerous references to Sophocles's *Oedipus Tyrannus* indicate that he wished to provide *The Mysterious Mother* with a clearcut precedent in classical tragedy. He was also acquainted with the incest tragedies of the Elizabethan, Jacobean, and Restoration dramatists, plays such as Francis Beaumont and John Fletcher's *A King and no King* (1611), John Ford's *'Tis Pity She's a Whore* (1633), and John Dryden's *Don Sebastian* (1689) with their situations of sibling and parental incest. Racine's *Phèdre*, a tragedy of maternal lust based on Euripides's *Hippolytus*, also caught Walpole's interest in its presentation of a mother's unconquerable desire for her son-in-law. Shakespeare's tragedies, particularly *Hamlet* with its haunted castle, violated specter of the father, incestuous mother figure, and sexual undercurrents dominating the center of the plot, also stimulated Walpole's imagination. But Walpole's most significant modification of the incest play involved his encrypting of the deed itself, its being withheld from the audience, as the Countess's concupiscence remained hidden until the final scene. The theme of the tragedy is placed in the mouth of one of the minor characters, Friar Martin, who asks the unbearable question: "What is this secret sin, this untold tale, That art cannot extract, nor penance cleanse?" (I.iii: 13-14).

The play was included in the 1798 collected edition of *The Works of Horatio Walpole*, but was not edited, studied or even admitted into the Gothic canon until the twentieth century. In Walpole's own day, it shocked Fanny Burney, who found its theme of "voluntary guilt ... atrocious and dreadful;" but it apparently did not offend Mrs. Radcliffe, who used the play's opening lines as a stately epigraph for Chapter Two of her novel, *The Romance of the Forest* (1791), then returned to its suspense and gloom in the epigraph for Chapter IV, of the first volume of her novel, *The Italian* (1797).[1] Sir Walter Scott included it in his 1811 collection of plays, *The Modern British Drama*, and Byron, who could often be cynical about the artistic successes of others, ranked *The Mysterious Mother* "a tragedy of the highest order, and not a puling love-play. [Walpole] is the father of the first romance and of the last tragedy in our language."[2] The novelist Mary Meeke showed that Walpole's incest drama still lingered in the popular memory when she used the title to entice the reader of her sentimental thriller, *The Veiled Protectress; or, The Mysterious Mother*, a Gothic novel published in 1819 by the Minerva-Press.

The play's stageworthiness and tragic depth were recognized by its first modern editor, Montague Summers, while later commentators have almost universally pointed out its bonding of the Gothic to the tragic in both diction and form. Summers concluded his Introduction by praising the play's "extraordinary merit ...

---

1 Epigraph from *The Romance of the Forest*, Chapter II reads: "How these antique towers and vacant courts / Chill the suspended soul! Till expectation / Wears the face of fear: and fear, half ready / To become devotion, mutters a kind / Of mental orison, it knows not wherefore. / What a kind of being is circumstance!" (*Mysterious Mother*, I.i: 1-7). Epigraph from *The Italian* reads: "Unfold th' impenetrable mystery, / That sets your soul and you at endless discord." (*Mysterious Mother*, I.v: 88-89). It is also probable that Radcliffe drew upon Walpole's Father Benedict in creating the nefarious profile of Father Schedoni, the confessor/oppressor of Ellena di Rosalba, in *The Italian*.

2 George Gordon, Lord Byron. Preface to *Marino Faliero, Doge of Venice, An Historical Tragedy in Five Acts* in *The Poetical Works of Lord Byron*, (London: Oxford UP, 1957), 408.

The blank verse is nervous and often beautiful; ... I know of no contemporary tragedy, nor, indeed, of any drama during many years before and after, which is in any way comparable to the vigour and spirit that moves these scenes ... The shadowed melancholy that broods over the accursed castle is suggested with the touch of a master."[1] Bertrand Evans, whose pioneering study *Gothic Drama from Walpole to Shelley* inaugurated the first serious study of Gothic theater in the twentieth century, thought that it was "the true beginning of the Gothic school of drama ... Dark word piled on dark word contributes to a mounting sense of gloom and terror ... The tragedy is constructed like a sentence in which each word deepens the mystery ... *The Mysterious Mother* devised a plan for exploiting selected materials, and established a new species."[2] Walpole's preeminent biographer, R.W. Ketton-Cremer, found the play to be full of masterful dramatic tension with its language occasionally rising to "Shakespearean reminiscence ... A nightmare of violent emotion and protracted suspense, it might have been thrown off at fever-heat as was *The Castle of Otranto.* Tense, powerful, and authentic, this extraordinary drama of incestuous passion is unlike anything else that Walpole wrote, and unlike anything else written in his century."[3] The play's most recent editor, Paul Baines, describes it as "an extreme version of incest narrative, even in literary terms.... [probing the] Œdipal dynamics of sex and power ... Its intense portrayal of family trauma, its fascination with verbal power, and its intertextual fusion of Greek and French dramatic material in a new Gothic form"[4] suggest Walpole's commitment to a fusion of the

---

1 Montague Summers, *Introduction* to *The Castle of Otranto* and *The Mysterious Mother* (London: Chiswick Press, Houghton Mifflin and Constable, 1925), lvi. For a view that contests Summer's laudatory estimate, see: Charles Beecher Hogan, "The Theatre of Geo. 3 [George III]" in *Horace Walpole: Writer, Politician, and Connoisseur; Essays on the 250th Anniversary of Walpole's Birth*, ed. Warren Hunting Smith. New Haven and London: Yale UP, 1967: 227-240. "*The Mysterious Mother* is not a satisfactory play because in it nothing, until the curtain is about to fall, happens. As drama, it is static, and its characters, one-dimensional" (232).

2 Bertrand Evans, *Gothic Drama from Walpole to Shelley* (Los Angeles: U of California P, 1947), 39.

3 R.W. Ketton-Cremer, *Horace Walpole: A Biography*, 1940 (Ithaca, NY: Cornell UP, 1964), 233.

4 Baines, "This Theatre of Monstrous Guilt," 287.

Gothic and the tragic. Walpole advances beyond the superficial and sensational Gothic of *The Castle of Otranto* to penetrate the deeper horrors of the soul in reviving one of the exalted themes of classical tragedy, the theme of "the family against itself."[1] Having fully developed the physics of Gothic space and action in *The Castle of Otranto*, Walpole turned his attention to the development of their metaphysics in *The Mysterious Mother*, thus bequeathing to his successors both the external and internal dynamics of Gothic fiction.

Both a solemn and suspenseful pageant of mounting horror and a problem play, *The Mysterious Mother* has strong scenic and dialogic appeal as well as an introspective depth of characterization totally lacking in *The Castle of Otranto*. Its Gothic qualities are almost totally a matter of mental horror and moral stress, a psychodramatic Gothic not dependent on gadgetry to achieve its horrifying picture of a fated family falling into its own private hells. No pictures stray from their frames, no restless helmets descend from the sky, no maidens scurry shrieking through the underground "gloomth," and no supernatural protuberances poke through the castle walls. Only the sinister Castle of Narbonne, the visible architectural symbol of the Countess's sexual secret, survives from the properties kit of *The Castle of Otranto*. With its "antique towers and vacant courts [that] chill the suspended soul, / Till expectation wears the cast of fear," (the play's opening speech, spoken by Florian), the castle has lost none of its power of entrapment, but there is no violent, half-mad tyrant like Manfred lurking within. Nevertheless, as an architectural metaphor for the Countess's concealed crime and Father Benedict's evil machinations, the dark and lonely Castle of Narbonne is a nearly perfect Gothic set. Walpole restricted the supernatural to an atmospheric role in *The Mysterious Mother*, allowing the ominous potency of the weather and the sinister spaces of the Castle of Narbonne to supplement the mounting horror of the incest theme, thus backgrounding the phantasmagoric element that he had foregrounded in *The Castle of Otranto*. As for direct instances of the supernatural in the play, the spectral element is reduced to the residual status of

---

1   Baines, "Introduction: Horace Walpole, *The Mysterious Mother*," in *Five Romantic Plays 1768-1821* (Oxford & New York: Oxford UP, 2000), xi-xiv.

omens, portents, and eerie phenomena. A crucifix topples mysteriously from an altar during a terrible storm and the chorus of orphans trembles at the prospect of the Count's ghost "with clotted locks, and eyes like burning stars" (II.ii.54) lurking about the church porch. Lightning shatters the Count's coat-of-arms, terrifying one of the orphans: "The shield of arms / Shiver'd to splinters. E'er I could repeat / An Ave-Mary, down with hideous crash / The cross came tumbling—then I fled—" (II.ii.114-117). But except for such foreboding touches and offstage acoustics, the Gothic of *The Mysterious Mother* has been almost entirely desupernaturalized.

With physical action and Gothic paraphernalia held to a minimum, the focus shifts totally to the anguished emotional interiors of the characters who undergo that "constant vicissitude of interesting passions" (*Otranto*, 60) that Walpole had recommended in the Preface to *The Castle of Otranto*. The plot relates the last days and suicide of the Countess of Narbonne, the mysterious and incestuous mother of the title. She is known throughout the play only by her aristocratic title of Countess, never by her personal name, a significant fact given the loss of human identity in her brutish fall to carnality. For sixteen years since the death of the Count she has resided in gloomy reclusion within the castle, passing her days in self-mortification and the performance of strange rituals of grief and mourning. While she practices Christian charity by being generous to the poor, praying sincerely, and supporting a local orphanage, she refuses all ministrations of the clergy, not permitting her confessor Father Benedict any access to her tormented soul through confession. It is this resistance to official absolution by the Church, and by extension, a defiance of the Church's power, that has turned Father Benedict into her antagonist and planted the seed of hatred in this determined villain, who conceals his dark motives like Shakespeare's Iago or the Edmund of *King Lear* beneath his "benediction" or "good speech." He connives to gain power over the Countess by prying her secret from her during confession, and failing this, to destroy her and her whole line in some other way. Like future Gothic villains such as Father Schedoni in Radcliffe's *The Italian*, Walpole's monastic Machiavel not only revels in his evil schemes but enjoys verbalizing his wickedness. He brags to Father Martin of his intent to enmesh them all:

> So be it—therefore interest bids us crush
> This cockatrice and her egg: or we shall see
> The singing saints of Savoy's neighb'ring vale
> Fly to the covert of her shadowy wings,
> And foil us at our own dexterity.
> Already to those vagrants she inclines;
> As if the rogues, that preach reform to others,
> Like idiots, minded to reform themselves.
> She is already lost—or ne'er was ours.
> I cannot dupe, and therefore must destroy her;
> Involve her house in ruin so prodigious,
> That neither she nor Edmund may survive it
>
> (IV.i.59-71).

Having surrendered to unspeakable sexual urges, the Countess has deceived her son, Edmund, into sleeping with her out of pure lust, then banished him for having an assignation (or so he has been led to believe) with her maid, Beatrice. But Edmund's partner was his mother, not her maid, thus adding to the gruesome burden of guilt she has borne during his sixteen-year exile since she had punished her son for the very crime of lasciviousness she herself had committed and then concealed. Her terrible crime is compounded by the fact that, never having loved the Count, she lusted after the son and, sated her sexual appetite on the very night of the Count's death. The concealment of her crime is the tragic fulcrum of the play. If *Hamlet* is about the catching of the conscience of a guilt-ridden king and queen living in a castle haunted by a revenge-demanding ghost, *The Mysterious Mother* is Walpole's variation on this traumatic situation, a retelling of the fable of the fall from innocence that requires no additional Gothification to extrapolate its horrors. In her initial interview with Father Benedict, while the wily confessor tries to catch the conscience of the Countess through intimidation and innuendo, she informs him that her character has already determined her fate, and that her damnation is of the here and now, not the hereafter, but temporal and self-inflicted:

> Father, we no prophetic dæmon bear
> Within our breast, but conscience. *That* has spoken
> Words more tremendous than this acted zeal,
> This poetry of fond enthusiasm
> Can conjure up. It is the still small voice
> That breathes conviction. 'Tis that voice has told me,
> 'Twas my son's birth, not his mortality,
> Must drown my soul in woe.—Those tears are shed
>
> (I.v.59–66).

Returning like Orestes to a house polluted, Edmund the unwitting victim of her crime, has come back secretly from the wars to find the castle and his mother afflicted by some inscrutable pall of gloom. When he confronts the Countess with his love for Adeliza, the Countess's ward and the child of incest, she repulses him in a fit of violent passion, unable to break the chain of guilt that is her awful legacy to her sin-stained offspring. The revelation that her incestuous sin is about to repeat itself in the incestuous union of her children drives her to what amounts to an aria-like lament:

> Edmund wed Adeliza! quick, unsay
> The monstrous tale—oh! prodigy of ruin!
> Does my own son then boil with fiercer fires
> Than scorch'd his impious mother's madding veins?
> Did reason reassume its shatter'd throne,
> But as a spectatress of this last of horrors?
> Oh! let my dagger drink my heart's black blood,
> And then present my hell-born progeny
> With drops of kindred sin!—*that* were a torch
> Fit to light up such loves! and fit to quench them!
>
> (V.v.66–75)

Having taken sadistic advantage of the situation to exert his power over the Countess, the vengeful priest has arranged the marriage of Edmund and Adeliza after deceiving the Countess into believing that her ward will wed Florian, Edmund's companion in battle. Throughout these intrigues, Edmund remains unaware that his partner on that fateful night was his mother, and that his destined bride, Adeliza, is both his sister and the daughter of their incestuous liaison, although the terrible facts of the case are certainly in Father Benedict's possession. For him, the problem becomes not how to expose the crime of the Countess, but how to use her guilt to rack her soul by "nurs[ing] her in new horrors" (I.iii.75). What he did not reckon on in all his sinister casuistry is the Countess's self-expiation through suicide.

To prolong and intensify the dual tension created by the Countess's hidden guilt and Benedict's expanding villainy, Walpole withholds all information until the play's final scenes, when the full horror is unveiled. Walpole also departs from the convention of keeping the violence offstage that characterizes the dramaturgy of Sophocles and Euripides, allowing the Countess to stage-manage her suicide with a bloody sensationalism. Her revelation to Edmund is almost a provocation as she finishes what he begins by taking the dagger from him as she "confesses":

> Grief, disappointment, opportunity,
> Rais'd such a tumult in my madding blood,
> I took the damsel's place; and while thy arms
> Twin'd, to thy thinking, round another's waist,
> Hear, hell, and tremble!—thou didst clasp thy mother!
> (V.vi.67-71).

By the end, her incest has become merely the ulterior expression of the deeper evil at large within this ill-fated family. While the Countess's crime against the self is horrible enough, both she and her tormentor Father Benedict remain unredeemed of deeper and more repulsive crimes in their willing violation of the sanctity of the human heart. Both the protagonist and the antagonist damn themselves, and in the process, bring about the damnation of others. At the play's Œedipal climax, both the characters and the audience learn these horrid truths as the Countess stabs herself before Edmund can kill her to bring down the black curtain on what he himself calls, in elegiac despair, "This theatre of monstrous guilt," a bad melodrama in which he had been duped into playing such a monstrous role to drive home the unassuaged horror of it all. For Edmund, as for all others condemned to the castle, there is no exit from this "theatre." Peace of soul, if not a resolution of his mother's malediction, can come for him only through death in battle.

Unlike the first Gothic novel, the first Gothic drama consigns its characters permanently to the outer darkness. *The Mysterious Mother* is not only the darkest work that Walpole himself ever wrote, it is probably the darkest tragedy written on incest or any other subject of sexual transgression in the entire eighteenth century. In later forms of the high Gothic, the soul often dies before the body dies and evil supplants good. Surely, this tragic fact is what moved the publisher of the 1798 edition of the play to celebrate Walpole's achievement in these terms: "Of the present tragedy we may boldly pronounce, that for nervous, simple, and pathetic language, each appropriated to the several persons of the drama; for striking incidents; for address in conducting the plot; and for consistency of character uniformly preserved through the whole piece; it is equal, if not superior, to any play of the present century" (*Mysterious Mother*, Advertisement from the Publishers, 174).

Horace Walpole: A Brief Chronology

1717   24 September (old style),[1] Horatio Walpole (contracted
to Horace), third son of Sir Robert Walpole and
Catherine Shorter, is born at their home on Arlington
Street, London. Sir Robert Walpole (1676–1745) of
Houghton Hall is one of the most prominent and powerful politicians of his time and served as Prime Minister from 1721 to 1742.

1727   26 April (old style), Walpole enters Eton at age nine-
and-a-half after living with the Walpoles at Chelsea and
his Townshend cousins at Bexley in Kent; at Eton, that
"brutal, rowdy, vigorous nursery of so many great men,"
he establishes lifelong intellectual companionships with
Thomas Gray, Richard West, Thomas Ashton, George
Montagu, William Cole, George Selwyn, and Charles
Lyttelton. He cultivates an early interest in art and literature by forming two clubs or "confederacies," the
Quadruple Alliance and the Triumvirate.

1734   23 September (old style), Walpole leaves Eton, one day
prior to his seventeenth birthday. Maintains his intellectual friendships through letters, especially with Gray and
West. Begins to develop artistic skills as an epistolarian.
He will elevate letter-writing to a fine art throughout a
lifetime of voluminous correspondence.

1735   11 March (old style), Walpole enters Kings College,
Cambridge University as a Fellow-Commoner and is
reunited with Gray and Ashton; he is influenced by the
Dissenting theologian, Dr. Conyers Middleton.

1736   July, enjoys a summer with his father, Sir Robert Walpole, at his newly built manor house at Houghton in
Norfolk, the estate filled with a magnificent collection
of art.

1737   20 August (old style), death of his mother, Lady Wal-

---

1   In 1752, England shifted from the Julian to the Gregorian Calendar, adding eleven
days.

pole; Walpole continues his studies at Kings College, Cambridge.

1739 Ceases academic residence at Cambridge and leaves the University without taking a degree. 29 March (old style), with Gray as his travelling companion, Walpole embarks on a Grand Tour of France and Italy; they tour Boulogne, Amiens, and St. Denis, arriving in Paris on 4 April; 9 September, after leaving Rheims they arrive in Dijon; 18 September, to Geneva and the mountains of Savoy to visit the Carthusian Monastery of the Grand Chartreuse; for the remainder of 1739, they visit the Italian cities of Turin, Genoa, Piacenza, Parma, Reggio, Bologna, and Modena, arriving in Florence on 16 December. Gray and Walpole will remain close friends, but there is some incompatibility and friction.

1740 The Grand Tour continues. Walpole and Gray sojourn in Rome and visit Sir Horace Mann at Casa Manetti in Florence; Mann becomes one of Walpole's lifelong correspondents; differences in temperament and taste exacerbate the friction between Gray and Walpole.

1741 April, Walpole and Gray depart from Florence for Reggio in May, Walpole and Gray quarrel and fall out; Gray leaves Walpole in Reggio, then goes alone to Venice, and finally home to England. 12 September (old style), Walpole returns to England by himself, landing at Dover. 14 September, Walpole returns to London after a two-and-one-half year absence; while away on the Grand Tour, he had been elected to Parliament for the borough of Carlington in Cornwall and will serve in Parliament for various boroughs until 1768.

1742 January, opposition in Parliament strives to bring down the Walpole ministry; Sir Robert Walpole resigns and retires to his Houghton estate, having been given the title Earl of Orford.

1743 Walpole prepares a catalogue of the paintings in his father's art collection at Houghton, *Ædes Walpoliana*, his first book. Walpole pursues an urbane "career" as a London socialite, attending the theater and the opera and corresponding with an ever-widening circle of friends and acquaintances.

1745   28 March (old style), Sir Robert Walpole dies at his home in Arlington Street, London, leaving his son a comfortable legacy in the form of various crown patents and sinecures. November, Horace Walpole and Thomas Gray resolve their quarrel, rebuild their friendship and resume correspondence.

1746   July, Walpole rents a small house near Windsor Castle ("a little tub of forty pounds a year") where he retires from London at intervals through the remainder of the year to try out country living and to entertain friends in a pleasant setting near a river.

1747   April, Walpole is attracted by and leases a small country house near Hampton Court at Twickenham on the upper Thames from Mrs. Chenevix, a London toy-and-china shop owner. Walpole renames the house and its surroundings "Strawberry Hill." The villa of Alexander Pope is located nearby; the house will become the focal point of Walpole's social, artistic, and antiquarian passions for the remainder of his life as well as a proving ground for his architectural experiments in the Gothic style. *Ædes Walpoliana* is published.

1748   18 September, Walpole plans to retrieve his letters from various correspondents in order to make them the basis for his *Memoirs* and writes to Sir Horace Mann of his intentions. He refurbishes the gardens and walks of Strawberry Hill and purchases the lease from Mrs. Chenevix to become the owner.

1749   Walpole begins to remodel his house informing Horace Mann that "I am going to build a little Gothic castle at Strawberry Hill. If you can pick me up any fragments of old painted glass, arms or anything, I shall be excessively obliged to you." Showing witty eccentricity, he tells Montagu that he has found "a text in *Deuteronomy* to authorize my future battlements."

1750   June, while musing over his elaborate schemes for medievalizing and Gothifying Strawberry Hill, Walpole receives a copy of Thomas Gray's poem "Elegy Written in a Country Churchyard." Impressed by the poem's somber landscape and its other Gothic moods, he finds a publisher and sees it through the press.

1751   To promote his Gothic project, Walpole organizes a "Committee of Taste" consisting of Richard Bentley, John Chute and himself. Chute and Bentley contribute designs and medieval notions for everything from furnishings, bookcases, and galleries to sham battlements. Having now retrieved some of his own letters, Walpole begins composing his *Memoirs*.

1753   While redecorating Strawberry Hill, Walpole contributes articles to *The World*, a magazine of London fashion; one of these papers is a light treatment of his nearly fatal encounter with the highwayman, John Maclean, who had robbed and nearly killed Walpole in Hyde Park in 1749. Outside and inside, the little Gothic villa fills up with pictures, porcelain, armor, and stained glass.

1754   A library and a refectory (monastery dining hall) are added to the little Gothic castle.

1757   25 June 1757 (new style), Walpole establishes a printing press (Officina Arbuteana or the Mayflower Workshop) in a separate building at Strawberry Hill and employs William Robinson as printer; 8 August, the press publishes two poems by Thomas Gray, *The Progress of Poesy* and *The Bard*.

1758   April, *Catalogue of the Royal and Noble Authors of England, with Lists of their Works* is published at the Strawberry Hill Press in a private edition of 300 copies; The Officina Arbuteana also published Lord Charles Whitworth's *An Account of Russia as it was in the Year 1710* and a pamphlet by Joseph Spence to raise money for the impoverished classics scholar, Robert Hill.

1760   1 January, Walpole begins writing *Anecdotes of Painting in England*, a history of English art. Construction begins on a cloister, gallery, and tower to give the house at Strawberry Hill a permanent Gothic facade and interior.

1763   The gallery, round tower, larger cloister and a cabinet "in the manner of a little chapel," all new additions to Strawberry Hill, are completed, doubling the size of the original house and changing its original square floor-plan into an oblong "Gothic" architectural fantasy; Thomas Pitt, a new member of "the committee of taste" contributes to the decorating of these additions: "His fantasies found concrete form; the little house called Strawberry Hill was fast assuming the splendours of the Castle of Otranto. He felt that he had achieved a triumphant illusion of barbarism and gloom." (Ketton-Cremer, *Horace Walpole: A Biography*, 124).

1764   April, the dismissal of Walpole's cousin, Henry Seymour Conway, from his post as groom of the royal bedchamber and from command of his regiment provokes Walpole's anger toward and resentment of King George III and the policies of the Court faction in Parliament. June, commences writing *The Castle of Otranto* directly after completing an irate pamphlet defending Conway; 6 August, finishes writing *The Castle of Otranto*; 24 December, encouraged by Thomas Gray to publish the work, 500 copies are published on Christmas Eve 1764 but are dated 1765.

1765   11 April, second edition of *The Castle of Otranto* is published, adding "Gothic" to the subtitle (*A Gothic Story*). July, to Walpole's satisfaction, Henry Seymour Conway is vindicated and becomes Secretary of State and Leader of the House of Commons. Walpole engages Thomas Kirgate to supervise his printing press at Strawberry Hill. September, Walpole sojourns in Paris and begins an intensive friendship with Madame du Deffand and becomes active in her salon.

1766   22 April, Walpole returns to London and is enmeshed in political intrigues in the aftermath of the Conway affair. August, begins writing the six *Hieroglyphic Tales*, "mere whimsical trifles, written chiefly for private entertainment." 25 December, commences the writing of *The Mysterious Mother*, a five act tragedy, working on the drama intermittently for the next fifteen months;

also begins *Historic Doubts on the Life and Reign of King Richard the Third*, an historical vindication of the villainous monarch.

1768   1 February, *Historic Doubts on the Life and Reign of King Richard the Third* published; 15 March, finishes the writing of *The Mysterious Mother*; the drama is printed at Strawberry Hill in a limited edition of fifty copies and circulated among a few close friends, including John Chute and Thomas Gray. Walpole retires from Parliament.

1769   28 March, Thomas Chatterton (1752-1770), "the marvellous boy" poet and author of the *Rowley Poems*, writes to Walpole concerning antiquarian interests and a correspondence between the two ensues. Walpole rejects the authenticity of the *Rowley Poems* as medieval forgeries; Chatterton condemns Walpole, writing: "Walpole! thou hadst not dared/ Thus to insult. But I shall live and stand/ By Rowley's side—when *Thou* are dead and damned." (Ketton-Cremer, *Horace Walpole: A Biography*, 246).

1770   Deaths of Thomas Gray and Thomas Chatterton; Walpole is unjustly accused of having caused Chatterton's untimely death by his own hand. Walpole is estranged from George Montagu, a friend of thirty years. ("He had dropped me, partly from politics and partly from caprice, for we never had any quarrel.") Walpole's epistolary friendship with the Reverend William Mason, reviser of *The Mysterious Mother*, now intensifies.

1772   Walpole writes six fairytales (*The Hieroglyphic Tales*) to entertain Caroline Campbell, the niece of Lady Ailesbury.

1774   Walpole prints *Description of Strawberry Hill*, a sort of catalogue of his collections of paintings, miniatures, bronzes, porcelains, ivories, enamels and curios such as the dagger of Henry VIII, the mourning ring of Charles I, and the spurs worn by William III at the Battle of the Boyne.

1776   Death of John Chute. Construction of the "Flemish" tower in the angle between the Round Tower and the main body of the house; Lady Diana Beauclerc's seven illustrations for *The Mysterious Mother* are placed in the Flemish Tower.

1777 April, *The Monthly Review* implicates Walpole in the suicide of Chatterton; Walpole attempts to avoid controversy but will later explain and justify his conduct in *The Gentleman's Magazine*.

1778 Walpole's affliction with gout becomes more severe. 25 April, James Boswell visits Strawberry Hill, one of numerous curious sightseers. 11 August, concerned with the future fate of his little Gothic castle, Walpole tells Lady Ossory "but alas! I am no poet, and my Castle is of paper, and my Castle and my attachments and I shall soon vanish and be forgotten together." (Ketton-Cremer, *Horace Walpole: A Biography*, 278).

1781 17 November, Robert Jephson's dramatic version of *The Castle of Otranto, The Count of Narbonne*, is produced at Covent Garden Theater; Walpole tells the actress Mrs. Elizabeth Pope that "Mr. Jephson, who has long been my friend, ... has proved himself so by making a rational and interesting tragedy out of my wild *Castle of Otranto*."

1782 Death of William Cole. Fourth edition of *The Castle of Otranto* is published.

1785 Two hundred bilingual (English and French) copies of Walpole's *Essay on Modern Gardening* are printed; six copies of the six stories in his *Hieroglyphic Tales* are printed.

1786 16 November, death of Horace Mann after an unbroken epistolary relationship with Walpole of forty-five years.

1788 Walpole makes the acquaintance of Robert Berry and his intellectual daughters, Mary and Agnes Berry, who take up residence near Strawberry Hill. Robert Berry becomes Walpole's literary executor; Mary Berry will later edit and oversee the 1798 edition of Walpole's *Works*. Walpole writes his final literary work, *Reminiscences, written in 1788, for the amusement of Miss Mary and Miss Agnes Berry*.

1791 November, Walpole is created the fourth Earl of Orford

to discover that the title is debt-ridden and Houghton "a mortifying ruin"; he tells Lady Ossory in a letter of 18 January 1792 that he has become the poorest Earl in England. Close friendship between Walpole and the Berry family who live at Cliveden house adjoining the Strawberry Hill estate.

1793 Walpole reacts with revulsion and despair over the events of the French Revolution and the Reign of Terror; he tells Mary Berry, "It remained for the enlightened eighteenth century to baffle language and invent horrors that can be found in no vocabulary. What tongue could be prepared to paint a Nation that should avow Atheism, profess Assassination, and practice Massacres on Massacres for four years together." (Ketton-Cremer, *Horace Walpole: A Biography*, 287).

1796 November, in poor health, Walpole is taken to Berkeley Square, London, leaving Strawberry Hill for the final time. During his final days, Mary and Agnes Berry "are in constant attendance."

1797 15 January, Walpole writes his final letter to Lady Ossory; 2 March, Walpole dies quietly and is buried eleven days later at Houghton Church beside his father and brothers. The villa at Strawberry Hill passes by Walpole's will to his niece, Anne Seymour Damer.

1798 *The Works of Horatio Walpole, Earl of Orford* is published in five quarto volumes edited by Mary Berry.

1810 Anne Seymour Damer relinquishes Strawberry Hill to Lady Waldegrave, granddaughter of Edward Walpole, Horace Walpole's brother.

1842 April–May, Walpole's art collections and other contents of Strawberry Hill are sold at general auction for 33,450 pounds; the house is allowed to fall into dereliction.

1883 Strawberry Hill is purchased by Baron de Stern after nearly being acquired by an American hotel company.

1923 Strawberry Hill is sold again to the Catholic Education Council; the house and grounds become St. Mary's Catholic Teacher Training College, later named St. Mary's University College.

1927   Sebastian Pugin Powell designs new rooms for the house, which becomes quarters for the Vincentian priests of the faculty.

1940   The site undergoes a destructive firebombing by the German airforce.

1950   Renovation continues; the home of the first Gothicist attracts individual visitors and conferences, including the second biannual meeting of the International Gothic Association in July, 1997.

Publication History of The Castle of Otranto *and* The Mysterious Mother

Nine editions, a French translation, a German translation, and an Italian translation of *The Castle of Otranto* were published during Walpole's lifetime. Some of these were not authorized. The last edition in which Walpole had a direct editorial involvement was the fourth edition, published by Dodsley in 1782. The novel was reprinted many times throughout the nineteenth century in both separate form and as part of publishers' novel series and anthologies. There were also abridgements and dramatic adaptations, such as the "Grand Romantic Extravaganza" of 1848 and the 1854 pantomime play, *The Castle of Otranto*; or, *Harlequin and the Great Helmet*, and numerous translations into many languages. The *National Union Catalogue* records thirty-four printings in the nineteenth century. Three authorized and one unauthorized (pirated) editions of *The Mysterious Mother* appeared during Walpole's lifetime along with private "readings" of the play, but there were no stage performances.

The Castle of Otranto

1764   Five hundred copies of the first edition of *The Castle of Otranto. A Story* were printed at the Strawberry Hill press on 24 December 1764. The title page reads "Printed for Tho.[mas] Lownds in Fleet Street."

1765   The second edition was printed at the Strawberry Hill Press on 11 April. The title page reads "Printed for William Bathoe in the Strand, and Thomas Lownds in Fleet Street. The subtitle now reads *A Gothic Story* and omits the fabricated authors, Onuphrio Muralto and William Marshal.

1767   First French translation. Amsterdam & Paris: Prault. Titled *Le Château d'Otrante, Histoire Gothique*, par M. Horace Walpole, traduite sur la seconde édition angloise par M.[arc Antoine] E.[idous].

1769   The third edition. London: John Murray.

1782   The fourth edition. London: J. Dodsley.

1786   The fifth edition. London: J. Dodsley. .

1791   The sixth edition. London: J. Dodsley. Another sixth
edition was published in Parma, Italy: Printed by
Bodoni for J. Edwards, Bookseller of London.

1793   The seventh edition. London: Wenman & Hodgson.

1794   The eighth edition. London: J. Wright for C. Cooke.

1794   German translation titled *Die Burg von Otranto. Eine
gotische Geschichte*. Berlin: C.F. Himburg.

1795   First Italian translation, *Il Castello di Otranto. Storia
Gotica*. Londra: Presso Molini, Polidori, Molini e Co.
Hay-Market; Edwards, Pall-Mall. Translated by Gio-
vanne Sivrac. The edition contains seven illustrations.

1796   The ninth edition. London: Cooper & Graham. Titled
H. Jeffery's Edition of *The Castle of Otranto. A Gothic
Story*. Contains colored plates.

1797   *Isabelle et Theodore, histoire traduite d'anglais*. Paris: Lep-
etit. An apparently unauthorized anonymous trans-
lation.

1798   Included in Mary Berry's edition of *The Works of Horatio Walpole, Earl of Orford*. London: G.G. & J. Robinson
& J. Edwards. *The Castle of Otranto* is Volume 2, 1-90.
The Mysterious Mother is Volume I, 38-127. Summary of
contents: Volume 1. *Fugitive pieces. The Mysterious
Mother. A Tragedy. Catalogue of the Royal and Noble
Authors of England.* Volume 2. *The Castle of Otranto. An
account of the Giants Lately Discovered. Historic doubts on
the Life and Reign of Richard III, with supplement, observations, etc. Ædes Walpolianæ; or, A Description of the Pictures
at Houghton Hall. Sermon on Painting. Nature Will Prevail:
A Moral Entertainment. Thoughts on Tragedy. Thoughts on
Comedy. Detection of a Late Forgery, Called Testament Poli-
tique du Chevalier Robert Walpole. Life of Rev. Thomas
Baker. Account of my Conduct Relative to the Places I Hold
under Government. Letters to and from Ministers. Description
of Strawberry Hill. On Modern Gardening. On the Late Dis-
mission of a General Officer.* Volume 3. *Anecdotes of Paint-*

ing [and the other fine arts]. Volume 4. *Catalogue of Engravers in England. Life of George Vertue, with list of works. Appendix to Anecdotes of Painting. Chatterton Papers. Narrative of the Quarrel of Mr. David Hume and J.J. Rousseau, as far as Mr. Horace Walpole was concerned in it. Letters between D. Hume and H. Walpole, Relative to Rousseau. Reminiscences, written in 1788. Hieroglyphic Tales. Parody on Chesterfield's Letters. Criticism on Dr. Johnson's Writings. Strange Occurrences: A Continuation of Baker's Chronicle. Detached Thoughts. Miscellaneous Verses. Prologues and Epilogues. Epigrams. Index to Catalogue of Engravers.* Volume 5. *Letters.*

1800   Reprinting of Jeffery's 1796 edition. London: W. Blackader.

1811   Edinburgh: Printed by James Ballantyne for John Ballantyne. Critical Preface by Sir Walter Scott.

1825   Manchester: J. Gleave, 1825. Has a biographical preface.

1834   Printed with William Beckford's *Vathek* and M.G. Lewis's translation of Heinrich Zschokke's *The Bravo of Venice* as Bentley's Standard Novels Number 41. London: R. Bentley.

1848   A dramatic version or "Grand Romantic Extravaganza" by Gilbert A'Beckett produced at the Haymarket Theatre on 24 April.

1854   Philadelphia: H.C. Baird.

1854   *The Castle of Otranto; or, Harlequin and the Giant Helmet. A New Romantic Comic Pantomime.* London: J.K. Green.

1872   Included in The Cottage Library series. London & Halifax, Nova Scotia: Milner.

1886   Included in Cassell's National Library series. London: Cassell.

1907   Included in the King's Classics series. London: Chatto & Windus. Reprints Sir Walter Scott's Introduction and has a Preface by Caroline F.E. Spurgeon.

1925   Montague Summers's limited edition of *The Castle of Otranto* and *The Mysterious Mother*, "embellished with coloured engravings," is published at the Chiswick Press for Houghton Mifflin Company and Constable and

Company.

1929 Oswald Doughty's edition of *The Castle of Otranto*. London: Scholartis.

1930 Included in *Shorter Novels of the Eighteenth Century*. London & New York: J.M Dent, E.P. Dutton; Everyman's Library 856. Printed with Samuel Johnson's *Rasselas* and William Beckford's *Vathek*.

1931 Included in *Three Eighteenth Century Romances*. New York: Scribner's. Printed with William Beckford's *Vathek* and Ann Radcliffe's *The Romance of the Forest*.

1936 Included in *An Eighteenth Century Miscellany; The Classics of the Eighteenth Century which Typify and Reveal an Era: Jonathan Swift, Alexander Pope, John Gay ... [and others]*. Edited and selected by Louis Kronenberger. New York: G.P. Putnam's Sons.

1950 London: Gray Walls Press.

1963 Marvin Mudrick's edition. New York: Macmillan. Includes Sir Walter Scott's 1811 Preface.

1963 Included in the paperback anthology, *Seven Masterpieces of Gothic Horror* edited by Robert D. Spector. New York: Bantam.

1963 Included with Jane Austen's *Northanger Abbey* and Ann Radcliffe's *The Mysteries of Udolpho* [abridged] and edited by Andrew Wright. New York: Holt, Rinehart & Winston.

1964 Wilmarth S. Lewis's edition for the Oxford English Novels series. London: Oxford University Press. Based on the 1798 text of the novel.

1966 Included in E.F. Bleiler's edition of *Three Gothic Novels*. New York: Dover Publishing. Printed with William Beckford's *Vathek* and John Polidori's *The Vampyre*.

1968 Included in Mario Praz's edition of *Three Gothic Novels*. Baltimore: Penguin Books. Printed with William Beckford's *Vathek* and Mary Shelley's *Frankenstein*.

1975 A leatherbound quarto volume with decorated, paper covered boards and gold stamping for The Limited Editions Club of New York. Elegant edition in 2000 copies published by Westerham Press.

1976 Devendra P. Varma's edition with lithographs. London:

Folio Society.

1993   Robert Mack's edition of *The Castle of Otranto* and *Hieroglyphic Tales*. London: J.M. Dent.

1996   E.J. Clery's edition based on W.S. Lewis's 1964 edition for the Oxford English Novels series. Oxford & New York: Oxford University Press.

1998   *The Works of Horatio Walpole, Earl of Orford, from the 1798 edition.* 5 volumes. Edited by Peter Sabor. London: Pickering & Chatto, 1998.

The Mysterious Mother

1768   The first edition, limited to fifty copies, was published at Walpole's Strawberry Hill Press.

1770   Included in the two-volume *Collected Works of Horace Walpole*, published at the Strawberry Hill Press.

1781   An authorized edition of the play is published by Dodsley in London.

1791   Unauthorized (pirated) editions based on the Dodsley edition of 1781 are published in London and Dublin, Ireland by J. Archer, W. Jones & R. White. The edition was not suppressed by Walpole. See: Richard H. Perkinson, "Walpole and a Dublin Pirate," *Philological Quarterly* 15 (1936): 391-400.

1798   Included in Mary Berry's edition of *The Works of Horatio Walpole, Earl of Orford*. London: G.G. & J. Robinson & J. Edwards. *The Mysterious Mother* is Volume I, 38-127.

1811   Included in Volume 2: *Tragedies* of Sir Walter Scott's anthology, *The Modern British Drama*. Edinburgh: Miller & Ballantyne.

1881   Included in *Dicks' Standard Plays*, circa 1881.

1925   First twentieth century edition of the play edited by Montague Summers and printed at the Chiswick Press for Houghton Mifflin and Constable Limited. Printed with *The Castle of Otranto* and extensive notes on both works.

1971   An edition of the play submitted as a doctoral dissertation at the University of Arizona by Janet A. Dolan. "Horace Walpole's *The Mysterious Mother:* A Critical Edition," *Dissertation Abstracts International* 31 (1971): 4115A-4116A.

2000   *The Mysterious Mother* is included in an anthology of *Five Romantic Plays, 1768-1821.* Edited by Paul Baines. Oxford & New York: Oxford UP, 2000. The other Gothic plays are Joanna Baillie's *De Monfort*, Robert Southey's *Wat Tyler*, Elizabeth Inchbald's *Lovers' Vows*, and Lord Byron's *Two Foscari*.

Using the Edition

This edition of the two founding texts of the Gothic movement has been prepared with two audiences in mind: students studying Gothic fiction in the formal setting of the classroom and general readers who are drawn to the Gothic by the pleasures inherent in the form. No attempt has been made to produce definitive scholarly or exhaustive variorum editions of the first Gothic novel and the first Gothic play. In each case, the edition furnishes the reader with reliable texts, with minimal notes mainly of an explanatory rather than explicative type, and a collection of source materials and historical commentaries intended to contextualize Walpole's Gothic writings. The edition is organized so as to enable the user to understand the aesthetic climate that propagated these first Gothics and to select from the four Appendices those documents most relevant to his or her purposes. The basis for the two texts is the 1798 edition of *The Works of Horatio Walpole, Earl of Orford*, which had Walpole's sanction as well as his corrections of earlier errors and misprints. Scanning the publication histories of the two works reveals opposite histories. The preeminent Gothic model, *The Castle of Otranto* has been reissued many times and has never been out of print; in contrast, *The Mysterious Mother* is a shadowy text backshelved and forgotten throughout the nineteenth century, but recovered by the zealous bibliophile Montague Summers in his 1925 combined edition of the novel and the play. Only recently has the first Gothic drama risen to canonical status as part of the remarkable renaissance of Gothic studies in general that began in the 1950s.

Prior to reading both the novel and the play, it is suggested that the user review thoroughly the Chronology of Walpole's life to grasp the unusual and occasionally eccentric personality of the author as well as his consciously manipulated public and private personae. Critics have sometimes disagreed about the degree of authorial presence in the two works, but most readers have concurred that various aspects of Walpole himself imbue and inform both the novel and the play, both works exhibiting a fair amount of what Donald Mack, in the introduction to his 1990 edition of

The Castle of Otranto, calls "personal subtexts."[1] Certainly Walpole, the Gothic architectural fanatic and fantasist, is present if not omnipresent throughout both works.

Modern responses to the novel and the drama will be enhanced by reading them in tandem with the letters found in Appendix A. These record the process of transcription by which his fantasy castle of ersatz stone at Strawberry Hill became the paper castle of the first Gothic novel. The letters discussing his decision to write a drama on a forbidden and risqué subject reveal a high seriousness toward his developing Gothic art. The letters not only chart the progress of Walpole's imagination toward a Gothic ideal, but also reflect the self-irony, self-effacement, and sly autobiography that haunt both works.

Walpole's lifelong interest in the visual arts and their Gothic literary accomplishments can best be appreciated by studying the seventeen plates that accompany the text. Eight of these illustrations are drawings and engravings of the exterior and interior of the castle at Strawberry Hill and will allow the reader visual access to some of the Gothic magnificence with which Walpole surrounded himself and which he displayed so proudly to a curious public. While reading the *Castle of Otranto* and the *Mysterious Mother*, the reader is urged to return frequently to the illustrations placed in Appendix A:3, if only because Walpole's memory made constant imaginative use of the decor of his "little Gothic villa" in the building of the novel and the drama and in visualizing their scenes of terror. There is scarcely a scene in the novel which is not directly related to a chamber, gallery, or staircase of the castellated villa at Strawberry Hill. The exterior views of the north, south, and east fronts of the building (pp. 282-83) should make a powerful statement to the reader about Walpole's imaginative "approaches" to the Gothic by giving a perspective on what the eighteenth-century visitors saw as they strolled the grounds and gardens or prepared to tour the house. Elsewhere throughout the edition, illustrations of major scenes in the novel and the play have been placed for their effect at various points of the text.

---

1 Donald Mack, Introduction to *The Castle of Otranto and Hieroglyphic Tales* (London: J.M. Dent; Rutland, VT: Charles E. Tuttle, 1993), xxi.

Illustrations such as the death of Conrad beneath the enormous helmet and Frederic's hair-raising encounter with the skeletal monk provide the reader with a visual index of Walpole's love of irregularity, surprise, and supernatural excitement. The seven drawings made by Lady Diana Beauclerc for *The Mysterious Mother* held a special charm for Horace Walpole. Hence, two of these seven drawings have been placed in the text of *The Mysterious Mother* for the similar enjoyment of the reader. Of the many portraits of Horace Walpole, I thought that the user of the edition would gain the most insight into the man behind these Gothics from one full-face painting done just as the towers of Strawberry Hill began to rise in the 1750s and one profile done just as the play was being published privately at the Strawberry Hill press in 1768. One can sense the passionate commitment to the highly visual aesthetics of the Gothic in the intelligent face of a young Horace Walpole in the Allan Ramsay portrait (p. 5). The pose seems to catch him in the midst of a not-yet-fulfilled Gothic daydream. The profile of Walpole in Pariset's engraving suggests a man whose Gothic ideal has deepened and in some ways matured. Although seventeen plates may seem a large number, they are but a minute sampling of the charms and wonders of Strawberry Hill and its master's moods. Because the Gothic is itself a highly visual medium, the optical nature of Walpole's Gothic made it nearly impossible to offer an appealing edition of the first Gothic novel and the first Gothic drama without an array of illustrations to contextualize properly the literary experience.[1]

The material in Appendices B, C, and D may be consulted at the discretion of the individual reader in no special order, but with individual needs in mind, such as an interest in the relationship of Gothic texts to current reader-reception theory. The

---

[1] For the user who desires detailed descriptions of the paintings, drawings, and engravings that have been included, as well as guidance on where to locate other portraits of Horace Walpole and the pictorialization of Strawberry Hill with its unique contents of armour, porcelain, and historical curios and memorabilia, the superlative source is: Wilmarth Sheldon Lewis, *Horace Walpole: The A.W. Mellon Lectures in the Fine Arts*. Bollingen Series XXXV-9; New York: Pantheon Books, 1960, 1961. Along with a full description of the Beauclerc Cabinet containing all seven drawings made for *The Mysterious Mother*, the book offers full-page reproductions of seven other portraits of Walpole by J.C. Eccardt (1754), George Dance (1793), Philip Mercier (1727), Rosalba Carriera (1741), Richard Bentley (1755), James McCardell (1757), and John Carter (1788).

views of Walpole's contemporaries, the later reactions of the Romantic and Victorian writers, and anecdotal asides such as the verse commemorations by Ann Yearsley and John Courtenay are valuable for determining the cultural reputation of Walpole's Gothic achievement, but not crucial to an appreciation of that achievement.

Appendix C, "Aesthetic and Intellectual Backgrounds," is imperative reading for those users who wish to comprehend the literary forces and philosophical crosscurrents that gave rise to Walpole's two Gothics in the first place. The Graveyard Poets, beginning with Walpole's neighbor, Alexander Pope, supplied Walpole with the idiom and the mood as well as setting and character for his Gothic endeavors. The importance of Walpole's friendship with Thomas Gray, a leading figure of the Graveyard School, should be stressed. Ample selections from Gray and other Graveyard Poets, arranged in a timeline from the 1720s to the 1760s, put the reader in touch with this rich vein of Gothic feeling that made the cult of death, the beautification of decay, the mysteries of the tomb and charnel house, mortuarial loveliness, architectural cataclysm and ancient "gloomth," so attractive to Walpole.

Some acquaintance with Burke's theory of fearful pleasure as an inducement to the sublime and Hurd's practical criticism of the Gothic mood and mode that made the case for the revival of "Gothic romance" is imperative for any full realization of Walpole's artistic success in an untried field. Burkean theory is applied by Walpole to produce the Gothic terrors of both the novel and the drama. Referring to the excerpts from Burke's *Enquiry* will also verify the prescience of Walpole's remark that "terror" is the author's "principal engine."

Bishop Hurd's *Letters on Chivalry and Romance* had called for an unblocking of the imagination and a restoration of dark fantasy, exactly what Walpole accomplished in giving form to his medieval daydreams. Hurd's *Letters* are the practical counterpart to Burke's arguments. Walpole's two first Gothics would validate Hurd's notions of the power of Gothic literature to elevate the imagination and lead to the establishment of the new genres of the Gothic novel and the Gothic drama.

Written three years before the publication of his first novel,

Waverley (1814), Scott's introduction to the 1811 edition of *The Castle of Otranto* is a perceptive critique of Walpole's accomplishment. An overlooked document in the history of Walpole criticism, Scott saw Walpole's novel as more than merely a technical resource for later Gothic writers: "Horace Walpole ... led the way in this new species of composition.... More will yet remain with him than the single merit of originality and invention" (Scott, Introduction, 340). Scott also recognized Walpole's genius in combining ancient and modern modes of composition as he moved from the building of Strawberry Hill to the prose architecture of *The Castle of Otranto*. "Mr. Walpole," Scott noted, "resolved to give the public a specimen of the Gothic style adapted to modern literature, as he had already exhibited its application to modern architecture" (Scott, Introduction, 332). In his assertion of the intrinsic merit of the first Gothic novel, Scott opened a line of inquiry which engages critics of Walpole's works down to present day. Are the first Gothic novel and first Gothic drama important solely for their influence, or do the two works have any intrinsic merit, any value as works of art *per se*?

Consulting the "Glossary of Gothic Terms" will reveal the magnitude of Walpole's donations to the mechanics and the psychodynamics of the Gothic form. Many terms in the Glossary have been keyed to events, characters, and settings in *The Castle of Otranto* to demonstrate the widespread influence of the first Gothic novel and the first Gothic drama.

Many of the entries in the "Bibliographies and Checklists of Criticism" relate to the ongoing debate over Walpole's proper place in the literary movement that he launched. He has been called "the first surrealist writer"[1] and his work celebrated "as a notable landmark in the history of English taste and English literature."[2] Dissenting opinions range from outright dismissal of Walpole's novel as "frivolous, lightweight, and escapist"[3] to denials of

---

1   Bonamy Dobrée, "Introduction," *From Anne to Victoria; Essays by Various Hands* (New York: Charles Scribner's Sons, 1937), viii. One of the essays is Romney Sedgwick's "Horace Walpole (1717-1797)" : 265-278.

2   Montague Summers, *The Gothic Quest: A History of the Gothic Novel*, 1938 (New York: Russell & Russell, 1964), 184.

3   Valdine Clemens, "Sexual Violence and Woman's Place: *The Castle of Otranto*," in *The Return of the Repressed: Gothic Horror from The Castle of Otranto to Alien* (Albany: State U of New York P, 1999), 40.

its seriousness in the exaggerated claim that "comedy is its basis,"[1] and "burlesque derision" its predominant tone; any reader who takes anything in *The Castle of Otranto* seriously has been victimized by the satirist's cunning irony.

Critical commentaries on *The Mysterious Mother*, many of which are source and influence studies, tend to emphasize the Sophoclean and Shakespearean dimensions of the play and find a compatibility of the Gothic and the tragic at the core of the drama. The Freudian "decoding" of the script to yield the sexual secrets of Walpole's subconscious mind, such as the possible fear that he was an illegitimate son of Sir Robert Walpole, has its uses, but it also has its limits: "a psychoanalytic reading can do nothing except use the play to analyze Walpole's personality"[2] leading to an overvaluation of the subtext at the expense of the text. Recent criticism has begun to appreciate the process of refinement in his conception of the Gothic in moving from external configurations of horror to internal ones. Whether Walpole also reformed as well as refined his vision of the Gothic when he came to write *The Mysterious Mother*, and if so, exactly what direction his Gothic took after *Otranto*, remains an engaging critical question.

Since the early 1980s, much of the criticism written on early Gothic fiction has emphasized its ideological basis as well as its polemical or subversive spirit. Allegedly, the Gothic speaks out against the violated rights of women or it sounds the call for revolutions that would radicalize society and alter the power roles. But as Rictor Norton has observed in his Introduction to selections from Walpole's first Gothic novel in *Gothic Readings: The First Wave, 1764-1840*, "by 'foregrounding' ideology, we risk forgetting that the Gothic is grounded in the desire to entertain the reader through the use of literary devices,"[3] an absolute of its enduring appeal that Walpole mastered brilliantly and never forgot.

---

1   Richard Davenport-Hines, *Gothic: 400 Years of Excess, Horror, Evil and Ruin* (London: Fourth Estate, 1998), 136.

2   Baines, "'This Theatre of Monstrous Guilt,'" 289.

3   Rictor Norton, Introduction to *Gothic Readings, The First Wave, 1764-1840* (London & New York: Leicester UP, 2000), xi.

The Castle of Otranto, 1795. Italian Edition.

Castle of Otranto,

A

S T O R Y.

Translated by

WILLIAM MARSHAL, Gent.

From the Original ITALIAN of

ONUPHRIO MURALTO,

Canon of the Church of St. Nicholas
at Otranto.

L O N D O N:

Printed for Tho. Lownds in Fleet-Street.
MDCCLXV.

PREFACE TO THE FIRST EDITION

THE following work was found in the library of an ancient Catholic family in the north of England. It was printed at Naples, in the black letter,[1] in the year 1529. How much sooner it was written does not appear. The principal incidents are such as were believed in the darkest ages of Christianity; but the language and conduct have nothing that savors of that barbarism. The style is the purest Italian. If the story was written near the time when it is supposed to have happened, it must have been between 1095, the era of the first crusade, and 1243, the date of the last, or not long afterwards. There is no other circumstance in the work, that can lead us to guess at the period in which the scene is laid. The names of the actors[2] are evidently fictitious, and probably disguised on purpose: yet the Spanish names of the domestics seem to indicate that this work was not composed until the establishment of the Arragonian kings in Naples[3] had made Spanish appellations familiar in that country. The beauty of the diction, and the zeal of the author (moderated, however, by singular judgement), concur to make me think, that the date of the composition was little antecedent to that of the impression. Letters were then in their most flourishing state in Italy, and contributed to dispel the empire of superstition, at that time so forcibly attacked by the reformers. It is not unlikely, that an artful priest might endeavour to turn their own arms on the innovators; and might avail himself of his abilities as an author to confirm the populace in their ancient errors and superstitions. If this was his view, he has certainly acted with signal address. Such a work as the following would enslave a hundred vulgar minds, beyond half the books of controversy that have been written from the days of Luther[4] to the present hour.

---

1 A Gothic typeface, e.g. 𝕿𝖍𝖊 𝕮𝖆𝖘𝖙𝖑𝖊 𝖔𝖋 𝕺𝖙𝖗𝖆𝖓𝖙𝖔.

2 Several of the characters' names are taken from Shakespeare. Bianca is taken from *Othello*; Isabella is taken from *Measure for Measure*. Hippolita is taken from *A Midsummer Night's Dream*. Manfred and Conrad were taken from historical accounts of the Italian kingdom of Sicily in the period 1200-1300.

3 These kings assumed the rule of the Neapolitan kingdom after the defeat and death of King Manfred in 1266.

4 Martin Luther (1483-1546), German Protestant religious reformer.

This solution of the author's motives is, however, offered as a mere conjecture. Whatever his views were, or whatever effects the execution of them might have, his work can only be laid before the public at present as a matter of entertainment. Even as such, some apology for it is necessary. Miracles, visions, necromancy, dreams, and other preternatural events, are exploded now even from romances. That was not the case when our author wrote; much less when the story itself is supposed to have happened. Belief in every kind of prodigy was so established in those dark ages, that an author would not be faithful to the manners of the time who should omit all mention of them. He is not bound to believe them himself, but he must represent his actors as believing them.

If this air of the miraculous is excused, the reader will find nothing else unworthy of his perusal. Allow the possibility of the facts, and all the actors comport themselves as persons would do in their situation. There is no bombast, no similes, flowers, digressions, or unnecessary descriptions. Everything tends directly to the catastrophe. Never is the reader's attention relaxed. The rules of the drama[1] are almost observed throughout the conduct of the piece. The characters are well drawn, and still better maintained. Terror, the author's principal engine, prevents the story from ever languishing; and it is so often contrasted by pity, that the mind is kept up in a constant vicissitude of interesting passions.

Some persons may, perhaps, think the characters of the domestics too little serious for the general cast of the story; but, besides their opposition to the principal personages, the art of the author is very observable in his conduct of the subalterns. They discover many passages essential to the story, which could not be well brought to light but by their *naïveté* and simplicity: in particular, the womanish terror and foibles of Bianca, in the last chapter, conduce essentially towards advancing the catastrophe.

It is natural for a translator to be prejudiced in favour of his adopted work. More impartial readers may not be so much struck with the beauties of this piece as I was. Yet I am not blind to my

---

1   Refers to the three unities assigned by Aristotle in *The Poetics* to the drama, unity of time; unity of place; and unity of action.

author's defects. I could wish he had grounded his plan on a more useful moral than this: that *"the sins of fathers are visited on their children to the third and fourth generation."*[1] I doubt whether, in his time, any more than at present, ambition curbed its appetite of dominion from the dread of so remote a punishment. And yet this moral is weakened by that less direct insinuation, that even such anathema may be diverted, by devotion to saint Nicholas.[2] Here, the interest of the monk plainly gets the better of the judgment of the author. However, with all its faults, I have no doubt but the English reader will be pleased with a sight of this performance. The piety that reigns throughout, the lessons of virtue that are inculcated, and the rigid purity of the sentiments, exempt this work from the censure to which romances are but too liable. Should it meet with the success I hope for, I may be encouraged to reprint the original Italian, though it will tend to depreciate my own labour. Our language falls far short of the charms of the Italian, both for variety and harmony. The latter is particularly excellent for simple narrative. It is difficult, in English, to relate without falling too low, or rising too high; a fault obviously occasioned by the little care taken to speak pure language in common conversation. Every Italian or Frenchman, of any rank, piques himself on speaking his own tongue correctly and with choice. I cannot flatter myself with having done justice to my author in this respect: his style is as elegant, as his conduct of the passions is masterly. It is a pity that he did not apply his talents to what they were evidently proper for, the theatre.

I will detain the reader no longer, but to make one short remark. Though the machinery is invention, and the names of the actors imaginary, I cannot but believe, that the ground work of the story is founded on truth. The scene is undoubtedly laid in some real castle.[3] The author seems frequently, without design, to describe particular parts. *"The chamber,"* says he, *"on the right hand; the door on the left hand; the distance from the chapel to Conrad's apart-*

---

1   A paraphrase of Exodus 34: 6-7.

2   Important fourth-century saint whose shrine is at Bari near Otranto.

3   The architectural model for the castle was Walpole's "little Gothic" villa at Strawberry Hill. Also, his memories of Trinity College at Cambridge University played an imaginative role.

ment." These and other passages, are strong presumptions that the author had some certain building in his eye. Curious persons, who have leisure to employ in such researches, may possibly discover in the Italian writers the foundation on which our author has built. If a catastrophe, at all resembling that which he describes, is believed to have given rise to this work, it will contribute to interest the reader, and will make *The Castle of Otranto* a still more moving story.

Horace Walpole, 1764

CASTLE of OTRANTO

A

GOTHIC STORY[1]

——— *Vanæ*
Fingentur fpecies, tamen ut Pes, & Caput uni
Reddantur formæ. ———

H O R.

THE SECOND EDITION.

L O N D O N:

Printed for W I L L I A M B A T H O E in the *Strand*,
and T H O M A S L O W N D S in *Fleet-Street*.

M. DCC. LXV.

---

1 In the first edition, Walpole subtitled the novel "A Story." The second edition added the word "Gothic" to the subtitle and included a Latin epigraph taken from Horace's *Ars Poetica*, 7-9: "Idle fancies shall be shaped like a sick man's dream so that neither foot nor head can be assigned a single shape." In the novel the *disjecta membra*, or scattered body parts, of Alfonso are eventually consolidated into one gigantic form, thus inverting the words of Horace.

PREFACE TO THE SECOND EDITION

THE favourable manner in which this little piece has been received by the public, calls upon the author to explain the grounds on which he composed it. But, before he opens those motives, it is fit that he should ask pardon of his readers for having offered his work to them under the borrowed personage of a translator. As diffidence of his own abilities, and the novelty of the attempt, were the sole inducements to assume the disguise, he flatters himself he shall appear excusable. He resigned the performance to the impartial judgement of the public; determined to let it perish in obscurity, if disproved; nor meaning to avow such a trifle, unless better judges should pronounce that he might own it without blush.

It was an attempt to blend the two kinds of romance, the ancient and the modern.[1] In the former, all was imagination and improbability: in the latter, nature is always intended to be, and sometimes has been, copied with success. Invention has not been wanting; but the great resources of fancy have been dammed up, by a strict adherence to common life. But if, in the latter species, Nature has cramped imagination, she did but take her revenge, having been totally excluded from old romances. The actions, sentiments, and conversations, of the heroes and heroines of ancient days, were as unnatural as the machines employed to put them in motion.

The author of the following pages thought it possible to reconcile the two kinds. Desirous of leaving the powers of fancy at liberty to expatiate through the boundless realms of invention, and thence of creating more interesting situations, he wished to conduct the mortal agents in his drama[2] according to the rules of probability; in short, to make them think, speak, and act, as it might be supposed mere men and women would do in extraordinary positions. He had observed, that, in all inspired writings, the

Bacon - We like rules / regularity.

---

1 The narrative will amalgamate the marvellous with the probable and the natural with the supernatural.

2 Walpole conceives of the novel in dramatic terms complete with stage directions, props, and asides. This applies to the supernatural as well as the natural characters. *Otranto* was adapted for the stage by Robert Jephson in *The Count of Narbonne* (1786).

personages under the dispensation of miracles, and witness to the most stupendous phenomena, never lose sight of their human character: whereas, in the productions of romantic story, an improbable event never fails to be attended by an absurd dialogue. The actors seem to lose their senses, the moment the laws of nature have lost their tone. As the public have applauded the attempt, the author must not say he was entirely unequal to the task he had undertaken: yet, if the new route he has struck out shall have paved a road for men of brighter talents, he shall own, with pleasure and modesty, that he was sensible the plan was capable of receiving greater embellishments than his imagination, or conduct of the passions, could bestow on it.

With regard to the deportment of the domestics, on which I have touched in the former preface, I will beg leave to add a few words. — The simplicity of their behaviour, almost tending to excite smiles, which, at first, seems not consonant to the serious cast of the work, appeared to me not only improper, but was marked designedly in that manner. My rule was nature. However grave, important, or even melancholy, the sensations of the princes and heroes may be, they do not stamp the same affections on their domestics: at least the latter do not, or should not be made to express their passions in the same dignified tone. In my humble opinion, the contrast between the sublime of the one and the *naïveté* of the other, sets the pathetic of the former in a stronger light. The very impatience which a reader feels, while delayed, by the coarse pleasantries of vulgar actors, from arriving at the knowledge of the important catastrophe he expects, perhaps heightens, certainly proves that he has been artfully interested in, the depending event. But I had higher authority than my own opinion for this conduct. The great master of nature, Shakespeare,[1] was the model I copied. Let me ask, if his tragedies of Hamlet and Julius Cæsar would not lose a considerable share of their spirit and wonderful beauties, if the humour of the gravedig-

---

1 Shakespeare included the supernatural as an aspect of nature. Along with *Hamlet, Julius Caesar, Macbeth,* and *Richard III*, all plays that use ghosts, Walpole also drew upon the tragicomedies, *A Winter's Tale* and *Cymbeline* for preternatural decor and supernatural excitement.

gers, the fooleries of Polonius [in Shakespeare's *Hamlet*], and the clumsy jests of the Roman citizens, were omitted, or vested in heroics? Is not the eloquence of Antony, the nobler and affected-ly-unaffected oration of Brutus [in Shakespeare's *Julius Caesar*], artificially exalted by the rude bursts of nature from the mouths of their auditors? These touches remind one of the Grecian sculptor, who, to convey the idea of a Colossus, within the dimensions of a seal, inserted a little boy measuring his thumb.

"No," says Voltaire, in his edition of Corneille,[1] "this mixture of buffoonery and solemnity is intolerable." — Voltaire is a genius — but not of Shakespeare's magnitude. Without recurring to disputable authority, I appeal from Voltaire to himself. I shall not avail myself of his former encomiums on our mighty poet; though the French critic has twice translated the same speech in Hamlet, some years ago in admiration, latterly in derision; and I am sorry to find that his judgment grows weaker when it ought to be farther matured. But I shall make use of his own words, delivered on the general topic of the theatre, when he was neither thinking to recommend or decry Shakespeare's practice; consequently, at a moment when Voltaire was impartial. In the preface to his *Enfant prodigue*,[2] that exquisite piece, of which I declare my admiration, and which, should I live twenty years longer, I trust I shall never attempt to ridicule, he has these words, speaking of comedy [but equally applicable to tragedy, if tragedy is, as surely it ought to be, a picture of human life; nor can I conceive why occasional pleasantry ought more to be banished from the tragic scene than pathetic seriousness from the comic], "*On y voit un mélange de sérieux et de plaisanterie, de comique et de touchant; souvent même une seule aventure produit tous ces contrastes. Rien n'est si communqu'une maison dans laquelle un père gronde, une fille occupée de sa passion pleure; le fils se moque des deux, et quelques parents prennent différemment part à la scène &c. Nous n'inférons pas de là que toute comédie*

---

1 The French philosopher of the Enlightenment, Voltaire (1694-1778) regarded Shakespeare as a rough and primitive genius who lacked the dramatic purity of the French tragedian, Pierre Corneille (1606-1684).

2 Voltaire's comedy, *L'Enfant prodigue* (*The Prodigal Son*, 1736) violated Voltaire's own dicta of dramatic purity by mixing the comic with the serious, a conjunction sometimes found in *Otranto* as with the nosebleed of Alfonso's statue (*Otranto*, 158).

*doive avoir des scènes de bouffonnerie et des scènes attendrissantes: il y a
beaucoup de très bonnes pièces où il ne règne que de la gaieté; d'autres
toutes sérieuses; d'autres mélangèes: d'autres où l'attendrissement va
jusques aux larmes: il ne faut donner l'exclusion à aucun genre; et si on
me demandoit, quel genre est le meilleur, je répondrois, celui qui est le
mieux traité.*"[1] Surely if comedy may be *toute sérieuse,* tragedy may
now and then, soberly, be indulged in a smile. Who shall pro-
scribe it? Shall the critic, who, in self-defence, declares, that no
kind ought to be excluded from comedy, give laws to Shakespeare?

. I am aware that the preface from whence I have quoted these
passages does not stand in Monsieur de Voltaire's name, but in that
of his editor; yet who doubts that the editor and the author were
the same person?[2] or where is the editor, who has so happily possessed himself of his author's style, and brilliant ease of argument?
These passages were indubitably the genuine sentiments of that
great writer. In his epistle to Maffei,[3] prefixed to his *Mérope,* he
delivers almost the same opinion, though, I doubt, with a little
irony. I will repeat his words, and then give my reason for quoting
them. After translating a passage in Maffei's *Mérope,* Monsieur de
Voltaire adds, "*Tous ces traits sont naïfs; tout y est convenable à ceux que
vous introduisez sur la scène, et aux moeurs que vous leur donnez. Ces
familiarités naturelles eussent été, à ce que je crois, bien reçues dans*

---

1   Quoting Voltaire, Walpole explains how a joining of the comic and the serious can
    enhance the artistic success of the whole work as demonstrated by Voltaire's comedy in
    which; [Translation: This work reveals a mix of seriousness and humor, comedy and
    emotion, these contrasts being often produced by a single event. Nothing is as com-
    mon as a house in which a father scolds, a daughter sheds tears because of her passion-
    ate love, the son makes fun of both of them, and various relatives take part in the action
    in different ways. By this, I am not suggesting that every comedy must contain farcical
    or touching scenes: many very good plays display nothing but cheerfulness; others are
    serious throughout; other mix both modes: in others still, emotions command tears.
    No style must be excluded and if anyone asked me what the best one is, I would
    answer, "it is the one that is presented in the best manner."]
2   The editor of *L'Enfant prodigue* was indeed Voltaire himself as indicated in the play's
    "Advertisement": "Corrigé par L'Auteur ... Nous assurons le public, que cette pièce
    est de M. de Voltaire" [corrected by the author ... We assure the public, that this play is
    by Mr. Voltaire]. See: Voltaire, *L'Enfant Prodigue: Comédie en Vers Dissyllabes, Représenté
    sur le Théâtre de La Comédie Française le 10 Octobre 1736.* Paris: Chez Prault Fils, 1738. 96.
3   Count Scipione Maffei (1675-1755) wrote the highly successful tragedy *Mérope* (1713).

Athènes; mais Paris et notre parterre veulent une autre espèce de simplicité.[1] I doubt, I say, whether there is not a grain of sneer in this and other passages of that epistle; yet the force of truth is not damaged by being tinged with ridicule. Maffei was to represent a Grecian story: surely the Athenians were as competent judges of Grecian manners, and of the propriety of introducing them, as the parterre of Paris. "On the contrary," says Voltaire (and I cannot but admire his reasoning), "there were but ten thousand citizens at Athens and Paris has near eight hundred thousand inhabitants, among whom one may reckon thirty thousand judges of dramatic works."—indeed!—but allowing so numerous a tribunal, I believe this is the only instance in which it was ever pretended that thirty thousand persons, living near two thousand years after the era in question, were, upon the mere face of the poll, declared better judges than the Grecians themselves, of what ought to be the manners of a tragedy written on a Grecian story.

I will not enter into a discussion of the *espèce de simplicité*, which the *parterre* of Paris demands, nor of the shackles with which the thirty thousand judges have cramped their poetry, the chief merit of which, as I gather from repeated passages in The New Commentary on Corneille, consists in vaulting in spite of those fetters; a merit which, if true, would reduce poetry from the lofty effort of imagination, to a puerile and most contemptible labour—*difficiles nugæ*[2] with witness! I cannot, however, help mentioning a couplet, which, to my English ears, always sounded as the flattest and most trifling instance of circumstantial propriety, but which Voltaire, who has dealt so severely with nine parts in ten of Corneille's works, has singled out to defend in Racine;[3]

---

1 The "sort of simplicity" on stage that the Parisian audience requires. Literally, *parterre* is a flowerbed, but in the theater, it is the pit or area in front of the stage where spectators with less money and less taste stand. [Translation: All these features are artless; everything in them matches the characters you bring to the stage and the customs you attribute to them. These sorts of true-to-life commonplaces would have been, I believe, well received in Athens, but Paris and those who sit in our stalls want a different kind of simplicity.]

2 Laborious trifles.

3 Jean Baptiste Racine (1639-1699). French tragic dramatist. His tragedy *Phèdre* is a model of neoclassic tragedy.

De son appartement cette porte est prochaine,
Et cette autre conduit dans celui de la Reine.

In English,

To Cæsar's *closet through this door you come.*
And t'other leads to the Queen's drawing-room.

Unhappy Shakespeare! hadst thou made Rosencrantz inform his compeer, Guildenstern, of the ichonography[1] of the palace of Copenhagen, instead of presenting us with a moral dialogue between the Prince of Denmark and the grave-digger,[2] the illuminated pit of Paris would have been instructed *a second time* to adore thy talents.

The result of all I have said, is, to shelter my own daring under the canon of the brightest genius this country, at least, has produced. I might have pleaded that, having created a new species of romance, I was at liberty to lay down what rules I thought fit for the conduct of it: but I should be more proud of having imitated, however faintly, weakly, and at a distance, so masterly a pattern, than to enjoy the entire merit of invention, unless I could have marked my work with genius, as well as with originality. Such as it is, the public have honoured it sufficiently, whatever rank their suffrages allot to it.

---

1 Floor plan or scale drawing of a building's ground plan.
2 Refers to the scene in Shakespeare's *Hamlet*.v.i. in which Hamlet plays a game of wits with the gravedigger.

SONNET[1]

To the Right Honourable
LADY MARY COKE

The gentle maid, whose hapless tale
These melancholy pages speak;
Say, gracious lady, shall she fail
To draw the tear adown thy cheek?

No; never was thy pitying breast
Insensible to human woes;
Tender, though firm, it melts distrest
For weaknesses it never knows.

Oh! Guard the marvels I relate
Of fell ambition scourg'd by fate,
    From reason's peevish blame:
Blest with thy smile, thy dauntless sail
I dare expand to fancy's gale,
    For sure thy smiles are fame.

H.W.

---

1   The dedicatory sonnet was added to the second edition of *Otranto*. Lady Mary [Campbell] Coke (1726-1811), daughter of the Duke of Argyll, was an eccentric and ultrasentimental friend and correspondent of Walpole. The sonnet's bantering tone gently mocks her extreme sensibility.

The death of Conrad beneath the helmet, chapter one,
The Castle of Otranto

CHAPTER ONE

MANFRED, Prince of Otranto, had one son and one daughter; the latter a most beautiful virgin, aged eighteen, was called Matilda. Conrad, the son, was three years younger, a homely youth, sickly, and of no promising disposition; yet he was the darling of his father, who never showed any symptoms of affection to Matilda. Manfred had contracted a marriage for his son with the Marquis of Vicenza's daughter, Isabella; and she had already been delivered by her guardians into the hands of Manfred, that he might celebrate the wedding as soon as Conrad's infirm state of health would permit. Manfred's impatience for this ceremonial was remarked by his family and neighbours. The former, indeed, apprehending the severity of their prince's disposition, did not dare to utter their surmises on this precipitation. Hippolita, his wife, an amiable lady, did sometimes venture to represent the danger of marrying their only son so early, considering his great youth, and greater infirmities; but she never received any other answer than reflections on her own sterility,[1] who had given him but one heir. His tenants and subjects were less cautious in their discourses: they attributed this hasty wedding to the prince's dread of seeing accomplished an ancient prophecy, which was said to have pronounced, *That the Castle and Lordship of Otranto should pass from the present family, whenever the real owner should be grown too large to inhabit it.* It was difficult to make any sense of this prophecy; and still less easy to conceive what it had to do with the marriage in question. Yet these mysteries, or contradictions, did not make the populace adhere the less to their opinion.

Young Conrad's birth-day was fixed for his espousals. The company was assembled in the chapel of the castle, and everything ready for beginning the divine office, when Conrad himself was missing. Manfred, impatient of the least delay, and who had not observed his son retire, dispatched one of his attendants to summon the young prince. The servant, who had not staid long enough to have crossed the court to Conrad's apartment, came

---

1   The sexual ambiguity is obvious since it opens the possibility of Manfred's impotency as the cause.

running back breathless, in a frantic manner, his eyes staring, and foaming at the mouth. He said nothing, but pointed to the court. The company were struck with terror and amazement.[1] The princess Hippolita, without knowing what was the matter, but anxious for her son, swooned away. Manfred, less apprehensive than enraged at the procrastination of the nuptials, and at the folly of his domestic, asked imperiously, what was the matter? The fellow made no answer, but continued pointing towards the court-yard; and at last, after repeated questions put to him, cried out, Oh, the helmet! the helmet! In the mean time, some of the company had run into the court, from whence was heard a confused noise of shrieks, horror,[2] and surprise. Manfred, who began to be alarmed at not seeing his son, went himself to get information of what occasioned this strange confusion. Matilda remained endeavouring to assist her mother, and Isabella staid for the same purpose, and to avoid showing any impatience for the bride-groom, for whom, in truth, she had conceived little affection.

The first thing that struck Manfred's eyes was a group of his servants endeavouring to raise something that appeared to him a mountain of sable plumes. He gazed without believing his sight. What are ye doing? cried Manfred, wrathfully: Where is my son? A volley of voices replied, Oh, my lord! the prince! the prince! the helmet! the helmet! Shocked with these lamentable sounds and dreading he knew not what, he advanced hastily—But what a sight for a father's eyes! — He beheld his child dashed to pieces, and almost buried under an enormous helmet, an hundred times more large than any casque[3] ever made for human being, and shaded with a proportionable quantity of black feathers.

---

1   By the time of *Otranto*, the words terror and horror had already taken on disparate meanings partly as a result of Edmund Burke's aesthetic theories in *A Philosophical Enquiry into the Origin of Our Ideas of the Sublime and Beautiful*. Terror indicated an anticipated dread of something fearful, the emotion often mingled with awe or amaze-ment.

2   The emotion of horror in Gothic fiction occurs when the terror that is anticipated or dreaded is horribly realized by being seen, touched, or experienced as a hideous physi-cal sensation. *Otranto* makes ample use of both responses.

3   A helmet, frequently the outer plated helmet worn over chain mail for jousting or combat. Walpole may have obtained the idea for an immense helmet from Jonathan Swift's *Battle of the Books* (1704) where the poet John Dryden does battle wearing a helmet nine times larger than his head. "For the Helmet was nine times too large for the Head, which appeared Situate far in the hinder Part."

The horror of the spectacle, the ignorance of all around how this misfortune happened, and above all, the tremendous phænomenon before him, took away the prince's speech. Yet his silence lasted longer than even grief could occasion. He fixed his eyes on what he wished in vain to believe a vision; and seemed less attentive at his loss, than buried in meditation on the stupendous object that had occasioned it. He touched, he examined the fatal casque; nor could even the bleeding mangled remains of the young prince divert the eyes of Manfred from the portent before him. All who had known his partial fondness for young Conrad, were as much surprised at their prince's insensibility, as thunderstruck themselves at the "miracle" of the helmet. They conveyed the disfigured corpse into the hall, without receiving the least direction from Manfred. As little was he attentive to the ladies who remained in the chapel: on the contrary, without mentioning the unhappy princesses his wife and daughter, the first sounds that dropped from Manfred's lips were, Take care of the Lady Isabella.

The domestics, without observing the singularity of this direction, were guided by their affection to their mistress to consider it as peculiarly addressed to her situation, and flew to her assistance. They conveyed her to her chamber more dead than alive, and indifferent to all the strange circumstances she heard, except the death of her son. Matilda, who doted on her mother, smothered her own grief and amazement, and thought of nothing but assisting and comforting her afflicted parent. Isabella, who had been treated by Hippolita like a daughter, and who returned that tenderness with equal duty and affection, was scarce less assiduous about the princess; at the same time endeavouring to partake and lessen the weight of sorrow which she saw Matilda strove to suppress, for whom she had conceived the warmest sympathy of friendship. Yet her own situation could not help finding its place in her thoughts. She felt no concern for the death of young Conrad, except commiseration; and she was not sorry to be delivered from a marriage which had promised her little felicity, either from her destined bridegroom, or from the severe temper of Manfred, who, though he had distinguished her by great indulgence, had imprinted her mind with terror, from his causeless rigour to such amiable princesses as Hippolita and Matilda.

While the ladies were conveying the wretched mother to her

bed, Manfred remained in the court, gazing on the ominous casque, and regardless of the crowd which the strangeness of the event had now assembled around him. The few words he articulated tended solely to enquiries, whether any man knew from whence it could have come? Nobody could give him the least information. However, as it seemed to be the sole object of his curiosity, it soon became so to the rest of the spectators, whose conjectures were as absurd and improbable as the catastrophe itself was unprecedented. In the midst of their senseless guesses a young peasant, whom rumour had drawn thither from a neighbouring village, observed that the miraculous helmet was exactly like that on the figure in black marble of Alfonso the Good, one of their former princes, in the church of St. Nicholas. Villain! what sayest thou? cried Manfred, starting from his trance in a tempest of rage, and seizing the young man by the collar: How darest thou utter such treason? Thy life shall pay for it. The spectators, who as little comprehended the cause of the prince's fury as all the rest they had seen, were at a loss to unravel this new circumstance. The young peasant himself was still more astonished, not conceiving how he had offended the prince: yet recollecting himself, with a mixture of grace and humility, he disengaged himself from Manfred's gripe, and then, with an obeisance which discovered more jealousy of innocence, than dismay, he asked with respect, of what he was guilty? Manfred, more enraged at the vigour, however decently exerted, with which the young man had shaken off his hold, than appeased by his submission, ordered his attendants to seize him, and, if he had not been withheld by his friends whom he had invited to the nuptials, would have poignarded[1] the peasant in their arms.

During this altercation, some of the vulgar spectators had run to the great church which stood near the castle, and came back open-mouthed, declaring the helmet was missing from Alfonso's statue. Manfred, at this news, grew perfectly frantic; and, as if he sought a subject on which to vent the tempest within him, he rushed again on the young peasant, crying, Villain! monster! sorcerer! 'tis thou hast slain my son! The mob, who wanted some object within the scope of their capacities on whom they might

1 A poignard is a dagger. Used as a verb, it means "stabbed."

discharge their bewildered reasonings, caught the words from the mouth of their lord, and re-echoed, Ay, ay, 'tis he, 'tis he: he has stolen the helmet from good Alfonso's tomb, and dashed out the brains of our young prince with it: — never reflecting, how enormous the disproportion was between the marble helmet that had been in the church, and that of steel before their eyes; nor how impossible it was for a youth, seemingly not twenty, to wield a piece of armour of so prodigious a weight.

The folly of these ejaculations brought Manfred to himself: yet whether provoked at the peasant having observed the resemblance between the two helmets, and thereby led to the farther discovery of the absence of that in the church; or wishing to bury any fresh rumour under so impertinent a supposition; he gravely pronounced that the young man was certainly a necromancer, and that till the church could take cognizance of the affair, he would have the magician, whom they had thus detected, kept prisoner under the helmet itself,[1] which he ordered his attendants to raise, and place the young man under it; declaring he should be kept there without food, with which his own infernal art might furnish him.

It was vain for the youth to represent against this preposterous sentence: in vain did Manfred's friends endeavour to divert him from this savage and ill-grounded resolution. The generality were charmed with their lord's decision, which to their apprehensions carried great appearance of justice, as the magician was to be punished by the very instrument with which he had offended: nor were they struck with the least compunction at the probability of the youth being starved, for they firmly believed that by his diabolical skill he could easily supply himself with nutriment.

Manfred thus saw his commands even cheerfully obeyed; and appointing a guard with strict orders to prevent any food being conveyed to the prisoner, he dismissed his friends and attendants, retired to his own chamber, after locking the gates of the castle, in which he suffered none but his domestics to remain.

In the mean time, the care and zeal of the young ladies had

---

1   Theodore's odd punishment is an example of the "extraordinary positions" discussed by Walpole in the Preface to the second edition. Later Gothic fiction would offer many variations of "extraordinary positions" to generate fear and trembling.

brought the princess Hippolita to herself, who amidst the transports of her own sorrow frequently demanded news of her lord, would have dismissed her attendants to watch over him, and at last enjoined Matilda to leave her, and visit and comfort her father. Matilda, who wanted no affectionate duty to Manfred, though she trembled at his austerity, obeyed the orders of Hippolita, whom she tenderly recommended to Isabella; and enquiring of the domestics for her father, was informed that he was retired to his chamber, and had commanded that nobody should have admittance to him. Concluding that he was immersed in sorrow for the death of her brother, and fearing to renew his tears by the sight of his sole remaining child, she hesitated whether she should break in upon his affliction; yet solicitude for him, backed by the commands of her mother, encouraged her to venture disobeying the orders he had given; a fault she had never been guilty of before. The gentle timidity of her nature made her pause for some minutes at his door. She heard him traverse his chamber backwards and forwards with disordered steps; a mood which increased her apprehensions. She was however just going to beg admittance, when Manfred suddenly opened the door; and as it was now twilight, concurring with the disorder of his mind, he did not distinguish the person, but asked angrily who it was? Matilda replied trembling, My dearest father, it is I, your daughter. Manfred, stepping back hastily, cried, Begone, I do not want a daughter; and, flinging back abruptly, clapped the door against the terrified Matilda.

She was too well acquainted with her father's impetuosity to venture a second intrusion. When she had a little recovered the shock of so bitter a reception, she wiped away her tears, to prevent the additional stab that the knowledge of it would give to Hippolita, who questioned her in the most anxious terms on the health of Manfred, and how he bore his loss. Matilda assured her he was well, and supported his misfortune with manly fortitude. But will he not let me see him? said Hippolita mournfully: Will he not permit me to blend my tears with his, and shed a mother's sorrows in the bosom of her lord? Or do you deceive me, Matilda? I know how Manfred doted on his son: Is not the stroke too heavy for him? Has he not sunk under it?—You do not answer me—Alas, I dread the worst!—Raise me, my maidens: I will, I will see my lord. Bear me to him instantly; he is dearer to me even than my children. Matilda made signs to Isabella to prevent Hippolita's rising; and both these lovely young women were using their gentle violence to stop and calm the princess, when a servant on the part of Manfred arrived, and told Isabella that his lord demanded to speak with her.

With me! cried Isabella. Go, said Hippolita, relieved by a message from her lord: Manfred cannot support the sight of his own family. He thinks you less disordered than we are, and dreads the shock of my grief. Console him, dear Isabella, and tell him I will smother my own anguish rather than add to his.

It was now evening; the servant who conducted Isabella, bore a torch before her. When they came to Manfred, who was walking impatiently about the gallery, he started and said hastily, Take away that light, and begone. Then shutting the door impetuously, he flung himself upon a bench against the wall, and bade Isabella sit by him. She obeyed trembling. I sent for you, lady, said he,—and then stopped under great appearance of confusion. My lord!— Yes, I sent for you on a matter of great moment, resumed he:— Dry your tears, young lady—you have lost your bridegroom:— yes, cruel fate, and I have lost the hopes of my race!—But Conrad was not worthy of your beauty.—How! my lord, said Isabella; sure you do not suspect me of not feeling the concern I ought? My duty and affection would have always—Think no more of him, interrupted Manfred; he was a sickly, puny child, and heaven has perhaps taken him away that I might not trust the honours of my house on so frail a foundation. The line of Manfred calls for numerous supports. My foolish fondness for that boy blinded the eyes of my prudence—but it is better as it is. I hope in a few years to have reason to rejoice at the death of Conrad.

Words cannot paint the astonishment of Isabella. At first she apprehended that grief had disordered Manfred's understanding. Her next thought suggested that this strange discourse was designed to ensnare her: she feared that Manfred had perceived her indifference for his son: and in consequence of that idea she replied, Good my lord, do not doubt my tenderness; my heart would have accompanied my hand. Conrad would have engrossed all my care; and wherever fate shall dispose of me, I shall always cherish his memory, and regard your highness and the virtuous Hippolita as my parents. Curse on Hippolita! cried Manfred: Forget her from this moment, as I do. In short, lady, you have missed a husband undeserving of your charms: they shall now be better disposed of. Instead of a sickly boy, you shall have a husband in the prime of his age,[1] who will know how to value your beauties, and who may expect a numerous offspring. Alas, my lord, said Isabella, my mind is too sadly engrossed by the recent catastrophe in your family to think of another marriage. If ever my father returns, and it shall be his pleasure, I shall obey, as I did when I consented to give my hand to your son: but until his return permit me to remain under your hospitable roof, and employ the melancholy hours in assuaging yours, Hippolita's, and the fair Matilda's affliction.

I desired you once before, said Manfred angrily, not to name that woman; from this hour she must be a stranger to you, as she must be to me:—in short, Isabella, since I cannot give you my son, I offer you myself.—Heavens! cried Isabella, waking from her delusion, what do I hear! You, my lord! You! My father in law! the father of Conrad! the husband of the virtuous and tender Hippolita!—I tell you, said Manfred imperiously, Hippolita is no longer my wife; I divorce her from this hour. Too long has she cursed me by her unfruitfulness: my fate depends on having sons,—and this night I trust will give a new date to my hopes. At those words he seized the cold hand of Isabella, who was half-dead with fright and horror. She shrieked, and started from him. Manfred rose to pursue her; when the moon, which was now up, and gleamed in at the opposite casement, presented to his sight the plumes of the fatal helmet, which rose to the height of the windows, waving backwards and forwards in a tempestuous manner, and accompanied with a hollow and rustling sound. Isabella, who gathered courage from her situation, and who dreaded nothing so much as Manfred's pursuit of his declaration, cried,

---

1 Manfred's remark is an assertion of virility but also reveals a fear of impotency. For a discussion of such sexual themes as fear of castration and impotency in the novel, see: George Haggerty, "Literature and Homosexuality in the Late Eighteenth Century: Walpole, Beckford, and Lewis" in *Homosexual Themes in Literary Studies*, eds. Wayne R. Dynes, Stephen Donaldson. New York: Garland, 1992: 167–178.

Look, my lord! see heaven itself declares against your impious intentions!—Heaven nor hell shall impede my designs, said Manfred, advancing again to seize the princess. At that instant the portrait of his grandfather, which hung over the bench where they had been sitting, uttered a deep sigh and heaved its breast. Isabella, whose back was turned to the picture, saw not the motion, nor knew whence the sound came, but started and said, Hark, my lord! what sound was that? and at the same time made towards the door. Manfred, distracted between the flight of Isabella, who had now reached the stairs, and his inability to keep his eyes from the picture, which began to move, had however advanced some steps after her, still looking backwards on the portrait, when he saw it quit its pannel,[1] and descend on the floor with a grave and melancholy air. Do I dream? cried Manfred returning, or are the devils themselves in league against me? Speak, infernal spectre! Or, if thou art my grandsire, why dost thou too conspire against thy wretched descendant, who too dearly pays for—Ere he could finish the sentence the vision sighed again, and made a sign to Manfred to follow him. Lead on! cried Manfred; I will follow thee to the gulph of perdition.[2] The spectre marched sedately, but dejected, to the end of the gallery, and turned into a chamber on the right hand. Manfred accompanied him at a little distance, full of anxiety and horror, but resolved. As he would have entered the chamber, the door was clapped-to with violence by an invisible hand.[3] The prince, collecting courage from this delay, would have forcibly burst open the door with his foot, but found that it resisted his utmost efforts. Since hell will not satisfy my curiosity, said Manfred, I will use the human means in my power for preserving my race; Isabella shall not escape me.

That lady, whose resolution had given way to terror the

---

1   I.e. panel. Although it became a commonplace of Gothic fiction, Walpole was the first to introduce the walking portrait, later an almost mandatory tool of terror. The portrait of Lord Falkland by Paul van Somer at Strawberry Hill furnished Walpole with a working model.

2   Manfred's remark recalls Hamlet's encounter with his father's ghost. *Hamlet* I.iv.79. "Go on, I'll follow thee."

3   Walpole was responsible for installing one of the most familiar acoustics of the Gothic tradition, the door that bangs shut by an unseen force. For the further history of this favorite Gothic acoustic see: Stefan Andriopoulos, "The Invisible Hand: Supernatural Agency in Political Economy and the Gothic Novel." *ELH* 66 (1999): 739-758.

moment she had quitted Manfred, continued her flight to the bottom of the principal staircase. There she stopped, not knowing whither to direct her steps, nor how to escape from the impetuosity of the prince. The gates of the castle she knew were locked, and guards placed in the court. Should she, as her heart prompted her, go and prepare Hippolita for the cruel destiny that awaited her, she did not doubt but Manfred would seek her there, and that his violence would incite him to double the injury he meditated, without leaving room for them to avoid the impetuosity of his passions. Delay might give him time to reflect on the horrid measures he had conceived, or produce some circumstance in her favour, if she could for that night at least avoid his odious purpose. — Yet where conceal herself! How avoid the pursuit he would infallibly make throughout the castle! As these thoughts passed rapidly through her mind, she recollected a subterraneous passage which led from the vaults of the castle to the church of St. Nicholas. Could she reach the altar before she was overtaken, she knew even Manfred's violence would not dare to profane the sacredness of the place; and she determined, if no other means of deliverance offered, to shut herself up for ever among the holy virgins, whose convent was contiguous to the cathedral. In this resolution, she seized a lamp that burned at the foot of the staircase, and hurried towards the secret passage.

The lower part of the castle was hollowed into several intricate cloisters; and it was not easy for one under so much anxiety to find the door that opened into the cavern. An awful silence reigned throughout those subterraneous regions, except now and then some blasts of wind that shook the doors she had passed, and which grating on the rusty hinges were re-echoed through that long labyrinth of darkness.[1] Every murmur struck her with new terror;— yet more she dreaded to hear the wrathful voice of Manfred urging his domestics to pursue her. She trod as softly as impatience would give her leave,— yet frequently stopped and lis-

---

1   Walpole's description of the Gothic maze through which innumerable victims will take flight puts in place the cryptonomic format of terror for Gothic fiction in general. See: Jerrold E. Hogle, "The Restless Labyrinth: Cryptonomy in the Gothic Novel." *Arizona Quarterly* 36 (1980): 330-358.

tened to hear if she was followed. In one of those moments she thought she heard a sigh. She shuddered, and recoiled a few paces. In a moment she thought she heard the step of some person. Her blood curdled; she concluded it was Manfred. Every suggestion that horror could inspire rushed into her mind. She condemned her rash flight, which had thus exposed her to his rage in a place where her cries were not likely to draw anybody to her assistance. — Yet the sound seemed not to come from behind;—if Manfred knew where she was, he must have followed her: she was still in one of the cloisters, and the steps she had heard were too distinct to proceed from the way she had come. Cheered with this reflection, and hoping to find a friend in whoever was not the prince; she was going to advance, when a door that stood a-jar, at some distance to the left, was opened gently; but ere her lamp, which she held up, could discover who opened it, the person retreated precipitately on seeing the light.

Isabella, whom every incident was sufficient to dismay, hesitated whether she should proceed. Her dread of Manfred soon outweighed every other terror. The very circumstance of the person avoiding her, gave her a sort of courage. It could only be, she thought, some domestic belonging to the castle. Her gentleness had never raised her an enemy, and conscious innocence made her hope that, unless sent by the prince's order to seek her, his servants would rather assist than prevent her flight. Fortifying herself with these reflections, and believing, by what she could observe, that she was near the mouth of the subterraneous cavern, she approached the door that had been opened; but a sudden gust of wind that met her at the door extinguished her lamp, and left her in total darkness.

Words cannot paint the horror of the princess's situation. Alone in so dismal a place, her mind imprinted with all the terrible events of the day, hopeless of escaping, expecting every moment the arrival of Manfred, and far from tranquil on knowing she was within reach of somebody, she knew not whom, who for some cause seemed concealed thereabouts, all these thoughts crowded on her distracted mind, and she was ready to sink under her apprehensions. She addressed herself to every saint in heaven, and inwardly implored their assistance. For a considerable time she remained in an agony of despair. At last, as softly as was possible, she felt for the door, and, having found it, entered trembling into the vault from whence she had heard the sigh and steps. It gave her a kind of momentary joy to perceive an imperfect ray of clouded moonshine gleam from the roof of the vault, which seemed to be fallen in, and from whence hung a fragment of earth or building, she could not distinguish which, that appeared to have been crushed inwards. She advanced eagerly towards this chasm, when she discerned a human form standing close against the wall.

She shrieked, believing it the ghost of her betrothed Conrad. The figure advancing, said in a submissive voice, Be not alarmed, lady; I will not injure you. Isabella, a little encouraged by the words and the tone of voice of the stranger, and recollecting that this must be the person who had opened the door, recovered her spirits enough to reply, Sir, whoever you are, take pity on a wretched princess standing on the brink of destruction: assist me to escape from this fatal castle, or in a few moments I may be made miserable for ever. Alas! said the stranger, what can I do to assist you? I will die in your defence; but I am unacquainted with the castle, and want—Oh! said Isabella, hastily interrupting him, help me but to find a trap-door that must be hereabout, and it is the greatest service you can do me; for I have not a minute to lose. Saying these words she felt about on the pavement, and directed the stranger to search likewise for a smooth piece of brass inclosed in one of the stones. That, said she, is the lock, which opens with a spring, of which I know the secret. If we can find that, I may escape—if not, alas, courteous stranger, I fear I shall have involved you in my misfortunes: Manfred will suspect you for the accomplice of my flight, and you will fall a victim to his resentment. I value not my life, said the stranger; and it will be some comfort to lose it in trying to deliver you from his tyranny. Generous youth, said Isabella, how shall I ever requite—As she uttered those words, a ray of moonshine streaming through a cranny of the ruin above shone directly on the lock they sought—Oh, transport! said Isabella, here is the trap-door! and taking out a key, she touched the spring, which starting aside discovered an iron ring. Lift up the door, said the princess. The stranger obeyed; and beneath appeared some stone steps descending into a vault totally dark.[1] We must go down here, said Isabella: follow me; dark and dismal as it is, we cannot miss our way; it leads directly to the church of saint Nicholas—But perhaps, added the princess modestly, you have no reason to leave the castle, nor have I farther occasion for your service; in a few minutes I shall be safe from Manfred's rage—only let me know to whom I am so much obliged. I will never quit you, said the stranger eagerly, till I have placed you in safety—nor think me, princess, more generous than I am: though you are my principal care—The stranger was interrupted by a sudden noise of voices that seemed approaching, and they soon distinguished these words: Talk not to me of necromancers; I tell you she must be in the castle; I will find her in spite of enchantment.—Oh, heavens! cried Isabella, it is the voice of Manfred! Make haste, or we are ruined! and shut the trap-door after you. Saying this, she descended the steps precipitately; and as the stranger hastened to follow her, he let the door slip out of his hands: it fell, and the spring closed over it. He tried in vain to open it, not having observed Isabella's method of touching the spring, nor had he many moments to make an essay.[2] The noise of the falling door had been heard by Manfred, who, directed by the sound, hastened thither, attended by his servants with torches. It must be Isabella, cried Manfred before he entered the vault; she is escaping by the subterraneous passage, but she cannot have got far.—What was the astonishment of the prince, when, instead of Isabella the light of the torches discovered to him the young peasant, whom he thought confined under the fatal helmet! Traitor! said Manfred, how camest thou here? I thought thee in durance[3] above in the court. I am no traitor, replied the young man boldly, nor am I answerable for your thoughts. Presumptuous villain! cried Manfred, dost

---

1 The primary Gothic motif of the descent into darkness is established here. Vaults and crypts need not be subterranean although in Gothic fiction they almost always are beneath the castle, abbey, or mansion. For a discussion of the mechanics of the castle interior, see: Thomas Meade Hartwell, "Toward a Gothic Metaphysic: Gothic Parts." *Publications of the Arkansas Philological Society* 12:2 (1986): 33-43.

2 An attempt.

3 Imprisoned or incarcerated.

thou provoke my wrath? Tell me; how hast thou escaped from above? Thou hast corrupted thy guards, and their lives shall answer it. My poverty, said the peasant calmly, will disculpate[1] them: though the ministers of a tyrant's wrath, to thee they are faithful, and but too willing to execute the orders which you unjustly imposed upon them. Art thou so hardy as to dare my vengeance? said the prince—but tortures shall force the truth from thee. Tell me, I will know thy accomplices. There was my accomplice! said the youth smiling, and pointing to the roof. Manfred ordered the torches to be held up, and perceived that one of the cheeks of the enchanted casque had forced its way through the pavement of the court, as his servants had let it fall over the peasant, and had broken through into the vault, leaving a gap through which the peasant had pressed himself some minutes before he was found by Isabella. Was that the way by which thou didst descend? said Manfred. It was, said the youth. But what noise was that, said Manfred, which I heard as I entered the cloister? A door clapped, said the peasant: I heard it as well as you. What door? said Manfred hastily. I am not acquainted with your castle, said the peasant; this is the first time I ever entered it, and this vault the only part of it within which I ever was. But I tell thee, said Manfred, [wishing to find out if the youth had discovered the trap-door] it was this way I heard the noise: my servants heard it too. —My lord, interrupted one of them officiously, to be sure it was the trap-door, and he was going to make his escape. Peace! blockhead, said the prince angrily; if he was going to escape, how should he come on this side? I will know from his own mouth what noise it was I heard. Tell me truly; thy life depends on thy veracity. My veracity is dearer to me than my life, said the peasant; nor would I purchase the one by forfeiting the other. Indeed! young philosopher! said Manfred contemptuously: tell me then, what was the noise I heard? Ask me what I can answer, said he, and put me to death instantly if I tell you a lie. Manfred, growing impatient at the steady valour and indifference of the youth, cried, Well then, thou man of truth! answer; was it the fall of the trap-door that I heard? It was, said the youth. It

---

1   Exonerate or clear from blame.

was! said the prince; and how didst thou come to know there was a trap-door here? I saw the plate of brass by a gleam of moonshine, replied he. But what told thee it was a lock? said Manfred: How didst thou discover the secret of opening it? Providence, that delivered me from the helmet, was able to direct me to the spring of a lock, said he. Providence should have gone a little farther, and have placed thee out of the reach of my resentment, said Manfred: when Providence had taught thee to open the lock, it abandoned thee for a fool, who did not know how to make use of its favours. Why didst thou not pursue the path pointed out for thy escape? Why didst thou shut the trap-door before thou hadst descended the steps? I might ask you, my lord, said the peasant, how I, totally unacquainted with your castle, was to know that those steps led to any outlet? but I scorn to evade your questions. Wherever those steps led to, perhaps I should have explored the way—I could not have been in a worse situation than I was. But the truth is, I let the trap-door fall: your immediate arrival followed. I had given the alarm—what imported it to me whether I was seized a minute sooner or a minute later? Thou art a resolute villain for thy years, said Manfred—yet on reflection I suspect thou dost but trifle with me: thou has not yet told me how thou didst open the lock. That I will show you, my lord, said the peasant; and taking up a fragment of stone that had fallen from above, he laid himself on the trap-door, and began to beat on the piece of brass that covered it; meaning to gain time for the escape of the princess. This presence of mind, joined to the frankness of the youth, staggered Manfred. He even felt a disposition towards pardoning one who had been guilty of no crime. Manfred was not one of those savage tyrants who wanton in cruelty unprovoked. The circumstances of his fortune had given an asperity to his temper, which was naturally humane; and his virtues were always ready to operate, when his passion did not obscure his reason.

While the prince was in this suspense, a confused noise of voices echoed through the distant vaults. As the sound approached, he distinguished the clamour of some of his domestics, whom he had dispersed through the castle in search of Isabella, calling out, Where is my lord? Where is the prince? Here I am, said Manfred, as they came nearer; have you found the princess?

The first that arrived replied, Oh, my lord! I am glad we have found you. — Found me! said Manfred: have you found the princess? We thought we had, my lord, said the fellow looking terrified — but — But what? cried the prince; has she escaped? — Jaquez and I, my lord — Yes, I and Diego, interrupted the second, who came up in still greater consternation — Speak one of you at a time, said Manfred; I ask you, where is the princess? We do not know, said they both together: but we are frightened out of our wits. — So I think, blockheads, said Manfred: what is it has scared you thus? — Oh, my lord! said Jaquez, Diego has seen such a sight! your highness would not believe our eyes. — What new absurdity is this? cried Manfred—give me a direct answer, or by heaven — Why, my lord, if it please your highness to hear me, said the poor fellow; Diego and I— Yes, I and Jaquez, cried his comrade — Did not I forbid you to speak both at a time? said the prince: You, Jaquez, answer; for the other fool seems more distracted than thou art; what is the matter? My gracious lord, said Jaquez, if it please your highness to hear me; Diego and I, according to your high-ness's orders, went to search for the young lady; but being comprehensive[1] that we might meet the ghost of my young lord, your highness's son, God rest his soul, as he has not received Christian burial — Sot! cried Manfred in a rage, is it only a ghost then that thou hast seen? Oh, worse! worse! my lord! cried Diego: I had rather have seen ten whole ghosts. — Grant me patience! said Manfred; these blockheads distract me. — Out of my sight, Diego! and thou, Jaquez, tell me in one word, art thou sober? art thou raving? Thou wast wont to have some sense: has the other sot frightened himself and thee too? Speak; what is it he fancies he has seen? Why, my lord, replied Jaquez trembling, I was going to tell your highness, that since the calamitous misfortune of my young lord, God rest his soul! not one of us your highness's faithful servants, indeed we are, my lord, though poor men; I say, not one of us has dared to set a foot about the castle, but two together: so Diego and I, thinking that my young lady might be in the great gallery, went up there to look for her, and tell her

---

[1] The servant Jaquez means "being apprehensive" or fearful. His malapropism recalls Dogberry's confused use of "comprehend" for "apprehend" in Shakespeare's *Much Ado About Nothing*, III.iii.24-25.

your highness wanted something to impart to her. — O blundering fools! cried Manfred: and, in the mean time she has made her escape, because you were afraid of goblins! Why, thou knave! she left me in the gallery; I came from thence myself. — For all that, she may be there still for aught I know, said Jaquez; but the devil shall have me before I seek her there again! — Poor Diego! I do not believe he will ever recover it! Recover what? said Manfred; am I never to learn what it is has terrified these rascals? But I lose my time; follow me, slave! I will see if she is in the gallery. — For heaven's sake, my dear good lord, cried Jaquez, do not go to the gallery! Satan himself I believe is in the great chamber next to the gallery. — Manfred, who hitherto had treated the terror of his servants as an idle panic, was struck at this new circumstance. He recollected the apparition of the portrait, and the sudden closing of the door at the end of the gallery — his voice faltered, and he asked with disorder, What is in the great chamber? My lord, said Jaquez, when Diego and I came into the gallery, he went first, for he said he had more courage than I. So when we came into the gallery, we found nobody. We looked under every bench and stool; and still we found nobody. — Were all the pictures in their places? said Manfred. Yes, my lord, answered Jaquez; but we did not think of looking behind them. — Well, well! said Manfred; proceed. When we came to the door of the great chamber, continued Jaquez, we found it shut. — And could not you open it? said Manfred. Oh! yes, my lord, would to heaven we had not! replied he. — Nay, it was not I neither, it was Diego: he was grown fool-hardy, and would go on, though I advised him not — If ever I open a door that is shut again — Trifle not, said Manfred shuddering, but tell me what you saw in the great chamber on opening the door. — I! My lord! said Jaquez, I saw nothing; I was behind Diego; — but I heard the noise. — Jaquez, said Manfred in a solemn tone of voice, tell me, I adjure thee by the souls of my ancestors, what was it thou sawest; what was it thou heardest? It was Diego saw it, my lord, it was not I, replied Jaquez; I only heard the noise. Diego had no sooner opened the door, than he cried out and ran back — I ran back too, and said, is it the ghost? The ghost! no, no, said Diego, and his hair stood on end — It is a giant, I believe; he is all clad in armour, for I saw his foot and part of his leg,[1] and they are as large as the helmet below in the court. As he said these words, my lord, we heard a violent motion and the rattling of armour, as if the giant was rising; for Diego has told me since, that he believes the giant was lying down, for the foot and leg were stretched at'length on the floor. Before we could get to the end of the gallery, we heard the door of the great chamber clap behind us, but we did not dare turn back to see if the giant was following us—Yet now I think on it, we must have heard him if he had pursued us.—But for heaven's sake, good my lord, send for the chaplain and have the castle exorcised, for, for certain, it is enchanted. Ay, pray do, my lord, cried all the servants at once, or we must leave your highness's service.—Peace, dotards! said Manfred, and follow me; I will know what all this means. We! my lord! cried they with one voice; we would not go up to the gallery for your highness's revenue. The young peasant, who had stood silent, now spoke. Will your highness, said he, permit me to try this adventure? My life is of consequence to nobody: I fear no bad angel, and have offended no good one. Your behavior is above your seeming, said Manfred; viewing him with surprise and admiration—hereafter I will reward your bravery—but now, continued he with a sigh, I am so circumstanced, that I dare trust no eyes but my own—However, I give you leave to accompany me.

Manfred, when he first followed Isabella from the gallery, had gone directly to the apartment of his wife, concluding the princess had retired thither. Hippolita, who knew his step, rose with anxious fondness to meet her lord, whom she had not seen since the death of their son. She would have flown in a transport mixed of joy and grief to his bosom; but he pushed her rudely off, and said, Where is Isabella? Isabella! my lord! said the astonished Hippolita. Yes, Isabella; cried Manfred imperiously; I want Isabella. My lord, replied Matilda, who perceived how much his behaviour had shocked her mother, she has not been with us since your highness summoned her to your apartment. Tell me where she is, said the prince; I do not want to know where she

---

1 The *disjecta membra* or scattered body parts of a colossal man residing within the castle walls is both terrifying and titillating. Walpole had dreamt of "a gigantic hand in armour" above a staircase in an ancient castle before beginning *Otranto*. Letter to William Cole, 9 March 1765.

The walking portrait, chapter one, *The Castle of Otranto.*

has been. My good lord, said Hippolita, your daughter tells you the truth: Isabella left us by your command, and has not returned since: but, my good lord, compose yourself: retire to your rest: this dismal day has disordered you. Isabella shall wait your orders in the morning. What, then you know where she is? cried Manfred: Tell me directly, for I will not lose an instant—And you, woman, speaking to his wife, order your chaplain to attend me forthwith. Isabella, said Hippolita calmly, is retired I suppose to her chamber: she is not accustomed to watch at this late hour. Gracious my lord, continued she, let me know what has disturbed you: has Isabella offended you? Trouble me not with questions, said Manfred, but tell me where she is. Matilda shall call her, said the princess—sit down, my lord, and resume your wonted fortitude. — What, art thou jealous of Isabella, replied he, that you wish to be present at our interview? Good heavens! my lord, said Hippolita, what is it your highness means? Thou wilt know ere many minutes are past, said the cruel prince. Send your chaplain to me, and wait my pleasure here. At these words he flung out of the room in search of Isabella; leaving the amazed ladies thunderstruck with his words and frantic deportment, and lost in vain conjectures on what he was meditating.

Manfred was now returning from the vault, attended by the peasant and a few of his servants whom he had obliged to accompany him. He ascended the stair-case without stopping till he arrived at the gallery, at the door of which he met Hippolita and her chaplain. When Diego had been dismissed by Manfred, he had gone directly to the princess's apartment with the alarm of what he had seen. That excellent lady, who no more than Manfred doubted of the reality of the vision, yet affected to treat it as a delirium of the servant. Willing, however, to save her lord from any additional shock, and prepared by a series of griefs not to tremble at any accession to it; she determined to make herself the first sacrifice, if fate had marked the present hour for their destruction. Dismissing the reluctant Matilda to her rest, who in vain sued for leave to accompany her mother, and attended only by her chaplain, Hippolita had visited the gallery and great chamber: and now, with more serenity of soul than she had felt for many hours, she met her lord, and assured him that the vision of the gigantic leg and foot was all a fable; and no doubt an impression made by fear, and the dark and dismal hour of the night, on the minds of the servants: She and the chaplain had examined the chamber, and found every thing in the usual order.

Manfred, though persuaded, like his wife, that the vision had been no work of fancy, recovered a little from the tempest of mind into which so many strange events had thrown him. Ashamed too of his inhuman treatment of a princess, who returned every injury with new marks of tenderness and duty, he felt returning love forcing itself into his eyes—but not less ashamed of feeling remorse towards one, against whom he was inwardly meditating a yet more bitter outrage, he curbed the yearnings of his heart, and did not dare to lean even towards pity. The next transition of his soul was to exquisite villainy.[1] Presuming on the unshaken submission of Hippolita, he flattered himself that she would not only acquiesce with patience to a divorce, but would obey, if it was his pleasure, in endeavouring to persuade Isabella to give him her hand. — But ere he could indulge this horrid hope, he reflected that Isabella was not to be found. Coming to himself, he gave orders that every avenue to the castle should be strictly guarded, and charged his domestics on pain of their lives to suffer nobody to pass out. The young peasant, to whom he spoke favourably, he ordered to remain in a small chamber on the stairs, in which there was a pallet-bed,[2] and the key of which he took away himself, telling the youth he would talk with him in the morning. Then dismissing his attendants, and bestowing a sullen kind of half-nod on Hippolita, he retired to his own chamber.

---

1 Manfred, the first Gothic villain, is a divided being whose personality is a compound of good and evil. The contradictory selves at war within him sets the pattern for Gothic villains throughout the tradition. Shakespeare's Macbeth, a noble figure corrupted by passion and "black and deep desires" is an immediate model for Manfred.
2 Bed of straw or coarse material.

CHAPTER TWO

MATILDA, who by Hippolita's order had retired to her apartment, was ill-disposed to take any rest. The shocking fate of her brother had deeply affected her. She was surprised at not seeing Isabella: but the strange words which had fallen from her father, and his obscure menace to the princess his wife, accompanied by the most furious behaviour, had filled her gentle mind with terror and alarm. She waited anxiously for the return of Bianca, a young damsel that attended her, whom she had sent to learn what was become of Isabella. Bianca soon appeared, and informed her mistress of what she had gathered from the servants, that Isabella was nowhere to be found. She related the adventure of the young peasant, who had been discovered in the vault, though with many simple additions from the incoherent accounts of the domestics; and she dwelled principally on the gigantic leg and foot which had been seen in the gallery-chamber. This last circumstance had terrified Bianca so much, that she was rejoiced when Matilda told her that she would not go to rest, but would watch till the princess should rise.

The young princess wearied herself in conjectures on the flight of Isabella, and on the threats of Manfred to her mother. But what business could he have so urgent with the chaplain? said Matilda. Does he intend to have my brother's body interred privately in the chapel? Oh! madam, said Bianca, now I guess. As you are become his heiress, he is impatient to have you married: he has always been raving for more sons; I warrant he is now impatient for grandsons. As sure as I live, madam, I shall see you a bride at last. Good madam, you won't cast off your faithful Bianca; you won't put Donna Rosara over me, now you are a great princess? My poor Bianca, said Matilda, how fast our thoughts amble! I a great princess! What hast thou seen in Manfred's behaviour since my brother's death that bespeaks any increase of tenderness to me? No, Bianca, his heart was ever a stranger to me—but he is my father, and I must not complain. Nay, if heaven shuts my father's heart against me, it over-pays my little merit in the tenderness of my mother—O that dear mother! Yes, Bianca, 'tis there I feel the rugged temper of Manfred. I can support his harshness to me with patience; but it wounds my soul when I am witness to his causeless severity towards her. Oh, madam, said Bianca, all men use their wives so, when they are weary of them.[1]—And yet you congratulated me but now, said Matilda, when you fancied my father intended to dispose of me. I would have you a great lady, replied Bianca, come what will. I do not wish to see you moped in a convent,[2] as you would be if you had your will, and if my lady your mother, who knows that a bad husband is better than no husband at all, did not hinder you. —Bless me! what noise is that? Saint Nicholas forgive me! I was but in jest. It is the wind, said Matilda, whistling through the battlements in the tower above: you have heard it a thousand times. Nay, said Bianca, there was no harm neither in what I said: it is no sin to talk of matrimony—And so, madam, as I was saying; if my lord Manfred should offer you a handsome young prince for a bridegroom, you would drop him a curtsy, and tell him you would rather take the veil. Thank heaven! I am in no such danger, said Matilda: you know how many proposals for me he has rejected. —And you thank him, like a dutiful daughter, do you madam?—But come, madam; suppose, to-morrow morning he was to send for you to the great council-chamber, and there you should find at his elbow a lovely young prince, with large black eyes, a smooth white forehead, and manly curling locks like jet; in short, madam, a young hero resembling the picture of the good Alfonso in the gallery, which you sit and gaze at for hours together. —Do not speak lightly of that picture, interrupted Matilda sighing: I know the adoration with which I look at that picture is uncommon—but I am not in love with a coloured pannel. The character of that virtuous prince, the veneration with which my mother has inspired me for his memory, the orisons[3] which I know not why she has enjoined me to pour forth at his tomb, all have concurred to persuade me that somehow or other my destiny is linked with something relating to him. —Lord! madam, how should that be? said Bianca: I have always heard that your family was in no way related to his: and I am sure I cannot con-

---

1   See Emilia's similar bitter remark about the selfish appetites of men in Shakespeare's *Othello*, III.iv.104-105. "They are all but stomachs, and we all but food."

2   Sequestered in gloomy surroundings.

3   Prayers, the action of praying; a speech, an oration.

ceive why my lady, the princess, sends you in a cold morning, or a damp evening, to pray at his tomb: he is no saint by the almanack. If you must pray, why does she not bid you address yourself to our great saint Nicholas? I am sure he is the saint I pray to for a husband. Perhaps my mind would be less affected, said Matilda, if my mother would explain her reasons to me: but it is the mystery she observes, that inspires me with this—I know not what to call it. As she never acts from caprice, I am sure there is some fatal secret at bottom—nay, I know there is: in her agony of grief for my brother's death she dropped some words that intimated as much. —Oh, dear madam, cried Bianca, what were they? No, said Matilda: if a parent lets fall a word, and wishes it recalled, it is not for a child to utter it. What! was she sorry for what she had said? asked Bianca. —I am sure, madam, you may trust me. —With my own little secrets, when I have any, I may, said Matilda; but never with my mother's: a child ought to have no ears or eyes but as a parent directs. Well, to be sure, madam, you was born to be a saint, said Bianca, and there is no resisting one's vocation: you will end in a convent at last. But there is my lady Isabella would not be so reserved to me: she will let me talk to her of young men; and when a handsome cavalier has come to the castle, she has owned to me that she wished your brother Conrad resembled him. Bianca, said the princess, I do not allow you to mention my friend disrespectfully. Isabella is of a cheerful disposition, but her soul is as pure as virtue itself. She knows your idle babbling humour, and perhaps has now and then encouraged it, to divert melancholy, and to enliven the solitude in which my father keeps us. —Blessed Mary! said Bianca starting, there it is again!—Dear madam, do you hear nothing?—This castle is certainly haunted![1]—Peace! said Matilda, and listen! I did think I heard a voice—but it must be fancy; your terrors I suppose have infected me. Indeed! indeed! madam, said Bianca, half weeping with agony, I am sure I heard a voice. Does anybody lie in the chamber beneath? said the princess. Nobody has dared lie there, answered

---

1   The influence of Elsinore Castle, haunted by the ghost of Hamlet's slain father in *Hamlet*, is evident throughout *Otranto*. The specter of the murdered relative at large within a ruined building is one of the prerequisite conditions of the Gothic. See: Railo, Eino. *The Haunted Castle: A Study of the Elements of English Romanticism.* New York: Humanities Press, 1964.

Bianca, since the great astrologer that was your brother's tutor drowned himself. For certain, madam, his ghost and the young prince's are now met in the chamber below—for heaven's sake let us fly to your mother's apartment! I charge you not to stir, said Matilda. If they are spirits in pain, we may ease their sufferings by questioning them.[1] They can mean no hurt to us, for we have not injured them—and if they should, shall we be more safe in one chamber than another? reach me my beads; we will say a prayer, and then speak to them. Oh, dear lady, I would not speak to a ghost for the world, cried Bianca. —As she said those words, they heard the casement of the little chamber below Matilda's open. They listened attentively, and in few minutes thought they heard a person sing, but could not distinguish the words. This can be no evil spirit, said the princess in a low voice: it is undoubtedly one of the family—open the window, and we shall know the voice. I dare not indeed, madam, said Bianca. Thou art a very fool, said Matilda, opening the window gently herself. The noise the princess made was however heard by the person beneath, who stopped; and, they concluded, had heard the casement open. Is any body below? said the princess: if there is, speak. Yes, said an unknown voice. Who is it? said Matilda. A stranger, replied the voice. What stranger? said she; and how didst thou come there at this unusual hour, when all the gates of the castle are locked? I am not here willingly, answered the voice—but pardon me, lady, if I have disturbed your rest: I knew not that I was overheard. Sleep had forsaken me: I left a restless couch, and came to waste the irksome hours with gazing on the fair approach of morning, impatient to be dismissed from this castle. Thy words and accents, said Matilda, are of a melancholy cast: if thou art unhappy, I pity thee. If poverty afflicts thee, let me know it; I will mention thee to the princess, whose beneficent soul ever melts for the distressed; and she will relieve thee. I am indeed unhappy, said the stranger; and I know not what wealth is: but I do not complain of the lot which heaven has cast for me: I am young and healthy, and am not ashamed of owing my support to myself—yet think me not proud, or that I disdain your generous offers. I will remember you in my orisons, *(prayers)* and will pray for blessings on your gracious self and

---

1 Restless ghosts might be relieved of their torment by questioning them.

your noble mistress — If I sigh, lady, it is for others, not for myself. Now I have it, madam, said Bianca whispering to the princess. This is certainly the young peasant; and by my conscience he is in love! — Well, this is a charming adventure! — Do, madam, let us sift him.[1] He does not know you, but takes you for one of my lady Hippolita's women. Art thou not ashamed, Bianca? said the princess: what right have we to pry into the secrets of this young man's heart? He seems virtuous and frank, and tells us he is unhappy: are those circumstances that authorize us to make a property of him? How are we entitled to his confidence? Lord! madam, how little you know of love! replied Bianca: why, lovers have no pleasure equal to talking of their mistress. And would you have *me* become a peasant's confidante? said the princess. Well then, let me talk to him, said Bianca: though I have the honour of being your highness's maid of honour, I was not always so great: besides, if love levels ranks, it raises them too: I have a respect for a young man in love. — Peace, simpleton! said the princess. Though he said he was unhappy, it does not follow that he must be in love. Think of all that has happened to-day, and tell me if there are no misfortunes but what love causes. Stranger, resumed the princess, if thy misfortunes have not been occasioned by thy own fault, and are within the compass of the princess Hippolita's power to redress, I will take upon me to answer that she will be thy protectress. When thou art dismissed from this castle, repair to holy father Jerome at the convent adjoining to the church of saint Nicholas, and make thy story known to him, as far as thou thinkest meet: he will not fail to inform the princess, who is the mother of all that want her assistance. Farewell: it is not seemly for me to hold farther converse with a man at this unwonted hour. May the saints guard thee, gracious lady! replied the peasant — but oh, if a poor and worthless stranger might presume to beg a minute's audience farther — am I so happy? — the casement is not shut — might I venture to ask — Speak quickly, said Matilda; the morning dawns apace:[2] should the labourers come into the fields and perceive us — what wouldst thou ask? — I know not how — I

---

1   To inspect or examine closely or to weigh evidence carefully.
2   Walpole adapts Shakespearean phrasing for the coming of dawn. See: *A Midsummer Night's Dream*, I.i.1–2; "our nuptial hour draws on apace."

know not if I dare, said the young stranger faltering—yet the humanity with which you have spoken to me emboldens—Lady! dare I trust you?—Heavens! said Matilda, What dost thou mean? with what wouldst thou trust me? Speak boldly, if thy secret is fit to be entrusted to a virtuous breast. — I would ask, said the peasant, recollecting himself, whether what I have heard from the domestics is true, that the princess is missing from the castle? What imports it to thee to know? replied Matilda. Thy first words bespoke a prudent and becoming gravity. Dost thou come hither to pry into the secrets of Manfred? Adieu, I have been mistaken in thee. —Saying these words she shut the casement hastily, without giving the young man time to reply. I had acted more wisely, said the princess to Bianca, with some sharpness, if I had let thee converse with this peasant: his inquisitiveness seems of a piece with thy own. It is not fit for me to argue with your highness, said Bianca; but perhaps the questions I should have put to him, would have been more to the purpose, than those you have been pleased to ask him. Oh, no doubt, said Matilda; you are a very discreet personage! May I know what you would have asked him? A by-stander often sees more of the game than those that play,[1] answered Bianca. Does your highness think, madam, that his question about my Lady Isabella was the result of mere curiosity? No, no, madam; there is more in it than you great folks are aware of. Lopez told me, that all the servants believe this young fellow contrived my Lady Isabella's escape—Now, pray, madam, observe—you and I both know that my Lady Isabella never much fancied the prince your brother. Well! he is killed just in the critical minute—I accuse nobody. A helmet falls from the moon—so my lord your father says; but Lopez and all the servants say that this young spark[2] is a magician, and stole it from Alfonso's tomb. — Have done with this rhapsody of imperti-

---

1 The adage means that those who watch a contest are in a better position to understand and judge than those who play. See: Madeleine Kahn. "'A By-Stander Often Sees More of the Game Than Those That Play': Ann Yearsley Reads *The Castle of Otranto*," *Bucknell Review* 42:1 (1998): 59-78.

2 Sneering term for an ostentatious young man whose manners and dress are highly affected. See the character, Sparkish, in William Wycherley's comedy, *The Country Wife* (1675).

nence, said Matilda. Nay, madam, as you please, cried Bianca—
yet it is very particular though, that my lady Isabella should be
missing the very same day, and this young sorcerer should be
found at the mouth of the trap-door—I accuse nobody—but if
my young lord came honestly by his death—Dare not on thy
duty, said Matilda, to breathe a suspicion on the purity of my dear
Isabella's fame. —Purity, or not purity, said Bianca, gone she is: a
stranger is found that nobody knows: you question him yourself:
he tells you he is in love, or unhappy, it is the same thing—nay, he
owned he was unhappy about others; and is any body unhappy
about another, unless they are in love with them? And at the very
next word he asks innocently, poor soul! if my Lady Isabella is
missing. —To be sure, said Matilda, thy observations are not totally without foundation—Isabella's flight amazes me: the curiosity
of this stranger is very particular—yet Isabella never concealed a
thought from me. —So she told you, said Bianca, to fish out your
secrets—but who knows, madam, but this stranger may be some
prince in disguise?—Do, madam, let me open the window, and
ask him a few questions. No, replied Matilda, I will ask him
myself, if he knows aught of Isabella: he is not worthy that I
should converse farther with him. She was going to open the
casement, when they heard the bell ring at the postern-gate[1] of
the castle, which is on the right hand of the tower, where Matilda
lay. This prevented the princess from renewing the conversation
with the stranger.

After continuing silent for some time; I am persuaded, said she
to Bianca, that whatever be the cause of Isabella's flight, it had no
unworthy motive. If this stranger was accessary to it, she must be
satisfied of his fidelity and worth. I observed, did not you, Bianca?
that his words were tinctured with an uncommon infusion of
piety. It was no ruffian's speech: his phrases were becoming a man
of gentle birth. I told you, madam, said Bianca, that I was sure he
was some prince in disguise. —Yet, said Matilda, if he was privy
to her escape, how will you account for his not accompanying her
in her flight? Why expose himself unnecessarily and rashly to my
father's resentment? As for that, madam, replied she, if he could

---

1   A rear gate, especially in a castle or fortress.

get from under the helmet, he will find ways of eluding your father's anger. I do not doubt but he has some talisman[1] or other about him. —You resolve every thing into magic, said Matilda— but a man who has any intercourse with infernal spirits does not dare to make use of those tremendous and holy words which he uttered. Didst thou not observe with what fervour he vowed to remember *me* to heaven in his prayers? Yes, Isabella was undoubtedly convinced of his piety. —Commend me to the piety of a young fellow and a damsel that consult to elope! said Bianca. No, no, madam; my lady Isabella is of another guess-mould[2] than you take her for. She used indeed to sigh and lift up her eyes in your company, because she knows you are a saint—but when your back was turned—You wrong her, said Matilda; Isabella is no hypocrite: she has a due sense of devotion, but never affected a call she has not. On the contrary, she always combated my inclination for the cloister: and though I own the mystery she has made to me of her flight confounds me; though it seems inconsistent with the friendship between us; I cannot forget the disinterested warmth with which she always opposed my taking the veil: she wished to see me married, though my dower would have been a loss to her and my brother's children. For her sake I will believe well of this young peasant. Then you do think there is some liking between them? said Bianca. —While she was speaking, a servant came hastily into the chamber, and told the princess that the lady Isabella was found. Where? said Matilda. She has taken sanctuary in saint Nicholas's church, replied the servant: father Jerome has brought the news himself: he is below with his highness. Where is my mother? said Matilda. She is in her own chamber, madam, and has asked for you.

Manfred had risen at the first dawn of light, and gone to Hippolita's apartment, to enquire if she knew aught of Isabella. While he was questioning her, word was brought that Jerome demanded to speak with him. Manfred, little suspecting the cause of the friar's arrival, and knowing he was employed by Hippolita in her charities, ordered him to be admitted, intending to leave them together, while he pursued his search after Isabella. Is your busi-

---

1 A charm or object possessing magical powers.
2 Of another kind or type.

ness with me or the princess? said Manfred. With both, replied the holy man. The Lady Isabella—What of her? interrupted Manfred eagerly—is at saint Nicholas's altar, replied Jerome. That is no business of Hippolita, said Manfred with confusion: let us retire to my chamber, father; and inform me how she came thither. No, my lord, replied the good man with an air of firmness and authority that daunted even the resolute Manfred, who could not help revering the saint-like virtues of Jerome: my commission is to both; and, with your highness's good-liking, in the presence of both I shall deliver it—But first, my lord, I must interrogate the princess, whether she is acquainted with the cause of the lady Isabella's retirement from your castle. —No, on my soul, said Hippolita; does Isabella charge me with being privy to it?—Father, interrupted Manfred, I pay due reverence to your holy profession; but I am sovereign here, and will allow no meddling priest to interfere in the affairs of my domestic. If you have aught to say, attend me to my chamber—I do not use to let my wife be acquainted with the secret affairs of my state; they are not within a woman's province. My lord, said the holy man, I am no intruder into the secrets of families. My office is to promote peace, to heal divisions, to preach repentance, and teach mankind to curb their headstrong passions. I forgive your highness's uncharitable apostrophe: I know my duty, and am the minister of a mightier prince than Manfred. Hearken to him who speaks through my organs. Manfred trembled with rage and shame. Hippolita's countenance declared her astonishment, and impatience to know where this would end: her silence more strongly spoke her observance of Manfred.

The lady Isabella, resumed Jerome, commends herself to both your highnesses; she thanks both for the kindness with which she has been treated in your castle: she deplores the loss of your son, and her own misfortune in not becoming the daughter of such wise and noble princes, whom she shall always respect as *parents*: she prays for uninterrupted union and felicity between you: [Manfred's colour changed] but as it is no longer possible for her to be allied to you, she entreats your consent to remain in sanctuary till she can learn news of her father; or, by the certainty of his death, be at liberty, with the approbation of her guardians, to dispose of herself in suitable marriage. I shall give no such consent, said the prince; but insist on her return to the castle without delay: I am answerable for her person to her guardians, and will not brook her being in any hands but my own. Your highness will recollect whether that can any longer be proper, replied the friar. I want no monitor, said Manfred colouring; Isabella's conduct leaves room for strange suspicions — and that young villain, who was at least the accomplice of her flight, if not the cause of it — The cause! interrupted Jerome: was a *young* man the cause? — This is not to be borne! cried Manfred. Am I to be bearded in my own palace by an insolent monk? Thou art privy, I guess, to their amours. I would pray to heaven to clear up your uncharitable surmises, said Jerome, if your highness were not satisfied in your conscience how unjustly you accuse me. I do pray to heaven to pardon that uncharitableness: and I implore your highness to leave the princess at peace in that holy place, where she is not liable to be disturbed by such vain and worldly fantasies as discourses of love from any man. Cant[1] not to me, said Manfred, but return, and bring the princess to her duty. It is my duty to prevent her return hither, said Jerome. She is where orphans and virgins are safest from the snares and wiles of this world; and nothing but a parent's authority shall take her thence. I am her parent, cried Manfred, and demand her. She wished to have you for her parent, said the friar; but heaven, that forbade that connexion, has for ever dissolved all ties betwixt you: and I announce to your highness — Stop! audacious man, said Manfred, and dread my displeasure. Holy father, said Hippolita, it is your office to be no respecter of persons: you must speak as your duty prescribes: but it is my duty to hear nothing that it pleases not my lord I should hear. I will retire to my oratory, and pray to the blessed Virgin to inspire you with her holy counsels, and to restore the heart of my gracious lord to its wonted peace and gentleness. Excellent woman! said the friar. — My lord, I attend your pleasure.

Manfred, accompanied by the friar, passed to his own apartment; where shutting the door, I perceive, father, said he, that Isabella has acquainted you with my purpose. Now hear my resolve, and obey. Reasons of state, most urgent reasons, my own and the safety of my people, demand that I should have a son. It is

---

1 Don't be hypocritical. The noun "cant" means insincerity or empty talk.

in vain to expect an heir from Hippolita. I had made choice of Isabella. You must bring her back; and you must do more. I know the influence you have with Hippolita: her conscience is in your hands. She is, I allow, a faultless woman: her soul is set on heaven, and scorns the little grandeur of this world: you can withdraw her from it entirely. Persuade her to consent to the dissolution of our marriage, and to retire into a monastery — she shall endow one if she will; and she shall have the means of being as liberal to your order as she or you can wish. Thus you will divert the calamities that are hanging over our heads, and have the merit of saving the principality of Otranto from destruction. You are a prudent man; and though the warmth of my temper betrayed me into some unbecoming expressions, I honour your virtue, and wish to be indebted to you for the repose of my life and the preservation of my family.

The will of heaven be done! said the friar. I am but its worth-less instrument. It makes use of my tongue to tell thee, prince, of thy unwarrantable designs. The injuries of the virtuous Hippolita have mounted to the throne of pity. By me thou art reprimanded for thy adulterous intention of repudiating her: by me thou art warned not to pursue thine incestuous design on thy contracted daughter. Heaven, that delivered her from thy fury, when the judgments so recently fallen on thy house ought to have inspired thee with other thoughts, will continue to watch over her. Even I, a poor and despised friar, am able to protect her from thy violence. — I, sinner as I am, and uncharitably reviled by your highness as an accomplice of I know not what amours, scorn the allurements with which it has pleased thee to tempt mine hon-esty. I love my order; I honour devout souls; I respect the piety of thy princess — but I will not betray the confidence she reposes in me, nor serve even the cause of religion by foul and sinful com-pliances — But forsooth! the welfare of the state depends on your highness having a son. Heaven mocks the short-sighted views of man. But yester-morn, whose house was so great, so flourishing as Manfred's? — Where is young Conrad now? — My lord, I respect your tears — but I mean not to check them — Let them flow, prince! they will weigh more with heaven toward the welfare of thy subjects, than a marriage, which, founded on lust or policy, could never prosper. The sceptre, which passed from the race of

Alfonso to thine, cannot be preserved by a match which the church will never allow. If it is the will of the Most High that Manfred's name must perish, resign yourself, my lord, to its decrees; and thus deserve a crown that can never pass away. — Come, my lord, I like this sorrow — Let us return to the princess: she is not apprised of your cruel intentions; nor did I mean more than to alarm you. You saw with what gentle patience, with what efforts of love, she heard, she rejected hearing the extent of your guilt. I know she longs to fold you in her arms, and assure you of her unalterable affection. Father, said the prince, you mistake my compunction: true; I honour, Hippolita's virtues; I think her a saint; and wish it were for my soul's health to tie faster the knot that has united us. — But alas! father, you know not the bitterest of my pangs! It is some time that I have had scruples on the legality of our union: Hippolita is related to me in the fourth degree[1] — It is true, we had a dispensation; but I have been informed that she had also been contracted to another. This it is that sits heavy at my heart: to this state of unlawful wedlock I impute the visitation that has fallen on me in the death of Conrad! — Ease my conscience of this burden: dissolve our marriage, and accomplish the work of godliness which your divine exhortations have commenced in my soul.

How cutting was the anguish which the good man felt, when he perceived this turn in the wily prince! He trembled for Hippolita, whose ruin he saw was determined; and he feared, if Manfred had no hope of recovering Isabella, that his impatience for a son would direct him to some other object, who might not be equally proof against the temptation of Manfred's rank. For some time the holy man remained absorbed in thought. At length, conceiving some hope from delay, he thought the wisest conduct would be to prevent the prince from despairing of recovering Isabella. Her the friar knew he could dispose, from her affection to Hippolita, and from the aversion she had expressed to him for Manfred's addresses, to second his views, till the censures of the

---

1   "Degree" is a genealogical term referring to the place or step in a family tree. By "fourth degree," Manfred infers that his marriage to Hippolita is incestuous, a spurious accusation.

church could be fulminated[1] against a divorce. With this intention, as if struck with the prince's scruples, he at length said, My lord, I have been pondering on what your highness has said; and if in truth it is delicacy of conscience that is the real motive of your repugnance to your virtuous lady, far be it from me to endeavour to harden your heart! The church is an indulgent mother; unfold your griefs to her: she alone can administer comfort to your soul, either by satisfying your conscience, or, upon examination of your scruples, by setting you at liberty, and indulging you in the lawful means of continuing your lineage. In the latter case, if the lady Isabella can be brought to consent—Manfred, who concluded that he had either overreached[2] the good man, or that his first warmth had been but a tribute paid to appearance, was overjoyed at his sudden turn, and repeated the most magnificent promises, if he should succeed by the friar's mediation. The well-meaning priest suffered him to deceive himself, fully determined to traverse his views,[3] instead of seconding them.

Since we now understand one another, resumed the prince, I expect, father, that you satisfy me in one point. Who is the youth that we found in the vault? He must have been privy to Isabella's flight: tell me truly; is he her lover? or is he an agent for another's passion? I have often suspected Isabella's indifference to my son: a thousand circumstances crowd on my mind that confirm that suspicion. She herself was so conscious of it, that, while I discoursed her in the gallery, she outran my suspicions, and endeavoured to justify herself from coolness to Conrad. The friar, who knew nothing of the youth but what he had learnt occasionally from the princess, ignorant what was become of him, and not sufficiently reflecting on the impetuosity of Manfred's temper, conceived that it might not be amiss to sow the seeds of jealousy in his mind: they might be turned to some use hereafter, either by prejudicing the prince against Isabella, if he persisted in that union; or, by diverting his attention to a wrong scent, and em-

---

1 Denounced in a thundering or explosive judgement.
2 Usually the word means to "overextend" and miss or fail, but Walpole seems to mean that Manfred had "misjudged" or "underestimated" the friar's usefulness to his schemes.
3 To block or foil his schemes.

ploying his thoughts on a visionary intrigue, prevent his engaging in any new pursuit. With this unhappy policy, he answered in a manner to confirm Manfred in the belief of some connection between Isabella and the youth. The prince, whose passions wanted little fuel to throw them into a blaze, fell into a rage at the idea of what the friar had suggested. I will fathom to the bottom of this intrigue, cried he; and quitting Jerome abruptly, with a command to remain there till his return, he hastened to the great hall of the castle, and ordered the peasant to be brought before him.

Thou hardened young imposter! said the prince, as soon as he saw the youth; what becomes of thy boasted veracity now? it was Providence, was it, and the light of the moon, that discovered the lock of the trap-door to thee? Tell me, audacious boy, who thou art, and how long thou has been acquainted with the princess — and take care to answer with less equivocation that thou didst last night, or tortures shall wring the truth from thee. The young man, perceiving that his share in the flight of the princess was discovered, and concluding that any thing he should say could no longer be of service or detriment to her, replied, I am no imposter, my lord; nor have I deserved opprobrious language. I answered every question your highness put to me last night with the same veracity that I shall speak now: and that will not be from fear of your tortures, but because my soul abhors a falsehood. Please to repeat your questions, my lord; I am ready to give you all the satisfaction in my power. You know my questions, replied the prince, and only want time to prepare an evasion. Speak directly; who art thou? and how long has thou been known to the princess? I am a labourer at the next village, said the peasant; my name is Theodore.[1] The princess found me in the vault last night: before that hour I never was in her presence. — I may believe as much or as little as I please of this, said Manfred; but I will hear thy own story, before I examine into the truth of it. Tell me, what reason did the princess give thee for making her escape? thy life depends on thy answer. She told me, replied Theodore,

---

1   The noble peasant's name is in keeping with the providential themes of the novel since it means "God's gift." See: Leigh A. Ehlers. "The Gothic World as Stage: Providence and Character in *The Castle of Otranto*," *Wascana Review* 14:2 (1980): 17-30.

that she was on the brink of destruction; and that, if she could not escape from the castle, she was in danger in a few moments of being made miserable for ever. And on this slight foundation, on a silly girl's report, said Manfred, thou didst hazard my displeasure? I fear no man's displeasure, said Theodore, when a woman in distress puts herself under my protection. —During this examination, Matilda was going to the apartment of Hippolita. At the upper end of the hall, where Manfred sat, was a boarded gallery[1] with latticed windows, through which Matilda and Bianca were to pass. Hearing her father's voice, and seeing the servants assembled round him, she stopped to learn the occasion. The prisoner soon drew her attention: the steady and composed manner in which he answered, and the gallantry of his last reply, which were the first words she heard distinctly, interested her in his favour. His person was noble, handsome and commanding, even in that situation: but his countenance soon engrossed her whole care. Heavens! Bianca, said the princess softly, do I dream? or is not that youth the exact resemblance of Alfonso's picture in the gallery? She could say no more, for her father's voice grew louder at every word. This bravado, said he, surpasses all thy former insolence. Thou shalt experience the wrath with which thou darest to trifle. Seize him, continued Manfred, and bind him—the first news the princess hears of her champion shall be, that he has lost his head for her sake. The injustice of which thou art guilty towards me, said Theodore, convinces me that I had done a good deed in delivering the princess from thy tyranny. May she be happy, whatever becomes of me! —This is a lover! cried Manfred in a rage: a peasant within sight of death is not animated by such sentiments. Tell me, tell me, rash boy, who thou art, or the rack shall force thy secret from thee. Thou has threatened me with death already, said the youth, for the truth I have told thee: if that is all the encouragement I am to expect for sincerity, I am not tempted to indulge thy vain curiosity farther. Then thou wilt not speak? said Manfred. I will not, replied he. Bear him away into the courtyard, said Manfred; I will see his head this instant severed from his body. —Matilda fainted at hearing these words. Bianca shrieked,

---

1   A panelled gallery, again reminiscent of the interior of Strawberry Hill.

and cried, Help! help! the princess is dead! Manfred started at this ejaculation, and demanded what was the matter. The young peasant, who heard it too, was struck with horror, and asked eagerly the same question; but Manfred ordered him to be hurried into the court, and kept there for execution, till he had informed himself of the cause of Bianca's shrieks. When he learned the meaning, he treated it as a womanish panic; and ordering Matilda to be carried to her apartment, he rushed into the court, and, calling for one of his guards, bade Theodore kneel down and prepare to receive the fatal blow. The undaunted youth received the bitter sentence with a resignation that touched every heart but Manfred's. He wished earnestly to know the meaning of the words he had heard relating to the princess; but, fearing to exasperate the tyrant more against her, he desisted. The only boon he deigned to ask was, that he might be permitted to have a confessor, and make his peace with heaven. Manfred, who hoped by the confessor's means to come at the youth's history,[1] readily granted his request: and being convinced that father Jerome was now in his interest, he ordered him to be called and shrieve[2] the prisoner. The holy man, who had little foreseen the catastrophe that his imprudence occasioned, fell on his knees to the prince, and adjured him in the most solemn manner not to shed innocent blood. He accused himself in the bitterest terms for his indiscretion, endeavoured to disculpate[3] the youth, and left no method untried to soften the tyrant's rage. Manfred, more incensed than appeased by Jerome's intercession, whose retractation now made him suspect he had been imposed upon by both, commanded the friar to do his duty, telling him he would not allow the prisoner many minutes for confession. Nor do I ask many, my lord, said the unhappy young man. My sins, thank heaven! have not been numerous; nor exceed what might be expected at my years. Dry your tears, good father, and let us dispatch: this is a bad world; nor have I had cause to leave it with regret. Oh! wretched youth! said

---

1 Manfred plans to manipulate Theodore's confession to Father Jerome to obtain information about his heritage. In much later Gothic fiction, it will be the priest himself who abuses the privacy of the confession to gain power over a victim.

2 To hear a confession and prescribe a penance.

3 Archaic form of "exculpate," to clear of blame or prove innocent.

Jerome; how canst thou bear the sight of me with patience? I am thy murderer! It is I have brought this dismal hour upon thee! — I forgive thee from my soul, said the youth, as I hope heaven will pardon me. Hear my confession, father; and give me thy blessing. How can I prepare thee for thy passage, as I ought? said Jerome. Thou canst not be saved without pardoning thy foes — and canst thou forgive that impious man there? I can, said Theodore; I do. — And does not this touch thee, cruel prince? said the friar. I sent for thee to confess him, said Manfred sternly; not to plead for him. Thou didst first incense me against him — his blood be upon thy head! — It will! it will! said the good man in an agony of sorrow. Thou and I must never hope to go where this blessed youth is going. — Dispatch! said Manfred: I am no more to be moved by the whining of priests, than by the shrieks of women. What! said the youth, is it possible that my fate could have occasioned what I heard? Is the princess then again in thy power? — Thou dost but remember me of my wrath, said Manfred: prepare thee, for this moment is thy last. The youth, who felt his indignation rise, and who was touched with the sorrow which he saw had infused into all the spectators, as well as into the friar, suppressed his emotions, and putting off his doublet and unbuttoning his collar, knelt down to his prayers. As he stooped, his shirt slipped down below his shoulder, and discovered the mark of a bloody arrow.[1] Gracious heaven! cried the holy man starting, what do I see? It is my child! my Theodore!

The passions that ensued must be conceived; they cannot be painted. The tears of the assistants were suspended by wonder, rather than stopped by joy. They seemed to enquire in the eyes of their lord what they ought to feel. Surprise, doubt, tenderness, respect, succeeded each other in the countenance of the youth. He received with modest submission the effusion of the old man's tears and embraces: yet afraid of giving a loose to hope, and suspecting from what had passed the inflexibility of Manfred's temper, he cast a glance towards the prince, as if to say, Canst thou be unmoved at such a scene as this?

---

1   The mark of royalty or nobility is an ancient motif of folklore and myth. The scar of Odysseus is one example of the sign of identity.

Manfred's heart was capable of being touched.[1] He forgot his anger in his astonishment; yet his pride forbad his owning himself affected. He even doubted whether this discovery was not a contrivance of the friar to save the youth. What may this mean? said he. How can he be thy son? Is it consistent with thy profession or reputed sanctity to avow a peasant's offspring for the fruit of thy irregular amours?—Oh God! said the holy man, dost thou question his being mine? Could I feel the anguish I do, if I were not his father? Spare him! good prince, spare him! and revile me as thou pleasest.—Spare him! spare him! cried the attendants, for this good man's sake!—Peace! said Manfred sternly: I must know more, ere I am disposed to pardon. A saint's bastard may be no saint himself.—Injurious lord! said Theodore: add not insult to cruelty. If I am this venerable man's son, though no prince as thou art, know, the blood that flows in my veins—Yes, said the friar, interrupting him, his blood is noble: nor is he that abject thing, my lord, you speak him. He is my lawful son; and Sicily can boast few houses more ancient than that of Falconara—but alas, my lord, what is blood! what is nobility! we are all reptiles, miserable, sinful creatures. It is piety alone that can distinguish us from the dust whence we sprung, and whither we must return. Truce to your sermon, said Manfred; you forget, you are no longer friar Jerome, but the Count of Falconara. Let me know your history; you will have time enough to moralize hereafter, if you should not happen to obtain the grace of that sturdy criminal there. Mother of God! said the friar, is it possible my lord can refuse a father the life of his only, his long-lost child! Trample me, my lord, scorn, afflict me, accept my life for his, but spare my son!— Thou canst feel then, said Manfred, what it is to lose an only son? A little hour ago thou didst preach up resignation to me: *my* house, if fate so pleased, must perish—but the count of Falconara—Alas! my lord, said Jerome, I confess I have offended; but aggravate not an old man's sufferings. I boast not of my family,

---

1 Unlike the vampire, a demonic being without conscience or pity, the Gothic villain beginning with Manfred is never totally evil and remorseless and is capable of virtuous feelings. Later Gothic villains often exhibit a mixture of the inhuman, the superhuman, and the pitiable human in their makeups.

nor think of such vanities — it is nature that pleads for this boy; it is the memory of the dear woman that bore him— Is she, Theodore, is she dead? — Her soul has long been with the blessed, said Theodore. Oh how? cried Jerome, tell me — No — she is happy! Thou art all my care now! — Most dread lord! will you — will you grant me my poor boy's life? Return to thy convent, answered Manfred; conduct the princess hither; obey me in what else thou knowest; and I promise thee the life of thy son. Oh! my lord, said Jerome, is my honesty the price I must pay for this dear youth's safety? For me! cried Theodore: let me die a thousand deaths, rather than stain thy conscience. What is it the tyrant would exact of thee? is the princess still safe from his power? protect her, thou venerable old man; and let all the weight of his wrath fall on me. Jerome endeavoured to check the impetuosity of the youth, and ere Manfred could reply, the trampling of horses was heard, and a brazen trumpet,[1] which hung without the gate of the castle, was suddenly sounded. At the same instant, the sable plumes on the enchanted helmet, which still remained at the other end of the court, were tempestuously agitated, and nodded thrice, as if bowed by some invisible wearer.

---

1   A loud or harsh trumpet call.

CHAPTER THREE

MANFRED's heart misgave him when he beheld the plumage on the miraculous casque shaken in concert with the sounding of the brazen trumpet. Father! said he to Jerome, whom he now ceased to treat as Count of Falconara, what mean these portents? If I have offended—[the plumes were shaken with greater violence than before][1] Unhappy prince that I am! cried Manfred—Holy father! will you not assist me with your prayers?—My lord, replied Jerome, heaven is no doubt displeased with your mockery of its servants. Submit yourself to the church; and cease to persecute her ministers. Dismiss this innocent youth; and learn to respect the holy character I wear: heaven will not be trifled with: you see—[the trumpet sounded again] I acknowledge I have been too hasty, said Manfred. Father, do you go to the wicket,[2] and demand who is at the gate. Do you grant me the life of Theodore? replied the friar. I do, said Manfred; but inquire who is without.

Jerome, falling on the neck of his son, discharged a flood of tears, that spoke the fulness of his soul. You promised to go to the gate, said Manfred. I thought, replied the friar, your highness would excuse my thanking you first in this tribute of my heart. Go, dearest sir, said Theodore, obey the prince; I do not deserve that you should delay his satisfaction for me.

Jerome, inquiring who was without, was answered, a Herald. From whom? said he. From the knight of the gigantic sabre, said the herald: and I must speak with the usurper of Otranto. Jerome returned to the prince, and did not fail to repeat the message in the very words it had been uttered. The first sounds struck Manfred with terror; but when he heard himself styled usurper, his rage rekindled, and all his courage revived. Usurper!—Insolent villain! cried he, who dares to question my title? Retire, father; this is no business for monks: I will meet this presumptuous man myself. Go to your convent, and prepare the princess's return:

---

1   Square brackets [ ] are used in the text to indicate stage directions and sound effects. Walpole conceived of the novel in highly dramatic terms.

2   In a castle, a small gate or door sometimes located within a larger gate or door.

your son shall be a hostage for your fidelity; his life depends on your obedience. — Good heaven! my lord, cried Jerome, your highness did but this instant freely pardon my child—have you so soon forgot the interposition of heaven? — Heaven, replied Manfred, does not send heralds to question the title of a lawful prince—I doubt whether it even notifies its will through friars—but that is your affair, not mine. At present you know my pleasure; and it is not a saucy herald that shall save your son, if you do not return with the princess.

It was in vain for the holy man to reply. Manfred commanded him to be conducted to the postern gate, and shut out from the castle: and he ordered some of his attendants to carry Theodore to the top of the black tower, and guard him strictly; scarce permitting the father and son to exchange a hasty embrace at parting. He then withdrew to the hall, and, seating himself in princely state, ordered the herald to be admitted to his presence.

Well, thou insolent! said the prince, what wouldst thou with me? I come, replied he, to thee, Manfred, usurper of the principality of Otranto, from the renowned and invincible knight, the knight of the gigantic sabre: in the name of his lord, Frederic marquis of Vicenza, he demands the Lady Isabella, daughter of that prince, whom thou has basely, and traitorously got into thy power, by bribing her false guardians during his absence: and he requires thee to resign the principality of Otranto, which thou hast usurped from the said lord Frederic, the nearest of blood to the last rightful lord Alfonso the Good. If thou dost not instantly comply with these just demands, he defies thee to single combat to the last extremity. And so saying, the herald cast down his warder.[1]

And where is this braggart, who sends thee? said Manfred. At the distance of a league, said the herald: he comes to make good his lord's claim against thee, as he is a true knight, and thou an usurper and ravisher.

Injurious as this challenge was, Manfred reflected that it was not his interest to provoke the Marquis. He knew how well-founded the claim of Frederic was; nor was this the first time he

---

1   A staff of authority or baton of office. Casting down the warder was the signal to begin the combat at tournaments.

had heard of it. Frederic's ancestors had assumed the style of princes of Otranto, from the death of Alfonso the Good without issue: but Manfred, his father, and grandfather, had been too powerful for the house of Vicenza to dispossess them. Frederic, a martial and amorous young prince, had married a beautiful young lady, of whom he was enamoured, and who had died in childbed of Isabella. Her death affected him so much, that he had taken the cross and gone to the Holy Land,[1] where he was wounded in an engagement against the infidels, made prisoner, and reported to be dead. When the news reached Manfred's ears, he bribed the guardians of the lady Isabella to deliver her up to him as a bride for his son Conrad, by which alliance he had purposed to unite the claims of the two houses. This motive, on Conrad's death, had co-operated to make him so suddenly resolve on espousing her himself; and the same reflection determined him now to endeavour at obtaining the consent of Frederic to this marriage. A like policy inspired him with the thought of inviting Frederic's champion into his castle, lest he should be informed of Isabella's flight, which he strictly enjoined his domestics not to disclose to any of the knight's retinue.

Herald, said Manfred, as soon as he had digested these reflections, return to thy master, and tell him, ere we liquidate our differences by the sword, Manfred would hold some converse with him. Bid him welcome to my castle, where, by my faith, as I am a true knight, he shall have courteous reception, and full security for himself and followers. If we cannot adjust our quarrel by amicable means, I swear he shall depart in safety, and shall have full satisfaction according to the law of arms: so help me God and his holy Trinity! — The herald made three obeisances, and retired.

During this interview Jerome's mind was agitated by a thousand contrary passions. He trembled for the life of his son, and his first idea was to persuade Isabella to return to the castle. Yet he was scarce less alarmed at the thought of her union with Manfred. He dreaded Hippolita's unbounded submission to the will of her lord: and though he did not doubt but he could alarm her piety not to consent to a divorce, if he could get access to her; yet should Manfred discover that the obstruction came from him, it

---

1   Consecrated his life to God by going on a crusade.

might be equally fatal to Theodore. He was impatient to know whence came the herald, who with so little management had questioned the title of Manfred: yet he did not dare absent himself from the convent, lest Isabella should leave it, and her flight be imputed to him. He returned disconsolately to the monastery, uncertain on what conduct to resolve. A monk, who met him in the porch and observed his melancholy air, said, Alas! brother, is it then true that we have lost our excellent princess Hippolita? The holy man started, and cried, What meanest thou, brother? I come this instant from the castle, and left her in perfect health. Martelli, replied the other friar, passed by the convent but a quarter of an hour ago on his way from the castle, and reported that her highness was dead. All our brethren are gone to the chapel to pray for her happy transit to a better life, and willed me to wait thy arrival. They know thy holy attachment to that good lady, and are anxious for the affliction it will cause in thee—Indeed we have all reason to weep; she was a mother to our house—But this life is but a pilgrimage; we must not murmur—we shall all follow her; may our end be like hers!—Good brother, thou dreamest, said Jerome: I tell thee I come from the castle, and left the princess well—Where is the lady Isabella?—Poor gentlewoman! replied the friar; I told her the sad news, and offered her spiritual comfort; I reminded her of the transitory condition of mortality, and advised her to take the veil: I quoted the example of the holy princess Sanchia of Arragon.[1] Thy zeal was laudable, said Jerome impatiently; but at present it was unnecessary: Hippolita is well— at least I trust in the Lord she is; I heard nothing to the contrary — Yet methinks, the prince's earnestness — Well, brother, but where is the lady Isabella? — I know not, said the friar: she wept much, and said she would retire to her chamber. Jerome left his comrade abruptly, and hasted to the princess, but she was not in her chamber. He enquired of the domestics of the convent, but could learn no news of her. He searched in vain throughout the monastery and the church, and dispatched messengers round the neighbourhood, to get intelligence if she had been seen; but to no

---

1 Saint Sanchia (1182–1229), daughter of Sancho I of Portugal. She was a dedicated virgin and became a Cistercian nun in 1223. Father Jerome urges Isabella to guard her chastity by renouncing the world and taking holy orders.

purpose. Nothing could equal the good man's perplexity. He judged that Isabella, suspecting Manfred of having precipitated his wife's death, had taken the alarm, and withdrawn herself to some more secret place of concealment. This new flight would probably carry the prince's fury to the height. The report of Hippolita's death, though it seemed almost incredible, increased his consternation; and though Isabella's escape bespoke her aversion of Manfred for a husband, Jerome could feel no comfort from it, while it endangered the life of his son. He determined to return to the castle, and made several of his brethren accompany him, to attest his innocence to Manfred, and, if necessary, join their intercession with his for Theodore.

The prince, in the mean time, had passed into the court, and ordered the gates of the castle to be flung open for the reception of the stranger knight and his train. In a few minutes the cavalcade arrived. First came two harbingers with wands.[1] Next a herald, followed by two pages and two trumpets. Then an hundred foot-guards. These were attended by as many horse. After them fifty footmen, clothed in scarlet and black, the colours of the knight. Then a led horse.[2] Two heralds on each side of a gentleman on horseback bearing a banner with the arms of Vicenza and Otranto quarterly[3]—a circumstance that much offended Manfred —but he stifled his resentment. Two more pages. The knight's confessor telling his beads.[4] Fifty more footmen, clad as before. Two knights habited in complete armour, their beavers[5] down, comrades to the principal knight. The 'squires of the two knights, carrying their shields and devices. The knight's own squire. An hundred gentlemen bearing an enormous sword,[6] and seeming to faint under the weight of it. The knight himself on a chestnut

---

1 Two messengers with batons.
2 An unridden extra mount.
3 An heraldic term referring to the four quarters division of a coat of arms.
4 Saying his rosary.
5 On a medieval helmet, the lower facial or chin visor.
6 An appropriate weapon for a huge hand, the weapon is a common object in Arthurian legendry. See King Arthur's sword, Excalibur and the sword bridge over which Sir Lancelot's crawls in Chrétien de Troyes's romance, *Lancelot, The Knight of the Cart*. "Never did so terrible a bridge or foot-crossing exist. This bridge over the cold water consisted of a polished, gleaming sword as long as two lances. This bridge is wickedly made and formed; an evil structure."

steed, in complete armour, his lance in the rest, his face entirely concealed by his vizor, which was surmounted by a large plume of scarlet and black feathers. Fifty foot-guards with drums and trumpets closed the procession, which wheeled off to the right and left to make room for the principal knight.

As soon as he approached the gate, he stopped; and the herald advancing, read again the words of the challenge. Manfred's eyes were fixed on the gigantic sword, and he scarce seemed to attend to the cartel:[1] but his attention was soon diverted by a tempest of wind that rose behind him. He turned, and beheld the plumes of the enchanted helmet agitated in the same extraordinary manner as before. It required intrepidity like Manfred's not to sink under a concurrence of circumstances that seemed to announce his fate. Yet scorning in the presence of strangers to betray the courage he had always manifested, he said boldly, Sir knight, whoever thou art, I bid thee welcome. If thou art of mortal mould, thy valour shall meet its equal: and if thou art a true knight, thou wilt scorn to employ sorcery to carry thy point. Be these omens from heaven or hell, Manfred trusts to the righteousness of his cause and to the aid of saint Nicholas, who has ever protected his house. Alight, Sir knight, and repose thyself. To-morrow thou shalt have a fair field; and heaven befriend the juster side!

The knight made no reply, but, dismounting, was conducted by Manfred to the great hall of the castle. As they traversed the court, the knight stopped to gaze at the miraculous casque; and, kneeling down, seemed to pray inwardly for some minutes. Rising, he made a sign to the prince to lead on. As soon as they entered the hall, Manfred proposed to the stranger to disarm; but the knight shook his head in token of refusal. Sir knight, said Manfred, this is not courteous; but by my good faith I will not cross thee! nor shalt thou have cause to complain of the prince of Otranto. No treachery is designed on my part: I hope none is intended on thine. Here take my gage:[2] [giving him his ring] your friends and you shall enjoy the laws of hospitality. Rest here until refreshments are brought: I will but give orders for the accommodation of your train and return to you. The three knights bowed,

---

1 In tournament or battle protocol, a written challenge.
2 A pledge or the physical token of a pledge as is the ring given here.

as accepting his courtesy. Manfred directed the stranger's retinue to be conducted to an adjacent hospital,[1] founded by the princess Hippolita for the reception of pilgrims. As they made the circuit of the court to return towards the gate, the gigantic sword burst from the supporters,[2] and, falling to the ground opposite to the helmet, remained immoveable. Manfred, almost hardened to preternatural appearances, surmounted the shock of this new prodigy; and returning to the hall, where by this time the feast was ready, he invited his silent guests to take their places. Manfred, however ill his heart was at ease, endeavoured to inspire the company with mirth. He put several questions to them, but was answered only by signs. They raised their vizors but sufficiently to feed themselves, and that but sparingly. Sirs, said the prince, ye are the first guests I ever treated within these walls, who scorned to hold intercourse with me: nor has it oft been customary, I ween, for princes to hazard their state and dignity against strangers and mutes. You say you come in the name of Frederic of Vicenza: I have ever heard that he was a gallant and courteous knight; nor would he, I am bold to say, think it beneath him to mix in social converse with a prince that is his equal, and not unknown by deeds in arms. — Still ye are silent — Well! be it as it may — by the laws of hospitality and chivalry ye are masters under this roof: ye shall do your pleasure — but come, give me a goblet of wine; ye will not refuse to pledge me to the healths of your fair mistresses. The principal knight sighed and crossed himself, and was rising from the board — Sir knight, said Manfred, what I said was but in sport: I shall constrain you in nothing: use your good liking. Since mirth is not your mood, let us be sad. Business may hit your fancies better: let us withdraw; and hear if what I have to unfold may be better relished than the vain efforts I have made for your pastime.

Manfred, then, conducting the three knights into an inner chamber, shut the door, and, inviting them to be seated, began thus, addressing himself to the chief personage: You come, Sir

---

1   An inn, hospice, or lodging house for travelers and strangers.
2   The animation and mobility of inanimate objects became a major supernatural convention of Gothic fiction after *Otranto*. Cf. the aerial mobility of the enormous helmet at the outset of the novel.

knight, as I understand, in the name of the marquis of Vicenza, to re-demand the Lady Isabella, his daughter, who has been contracted in the face of the holy church to my son, by the consent of her legal guardians; and to require me to resign my dominions to your lord, who gives himself for the nearest of blood to prince Alfonso, whose soul God rest! I shall speak to the latter article of your demands first. You must know, your lord knows, that I enjoy the principality of Otranto from my father Don Manuel, as he received it from his father Don Ricardo. Alfonso, their predecessor, dying childless in the Holy Land, bequeathed his estates to my grandfather Don Ricardo, in consideration of his faithful services —[The stranger shook his head]— Sir knight, said Manfred warmly, Ricardo was a valiant and upright man; he was a pious man; witness his munificent foundation of the adjoining church and two convents. He was peculiarly patronised by saint Nicholas — My grandfather was incapable — I say, sir, Don Ricardo was incapable — Excuse me, your interruption has disordered me — I venerate the memory of my grandfather — Well, sirs! he held this estate; he held it by his good sword, and by the favour of saint Nicholas — so did my father; and so, sirs, will I, come what come will. — But Frederic, your lord, is nearest in blood — I have consented to put my title to the issue of the sword — does that imply a vitious title?[1] I might have asked, where is Frederic, your lord? Report speaks him dead in captivity. You say, your actions say, he lives — I question it not — I might, sirs, I might — but I do not. Other princes would bid Frederic take his inheritance by force, if he can: they would not stake their dignity on a single combat: they would not submit it to the decision of unknown mutes![2] Pardon me, gentlemen, I am too warm: but suppose yourselves in my situation: as ye are stout knights, would it not move your choler to have your own and the honour of your ancestors called in question? — But to the point. Ye require me to deliver up the Lady Isabella — Sirs, I must ask if ye are authorized to receive her? [The knight nodded.] Receive her — continued Manfred: Well! you are authorised to receive her — But, gentle knight, may I ask if you have full powers? [The knight nodded.]

---

1   An illegitimate or unlawful title.

2   Manfred's sarcastic reference to Frederic's knightly retinue.

'Tis well, said Manfred: then hear what I have to offer—Ye see, gentlemen, before you the most unhappy of men! [he began to weep] afford me your compassion; I am entitled to it; indeed I am. Know, I have lost my only hope, my joy, the support of my house—Conrad died yester-morning. [The knights discovered signs of surprise.] Yes, sirs, fate has disposed of my son. Isabella is at liberty.—Do you then restore her, cried the chief knight, breaking silence. Afford me your patience, said Manfred. I rejoice to find, by this testimony of your good-will, that this matter may be adjusted without blood. It is no interest of mine dictates what little I have farther to say. Ye behold in me a man disgusted with the world:[1] the loss of my son has weaned me from earthly cares. Power and greatness have no longer any charms in my eyes. I wished to transmit the sceptre I had received from my ancestors with honour to my son—but that is over! Life itself is so indifferent to me, that I accepted your defiance with joy: a good knight cannot go to the grave with more satisfaction than when falling in his vocation. Whatever is the will of heaven, I submit; for, alas! sirs, I am a man of many sorrows. Manfred is no object of envy— but no doubt you are acquainted with my story. [The knight made signs of ignorance, and seemed curious to have Manfred proceed.] Is it possible, sirs, continued the prince, that my story should be a secret to you? Have you heard nothing relating to me and the princess Hippolita? [They shook their heads]—No! Thus then, sirs, it is. You think me ambitious: ambition, alas, is composed of more rugged materials.[2] If I were ambitious, I should not for so many years have been prey to all the hell of conscientious scruples—But I weary your patience: I will be brief. Know then, that I have long been troubled in mind on my union with the princess Hippolita.—Oh! sirs, if ye were acquainted with that excellent woman! if ye knew that I adore her like a mistress, and

---

1 Walpole's first Gothic villain also displays the traits of the Byronic hero in his exhibition of world weariness. His crime-stained career is a form of protest against the ennui and emptiness of existence. Compare with Lord Byron's gloomy hero, Manfred, in the Gothic drama, *Manfred* (1817). For connections between the Byronic hero and his immediate antecedent, see: Peter Thorslev, *The Byronic Hero: Types and Prototypes*, Minneapolis: University of Minnesota Press, 1962.

2 A near paraphrase of a line in Mark Antony's funeral oration for Cæsar in Shakespeare's *Julius Cæsar*. "Ambition should be made of sterner stuff." *Julius Cæsar*, III.ii.94, and another instance of Walpole's conscious use of Shakespearean language.

cherish her as a friend—but man was not born for perfect happiness! she shares my scruples, and with her consent I have brought this matter before the church, for we are related within the forbidden degrees.[1] I expect every hour the definitive sentence that must separate us forever. I am sure you feel for me—I see you do—Pardon these tears! [The knights gazed on each other, wondering where this would end.] Manfred continued: The death of my son betiding while my soul was under this anxiety, I thought of nothing but resigning my dominions, and retiring forever from the sight of mankind. My only difficulty was to fix on a successor, who would be tender of my people, and to dispose of the Lady Isabella, who is dear to me as my own blood. I was willing to restore the line of Alfonso, even in his most distant kindred: and though, pardon me, I am satisfied it was his will that Ricardo's lineage should take place of his own relations; yet where was I to search for those relations? I knew of none but Frederic, your lord: he was a captive to the infidels, or dead; and were he living, and at home, would he quit the flourishing state of Vicenza for the inconsiderable principality of Otranto? If he would not, could I bear the thought of seeing a hard unfeeling viceroy set over my poor faithful people?—for, sirs, I love my people, and thank heaven am beloved by them.—But ye will ask, Whither tends this long discourse? Briefly then, thus, sirs. Heaven in your arrival seems to point out a remedy for these difficulties and my misfortunes. The lady Isabella is at liberty: I shall soon be so. I would submit to any thing for the good of my people—Were it not the best, the only way to extinguish the feuds between our families, if I were to take the lady Isabella to wife?—You start—But though Hippolita's virtues will ever be dear to me, a prince must not consider himself; he is born for his people.—A servant at that instant entering the chamber, apprized Manfred that Jerome and several of his brethren demanded immediate access to him.

The prince, provoked at this interruption, and fearing that the friar would discover to the strangers that Isabella had taken sanctuary, was going to forbid Jerome's entrance. But recollecting that

---

1 Manfred has insinuated earlier that his marriage to Hippolita within the "fourth degree" was incestuous, thus allowing him to dissolve the marriage and advance his schemes.

he was certainly arrived to notify the princess's return, Manfred began to excuse himself to the knights for leaving them for a few moments, but was prevented by the arrival of the friars. Manfred reprimanded them for their intrusion, and would have forced them back from the chamber; but Jerome was too much agitated to be repulsed. He declared aloud the flight of Isabella, with protestations of his own innocence. Manfred, distracted at the news, and not less at its coming to the knowledge of the strangers, uttered nothing but incoherent sentences, now upbraiding the friar, now apologizing to the knights, earnest to know what was become of Isabella, yet equally afraid of their knowing; impatient to pursue her, yet dreading to have them join in the pursuit. He offered to dispatch messengers in quest of her: — but the chief knight, no longer keeping silence, reproached Manfred in bitter terms for his dark and ambiguous dealing, and demanded the cause of Isabella's first absence from the castle. Manfred, casting a stern look at Jerome, implying a command of silence, pretended that on Conrad's death he had placed her in sanctuary until he could determine how to dispose of her. Jerome, who trembled for his son's life, did not dare to contradict this falsehood; but one of his brethren, not under the same anxiety, declared frankly that she had fled to their church in the preceding night. The prince in vain endeavoured to stop this discovery, which overwhelmed him with shame and confusion. The principal stranger, amazed at the contradictions he heard, and more than half persuaded that Manfred had secreted the princess, notwithstanding the concern he expressed at her flight, rushing to the door, said, Thou traitor-prince! Isabella shall be found. Manfred endeavoured to hold him; but the other knights assisting their comrade, he broke from the prince, and hastened into the court, demanding his attendants. Manfred, finding it in vain to divert him from the pursuit, offered to accompany him; and summoning his attendants, and taking Jerome and some of the friars to guide them, they issued from the castle; Manfred privately giving orders to have the knight's company secured, while to the knight he affected to dispatch a messenger to require their assistance.

The company had no sooner quitted the castle, than Matilda, who felt herself deeply interested for the young peasant, since she had seen him condemned to death in the hall, and whose thoughts had been taken up with concerting measures to save him, was informed by some of the female attendants that Manfred had dispatched all his men various ways in pursuit of Isabella. He had in his hurry given this order in general terms, not meaning to extend it to the guard he had set upon Theodore, but forgetting it. The domestics, officious to obey so peremptory a prince, and urged by their own curiosity and love of novelty to join in any precipitate chace, had to a man left the castle. Matilda disengaged herself from her women, stole up to the black tower, and, unbolting the door, presented herself to the astonished Theodore. Young man, she said, though filial duty and womanly modesty condemn the step I am taking, yet holy charity, surmounting all other ties, justifies this act. Fly; the doors of thy prison are open: my father and his domestics are absent; but they may soon return: begone in safety; and may the angels of heaven direct thy course! — Thou art surely one of those angels! said the enraptured Theodore: none but a blessed saint could speak, could act, could look like thee! — May I not know the name of my divine protectress? Methought thou namedst thy father: is it possible? can Manfred's blood feel holy pity? — Lovely lady, thou answerest not — But how art thou here thyself? Why dost thou neglect thy own safety, and waste a thought on a wretch like Theodore? Let us fly together: the life thou bestowest shall be dedicated to thy defence. Alas! thou mistakest, said Matilda sighing: I am Manfred's daughter, but no dangers await me. Amazement! said Theodore: but last night I blessed myself for yielding thee the service thy gracious compassion so charitably returns me now. Still thou art in an error, said the princess; but this is no time for explanation. Fly, virtuous youth, while it is in my power to save thee: should my father return, thou and I both should indeed have cause to tremble. How? said Theodore: thinkest thou, charming maid, that I will accept of life at the hazard of aught calamitous to thee? Better I endured a thousand deaths — I run no risk, said Matilda, but by thy delay. Depart: it cannot be known that I assisted thy flight. Swear by the saints above, said Theodore, that thou canst not be suspected; else here I vow to await whatever can befall me. Oh! thou art too generous, said Matilda; but rest assured that no suspicions can alight on me. Give me thy beauteous hand in token that thou dost not deceive me, said Theodore; and let me bathe it with the warm tears of gratitude. — Forbear, said the princess: this must not be. — Alas! said Theodore, I have never known but calamity until this hour — perhaps shall never know other fortune again: suffer the chaste raptures of holy gratitude: 'tis my soul would print its effusions on thy hand. — Forbear, and begone, said Matilda: how would Isabella approve of seeing thee at my feet? — Who is Isabella? said the young man with surprise. — Ah me! I fear, said the princess, I am serving a deceitful one! Hast thou forgot thy curiosity this morning? — Thy looks, thy actions, all thy beauteous self seems an emanation of divinity, said Theodore, but thy words are dark and mysterious — Speak, lady, speak to thy servant's comprehension. — Thou understandest but too well, said Matilda: but once more I command thee to be gone: thy blood, which I may preserve, will be on my head, if I waste the time in vain discourse. I go, lady, said Theodore, because it is thy will, and because I would not bring the grey hairs of my father with sorrow to the grave. Say but, adored lady, that I have thy gentle pity. — Stay, said Matilda; I will conduct thee to the subterraneous vault[1] by which Isabella escaped; it will lead thee to the church of saint Nicholas, where thou mayest take sanctuary. — What! said Theodore, was it another, and not thy lovely self, that I assisted to find the subterraneous passage? It was, said Matilda: but ask no more; I tremble to see thee still abide here: fly to the sanctuary. — To sanctuary! said Theodore: No, princess; sanctuaries are for helpless damsels, or for criminals. Theodore's soul is free from guilt, nor will wear the appearance of it. Give me a sword, lady, and thy father shall learn that Theodore scorns an ignominious flight. Rash youth! said Matilda, thou wouldst not dare to lift thy presumptuous arm against the prince of Otranto? Not against *thy* father; indeed, I dare not, said Theodore: excuse me, lady; I had forgotten — but could I gaze on thee, and remember thou art sprung from the tyrant Manfred? — But he is thy father, and from this moment my injuries are buried in oblivion. A deep and hollow groan, which seemed to come from above, startled the princess and Theodore. Good heaven! we are overheard! said the

---

1   Matilda's invitation to Theodore to descend to the underground inaugurates the motif of the Gothic journey, a subterranean course to be followed by scores of Gothic maidens, heroes, and villains to come.

princess. They listened; but perceiving no farther noise, they both concluded it the effect of pent-up vapours;[1] and the princess, preceding Theodore softly, carried him to her father's armoury; where equipping him with a complete suit, he was conducted by Matilda to the postern-gate. Avoid the town, said the princess, and all the western side of the castle: 'tis there the search must be making by Manfred and the strangers: but hie thee to the opposite quarter. Yonder, behind that forest to the east is a chain of rocks, hollowed into a labyrinth of caverns[2] that reach to the sea-coast. There thou mayest lie concealed, till thou canst make signs to some vessel to put on shore and take thee off. Go! heaven be thy guide!—and sometimes in thy prayers remember—Matilda! Theodore flung himself at her feet, and seizing her lily hand, which with struggles she suffered him to kiss, he vowed on the earliest opportunity to get himself knighted, and fervently entreated her permission to swear himself eternally her knight. — Ere the princess could reply, a clap of thunder was suddenly heard that shook the battlements. Theodore, regardless of the tempest, would have urged his suit; but the princess, dismayed, retreated hastily into the castle, and commanded the youth to be gone, with an air that would not be disobeyed. He sighed, and retired, but with eyes fixed on the gate, until Matilda closing it put an end to an interview, in which the hearts of both had drunk so deeply of a passion which both now tasted for the first time.

Theodore went pensively to the convent, to acquaint his father with his deliverance. There he learned the absence of Jerome, and the pursuit that was making after the Lady Isabella, with some particulars of whose story he now first became acquainted. The generous gallantry of his nature prompted him to wish to assist her; but the monks could lend him no lights to guess at the route she had taken. He was not tempted to wander far in search of her;

---

1   The natural explanation of seemingly supernatural phenomena (here, the eerie groan from above) anticipates the "explained" or rationalized Gothic of Mrs. Radcliffe. The supernatural in her Gothic romances is never real, but illusory, and is eventually explained or accounted for in rational ways.
2   Walpole introduces a highly useful floorplan for later Gothic writers, the maze of caves adjoining the haunted castle. Caves are sometimes sanctuaries but can also be horrible enclosures as in Charles Brockden Brown's novel of the night, *Edgar Huntly; or, The Memoirs of a Sleep-Walker* (1799).

for the idea of Matilda had imprinted itself so strongly on his heart, that he could not bear to absent himself at much distance from her abode. The tenderness Jerome had expressed for him concurred to confirm this reluctance; and he even persuaded himself that filial affection was the chief cause of his hovering between the castle and monastery. Until Jerome should return at night, Theodore at length determined to repair[1] to the forest that Matilda had pointed out to him. Arriving there, he sought the gloomiest shades, as best suited to the pleasing melancholy that reigned in his mind. In this mood he roved insensibly to the caves[2] which had formerly served as a retreat to hermits, and were now reported round the country to be haunted by evil spirits. He recollected to have heard this tradition; and being of a brave and adventurous disposition, he willingly indulged his curiosity in exploring the secret recesses of this labyrinth.[3] He had not penetrated far before he thought he heard the steps of some person who seemed to retreat before him. Theodore, though firmly grounded in all our holy faith enjoins to be believed, had no apprehension that good men were abandoned without cause to the malice of the powers of darkness. He thought the place more likely to be infested by robbers, than by those infernal agents who are reported to molest and bewilder travellers. He had long burned with impatience to approve his valour. Drawing his sabre, he marched sedately onwards, still directing his steps as the imperfect rustling sound before him led the way. The armour he wore was a like indication to the person who avoided him. Theodore, now convinced that he was not mistaken, redoubled his pace, and

---

1   To retreat or withdraw to a place.
2   Often the domain of monsters in mythology (e.g., the Cyclops, Polyphemus, in *The Odyssey* and the submarine grotto of Grendel's mother in *Beowulf*), the cave in eighteenth-century literature was often a haven for the contemplative melancholiac. Such is Walpole's usage here, but in later Gothic fiction, the cave is often less a haven than a horrible place. See: Clark Griffith, "Caves and Cave Dwellers: The Study of a Romantic Image," *Journal of English and Germanic Philology* 62 (1963): 551-568.
3   The phrase contains another versatile Gothic motif, that of the enclosure within the enclosure. The titling and action of Sophia Lee's historical Gothic, *The Recess* (1783) shows the influence of Walpole's phrase, "secret recesses." Poe put Walpole's recess and labyrinth to good use in the labyrinth that terminates in a recess in "The Cask of Amontillado." For the importance of the recess as a Gothic motif, see: Leonard Engel, "The Role of the Enclosure in the English and American Gothic Romance," *Essays in Arts and Sciences* 11 (1982): 59-68.

evidently gained on the person that fled; whose haste increasing, Theodore came up just as a woman fell breathless before him. He hasted to raise her; but her terror was so great, that he apprehended she would faint in his arms. He used every gentle word to dispel her alarms, and assured her that, far from injuring, he would defend her at the peril of his life. The lady recovering her spirits from his courteous demeanour, and gazing on her protector, said, Sure I have heard that voice before?—Not to my knowledge, replied Theodore, unless, as I conjecture, thou art the lady Isabella.—Merciful heaven! cried she, thou art not sent in quest of me, art thou? And saying those words she threw herself at his feet, and besought him not to deliver her up to Manfred. To Manfred! cried Theodore—No, lady: I have once already delivered thee from his tyranny, and it shall fare hard with me now, but I place thee out of the reach of his daring. Is it possible, said she, that thou shouldst be the generous unknown whom I met last night in the vault of the castle? Sure thou art not a mortal, but my guardian angel: On my knees let me thank—Hold, gentle princess, said Theodore, nor demean thyself before a poor and friendless young man. If heaven has selected me for thy deliverer, it will accomplish its work, and strengthen my arm in thy cause. But come, lady, we are too near the mouth of the cavern; let us seek its inmost recesses: I can have no tranquillity till I have placed thee beyond the reach of danger. — Alas! what mean you, sir? said she. Though all your actions are noble, though your sentiments speak the purity of your soul, is it fitting that I should accompany you alone into these perplexed retreats? Should we be found together, what would a censorious world think of my conduct?— I respect your virtuous delicacy, said Theodore; nor do you harbour a suspicion that wounds my honour. I meant to conduct you into the most private cavity of these rocks; and then, at the hazard of my life, to guard their entrance against every living thing. Besides, lady, continued he, drawing a deep sigh, beauteous and all-perfect as your form is, and though my wishes are not guiltless of aspiring, know, my soul is dedicated to another; and although—a sudden noise prevented Theodore from proceeding. They soon distinguished these sounds, Isabella! What ho! Isabella!—the trembling princess relapsed into her former agony of fear. Theodore endeavoured to encourage her, but in vain. He assured her he would die rather than suffer her to return under Manfred's power; and begging her to remain concealed, he went forth to prevent the person in search of her from approaching.

At the mouth of the cavern he found an armed knight discoursing with a peasant, who assured him he had seen a lady enter the passes of the rock. The knight was preparing to seek her, when Theodore, placing himself in his way, with his sword drawn, sternly forbad him at his peril to advance. And who art thou who darest to cross my way? said the knight haughtily. One who does not dare more than he will perform, said Theodore. I seek the lady Isabella, said the knight; and understand she has taken refuge among these rocks. Impede me not, or thou wilt repent having provoked my resentment. — Thy purpose is as odious as thy resentment is contemptible, said Theodore. Return whence thou camest, or we shall soon know whose resentment is most terrible. — The stranger, who was the principal knight that had arrived from the marquis of Vicenza, had galloped from Manfred as he was busied in getting information of the princess, and giving various orders to prevent her falling into the power of the three knights. Their chief had suspected Manfred of being privy to the princess's absconding; and this insult from a man who he concluded was stationed by that prince to secrete her, confirming his suspicions, he made no reply, but, discharging a blow with his sabre at Theodore, would soon have removed all obstruction, if Theodore, who took him for one of Manfred's captains, and who had no sooner given the provocation than prepared to support it, had not received the stroke on his shield. The valour that had so long been smothered in his breast, broke forth at once: he rushed impetuously on the knight, whose pride and wrath were not less powerful incentives to hardy deeds. The combat was furious, but not long. Theodore wounded the knight in three places, and at last disarmed him as he fainted by the loss of blood. The peasant, who had fled on the first onset, had given the alarm to some of Manfred's domestics, who by his orders were dispersed through the forest in pursuit of Isabella. They came up as the knight fell, whom they soon discovered to be the noble stranger. Theodore, notwithstanding his hatred to Manfred, could not behold the victory he had gained without emotions of pity and generosity; but he was more touched, when he learned the quality of his adversary, and was informed that he was no retainer, but an enemy of Manfred. He assisted the servants of the latter in disarming the knight, and in endeavouring to staunch the blood that flowed from his wounds. The knight, recovering his speech, said in a faint and faltering voice, Generous foe, we have both been in an error: I took thee for an instrument of the tyrant; I perceive thou has made the like mistake—It is too late for excuses—I faint.—If Isabella is at hand, call her—I have important secrets to—He is dying! said one of the attendants; has nobody a crucifix about them? Andrea, do thou pray over him.—Fetch some water, said Theodore, and pour it down his throat, while I hasten to the princess.—Saying this, he flew to Isabella; and in a few words told her modestly, that he had been so unfortunate by mistake as to wound a gentleman from her father's court, who wished ere he died to impart something of consequence to her. The princess, who had been transported at hearing the voice of Theodore as he called her to come forth, was astonished at what she heard. Suffering herself to be conducted by Theodore, the new proof of whose valour recalled her dispersed spirits, she came where the bleeding knight lay speechless on the ground—but her fears returned when she beheld the domestics of Manfred. She would again have fled, if Theodore had not made her observe that they were unarmed, and had not threatened them with instant death, if they should dare to seize the princess. The stranger, opening his eyes, and beholding a woman, said, Art thou—pray, tell me truly—art thou Isabella of Vicenza? I am, said she; good heaven restore thee!—Then thou—then thou—said the knight, struggling for utterance—seest—thy father!—Give me one—Oh! amazement! horror! what do I hear? what do I see? cried Isabella. My father! You my father! How came you here, sir? for heaven's sake speak!—Oh! run for help, or he will expire!—'Tis most true, said the wounded knight, exerting all his force; I am Frederic, thy father—Yes, I came to deliver thee—It will not be—Give me a parting kiss, and take—Sir, said Theodore, do not exhaust yourself: suffer us to convey you to the castle.—To the castle! said Isabella: Is there no help nearer than the castle? Would you expose my father to the tyrant? If he goes thither, I dare not accompany him.—And yet, can I leave him?—My child, said Frederic, it matters not for me whither I am carried: a few minutes will place me beyond danger: but while I have eyes to dote on thee, forsake me not, dear Isabella! This brave knight—I know not who he is—will protect thy innocence. Sir, you will not abandon my child, will you?—Theodore, shedding tears over his victim, and vowing to guard the princess at the expense of his life, persuaded Frederic to suffer himself to be conducted to the castle. They placed him on a horse belonging to one of the domestics, after binding up his wounds as well as they were able. Theodore marched by his side; and the afflicted Isabella, who could not bear to quit him, followed mournfully behind.

CHAPTER FOUR

THE sorrowful troop no sooner arrived at the castle, than they were met by Hippolita and Matilda, whom Isabella had sent one of the domestics before to advertise of their approach. The ladies, causing Frederic to be conveyed into the nearest chamber, retired, while the surgeons examined his wounds. Matilda blushed at seeing Theodore and Isabella together; but endeavoured to conceal it by embracing the latter, and condoling with her on her father's mischance. The surgeons soon came to acquaint Hippolita that none of the marquis's wounds were dangerous; and that he was desirous of seeing his daughter and the princesses. Theodore, under pretence of expressing his joy at being freed from his apprehensions of the combat being fatal to Frederic, could not resist the impulse of following Matilda. Her eyes were so often cast down on meeting his, that Isabella, who regarded Theodore as attentively as he gazed on Matilda, soon divined who the object was that he had told her in the cave engaged his affections. While this mute scene passed, Hippolita demanded of Frederic the cause of his having taken that mysterious course for reclaiming his daughter; and threw in various apologies to excuse her lord for the match contracted between their children. Frederic, however incensed against Manfred, was not insensible to the courtesy and benevolence of Hippolita: but he was still more struck with the lovely form of Matilda. Wishing to detain them by his bed-side, he informed Hippolita of his story. He told her, that, while prisoner to the infidels, he had dreamed that his daughter, of whom he had learned no news since his captivity, was detained in a castle, where she was in danger of the most dreadful misfortunes; and that if he obtained his liberty, and repaired to a wood near Joppa,[1] he would learn more. Alarmed at this dream, and incapable of obeying the direction given by it, his chains became more grievous than ever. But while his thoughts were occupied on the means of obtaining his liberty, he received the agreeable news that the confederate princes, who were warring in Palestine, had paid his ransom. He instantly set out for the wood that had been

---

1   Seaport on the coast of Palestine (now Jaffa in modern Israel) and an important landing
    and embarkation point during the Crusades.

marked in his dream. For three days he and his attendants had wandered in the forest without seeing a human form: but on the evening of the third they came to a cell, in which they found a venerable hermit in the agonies of death. Applying rich cordials, they brought the saint-like man to his speech. My sons, said he, I am bounden to your charity—but it is in vain—I am going to my eternal rest—yet I die with the satisfaction of performing the will of heaven. When first I repaired to this solitude, after seeing my country become a prey to unbelievers [it is, alas! above fifty years since I was witness to that dreadful scene!] saint Nicholas appeared to me, and revealed a secret, which he bade me never disclose to mortal man, but on my death-bed. This is that tremendous hour, and ye are no doubt the chosen warriors to whom I was ordered to reveal my trust. As soon as ye have done the last offices to this wretched corse,[1] dig under the seventh tree on the left hand of this poor cave, and your pains will—Oh! good heaven receive my soul! With those words the devout man breathed his last. By break of day, continued Frederic, when we had committed the holy relics to earth, we dug according to direction—But what was our astonishment, when about the depth of six feet we discovered an enormous sabre[2]—the very weapon yonder in the court! On the blade, which was then partly out of the scabbard, though since closed by our efforts in removing it, were written the following lines—No; excuse me, madam, added the marquis, turning to Hippolita, if I forbear to repeat them: I respect your sex and rank, and would not be guilty of offending your ear with sounds injurious to aught that is dear to you. —He paused: Hippolita trembled. She did not doubt but Frederic was destined by heaven to accomplish the fate that seemed to threaten her house. Looking with anxious fondness at Matilda, a silent tear stole down her cheek; but recollecting herself, she said, Proceed, my lord; heaven does nothing in vain: mortals must receive its divine behests with lowliness and submission. It is our part to deprecate its wrath, or bow to its decrees. Repeat

---

1 Archaic spelling of "corpse."
2 Swords bearing mystical inscriptions and cabalistic verses are one of the accouterments of medieval romance and are used to test the hero. The hugeness of the blade here suits the theme of gigantism that imbues the novel. There is also a hint of Walpole's interest in the new antiquarian science of archeology in the excavation of the sword relic.

the sentence, my lord: we listen resigned. — Frederic was grieved that he had proceeded so far. The dignity and patient firmness of Hippolita penetrated him with respect, and the tender silent affection, with which the princess and her daughter regarded each other, melted him almost to tears. Yet apprehensive that his forbearance to obey would be more alarming, he repeated in a faltering and low voice the following lines:

> Where'er a casque that suits this sword is found,
> With perils is thy daughter compass'd round:
> Alfonso's blood alone can save the maid,
> And quiet a long restless prince's shade.[1]

What is there in these lines, said Theodore impatiently, that affects these princesses? Why were they to be shocked by a mysterious delicacy, that has so little foundation? Your words are rude, young man, said the marquis; and though fortune has favoured you once — My honoured lord, said Isabella, who resented Theodore's warmth, which she perceived was dictated by his sentiments for Matilda, discompose not yourself for the glosing[1] of a peasant's son: he forgets the reverence he owes you; but he is not accustomed — Hippolita, concerned at the heat that had arisen, checked Theodore for his boldness, but with an air acknowledging his zeal; and, changing the conversation, demanded of Frederic where he had left her lord? As the marquis was going to reply they heard a noise without; and rising to inquire the cause, Manfred, Jerome, and part of the troop, who had met an imperfect rumour of what had happened, entered the chamber. Manfred advanced hastily towards Frederic's bed to condole with him on his misfortune, and to learn the circumstances of the combat; when starting in an agony of terror and amazement, he cried, Ha! what art thou, thou dreadful spectre! Is my hour come? — My dearest, gracious lord, cried Hippolita, clasping him in her arms, what is it you see? Why do you fix your eye-balls thus? — What! cried Manfred breathless — dost thou see nothing, Hippolita? Is this ghastly phantom sent to me alone — to me, who did not — For mercy's sweetest self, my lord, said Hippolita, resume your

---

1 Deceitful or evasive talk meant to flatter and mislead.

soul, command your reason. There is none here but we, your friends. — What, is not that Alfonso? cried Manfred; Dost thou not see him? Can it be my brain's delirium? — This! my lord, said Hippolita; this is Theodore, the youth who has been so unfortunate — Theodore! said Manfred mournfully, and striking his forehead — Theodore, or a phantom, he has unhinged the soul of Manfred. — But how comes he here? and how comes he in armour? I believe he went in search of Isabella, said Hippolita. Of Isabella? said Manfred, relapsing into rage — Yes, yes, that is not doubtful — but how did he escape from durance[1] in which I left him? Was it Isabella, or this hypocritical old friar, that procured his enlargement? — And would a parent be criminal, my lord, said Theodore, if he meditated the deliverance of his child? Jerome, amazed to hear himself in a manner accused by his son, and without foundation, knew not what to think. He could not comprehend how Theodore had escaped, how he came to be armed, and to encounter Frederic. Still he would not venture to ask any questions that might tend to inflame Manfred's wrath against his son. Jerome's silence convinced Manfred that he had contrived Theodore's release. — And is it thus, thou ungrateful old man, said the prince, addressing himself to the friar, that thou repayest mine and Hippolita's bounties? And not content with traversing my heart's nearest wishes, thou armest thy bastard, and bringest him into my own castle to insult me! — My lord, said Theodore, you wrong my father: nor he nor I is capable of harbouring a thought against your peace. Is it insolence thus to surrender myself to your highness's pleasure? added he, laying his sword respectfully at Manfred's feet. Behold my bosom; strike, my lord, if you suspect that a disloyal thought is lodged there. There is not a sentiment engraven on my heart, that does not venerate you and yours. The grace and fervour with which Theodore uttered these words, interested every person present in his favour. Even Manfred was touched — yet still possessed with his resemblance to Alfonso, his admiration was dashed with secret horror. Rise, said he; thy life is not my present purpose. — But tell me thy history, and how thou camest connected with this old traitor here. My lord, said Jerome eagerly. — Peace, imposter! said Manfred; I will not have him

---

1   Incarceration or close confinement.

prompted. My lord, said Theodore, I want no assistance; my story is very brief. I was carried at five years of age to Algiers, with my mother, who had been taken by corsairs[1] from the coast of Sicily. She died of grief in less than a twelve-month. — The tears gushed from Jerome's eyes, on whose countenance a thousand anxious passions stood expressed. Before she died, continued Theodore, she bound a writing about my arm under my garments, which told me I was the son of the Count Falconara. — It is most true, said Jerome; I am that wretched father. — Again, I enjoin thee silence, said Manfred: proceed. I remained in slavery, said Theodore, Until within these two years, when attending on my master in his cruizes, I was delivered by a Christian vessel, which overpowered the pirate; and discovering myself to the captain, he generously put me on shore in Sicily. But alas! instead of finding a father, I learned that his estate, which was situated on the coast, had during his absence been laid waste by the rover,[2] who had carried my mother and me into captivity: that his castle had been burnt to the ground: and that my father on his return had sold what remained, and was retired into religion in the kingdom of Naples, but where no man could inform me. Destitute and friendless, hopeless almost of attaining the transport of a parent's embrace, I took the first opportunity of setting sail for Naples; from whence within these six days I wandered into this province, still supporting myself by the labour of my hands; nor until yester-morn did I believe that heaven had reserved any lot for me but peace of mind and contented poverty. This, my lord, is Theodore's story. I am blessed beyond my hope in finding a father; I am unfortunate beyond my desert in having incurred your highness's displeasure. He ceased. A murmur of approbation gently arose from the audience. This is not all, said Frederic; I am bound in honour to add what he suppresses. Though he is modest, I must be generous — he is one of the bravest youths on Christian ground. He is warm too; and from the short knowledge I have of him, I will pledge myself for his veracity: if what he reports of himself were not true, he would not utter it — and for me, youth, I honour a frankness which becomes thy birth. But

---

1 Pirates, especially those of the Barbary Coast from Tripoli to Morocco.

2 A pirate or a pirate ship.

now, and thou didst offend me; yet the noble blood which flows in thy veins may well be allowed to boil out, when it has so recently traced itself to its source. Come, my lord, [turning to Manfred] If I can pardon him, surely you may: it is not the youth's fault, if you took him for a spectre. This bitter taunt galled the soul of Manfred. If beings from another world, replied he haughtily, have power to impress my mind with awe, it is more than living man can do; nor could a stripling's arm—My lord, interrupted Hippolita, your guest has occasion for repose; shall we not leave him to rest? Saying this, and taking Manfred by the hand, she took leave of Frederic, and led the company forth. The prince, not sorry to quit a conversation which recalled to mind the discovery he had made of his most secret sensations, suffered himself to be conducted to his own apartment, after permitting Theodore, though under engagement to return to the castle on the morrow, [a condition the young man gladly accepted] to retire with his father to the convent. Matilda and Isabella were too much occupied with their own reflections, and too little content with each other, to wish for farther converse that night. They separated each to her chamber, with more expressions of ceremony, and fewer of affection, than had passed between them since their childhood.

If they parted with small cordiality, they did but meet with greater impatience as soon as the sun was risen. Their minds were in a situation that excluded sleep, and each recollected a thousand questions which she wished she had put to the other overnight. Matilda reflected that Isabella had been twice delivered by Theodore in very critical situations, which she could not believe accidental. His eyes, it was true, had been fixed on her in Frederic's chamber; but that might have been to disguise his passion for Isabella from the fathers of both. It were better to clear this up. She wished to know the truth, lest she should wrong her friend by entertaining a passion for Isabella's lover. Thus jealousy prompted, and at the same time borrowed an excuse from friendship to justify its curiosity.

Isabella, not less restless, had better foundation for her suspicions. Both Theodore's tongue and eyes had told her his heart was engaged, it was true—yet perhaps Matilda might not correspond to his passion—She had ever appeared insensible to love;

all her thoughts were set on heaven — Why did I dissuade her? said Isabella to herself; I am punished for my generosity — But when did they meet? where? — It cannot be; I have deceived myself — Perhaps last night was the first time they ever beheld each other — it must be some other object that has prepossessed his affections — if it is, I am not so unhappy as I thought; if it is not my friend Matilda — How! can I stoop to wish for the affection of a man, who rudely and unnecessarily acquainted me with his indifference? and that at the very moment in which common courtesy demanded at least expressions of civility. I will go to my dear Matilda, who will confirm me in this becoming pride — Man is false — I will advise with her on taking the veil: she will rejoice to find me in this disposition; and I will acquaint her that I no longer oppose her inclination for the cloister. In this frame of mind, and determinied to open her heart entirely to Matilda, she went to that princess's chamber, whom she found already dressed, and leaning pensively on her arm. This attitude, so correspondent to what she felt herself, revived Isabella's suspicions, and destroyed the confidence she purposed to place in her friend. They blushed at meeting, and were too much novices to disguise their sensations with address. After some unmeaning questions and replies, Matilda demanded of Isabella the cause of her flight? The latter, who had almost forgotten Manfred's passion, so entirely was she occupied by her own, concluding that Matilda referred to her last escape from the convent, which had occasioned the events of the preceding evening, replied, Martelli brought word to the convent that your mother was dead. — Oh! said Matilda interrupting her, Bianca has explained that mistake to me: on seeing me faint, she cried out, The princess is dead! and Martelli, who had come for the usual dole[1] to the castle — And what made you faint? said Isabella, indifferent to the rest. Matilda blushed, and stammered — My father — he was sitting in judgment on a criminal. — What criminal? said Isabella eagerly. — A young man, said Matilda — I believe — I think it was that young man that — What, Theodore? said Isabella. Yes, answered she; I never saw him before; I do not know how he had offended my father — but, as he has been of service to you, I am glad my lord has pardoned him. Served me?

---

1   Charitable gift of food or money "doled out" by the lord of the castle.

replied Isabella: do you term it serving me, to wound my father, and almost occasion his death? Though it is but since yesterday that I am blessed with knowing a parent, I hope Matilda does not think I am such a stranger to filial tenderness as not to resent the boldness of that audacious youth, and that it is impossible for me ever to feel any affection for one who dared to lift his arm against the author of my being. No, Matilda, my heart abhors him; and if you still retain the friendship for me that you have vowed from your infancy, you will detest a man who has been on the point of making me miserable for ever. Matilda held down her head, and replied, I hope my dearest Isabella does not doubt her Matilda's friendship: I never beheld that youth until yesterday; he is almost a stranger to me: but as the surgeons have pronounced your father out of danger, you ought not to harbour uncharitable resentment against one who I am persuaded did not know the marquis was related to you. You plead his cause very pathetically, said Isabella, considering he is so much a stranger to you! I am mistaken, or he returns your charity. What mean you? said Matilda. Nothing, said Isabella; repenting that she had given Matilda a hint of Theodore's inclination for her. Then changing the discourse, she asked Matilda what occasioned Manfred to take Theodore for a spectre? Bless me, said Matilda, did not you observe his extreme resemblance to the portrait of Alfonso in the gallery? I took notice of it to Bianca even before I saw him in armour; but with the helmet on, he is the very image of that picture. I do not much observe pictures, said Isabella; much less have I examined this young man so attentively as you seem to have done. — Ah! Matilda, your heart is in danger — but let me warn you as a friend — He has owned to me that he is in love: it cannot be with you, for yesterday was the first time you ever met — was it not? Certainly, replied Matilda. But why does my dearest Isabella conclude from any thing I have said, that — She paused — then continuing, He saw you first, and I am far from having the vanity to think that my little portion of charms could engage a heart devoted to you. May you be happy, Isabella, whatever is the fate of Matilda! — My lovely friend, said Isabella, whose heart was too honest to resist a kind expression, it is you that Theodore admires; I saw it; I am persuaded of it; nor shall a thought of my own happiness suffer me to interfere with yours. This frankness drew tears from the gentle Matilda; and jealousy, that for a moment had raised a coolness between these amiable maidens, soon gave way to the natural sincerity and candour of their souls. Each confessed to the other the impression that Theodore had made on her; and this confidence was followed by a struggle of generosity, each insisting on yielding her claim to her friend. At length, the dignity of Isabella's virtue reminding her of the preference which Theodore had almost declared for her rival, made her determine to conquer her passion, and cede the beloved object to her friend.

During this contest of amity, Hippolita entered her daughter's chamber. Madam, said she to Isabella, you have so much tenderness for Matilda, and interest yourself so kindly in whatever affects our wretched house, that I can have no secrets with my child, which are not proper for you to hear. The princesses were all attention and anxiety. Know then, madam, continued Hippolita, and you, my dearest Matilda, that being convinced by all the events of these two last ominous days, that Heaven purposes[1] the sceptre of Otranto should pass from Manfred's hands into those of marquis Frederic, I have been perhaps inspired with the thought of averting our total destruction by the union of our rival houses. With this view I have been proposing to Manfred my lord to tender this dear dear child to Frederic your father—Me to lord Frederic! cried Matilda—Good heavens! my gracious mother—and have you named it to my father? I have, said Hippolita: he listened benignly to my proposal, and is gone to break it to the marquis.—Ah! wretched princess! cried Isabella, what hast thou done? What ruin has thy inadvertent goodness been preparing for thyself, for me, and for Matilda! Ruin from me to you and to my child! said Hippolita: What can this mean? Alas! said Isabella, the purity of your own heart prevents your seeing the depravity of others. Manfred, your lord, that impious man—Hold, said Hippolita; you must not in my presence, young lady, mention Manfred with disrespect; he is my lord and husband, and—Will not long be so, said Isabella, if his wicked purposes can be carried into

---

[1] Unlike much later Gothic fiction in which the universe is under demonic control, a just and benign God, working through the gigantic agency of Alfonso the Good, will restore order and thwart evil. See: Syndy M. Conger, "Faith and Doubt in *The Castle of Otranto*," *Gothic: The Review of Supernatural Horror Fiction* 1 (1979): 51–59.

execution. This language amazes me, said Hippoita. Your feeling, Isabella, is warm; but until this hour I never knew it betray you into intemperance. What deed of Manfred authorizes you to treat him as a murderer, an assassin? Thou virtuous and too credulous princess! replied Isabella; it is not thy life he aims at—it is to separate himself from thee! to divorce thee! To—to divorce me! To divorce my mother! cried Hippolita and Matilda at once.—Yes, said Isabella; and to complete his crime he meditates—I cannot speak it! What can surpass what thou hast already uttered? said Matilda. Hippolita was silent. Grief choked her speech; and the recollection of Manfred's late ambiguous discourses confirmed what she heard. Excellent, dear lady! madam! mother! cried Isabella, flinging herself at Hippolita's feet in a transport of passion; trust me, believe me, I will die a thousand deaths sooner than consent to injure you, than yield to so odious—oh!—This is too much! cried Hippolita: What crimes does one crime suggest! Rise, dear Isabella; I do not doubt your virtue. Oh! Matilda, this stroke is too heavy for thee! Weep not, my child; and not a murmur, I charge thee. Remember, he is *thy* father still.—But you are my mother too, said Matilda fervently; and *you* are virtuous, *you* are guiltless!—Oh! must not I, must not I complain? You must not, said Hippolita—Come, all will yet be well. Manfred, in the agony for the loss of thy brother, knew not what he said: perhaps Isabella misunderstood him: his heart is good—and, my child, thou knowest not all. There is a destiny hangs over us; the hand of Providence is stretched out—Oh! could I but save thee from the wreck!—Yes, continued she in a firmer tone; perhaps the sacrifice of myself may atone for all—I will go and offer myself to this divorce—it boots not what becomes of me. I will withdraw into the neighbouring monastery, and waste the remainder of life in prayers and tears for my child and—the prince! Thou art as much too good for this world, said Isabella, as Manfred is execrable—But think not, lady, that thy weakness shall determine for me. I swear—hear me, all ye angels—Stop, I adjure thee, cried Hippolita; remember, thou dost not depend on thyself; thou hast a father.—My father is too pious, too noble, interrupted Isabella, to command an impious deed. But should he command it, can a father enjoin a cursed act? I was contracted to the son; can I wed the father?—No, madam, no; force should not drag me to Manfred's hated bed. I loath him, I abhor him: divine and human laws forbid. — And my friend, my dearest Matilda! would I wound her tender soul by injuring her adored mother? my own mother — I never have known another. — Oh! she is the mother of both! cried Matilda. Can we, can we, Isabella, adore her too much? My lovely children, said the touched Hippolita, your tenderness overpowers me — but I must not give way to it. It is not ours to make election for ourselves; heaven, our fathers, and our husbands, must decide for us. Have patience until you hear what Manfred and Frederic have determined. If the marquis accepts Matilda's hand, I know she will readily obey. Heaven may interpose and prevent the rest. What means my child? continued she, seeing Matilda fall at her feet with a flood of speechless tears — But no; answer me not, my daughter; I must not hear a word against the pleasure of thy father. Oh! doubt not my obedience, my dreadful obedience to him and to you! said Matilda. But can I, most respected of women, can I experience all this tenderness, this world of goodness, and conceal a thought from the best of mothers? What art thou going to utter? said Isabella trembling. Recollect thyself, Matilda. No, Isabella, said the princess, I should not deserve this incomparable parent, if the inmost recesses of my soul harboured a thought without her permission — nay, I have offended her; I have suffered a passion to enter my heart without her avowal — But here I disclaim it; here I vow to heaven and her — My child! my child! said Hippolita, what words are these? What new calamities has fate in store for us? Thou, a passion! thou, in this hour of destruction! — Oh! I see all my guilt! said Matilda. I abhor myself, if I cost my mother a pang. She is the dearest thing I have on earth — Oh! I will never, never behold him more! — Isabella, said Hippolita, thou art conscious to this unhappy secret, whatever it is. Speak! — What! cried Matilda, have I so forfeited my mother's love that she will not permit me even to speak my own guilt? Oh! wretched, wretched Matilda! — Thou art too cruel, said Isabella to Hippolita: canst thou behold this anguish of a virtuous mind, and not commiserate it? Not pity my child! said Hippolita, catching Matilda in her arms — Oh! I know she is good, she is all virtue, all tenderness, and duty. I do forgive thee, my excellent, my only hope! The princesses then revealed to Hippolita their mutual inclination for Theodore, and the purpose of Isabella to resign him to Matilda. Hippolita blamed their imprudence, and shewed them the improbability that either father would consent to bestow his heiress on so poor a man, though nobly born. Some comfort it gave her to find their passion of so recent a date, and that Theodore had but little cause to suspect it in either. She strictly enjoined them to avoid all correspondence with him. This Matilda fervently promised: but Isabella, who flattered herself that she meant no more than to promote his union with her friend, could not determine to avoid him; and made no reply. I will go to the convent, said Hippolita, and order new masses to be said for a deliverance from these calamities. — Oh! my mother, said Matilda, you mean to quit us: you mean to take sanctuary, and to give my father an opportunity of pursuing his fatal intention. Alas! on my knees I supplicate you to forbear — Will you leave me a prey to Frederic? I will follow you to the convent. — Be at peace, my child, said Hippolita: I will return instantly. I will never abandon thee, until I know it is the will of heaven, and for thy benefit. Do not deceive me, said Matilda. I will not marry Frederic until thou commandest it. Alas! what will become of me? — Why that exclamation? said Hippolita. I have promised thee to return. — Ah! my mother, replied Matilda, stay and save me from myself. A frown from thee can do more than all my father's severity. I have given away my heart, and you alone can make me recall it. No more, said Hippolita: thou must not relapse, Matilda. I can quit Theodore, said she, but must I wed another? Let me attend thee to the altar, and shut myself from the world for ever. Thy fate depends on thy father, said Hippolita: I have ill bestowed my tenderness, if it has taught thee to revere aught beyond him. Adieu, my child! I go to pray for thee.

Hippolita's real purpose was to demand of Jerome, whether in conscience she might not consent to the divorce. She had oft urged Manfred to resign the principality, which the delicacy of her conscience rendered an hourly burthen[1] to her. These scruples concurred to make the separation from her husband appear less dreadful to her than it would have seemed in any other situation.

---

1 Burden.

Jerome, at quitting the castle overnight, had questioned Theodore severely why he had accused him to Manfred of being privy to his escape. Theodore owned it had been with the design to prevent Manfred's suspicion from alighting on Matilda; and added, the holiness of Jerome's life and character secured him from the tyrant's wrath. Jerome was heartily grieved to discover his son's inclination for that princess; and, leaving him to his rest, promised in the morning to acquaint him with important reasons for conquering his passion. Theodore, like Isabella, was too recently acquainted with parental authority to submit to its decisions against the impulse of his heart. He had little curiosity to learn the friar's reasons, and less disposition to obey them. The lovely Matilda had made stronger impressions on him than filial affection. All night he pleased himself with visions of love; and it was not till late after the morning-office,[1] that he recollected the friar's commands to attend him at Alfonso's tomb.

Young man, said Jerome, when he saw him, this tardiness does not please me. Have a father's commands already so little weight? Theodore made awkward excuses, and attributed his delay to having overslept himself. And on whom were thy dreams employed? said the friar sternly. His son blushed. Come, come, resumed the friar, inconsiderate youth, this must not be; eradicate this guilty passion from thy breast. — Guilty passion! cried Theodore: can guilt dwell with innocent beauty and virtuous modesty? It is sinful, replied the friar, to cherish those whom heaven has doomed to destruction. A tyrant's race must be swept from the earth to the third and fourth generation. Will heaven visit the innocent for the crimes of the guilty? said Theodore. The fair Matilda has virtues enough — To undo thee, interrupted Jerome. Hast thou so soon forgotten that twice the savage Manfred has pronounced thy sentence? Nor have I forgotten, sir, said Theodore, that the charity of his daughter delivered me from his power. I can forget injuries, but never benefits. The injuries thou hast received from Manfred's race, said the friar, are beyond what thou canst conceive. — Reply not, but view this holy image! Beneath this marble monument rest the ashes of the good Alfonso; a prince adorned with every

---

1   Matin or Mattins (British usage). Morning prayers.

virtue: the father of his people! the delight of mankind! kneel, head-strong boy, and list, while a father unfolds a tale of horror, that will expel every sentiment from thy soul, but sensations of sacred vengeance.[1] — Alfonso! much-injured prince! let thy unsatisfied shade[2] sit awful on the troubled air, while these trembling lips — Ha! who comes there? — The most wretched of women, said Hippolita, entering the choir. Good father, art thou at leisure? — But why this kneeling youth? what means the horror imprinted on each countenance? why at this venerable tomb — Alas! hast thou seen aught? We were pouring forth our orisons to heaven, replied the friar with some confusion, to put an end to the woes of this deplorable province. Join with us, lady! thy spotless soul may obtain an exemption from the judgments which the portents of these days but too speakingly denounce against thy house. I pray fervently to heaven to divert them, said the pious princess. Thou knowest it has been the occupation of my life to wrest a blessing for my lord and my harmless children — One, alas! is taken from me! would heaven but hear me for my poor Matilda! Father, intercede for her! — Every heart will bless her, cried Theodore with rapture. — Be dumb, rash youth! said Jerome. And thou, fond princess, contend not with the powers above! The Lord giveth, and the Lord taketh away: bless his holy name, and submit to his decrees. I do most devoutly, said Hippolita: but will he not spare my only comfort? must Matilda perish too? — Ah! father, I came — But dismiss thy son. No ear but thine must hear what I have to utter. May heaven grant thy every wish, most excellent princess! said Theodore retiring. Jerome frowned.

Hippolita then acquainted the friar with the proposal she had suggested to Manfred, his approbation of it, and the tender of Matilda that he was gone to make to Frederic. Jerome could not conceal his dislike of the motion, which he covered under the

---

1 Much of the passage is a rewording of Hamlet's encounter with his father's ghost. It was Walpole's artistic intention to link the style and themes of *The Castle of Otranto* to Shakespeare's tragedies. See: *Hamlet*, I.v.16-18. "I could a tale unfold whose lightest word/ Would harrow up thy soul, freeze thy young blood,/ Make thy two eyes, like stars,/ Start from their spheres." See: E.L. Burney, "Shakespeare in *Otranto*," *Manchester Review* 12 (1972): 61-64.

2 Specter or ghost.

pretence of the improbability that Frederic, the nearest of blood to Alfonso, and who was come to claim his succession, would yield to an alliance with the usurper of his right. But nothing could equal the perplexity of the friar, when Hippolita confessed her readiness not to oppose the separation, and demanded his opinion on the legality of her acquiescence. The friar catched eagerly at her request of his advice; and without explaining his aversion to the proposed marriage of Manfred and Isabella, he painted to Hippolita in the most alarming colours the sinfulness of her consent, denounced judgments against her if she complied, and enjoined her in the severest terms to treat any such proposition with every mark of indignation and refusal.

Manfred, in the mean time, had broken his purpose to Frederic, and proposed the double marriage. That weak prince, who had been struck with the charms of Matilda, listened but too early to the offer. He forgot his enmity to Manfred, whom he saw but little hope of dispossessing by force; and flattering himself that no issue might succeed from the union of his daughter with the tyrant, he looked upon his own succession to the principality as facilitated by wedding Matilda. He made faint opposition to the proposal; affecting, for form only, not to acquiesce unless Hippolita should consent to the divorce. Manfred took that upon himself. Transported with his success, and impatient to see himself in a situation to expect sons, he hastened to his wife's apartment, determined to extort her compliance. He learned with indignation that she was absent at the convent. His guilt suggested to him that she had probably been informed by Isabella of his purpose. He doubted whether her retirement to the convent did not import an intention of remaining there, until she could raise obstacles to their divorce; and the suspicions he had already entertained of Jerome, made him apprehend that the friar would not only traverse his views,[1] but might have inspired Hippolita with the resolution of taking sanctuary. Impatient to unravel this clue, and to defeat its success, Manfred hastened to the convent and arrived there as the friar was earnestly exhorting the princess never to yield to the divorce.

---

1   Frustrate his plans.

Madam, said Manfred, what business drew you hither? Why did you not await my return from the marquis? I came to implore a blessing on your councils, replied Hippolita. My councils do not need a friar's intervention, said Manfred—and of all men living is that hoary traitor the only one whom you delight to confer with?—Profane prince! said Jerome: is it at the altar that thou choosest to insult the servants of the altar?—But, Manfred, thy impious schemes are known. Heaven and this virtuous lady know them. Nay, frown not, prince. The church despises thy menaces. Her thunders will be heard above thy wrath. Dare to proceed in thy curst purpose of a divorce, until her sentence be known, and here I lance her anathema[1] at thy head. Audacious rebel! said Manfred, endeavouring to conceal the awe with which the friar's words inspired him; dost thou presume to threaten thy lawful prince? Thou art no lawful prince, said Jerome; thou art no prince—Go, discuss thy claim with Frederic; and when that is done—It is done, replied Manfred: Frederic accepts Matilda's hand, and is content to waive his claim, unless I have no male issue.—As he spoke those words three drops of blood fell from the nose of Alfonso's statue.[2] Manfred turned pale, and the princess sunk on her knees. Behold! said the friar: mark this miraculous indication that the blood of Alfonso will never mix with that of Manfred! My gracious lord, said Hippolita, let us submit ourselves to heaven. Think not thy ever obedient wife rebels against thy authority. I have no will but that of my lord and the church. To that revered tribunal let us appeal. It does not depend on us to burst the bonds that unite us. If the church shall approve the dissolution of our marriage, be it so—I have but few years, and those of sorrow, to pass. Where can they be worn away so well as at the foot of this altar, in prayers for thine and Matilda's safety?—But thou shalt not remain here until then, said Manfred. Repair with me to the castle, and there I will advise on the proper

---

1   To curse or damn Manfred for seeking a divorce. To anathematize in formal ecclesiastical sense meant to excommunicate from the church.

2   In his edition of *The Castle of Otranto*, Montague Summers cites many instances in drama where nosebleeding forebodes doom or forecasts disaster. Walpole's somewhat risible Gothic effect of the nosebleeding statue partially derives from Calpurnia's nightmare in Shakespeare's *Julius Cæsar*, II.ii.76-78: "She dreamt tonight she saw my statue, / Which, like a fountain with an hundred spouts, did run pure blood."

measures for a divorce. — But this meddling friar[1] comes not thither; my hospitable roof shall never more harbour a traitor — and for thy reverence's offspring, continued he, I banish him from my dominions. He, I ween, is no sacred personage, nor under the protection of the church. Whoever weds Isabella, it shall not be Father Falconara's started-up son. They start up, said the friar, who are suddenly beheld in the seat of lawful princes; but they wither away like the grass and their place knows them no more. Manfred, casting a look of scorn at the friar, led Hippolita forth; but at the door of the church whispered one of his attendants to remain concealed about the convent, and bring him instant notice, if any one from the castle should repair thither.

---

1 In later Gothic fiction, monks and friars are generally nefarious, villainous, hypocritical, and lecherous, as is the case with Walpole's portrayal of the churchman-as-villain, Father Benedict, in *The Mysterious Mother* and Mrs. Radcliffe's Father Schedoni in *The Italian* (1797). In Shakespeare's *Measure for Measure*, V.i.132-133, Lucio says "'tis a meddling friar./ I do not like the man."

CHAPTER FIVE

EVERY reflection which Manfred made on the friar's behaviour, conspired to persuade him that Jerome was privy to an amour between Isabella and Theodore. But Jerome's new presumption, so dissonant from his former meekness, suggested still deeper apprehensions. The prince even suspected that the friar depended on some secret support from Frederic, whose arrival coinciding with the novel appearance of Theodore seemed to bespeak a correspondence. Still more was he troubled with the resemblance of Theodore to Alfonso's portrait. The latter he knew had unquestionably died without issue. Frederic had consented to bestow Isabella on him. These contradictions agitated his mind with numberless pangs. He saw but two methods of extricating himself from his difficulties. The one was to resign his dominions to the marquis — Pride, ambition, and his reliance on ancient prophecies, which had pointed out a possibility of preserving them to his posterity, combated that thought. The other was to press his marriage with Isabella. After long ruminating on these anxious thoughts, as he marched silently with Hippolita to the castle, he at last discoursed with that princess on the subject of his disquiet, and used every insinuating and plausible argument to extract her consent to, even her promise of promoting, the divorce. Hippolita needed little persuasion to bend her to his pleasure. She endeavoured to win him over to the measure of resigning his dominions; but finding her exhortations fruitless, she assured him, that as far as her conscience would allow, she would raise no opposition to a separation, though, without better founded scruples than what he yet alleged, she would not engage to be active in demanding it.

This compliance, though inadequate, was sufficient to raise Manfred's hopes. He trusted that his power and wealth would easily advance his suit at the court of Rome, whither he resolved to engage Frederic to take a journey on purpose. That prince had discovered so much passion for Matilda, that Manfred hoped to obtain all he wished by holding out or withdrawing his daughter's charms, according as the marquis should appear more or less disposed to co-operate in his views. Even the absence of Frederic would be a material point gained, until he could take farther measures for his security.

SCENE FROM 'THE CASTLE OF OTRANTO,'
BY BERTIE GREATHEED, THE YOUNGER

Frederic encounters the skeletal monk, chapter five.

Dismissing Hippolita to her apartment, he repaired to that of the marquis; but crossing the great hall through which he was to pass, he met Bianca. That damsel he knew was in the confidence of both the young ladies. It immediately occurred to him to sift her[1] on the subject of Isabella and Theodore. Calling her aside into the recess of the oriel window[2] of the hall, and soothing her with many fair words and promises, he demanded of her whether she knew aught of the state of Isabella's affections. I! my lord? No, my lord — Yes, my lord — Poor lady! she is wonderfully alarmed about her father's wounds; but I tell her he will do well; don't your highness think so? I do not ask you, replied Manfred, what she thinks about her father: but you are in her secrets: come, be a good girl and tell me, is there any young man — ha! you under-stand me. Lord bless me! understand your highness? No, not I: I told her a few vulnerary herbs[3] and repose — I am not talking, replied the prince impatiently, about her father: I know he will do well. Bless me, I rejoice to hear your highness say so; for though I thought it right not to let my young lady despond, methought his greatness had a wan look, and a something — I remember when young Ferdinand was wounded by the Venetian. Thou answerest from the point, interrupted Manfred; but here, take this jewel, perhaps that may fix thy attention — Nay, no reverences; my favour shall not stop here — Come, tell me truly; how stands Isabella's heart? Well, your highness has such a way, said Bianca — to be sure — but can your highness keep a secret? If it should ever come out of your lips — It shall not, it shall not, cried Manfred. Nay, but swear, your highness — by my halidame,[4] if it should ever be known that I said it — Why, truth is truth, I do not think my Lady Isabella ever much affectioned my young lord, your son: yet he was a sweet youth as one should see. I am sure if I had been a princess — but bless me! I must attend my Lady Matilda; she will marvel what is become of me. — Stay, cried Manfred; thou hast not satisfied my question. Hast thou ever carried any message, any letter? — I! Good gracious! cried Bianca: I carry a letter? I would

---

not to be a queen. I hope your highness thinks, though I am poor, I am honest. Did your highness never hear what Count Marsigli offered me, when he came a-wooing to my lady Matilda? — I have not leisure, said Manfred, to listen to thy tales. I do not question thy honesty; but it is thy duty to conceal nothing from me. How long has Isabella been acquainted with Theodore? — Nay, there is nothing can escape your highness, said Bianca — not that I know anything of the matter. Theodore, to be sure, is a proper young man, and, as my lady Matilda says, the very image of good Alfonso: Has not your highness remarked it? Yes, yes — No — thou torturest me, said Manfred: Where did they meet? when? — Who, my Lady Matilda? said Bianca. No, no, not Matilda; Isabella: When did Isabella first become acquainted with this Theodore? — Virgin Mary! said Bianca, how should I know? Thou dost know, said Manfred; and I must know; I will. — Lord! your highness is not jealous of young Theodore? said Bianca. — Jealous! No, no: why should I be jealous? — Perhaps I mean to unite them — If I was sure Isabella would have no repugnance. — Repugnance! No, I'll warrant her, said Bianca: he is as comely a youth as ever trod on Christian ground: we are all in love with him: there is not a soul in the castle but would be rejoiced to have him for our prince — I mean, when it shall please heaven to call your highness to itself. — Indeed! said Manfred: has it gone so far? Oh! this cursed friar! — But I must not lose time — Go, Bianca, attend Isabella; but I charge thee, not a word of what has passed. Find out how she is affected towards Theodore; bring me good news, and that ring has a companion. Wait at the foot of the winding staircase: I am going to visit the marquis, and will talk farther with thee at my return.

Manfred, after some general conversation, desired Frederic to dismiss the two knights his companions, having to talk with him on urgent affairs. As soon as they were alone, he began in artful guise to sound the marquis on the subject of Matilda; and finding him disposed to his wish, he let drop hints on the difficulties that would attend the celebration of their marriage, unless — At that instant Bianca burst into the room, with a wildness in her look and gestures that spoke the utmost terror. Oh! my lord, my lord! cried she, we are all undone! It is come again! it is come again! — What is come again? cried Manfred amazed. — Oh! the hand! the giant! the hand!—Support me! I am terrified out of my senses, cried Bianca: I will not sleep in the castle to-night. Where shall I go? My things may come after me to-morrow.—Would I had been content to wed Francesco! This comes of ambition!—What has terrified thee thus, young woman? said the marquis; thou art safe here; be not alarmed. Oh! your greatness is wonderfully good, said Bianca, but I dare not—No, pray let me go—I had rather leave every thing behind me, than stay another hour under this roof. Go to, thou hast lost thy senses, said Manfred. Interrupt us not; we were communing on important matters.—My lord, this wench is subject to fits—Come with me, Bianca.—Oh! the saints! No, said Bianca—for certain it comes to warn your high-ness; why should it appear to me else? I say my prayers morning and evening—Oh! if your highness had believed Diego! 'Tis the same hand that he saw the foot to in the gallery-chamber—Father Jerome has often told us the prophecy would be out one of these days—Bianca, said he, mark my words.—Thou ravest, said Manfred in a rage: Begone, and keep these fooleries to fright-en thy companions. What! my lord, cried Bianca, do you think I have seen nothing? Go to the foot of the great stairs yourself—As I live I saw it. Saw what? Tell us, fair maid, what thou hast seen, said Frederic. Can your highness listen, said Manfred, to the delir-ium of a silly wench, who has heard stories of apparitions until she believes them? This is more than fancy, said the marquis; her terror is too natural and too strongly impressed to be the work of imagination. Tell us, fair maiden, what it is has moved thee thus. Yes, my lord; thank your greatness, said Bianca—I believe I look very pale; I shall be better when I have recovered myself.—I was going to my lady Isabella's chamber by his highness's order—We do not want the circumstances, interrupted Manfred: since his highness will have it so, proceed; but be brief.—Lord, your high-ness thwarts one so! replied Bianca—I fear my hair—I am sure I never in my life—Well! as I was telling your greatness, I was going by his highness's order to my Lady Isabella's chamber: she lies in the watchet-coloured[1] chamber, on the right hand, one pair of stairs: so when I came to the great stairs—I was looking on his

---

1   Azure-colored. Many readers of *Otranto* have noticed that there was a blue bedchamber at Strawberry Hill.

highness's present here. Grant me patience! said Manfred, will this wench never come to the point? What imports it to the marquis, that I gave thee a bauble for thy faithful attendance on my daughter? We want to know what thou sawest. I was going to tell your highness, said Bianca, if you would permit me. — So, as I was rubbing the ring[1] — I am sure I had not gone up three steps, but I heard the rattling of armour; for all the world such a clatter, as Diego says he heard when the giant turned him about in the gallery-chamber. — What does she mean, my lord? said the marquis. Is your castle haunted by giants and goblins? — Lord, what, has not your greatness heard the story of the giant in the gallery-chamber? cried Bianca. I marvel his highness has not told you — mayhap you do not know there is a prophecy — This trifling is intolerable, interrupted Manfred. Let us dismiss this silly wench, my lord: we have more important affairs to discuss. By your favour, said Frederic, these are no trifles: the enormous sabre I was directed to in the wood; yon casque, its fellow — are these visions of this poor maiden's brain? — So Jaquez thinks, may it please your greatness, said Bianca. He says this moon will not be out without our seeing some strange revolution. For my part I should not be surprised if it was to happen to-morrow; for, as I was saying, when I heard the clattering of armour, I was all in a cold sweat — I looked up, and, if your greatness will believe me, I saw upon the uppermost bannister of the great stairs a hand in armour[2] as big, as big — I thought I should have swooned — I never stopped until I came hither — would I were well out of this castle! My lady Matilda told me but yester-morning that her highness Hippolita knows something — Thou art an insolent! cried Manfred — Lord Marquis, it much misgives me that this scene is concerted to affront me. Are my own domestics suborned to spread tales injurious to my honour? Pursue your claim by manly daring; or let us bury our feuds, as was proposed, by the

---

1 Just previously, Manfred has given Bianca a jewel to get her to disclose information about Theodore and Isabella. She may have been rubbing the ring as a superstitious gesture of protection against ghosts.

2 Bianca's encounter with the huge hand in armor relates directly to the dream origins of the novel in Walpole's imagination. In a letter to William Cole of 9 March 1765, Walpole describes the sight of "a gigantic hand in armour" above a staircase in an ancient castle as the dream inspiration for the novel.

intermarriage of our children: but trust me, it ill becomes a prince of your bearing to practice on mercenary wenches. —I scorn your imputation, said Frederic; until this hour I never set eyes on this damsel: I have given her no jewel! —My lord, my lord, your conscience, your guilt accuses you, and would throw the suspicion on me—But keep your daughter, and think no more of Isabella: the judgments already fallen on your house forbid me matching into it.

Manfred, alarmed at the resolute tone in which Frederic delivered these words, endeavoured to pacify him. Dismissing Bianca, he made such submissions to the marquis, and threw in such artful encomiums on Matilda, that Frederic was once more staggered. However, as his passion was of so recent a date, it could not at once surmount the scruples he had conceived. He had gathered enough from Bianca's discourse to persuade him that heaven declared itself against Manfred. The proposed marriages too removed his claim to a distance: and the principality of Otranto was a stronger temptation, than the contingent reversion of it with Matilda.[1] Still he would not absolutely recede from his engagements; but purposing to gain time, he demanded of Manfred if it was true in fact that Hippolita consented to the divorce. The prince, transported to find no other obstacle, and depending on his influence over his wife, assured the marquis it was so, and that he might satisfy himself of the truth from her own mouth.

As they were thus discoursing, word was brought that the banquet was prepared. Manfred conducted Frederic to the great hall, where they were received by Hippolita and the young princesses. Manfred placed the marquis next to Matilda, and seated himself between his wife and Isabella. Hippolita comported herself with an easy gravity; but the young ladies were silent and melancholy. Manfred, who was determined to pursue his point with the marquis in the remainder of the evening, pushed on the feast until it waxed late; affecting unrestrained gaiety, and plying Frederic with

1   Frederic entertains the possibility of claiming Otranto for himself immediately by force of arms rather than marrying Matilda and then waiting for Manfred's death when the title would pass to her. Much later Gothic fiction features the conflict of rightful ownership of the castle, the mansion, or the ancient house. See: Ian P. Watt, "Time and the Family in the Gothic Novel: *The Castle of Otranto,*" *Eighteenth-Century Life* 10 (1986): 159-171.

repeated goblets of wine. The latter, more upon his guard than Manfred wished, declined his frequent challenges, on pretence of his late loss of blood; while the prince, to raise his own disordered spirits, and to counterfeit unconcern, indulged himself in plentiful draughts, though not to the intoxication of his senses.

The evening being far advanced, the banquet concluded. Manfred would have withdrawn with Frederic; but the latter, pleading weakness and want of repose, retired to his chamber, gallantly telling the prince, that his daughter should amuse his highness until himself could attend him. Manfred accepted the party; and, to the no small grief of Isabella, accompanied her to her apartment. Matilda waited on her mother, to enjoy the freshness of the evening on the ramparts of the castle.

Soon as the company were dispersed their several ways, Frederic, quitting his chamber, enquired if Hippolita was alone, and was told by one of her attendants, who had not noticed her going forth, that at that hour, she generally withdrew to her oratory, where he probably would find her. The marquis during the repast had beheld Matilda with increase of passion. He now wished to find Hippolita in the disposition her lord had promised. The portents that had alarmed him were forgotten in his desires. Stealing softly and unobserved to the apartment of Hippolita, he entered it with a resolution to encourage her acquiescence to the divorce, having perceived that Manfred was resolved to make the possession of Isabella an unalterable condition, before he would grant Matilda to his wishes.

The marquis was not surprised at the silence that reigned in the princess's apartment. Concluding her, as he had been advertised,[1] in her oratory, he passed on. The door was a-jar; the evening gloomy and overcast. Pushing open the door gently, he saw a person kneeling before the altar. As he approached nearer, it seemed not a woman, but one in a long woollen weed,[2] whose back was towards him. The person seemed absorbed in prayer. The marquis was about to return, when the figure rising, stood some moments fixed in meditation, without regarding him. The marquis, expecting the holy person to come forth, and meaning

---

1   Informed.
2   Garments of mourning, especially those worn by a widow.

to excuse his uncivil interruption, said, Reverend father, I sought the lady Hippolita. — Hippolita! replied a hollow voice: camest thou to this castle to seek Hippolita? — And then the figure, turning slowly round, discovered to Frederic the fleshless jaws and empty sockets of a skeleton, wrapt in a hermit's cowl.[1] Angels of grace, protect me! cried Frederic recoiling. Deserve their protection, said the spectre. Frederic, falling on his knees, adjured the phantom to take pity on him. Dost thou not remember me? said the apparition.[2] Remember the wood of Joppa! Art thou that holy hermit? cried Frederic trembling — can I do aught for thy eternal peace? — Wast thou delivered from bondage, said the spectre, to pursue carnal delights? Hast thou forgotten the buried sabre and the behest of heaven engraven on it? — I have not, I have not, said Frederic — But say, blest spirit, what is thy errand to me? what remains to be done? To forget Matilda! said the apparition — and vanished.

Frederic's blood froze in his veins. For some minutes he remained motionless. Then falling prostrate on his face before the altar, he besought the intercession of every saint for pardon. A flood of tears succeeded to this transport; and the image of the beauteous Matilda, rushing in spite of him on his thoughts, he lay on the ground in a conflict of penitence and passion. Ere he could recover from this agony of his spirits, the princess Hippolita, with a taper in her hand, entered the oratory alone. Seeing a man without motion on the floor, she gave a shriek, concluding him dead. Her fright brought Frederic to himself. Rising suddenly, his face bedewed with tears, he would have rushed from her presence; but Hippolita, stopping him, conjured him in the most plaintive accents to explain the cause of his disorder, and by what strange chance she had found him there in that posture. Ah! virtuous princess! said the marquis, penetrated with grief — and

---

1. The hooded phantom, living corpse, or animated skeleton viewed first from behind, then revealed in full by a ghastly turn is one of *Otranto's* best horrific effects and wrenches Frederic from skepticism to horror-struck belief.

2. The entire passage is struck through with the exact speeches of Hamlet in conversation with his father's ghost on the battlements of Elsinore castle. See: *Hamlet*, I.iv.39. "Angels and ministers of grace, defend us." Unlike Hamlet, who cannot decide whether the ghost is "a spirit of health" or "goblin damn'd," Frederic regards the skeletal monk as a messenger of God sent to warn him against his lustful and usurping ambitions.

stopped. For the love of heaven, my lord, said Hippolita, disclose the cause of this transport! what mean these doleful sounds, this alarming exclamation on my name? What woes has heaven still in store for the wretched Hippolita? — Yet silent? — By every pitying angel, I adjure thee, noble prince, continued she, falling at his feet, to disclose the purport of what lies at thy heart — I see thou feelest for me; thou feelest the sharp pangs that thou inflictest — Speak, for pity! — Does aught thou knowest concern my child? — I cannot speak, cried Frederic, bursting from her — Oh! Matilda!

Quitting the princess thus abruptly, he hastened to his own apartment. At the door of it he was accosted by Manfred, who, flushed by wine and love, had come to seek him, and to propose to waste some hours of the night in music and revelling. Frederic, offended at an invitation so dissonant from the mood of his soul, pushed him rudely aside, and, entering his chamber, flung the door intemperately against Manfred, and bolted it inwards. The haughty prince, enraged at this unaccountable behaviour, withdrew in a frame of mind capable of the most fatal excesses. As he crossed the court, he was met by the domestic whom he had planted at the convent as a spy on Jerome and Theodore. This man, almost breathless with the haste he had made, informed his lord, that Theodore and some lady from the castle were at that instant in private conference at the tomb of Alfonso in St. Nicholas's church. He had dogged Theodore thither, but the gloominess of the night had prevented his discovering who the woman was.

Manfred, whose spirits were inflamed, and whom Isabella had driven from her on his urging his passion with too little reserve, did not doubt but the inquietude she had expressed had been occasioned by her impatience to meet Theodore. Provoked by this conjecture, and enraged at her father, he hastened secretly to the great church. Gliding softly between the aisles, and guided by an imperfect gleam of moonshine that shone faintly through the illuminated windows, he stole towards the tomb of Alfonso, to which he was directed by indistinct whispers of the persons he sought. The first sounds he could distinguish were — Does it, alas, depend on me? Manfred will never permit our union. — No, this shall prevent it! cried the tyrant, drawing his dagger, and plunging

it over her shoulder into the bosom of the person that spoke—
Ah me, I am slain! cried Matilda sinking: Good heaven, receive
my soul!—Savage, inhuman monster! what hast thou done? cried
Theodore, rushing on him, and wrenching his dagger from
him.—Stop, stop thy impious hand, cried Matilda; it is my father!
Manfred, waking as from a trance, beat his breast, twisted his
hands in his locks, and endeavoured to recover his dagger from
Theodore to dispatch himself. Theodore, scarce less distracted,
and only mastering the transports of his grief to assist Matilda, had
now by his cries drawn some of the monks to his aid. While part
of them endeavoured in concert with the afflicted Theodore to
stop the blood of the dying princess, the rest prevented Manfred
from laying violent hands on himself.

Matilda, resigning herself patiently to her fate, acknowledged
with looks of grateful love the zeal of Theodore. Yet oft as her
faintness would permit her speech its way, she begged the assistants to comfort her father. Jerome by this time had learnt the
fatal news, and reached the church. His looks seemed to reproach
Theodore; but turning to Manfred, he said, Now, tyrant! behold
the completion of woe fulfilled on thy impious and devoted head!
The blood of Alfonso cried to heaven for vengeance; and heaven
has permitted its altar to be polluted by assassination, that thou
mightest shed thy own blood at the foot of that prince's sepul-
chre!—Cruel man! cried Matilda, to aggravate the woes of a parent! May heaven bless my father, and forgive him as I do! My
lord, my gracious sire, dost thou forgive thy child? Indeed I came
not hither to meet Theodore! I found him praying at this tomb,
whither my mother sent me to intercede for thee, for her—
Dearest father, bless your child, and say you forgive her.—Forgive
thee! Murderous monster! cried Manfred—can assassins forgive?
I took thee for Isabella; but heaven directed my bloody hand to
the heart of my child!—Oh! Matilda—I cannot utter it—canst
thou forgive the blindness of my rage?—I can, I do, and may
heaven confirm it! said Matilda—But while I have life to ask
it—oh, my mother! what will she feel!—Will you comfort her,
my lord? Will you not put her away? Indeed she loves you—Oh,
I am faint! bear me to the castle—can I live to have her close my
eyes?

Theodore and the monks besought her earnestly to suffer herself to be borne into the convent; but her instances were so pressing to be carried to the castle, that, placing her on a litter, they conveyed her thither as she requested. Theodore supporting her head with his arm, and hanging over her in an agony of despairing love, still endeavoured to inspire her with hopes of life. Jerome on the other side comforted her with discourses of heaven, and holding a crucifix before her, which she bathed with innocent tears, prepared her for the passage to immortality. Manfred, plunged in the deepest affliction, followed the litter in despair.

Ere they reached the castle, Hippolita, informed of the dreadful catastrophe, had flown to meet her murdered child; but when she saw the afflicted procession, the mightiness of her grief deprived her of her senses, and she fell lifeless to the earth in a swoon. Isabella and Frederic, who attended her, were overwhelmed in almost equal sorrow. Matilda alone seemed insensible to her own situation: every thought was lost in tenderness for her mother. Ordering the litter to stop, as soon as Hippolita was brought to herself, she asked for her father. He approached, unable to speak. Matilda, seizing his hand and her mother's, locked them in her own, and then clasped them to her heart. Manfred could not support this act of pathetic piety. He dashed himself on the ground, and cursed the day he was born. Isabella, apprehensive that these struggles of passion were more than Matilda could support, took upon herself to order Manfred to be borne to his apartment, while she caused Matilda to be conveyed to the nearest chamber. Hippolita, scarce more alive than her daughter, was regardless of every thing but her: but when the tender Isabella's care would have likewise removed her, while the surgeons examined Matilda's wound, she cried, Remove me? Never! never! I lived but in her, and will expire with her. Matilda raised her eyes at her mother's voice, but closed them again without speaking. Her sinking pulse, and the damp coldness of her hand, soon dispelled all hopes of recovery. Theodore followed the surgeons into the outer chamber, and heard them pronounce the fatal sentence with a transport equal to phrenzy—Since she cannot live mine, cried he, at least she shall be mine in death!—Father! Jerome! will you not join our hands? cried he to the friar, who with the marquis had accompanied the surgeons. What means thy distracted rashness?

said Jerome: is this an hour for marriage? It is, it is, cried Theodore: alas, there is no other! Young man, thou art too unadvised, said Frederic: dost thou think we are to listen to thy fond transports in this hour of fate? What pretensions hast thou to the princess? Those of a prince, said Theodore; of the sovereign of Otranto. This reverend man, my father, has informed me who I am. Thou ravest, said the marquis: there is no prince of Otranto but myself, now Manfred by murder, by sacrilegious murder, has forfeited all pretensions. My lord, said Jerome, assuming an air of command, he tells you true. It was not my purpose the secret should have been divulged so soon; but fate presses onward to its work. What his hot-headed passion has revealed, my tongue confirms. Know, prince, that when Alfonso set sail for the Holy Land—Is this a season for explanations? cried Theodore. Father, come and unite me to the princess: she shall be mine—in every other thing I will dutifully obey you. My life! my adored Matilda! continued Theodore, rushing back into the inner chamber, will you not be mine? will you not bless your—Isabella made signs to him to be silent, apprehending the princess was near her end. What, is she dead? cried Theodore: is it possible? The violence of his exclamations brought Matilda to herself. Lifting up her eyes, she looked round for her mother—Life of my soul! I am here, cried Hippolita: think not I will quit thee!—Oh! you are too good, said Matilda—but weep not for me, my mother! I am going where sorrow never dwells.—Isabella, thou hast loved me; will thou not supply my fondness to this dear, dear woman? Indeed I am faint!—Oh! my child! my child! said Hippolita in a flood of tears, can I not withhold thee a moment?—It will not be, said Matilda—Commend me to heaven—Where is my father? Forgive him, dearest mother—forgive him my death; it was an error—Oh! I had forgotten—Dearest mother, I vowed never to see Theodore more—Perhaps that has drawn down this calamity—but it was not intentional—can you pardon me?—Oh! wound not my agonizing soul! said Hippolita; thou never could'st offend me.—Alas, she faints! help! help!—I would say something more, said Matilda struggling; but it wonnot[1] be—Isabella—Theodore—for my sake—oh!—She expired. Isabella

---

1 Archaic form of "will not."

and her women tore Hippolita from the corse;[1] but Theodore threatened destruction to all who attempted to remove him from it. He printed a thousand kisses on her clay-cold hands, and uttered every expression that despairing love could dictate.

Isabella, in the mean time, was accompanying the afflicted Hippolita to her apartment; but in the middle of the court they were met by Manfred, who, distracted with his own thoughts, and anxious once more to behold his daughter, was advancing to the chamber where she lay. As the moon was now at its height, he read in the countenances of this unhappy company the event he dreaded. What! is she dead? cried he in wild confusion—A clap of thunder at this instant shook the castle to its foundations; the earth rocked, and the clank of more than mortal armour was heard behind. Frederic and Jerome thought the last day was at hand. The latter, forcing Theodore along with them, rushed into the court. The moment Theodore appeared, the walls of the castle behind Manfred were thrown down with a mighty force,[2] and the form of Alfonso, dilated to an immense magnitude, appeared in the centre of the ruins. Behold in Theodore, the true heir of Alfonso! said the vision: and having pronounced those words, accompanied by a clap of thunder, it ascended solemnly towards heaven, where the clouds parting asunder, the form of saint Nicholas was seen; and receiving Alfonso's shade[3] they were soon wrapt from mortal eyes in a blaze of glory.

The beholders fell prostrate on their faces, acknowledging the divine will. The first that broke silence was Hippolita. My lord, said she to the desponding Manfred, behold the vanity of human greatness! Conrad is gone! Matilda is no more! in Theodore we view the true prince of Otranto. By what miracle he is so, I know not—suffice it to us, our doom is pronounced! Shall we not, can

---

1   Archaic spelling of "corpse."

2   The fall of the House of Otranto as caused by a supernatural force inspired many Gothic climaxes to follow including the architectural collapse of the House in Poe's "The Fall of the House of Usher." *Otranto* terminates with Gothic fiction's first haunted ruin firmly in place. Later Gothic would replace the colossal figure of goodness with gigantic forces of evil reigning supreme over a fallen world. Commenting on the supernatural dénouement of *Otranto*'s climax, E.F. Bleiler has written: "It might be said that the Gothic novel is a primitive detective story in which God or fate is the detective." Introduction to *Three Gothic Novels*, New York: Dover, 1966, xv.

3   Phantom or ghost.

we but dedicate the few deplorable hours we have to live, in deprecating the farther wrath of heaven? Heaven ejects us — whither can we fly, but to yon holy cells that yet offer us a retreat? — Thou guiltless but unhappy woman! unhappy by my crimes! replied Manfred, my heart at last is open to thy devout admonitions. Oh! could — but it cannot be — ye are lost in wonder — let me at last do justice on myself! To heap shame on my own head is all the satisfaction I have left to offer to offended heaven. My story has drawn down these judgments: let confession atone — But ah! what can atone for usurpation and a murdered child? a child murdered in a consecrated place! — List, sirs, and may this bloody record be a warning to future tyrants!

Alfonso, ye all know, died in the Holy Land — ye would interrupt me; ye would say he came not fairly to his end — It is most true — why else this bitter cup which Manfred must drink to the dregs? Ricardo, my grandfather, was his chamberlain — I would draw a veil over my ancestor's crimes — but it is in vain: Alfonso

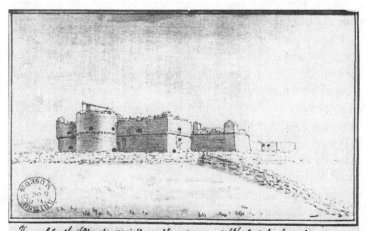

The real Castle of Otranto as existing on the eastern coast of Naples taken from the spot 1785.

REVELEY'S DRAWING OF THE CASTLE OF OTRANTO
AS IT EXISTED IN 1785

The real Castle of Otranto

died by poison. A fictitious will declared Ricardo his heir. His crimes pursued him—yet he lost no Conrad, no Matilda! I pay the price of usurpation for all! A storm overtook him. Haunted by his guilt, he vowed to saint Nicholas to found a church and two convents if he lived to reach Otranto. The sacrifice was accepted: the saint appeared to him in a dream, and promised that Ricardo's posterity should reign in Otranto until the rightful owner should be grown too large to inhabit the castle, and as long as issue-male from Ricardo's loins should remain to enjoy it.—Alas! alas! nor male nor female, except myself, remains of all his wretched race!—I have done—the woes of these three days speak the rest. How this young man can be Alfonso's heir I know not—yet I do not doubt it. His are these dominions; I resign them—yet I knew not Alfonso had an heir—I question not the will of heaven—poverty and prayer must fill up the woeful space, until Manfred shall be summoned to Ricardo.

What remains is my part to declare, said Jerome. When Alfonso set sail for the Holy Land, he was driven by a storm on the coast of Sicily. The other vessel, which bore Ricardo and his train, as your *lordship* must have heard, was separated from him. It is most true, said Manfred; and the title you give me is more than an outcast can claim—Well, be it so—proceed. Jerome blushed, and continued. For three months lord Alfonso was wind-bound in Sicily. There he became enamoured of a fair virgin named Victoria. He was too pious to tempt her to forbidden pleasures. They were married. Yet deeming this amour incongruous with the holy vow of arms by which he was bound, he determined to conceal their nuptials until his return from the crusade, when he purposed to seek and acknowledge her for his lawful wife. He left her pregnant. During his absence she was delivered of a daughter: but scarce had she felt a mother's pangs, ere she heard the fatal rumour of her lord's death, and the succession of Ricardo. What could a friendless, helpless woman do? Would her testimony avail?—Yet, my lord, I have an authentic writing.—It needs not, said Manfred; the horrors of these days, the vision we have but now seen, all corroborate thy evidence beyond a thousand parchments. Matilda's death and my expulsion—Be composed, my lord, said Hippolita; this holy man did not mean to recall your griefs. Jerome proceeded.

I shall not dwell on what is needless. The daughter of which Victoria was delivered, was at her maturity bestowed in marriage on me. Victoria died; and the secret remained locked in my breast. Theodore's narrative has told the rest.

The friar ceased. The disconsolate company retired to the remaining part of the castle.[1] In the morning Manfred signed his abdication of the principality, with the approbation of Hippolita, and each took on them the habit of religion in the neighbouring convents. Frederic offered his daughter to the new prince, which Hippolita's tenderness for Isabella concurred to promote: but Theodore's grief was too fresh to admit the thought of another love; and it was not until after frequent discourses with Isabella, of his dear Matilda, that he was persuaded he could know no happiness but in the society of one with whom he could forever indulge the melancholy that had taken possession of his soul.

---

1 Walpole structured *The Castle of Otranto* as a five-act drama of tragic fate. As in the final scene in Shakespeare's tragedies, the stage grows empty as the survivors retire solemnly.

THE

Mysterious Mother.

A

TRAGEDY.

By Mr. HORACE WALPOLE.

Sit mihi fas audita loqui! VIRGIL.[1]

PRINTED AT STRAWBERRY-HILL:
MDCCLXVIII.

---

1 Sit mihi fas audita loqui! "Let it be right for me to speak what I have heard." Virgil, *Æneid* VI, 266. In Book VI of the *Æneid*, Æneas visits the Sybil's cave, then at her bidding finds and plucks a golden bough that enables him to descend into the under-world. Walpole's incest tragedy "descends" into the hell of this darkest of subjects to

Mr. Horace Walpole.

penetrate the secrets of the damned. The playwright's journey into the darkness of the Countess's crime is as moral a journey as Æneas's dark descent. Hence, it is "right to speak" of these tragic and repulsive events. The same passage from Virgil is cited by Edmund Burke in *A Philosophical Enquiry into the Origin of Our Ideas of the Sublime and Beautiful* "where before he unlocks the secrets of the great deep, he seems to be seized with a religious horror, and to retire astonished at the boldness of his own design" (Burke, *Enquiry*, Part II, Section 6).

PREFACE TO THE 1781 EDITION

THE author of the following Tragedy is so far from thinking it worthy of being offered to the Public, that he has done everything in his power to suppress the publication—in vain. It is solely to avoid its being rendered still worse by surreptitious editions, that he is reduced to give it from his own copy. He is sensible that the subject is disgusting, and by no means compensated by the execution. It was written several years ago; and to prevent the trouble of reading, or having it transcribed, a few copies were printed and given away. One or two have been circulated, and different editions have been advertised, which occasion the present publication. All the favour the Author solicits or expects, is, to be believed how unwillingly he has submitted to its appearance: he cannot be more blamed than he blames himself for having undertaken so disagreeable a story, and for having hazarded the publicity by letting it out of his own hands. He respects the judgment of the Public too much to offer to them voluntarily what he does not think deserves their approbation.

April 19, 1781

ADVERTISEMENT FROM THE PUBLISHERS[1]

THE tragedy here offered to the Public, has long been known in private to a few individuals. The admiration it justly claimed, the continued praises of those who had been fortunate enough to peruse it, naturally excited curiosity. Intimation having been given to us of an hasty edition[2] intended, the idea suggested itself of anticipating that scheme, we were solicitous the piece should appear in a handsome form, and resolved that our best endeavours should be exerted to prevent its being printed incorrectly and in a manner unsuitable to its merit.

The impression was just completed, when hearing accidentally, that some persons, to whose opinion we wish to pay every deference, had expressed the greatest anxiety lest the feelings of the amiable author might be hurt, we determined, without hesitation, to suppress the edition. The expence already incurred, was, after such a hint, a consideration beneath our notice; we were glad to embrace the opportunity of testifying our sincere regard for the high rank, excellent character and eminence in literature of the gentleman who is the reputed author. Finding, however, after an interval of several months, that our well-meant intentions could not be effectual, and that our interference had only delayed, but could not prevent a publication eagerly demanded, we have been induced, reluctantly, to comply with the general wish, and to deliver for sale a work that has been a considerable time in readiness.

We had previously taken the precaution to apprize the accomplished author of the motives by which we had been influenced. We flatter ourselves he will be pleased to accept of our apology, and beg leave to assure him, we should esteem it a great misfortune to meet with his disapprobation, and so to stand well in his opinion is our highest ambition, so he is the last person in the world to whom we should be wanting in respect.

---

1 The publisher's advertisement appears only in a single edition of the play, the Dublin edition of 1791.
2 Refers to an unauthorized edition of play published in London in 1791.

MR. BAKER, in his *Biographia Dramatica*,[1] mentioning the following Poem, tells us it was distributed by the author to his particular friends only; and with such strict injunctions of secrecy, that knowing its merits, much astonishment was excited at its being withheld from the public. Mr. Walpole has given the story in the following words: "I had heard when very young, that a gentlewoman, under uncommon agonies of mind had waited on Archbishop Tillotson and besought his counsel. A damsel that served her had, many years before, acquainted her that she was importuned by the gentlewoman's son to grant him a private meeting. The mother ordered the maiden to make the assignation, when she said she would discover herself, and reprimand him for his criminal passion; but, being hurried away by a much more criminal passion herself, she kept the assignation without discovering herself. The fruit of this horrid artifice was a daughter, whom the gentlewoman caused to be educated very privately in the country; but proving very lovely, and being accidentally met by her father-brother, who never had the slightest suspicion of the truth, he had fallen in love with, and actually married her. The wretched guilty mother learning what had happened, and distracted with the consequence of her crime, had now resorted to the Archbishop to know in what manner she should act. The prelate charged her never to let her son and daughter know what had passed, as they were innocent of any criminal intention. For herself, he bade her almost despair."[2]

On this ground-work is Mr. Walpole's tragedy built, since the writing of which he has discovered a story wonderfully similar in many of its circumstances, in a book well known by the name of *Tales of the Queen of Navarre*;[3] it is the 30th tale of the first volume.

That the production of such a tragedy as the present, on the

---

1 Refers to David Erskine Baker's (1730-1767) history of the British theater published originally as *The Companion to the Play House* in 1764 and in a revised edition titled *Biographia Dramatica* in 1782.

2 The anecdote is a major real life source for the play's incest plot and the mother's deception of the son to satisfy her lust.

3 An allusion to an analogue for the play's incest plot, the Queen of Navarre's *Heptameron*, a collection of tales of love and intrigue written by Marguerite of Navarre, sister of Francis I and queen from 1544 to 1549. Walpole acknowledged the coincidental resemblance. See: *Horace Walpole's Correspondence*, letters to Walpole from Michael Lort, 5 July 1775, 11 June 1776, Vol. 16: 164-166.

modern stage, would be extremely hazardous, we are ready to admit; but we cannot but observe at the same time, that the delicacy of the present times is frequently carried to a ridiculous degree of affectation. Vices of greater magnitude are daily represented, and without exciting the smallest disgust in the spectator. We are by no means convinced that any consequences, unfavourable to the interests of society, could arise from the representation of the result of crimes even so shocking as those which are the basis of the present play, especially when they are painted in such colours as those in which Mr. Walpole's canvas exhibits them. It is certain, that writers of the last century would not have avoided the story for any of the reasons for which the present author has condemned his piece to oblivion; nor do we apprehend that a play, written with the pathos and energy of the present, would have then been refused by managers, or neglected by the town. That former authors, patentees, and audiences, were less scrupulous, may be inferred from this circumstance, that a contemptible performance, entitled, *The Fatal Discovery, or Love in Ruines*,[1] was actually brought before the public at Drury-lane in 1698. This tragedy is founded on the same circumstances which are the principal objects of the present. The heroine is guilty of incest in the same manner; has a daughter who is brought up unconscious of her real parents, banishes her son, who returns just at the opening of the play; he falls in love with his sister daughter, and marries her. The discovery is made, the lady goes mad, and in her frenzy kills her daughter, and afterwards herself. In the old play the incestuous commerce between the son and mother is softened, by making the latter ignorant of the person with whom she had been guilty, until after the horrid event. The same circumstance has been again introduced by Mr. Gould, in another worthless piece, called *Innocence Distressed, or the Royal Penitents*. 8vo. [octavo.] 1737.[2]

---

1 An anonymous incest drama performed at Drury Lane Theater in 1698. Walpole would also have known Euripides's tragedy *Hippolytus* (circa 423 B.C.), the classical source for Racine's *Phèdre* [*Phædra*]. In these plays, a mother falls in love with her stepson, then conceals her passion by being cold and hostile to the young man.

2 Incest play by a minor playwright, Robert Gould. It was printed in 1737, but never performed. Incest was also the subject of John Ford's tragedy *'Tis Pity She's a Whore* (1633) and Francis Beaumont's and John Fletcher's tragedy *A King and no King* (1611).

Of the present tragedy we may boldly pronounce, that for nervous, simple, and pathetic language, each appropriated to the several persons of the drama; for striking incidents; for address in conducting the plot; and for consistency of character uniformly preserved through the whole piece; it is equal, if not superior, to any play of the present century.

PERSONS

COUNTESS of Narbonne.
Count EDMUND, her Son.
FLORIAN, his Friend.
ADELIZA, an Orphan.
BENEDICT
MARTIN } Friars.
PETER, PORTER of the Castle.
MARIA } Damsels attending the Countess.
ELINOR } Mutes.
Chorus of Orphans.
Chorus of Friars.

The Scene lies at the Castle of Narbonne; partly on a Platform before the Gate, partly in a Garden within the Walls.

PROLOGUE

From no French model[1] breathes the muse to-night
The scene she draws is horrid, not polite.
She dips her pen in terror. Will ye shrink?
Shall foreign critics teach you how to think?
Had Shakespeare's magic dignified the stage,   5
If timid laws had school'd th' insipid age?
Had Hamlet's spectre[2] trod the midnight round?

---

1   Walpole repudiates the stiff and formalized French tragedies of Racine and Corneille, neoclassical dramas that had followed Aristotle's rigidly prescribed rules of time, place, and action. The play's sexual suspense "reënact[s] a kind of Oedipal pattern in the Sophoclean or dramatic sense of a secret whose teasing out is the source of theatrical tension." See: Paul Baines, "'This Theatre of Monstrous Guilt': Horace Walpole and the Drama of Incest," *Studies in Eighteenth-Century Culture* 28 (1999): 287-309. The Prologue did not appear in the 1768 edition but was first printed in 1798 in *The Works of Horatio Walpole*.

2   In Shakespeare's *Hamlet*, the ghost of Hamlet's father appears to him on the battlements of Elsinore Castle. (*Hamlet*.I.v). As in *The Castle of Otranto*, Walpole made liberal use of Shakespeare's *Hamlet* and *Macbeth* in *The Mysterious Mother*, borrowing the language of the soliloquies and adapting scenic elements. He limited the use of the supernatural in the drama having presented it *in extremis* in *Otranto*.

Or Banquo's issue[1] been in vision crown'd?
Free as your country, Britons, be your scene!
10   Be Nature now, and now Invention, queen!
Be Vice alone corrected and restrain'd.
Can crimes be punish'd by a bard enchain'd?
Shall the bold censor back be sent to school,
And told, This is not nice; That is not rule?
15   The French no crimes of magnitude admit;
They seldom startle, just alarm the pit.
At most, when dire necessity ordains
That death should sluice some King's or lover's veins,
A tedious confident appears, to tell
20   What dismal woes behind the scenes befell.
Chill'd with the drowsy tale, his audience fret,
While the starv'd piece concludes like a gazette.
The tragic Greeks with nobler licence wrote;
Nor veil'd the eye, but pluck'd away the mote.
25   Whatever passion prompted, was their game;
Not delicate, while chastisement their aim.
Electra[2] now a parent's blood demands;
Now parricide distains the Theban's hands,[3]
And love incestuous knots his nuptial bands.
30   Such is our scene; from real life it rose;
Tremendous picture of domestic woes.
If terror shake you, or soft pity move,
If dreadful pangs o'ertake unbridled love;
Excuse the bard who from your feelings draws
35   All the reward he aims at, your applause.

---

1   In Shakespeare's Macbeth, Macbeth vows the deaths of all of Banquo's descendants since
    they threaten his kingship: "For Banquo's issue have I fil'd my mind" (Macbeth. III.i.64.)
2   In Greek mythology and in tragic dramas by Sophocles and Euripides, she is the sister
    of Orestes and the daughter of Agamemnon and Clytemnestra. She aids her brother in
    his revenge for the murder of their father, Agamemnon, by their mother, Clytemnestra,
    and her lover, Aegisthus.
3   Refers to the parricidal and incestuous crimes of Œdipus, King of Thebes, who
    unknowingly murdered his father and unknowingly married his mother in Sophocles's
    tragedy, Œdipus Tyrannus. Unlike Œdipus, the Countess is fully aware of her incestu-
    ous deed.

THE MYSTERIOUS MOTHER

A TRAGEDY

ACT THE FIRST

SCENE I

A Platform before the Castle

FLORIAN. WHAT awful silence! How these antique towers
    And vacant courts chill the suspended soul,
    Till expectation wears the cast of fear;
    And fear, half-ready to become devotion,
    Mumbles a kind of mental orison,   5
    It knows not wherefore. What a kind of being
    Is circumstance!
    I am a soldier, and were yonder battlements
    Garnish'd with combatants, and cannon-mounted,
    My daring breast would bound with exultation,   10
    And glorious hopes enliven the drear scene.
    Now dare not I scarce tread to my own hearing,
    Lest echo borrow superstition's tongue,
    And seem to answer me, like one departed.
    I met a peasant, and enquir'd my way: 15
    The carle,[1] not rude of speech, but like the tenant
    Of some night-haunted ruin, bore an aspect
    Of horror, worn to habitude. He bade
    God bless me; and pass'd on. I urg'd him farther;
    Good master, cried he, go not to the castle;   20
    There sorrow ever dwells, and moping misery.
    I press'd him—None there, said he, are welcome,
    But now and then a mass-priest, and the poor;
    To whom the pious Countess deals her alms,

---

1 Archaic form of the derogatory term "churl," an ill-bred fellow or lowborn person.

On covenant, that each revolving night
They beg of heav'n the health of her son's soul
And of her own: but often as returns
The twentieth of September,[1] they are bound
Fast from the midnight watch to pray till morn.—
More would he not disclose, or knew not more.
—What precious mummery! Her son in exile,
She wastes on monks and beggars his inheritance,
For his soul's health! I never knew a woman
But lov'd our bodies or our souls too well.
Each master-whim maintains its hour of empire,
And obstinately faithful to its dictates,
With equal ardour, equal importunity,
They teaze us to be damn'd or to be sav'd.
I hate to love or pray too long.

SCENE II

PORTER of the castle, FLORIAN.

PORTER.   Methought
I heard a stranger's voice—What lack you, sir?
FLORIAN. Good fellow, who inhabits here?
PORTER.   I do.
FLORIAN. Belike this castle is not thine.
PORTER.   Belike so:
But be it whose it may, this is no haunt
For revellers and gallants—pass your way.
FLORIAN. Thou churl! Is this your Gallic hospitality?
Thy lady, on my life, would not thus rudely
Chide from her presence a bewilder'd knight.
PORTER. Thou know'st my lady then!—Thou know'st her not.
Canst thou in hair-clothes vex those dainty limbs?
Canst thou on reeking pavements and cold marble,
In meditation pass the livelong night?
Canst mortify that flesh, my rosy minion,

---

1   The date of the death of the Count of Narbonne.

And bid thy rebel appetite refrain
From goblets foaming wine, and costly viands?
These are deeds, my youngster, must draw down
My lady's ever heav'n-directed eye.   20

FLORIAN. In sooth, good friend, my knighthood is not school'd
In voluntary rigours—I can fast,
March supperless, and make cold earth my pillow,
When my companions know no choicer fare.
But seldom roost in churches, or reject   . 25
The ready banquet or a willing fair-one.

PORTER. Angels defend us! What a reprobate!
Yon mould'ring porch, for sixteen years and more
Has not been struck with such unhallow'd sounds.
Hence to thy lewd companions!   30

FLORIAN.   Father greybeard,
I cry you mercy; —nor was't my intention
To wound your reverence's saint-like organs.
But come, thou hast known other days—canst tell
Of banquetings and dancings—'twas not always thus.   35

PORTER. No, no—time was—my lord, the Count of Narbonne,[1]
A prosp'rous gentleman, were he alive,
We should not know these moping melancholies.
Heav'n rest his soul! I marvel not my lady
Cherishes his remembrance, for he was   40
Comely to sight, wond'rous and goodly built.
They say, his son, Count Edmund's mainly like him.
Would these old arms, that serv'd his grandfather,
Could once enfold him! I should part in peace.

FLORIAN. What, if I bring thee tidings of Count Edmund!   45

PORTER. Mercy befall me!—now my dream is out,
Last night the raven croak'd, and from the bars
Of our lodge-fire flitted a messenger—
I knew no good would follow—Bring you ill tidings,
Sir gentleman?   50

FLORIAN.   (This is a solemn fool,   [*Aside.*

---

1 A city in the south of France. Also used as the site of action by Robert Jephson in his
   dramatic adaptation of *The Castle of Otranto*, *The Count of Narbonne* (1781).

Or solemn knave). Shouldst thou indeed rejoice
To see Count Edmund? Would thy noble mistress
Spring with a mother's joy to clasp her son?

55 PORTER. Oh! no, no, no,—He must not here—alas!
He must not here set foot—But tell me, stranger,
I prithee say, does my old master's heir
Still breathe this vital air? Is he in France?
Is he within some ten, or twenty leagues,

60 Or fifty? I am hearty yet, have all my limbs,
And I would make a weary pilgrimage
To kiss his gracious hand, and at his feet
Lay my old bones—for here I ne'er must see him.   [*Weeps.*

FLORIAN. Thou good old man, forgive a soldier's mirth,

65 But say, why Narbonne's heir from Narbonne's lands
Is banish'd, driven by a ruthless mother?

PORTER. Ah! sir, 'tis hard indeed—but spare his mother;
Such virtue never dwelt in female form.
Count Edmund—but he was indeed a stripling,

70 A very lad—it was the trick of youth,
And we have all our sins, or we have had;
Yet still no pardon—Thinkst thou not, my lord,
My late kind master, e'er he knew my lady,
Wist not what woman was?—I warrant him—

75 But so—Count Edmund being not sixteen,
A lusty youth, his father's very image—
Oh! he has play'd me many a trick—good sir,
Does my young master ever name old Peter?
Well!—but I prate—you must forgive my age;

80 I come to th' point—Her name was Beatrice;
A rogish eye—she ne'er would look on me,
Or we had sav'd many a woefull day!
Mark you me well?

FLORIAN.   I do.

85 PORTER. This Beatrice—
But hark! my lady comes—retire awhile
Beyond those yews—anon I'll tell you more.

FLORIAN. May I not greet her?

PORTER.   For my office, no;

90 'Twere forfeit of my badge to hold a parley

With one of near thy years.   [FLORIAN *withdraws.*

[*The* COUNTESS *in weeds,*[1] *with a crucifix in her hand, issues from the castle, accompanied by two maidens, and passes over the stage. When she is gone,* FLORIAN *returns.*

                        'Tis ever thus.
At break of morn, she hies to yonder abbey,
And prostrate o'er some monumental stone,
Seems more to wait her doom, than ask to shun it.   95
The day is pass'd in minist'ring to wants
Of health or means; the closing eye beholds
New tears, new pray'rs, or haggar'd meditation.
But if cold moonshine, deep'ning ev'ry frown
Of these impending towers, invite her steps,   100
She issues forth.—Beshrew me, but I tremble,
When my own keys discharge the drawbridge chains,
And rattle thro' the castle's farmost vaults.
Then have I seen this sad, this sober mourner,
With frantic gesture and disorder'd step—   105
But hush—Who moves up yonder avenue?
It is—no—stay—i'faith! but it is he,
My lady's confessor, with friar Martin—
Quick hie thee hence—should that same meddling monk
Observe our con'frence, there were fine work toward.[2]   110
FLORIAN. You will not leave your tale unfinished?
PORTER. Mass! but I will[3]—A tale will pay no stipend.
These fifty winters have I borne this staff,
And will not lose my porridge for my prating.
FLORIAN. Well! but Count Edmund—wo't not hear of him?   115
PORTER. Aye, bless his name! at any leisure hour.
This ev'ning, e'er the shutting of the gates,
Loiter about yon grange; I'll come to thee.
So now, begone—away!   [*exeunt severally.*

---

1 Weeds are black garments of mourning. The fact that the Countess wears weeds sixteen years after the death of the Count indicates an unusually long period of grief.
2 Work going on or in progress.
3 The Porter blasphemes the Eucharist in this profane exclamation.

SCENE III

BENEDICT, MARTIN,

BENEDICT.   Ay! sift her, sift her—[1]
As if I had not prob'd her very soul,
And wound me round her heart—I tell thee, brother,
This woman was not cast in human mould.
5   Ten such would foil a council,[2] would unbuild
Our Roman church—In her, devotion's real.
Our beads, our hymns, our saints, amuse her not:
Nay, not confession, not repeating o'er
Her darling sins, has any charms for her.
10 I have mark'd her praying: not one wand'ring thought
Seems to steal meaning from her words.—She prays
Because she feels, and feels, because a sinner.
MARTIN. What is this secret sin; this untold tale,
That art cannot extract, nor penance cleanse?
15 Loss of a husband, sixteen years enjoy'd,
And dead as many, could not stamp such sorrow.
Nor could she be his death's artificer,
And now affect to weep it—I have heard,
That chasing, as he homeward rode, a stag,
20 Chas'd by the hounds, with sudden onset slew
Th' adventurous Count.
BENEDICT.   'Twas so; and yet, my brother,
My mind has more than once imputed blood
To this incessant mourner. Beatrice,
25 The damsel for whose sake she holds in exile
Her only son, has never, since the night
Of his incontinence, been seen or heard of.
MARTIN. 'Tis clear, 'tis clear; nor will her prudent tongue
Accuse its owner.
BENEDICT.   Judge not rashly, brother.
30 I oft have shifted my discourse to murder;

---

1   Carefully examine by questioning, especially during the confession.
2   Refers to a synod or council of churches or body of religious officials. The Countess's
    strength of mind could foil or thwart a learned assembly.

She notes it not. Her muscles hold their place,
Nor discompos'd, nor firm'd to steadiness.
No sudden flushing, and no faltering lip:
Nor, tho' she pities, lifts she to her eyes
Her handkerchief, to palliate her disorder. 35
There the wound rankles not.—I fix'd on love,
The failure of the sex, and aptest cause
Of each attendant crime.—
MARTIN.   Ay, brother, there
We master all their craft. Touch but that string—[1] 40
BENEDICT. Still, brother, do you err. She own'd to me,
That, tho' of nature warm, the passion love
Did ne'er anticipate her choice. The Count,
Her husband, so ador'd and so lamented,
Won not her fancy, till the nuptial rites 45
Had with the sting of pleasure taught her passion.
This, with such modest truth, and that truth's heighten'd
By conscious sense, that holds deceit a weakness,
She utter'd, I would pawn my order's credit[2]
On her veracity. 50
MARTIN.   Then whither turn
To worm her secret out?
BENEDICT.   I know not that.
She will be silent, but she scorns a falsehood.
And thus while frank on all things, but her secret, 55
I know, I know it not.
MARTIN.   Till she disclose it,
Deny her absolution.

---

1 Like *The Castle of Otranto*, the play is struck through with transcriptions of lines from
Shakespeare. Compare Father Martin's "touch but that string" with Ulysses's speech on
civil order and disorder and class structure in *Troilus and Cressida*, "Take but degree
away, untune that string,/And hark what discord follows" (*Troilus and Cressida*.
I.iii.109-110).

2 To exactly what monastic order Father Benedict belongs is not made clear, but since he
is a friar, his ministry is not reclusive. The unholy monks and friars of Gothic fiction
are frequently the obverse of the Benedictine rule of poverty, chastity, and obedience,
although the stereotype of the lecherous priest predates Gothic fiction. Since he is a
discredit to his order, his remark is highly ironic. See: Sister Mary Muriel Tarr, *Catholicism in Gothic Fiction: A Study of the Nature and Function of Catholic Materials in Gothic
Fiction in England (1762-1820)*. Washington, DC: Catholic University of America Press,
1946.

BENEDICT.   She will take none:

60   Offer'd, she scoffs it; and withheld, demands not.
Nay, vows she will not load her sinking soul
With incantations.

MARTIN.   This is heresy;
Rank heresy; and holy church should note it.

65 BENEDICT. Be patient, brother.—Tho' of adamant
Her reason, charity dissolves that rock,
   —And surely we have tasted of the stream.
Nay, one unguarded moment may disclose
This mystic tale—then, brother, what a harvest,

70   When masters of her bosom-guilt!—Age too
May numb her faculties.—Or soon, or late,
A praying woman must become our spoil.

MARTIN. Her zeal may falter.

BENEDICT.   Not in solitude.

75   I nurse her in new horrors;[1] form her tenants
To fancy visions, phantoms; and report them.
She mocks their fond credulity—but trust me,
Her memory retains their colouring.
Oft times it paints her dreams; and ebon night

80   Is no logician. I have known her call
For lights, e'er she could combat its impressions.
I too, tho' often scorn'd, relate my dreams,
And wond'rous voices heard; that she may think me,
At least an honest bigot; nor remember

85   I tried to practice on her fears, and foil'd,
Give o'er my purpose.

MARTIN.   This is masterly.

BENEDICT. Poor mastery! When I am more in awe
Of my own penitent than she of me.

90   My genius is command; art, but a tool
My groveling fortune forces me to use.
Oh! were I seated high as my ambition,

---

1   Monastic villainy, later a staple of terror in Gothic fiction and drama, makes an early appearance in the schemes of Benedict to intimidate and torment the Countess with supernatural and unnatural tales. Compare the scheming motives with the inept goodness of Father Jerome in *The Castle of Otranto*.

I'd place this nak'd foot on necks of monarchs,
And make them bow to creeds myself would laugh at.[1]
MARTIN. By humbler arts our mighty fabric rose.
 Win power by craft; wear it with ostentation;   95
 For confidence is half-security.
 Deluded men think boldness, conscious strength;
 And grow the slaves of their own want of doubt.
 Gain to the Holy See this fair domain;
 A crimson bonnet may reward your toils,   100
 And the rich harvest prove at last your own.
BENEDICT. Never, while Edmund lives. This steady woman
 Can ne'er be pious with so many virtues.
 Justice is interwoven in her frame;
 Nor will she wrong the son she will not see.   105
 She loves him not; yet mistress of his fortunes,
 His ample exhibition speaks her bounty.
 She destines him whate'er his father's love
 Gave blindly to her will. Her alms, her charities,
 Usurp'd from her own wants, she sets apart   110
 A scanty portion only for her ward,
 Young Adeliza.
MARTIN.   Say her son were dead,
 And Adeliza veil'd—
BENEDICT. I press the latter   115
 With fruitless ardour. Often as I urge it,
 She pleads the maiden's flushing cheek, and nature,
 That speaks in characters of glowing rose
 Its modest appetites and timid wishes.
 Her sex, she says, when gratified, are frail;   120
 When check'd, a hurricane of boundless passions.
 Then, with sweet irony and sad, she wills me
 Ask my own breast, if cowls and scapularies[2]
 Are charms all powerful to subdue desire?   125

---

1 Montague Summers notes that Benedict's speech on power for power's sake is modeled
 on the ruthless policies of Pope Sixtus V (reigned 1585-1590).
2 Parts of monks' habits. The cowl is a monk's hood. The scapulary is a monk's sleeve-
 less, outer garment that covers the shoulders and might designate the religious order to
 which he belongs.

MARTIN. 'Twere wiser school the maiden: lead the train
    Of young ideas to a fancied object.
    A mental spouse may fill her hov'ring thoughts,
    And bar their fixing on some earthly lover.
130 BENEDICT. This is already done—but Edmund's death
    Were hopes more solid—
MARTIN.   First report him dead;
    His letters intercepted—
BENEDICT.   Greatly thought!
135   Thou true son of the church!—and lo! where comes
    Our patroness—leave me; I will not lose
    An instant. I will sound her inmost soul,
    And mould it to the moment of projection.

                           [*Exit* MARTIN.
                  [BENEDICT *retires within the castle.*

SCENE IV

COUNTESS, TWO MAIDENS

COUNTESS. Haste thee, Maria, to the western tower,
    And learn if th' aged pilgrim dozes yet.
    You, Elinor, attend my little orphans,
    And when their task is done, prepare their breakfast,
5   But scant th' allowance of the red-hair'd urchin,
    That maim'd the poor man's cur.—Ah! happy me!

              [*The damsels go in.*]

    If sentiment, untutor'd by affliction,
    Had taught my temperate blood to feel for others,
    E'er pity, perching on my mangled bosom,
10   Like flies on wounded flesh, had made me shrink
    More with compunction than with sympathy!
    Alas! must guilt then ground our very virtues!
    Grow they on sin alone, and not on grace?
    While Narbonne liv'd, my fully-sated soul
15   Thought none unhappy—for it did not think!

In pleasures roll'd whole summer suns away;
And if a pensive visage cross'd my path,
I deem'd the wearer envious or ill-natur'd.
What anguish had I blessedly redress'd,
But that I was too bless'd!—Well! peace is fled,   20
Ne'er to return! nor dare I snap the thread
Of life, while misery may want a friend.
Despair and Hell must wait, while pity needs
My ministry—Eternity has scope
Enough to punish me, tho' I should borrow   25
A few short hours to sacrifice to charity.

SCENE V

BENEDICT, COUNTESS

BENEDICT. I sought you, lady.
COUNTESS.   Happily I'm found.
    Who needs the widow's mite?[1]
BENEDICT.   None ask your aid.
    Your gracious foresight still prevents occasion: 5
    And your poor beadsman[2] joys to meet your presence,
    Uncumber'd with a suit. It pains my soul,
    Oft as I tax your bounty, lest I seem
    A craving or immodest almoner.[3]
COUNTESS. No more of this, good father. I suspect not   10
    One of your holy order of dissembling:
    Suspect not me of loving flattery.
    Pass a few years, and I shall be a corpse—
    Will flattery then new cloath my skeleton,
    Fill out these hollow jaws? Will't give me virtues?   15
    Or at the solemn audit pass for truth,
    And varnish o'er my stains?

---

1   A small sum of money or coin of low value. Traditionally, a widow was deprived of a
    husband's income and could not contribute as much as a married woman to the
    Church.
2   Any person who prays for another's soul, especially one who is hired to do so.
3   A person who distributes alms or charity, sometimes, but not necessarily, a priest.

BENEDICT.   The church could seal
          Your pardon—but you scorn it. In your pride
20   Consists your danger. Yours are Pagan virtues:[1]
          As such I praise them—but as such condemn them.
COUNTESS. Father, my *crimes* are Pagan; my belief
          Too orthodox to trust to erring man.
          What! shall I, foul with guilt, and self-condemn'd,
25   Presume to kneel, where angels kneel appal'd,
          And plead a priest's certificate for pardon?
          While he, perchance, before my blasted eyes
          Shall sink to woes, endless, unutterable,
          For having fool'd me into that presumption.
30 BENEDICT. Is he to blame, trusting to what he grants?
COUNTESS. Am I to blame, not trusting what he grants?
BENEDICT. Yet faith—
COUNTESS.   I have it not—Why shakes my soul
          With nightly terrors? Courage such as mine
35   Would start at nought but guilt. 'Tis from within
          I tremble. Death would be felicity,
          Were there no retrospect. What joys have I?
          What pleasure softens, or what friendship sooths
          My aching bosom?—I have lost my husband:
40   My own decree has banish'd my own son.
BENEDICT. Last night I dreamt your son was with the blessed.
COUNTESS. Would heav'n he were!
BENEDICT.   Do you then wish his death?
COUNTESS. Should I not wish him blest?
45 BENEDICT.   Belike he is:
          I never knew my Friday's dreams[2] erroneous.

---

1   Pagan virtues. Virtuous pagans who lived before Christ such as the philosophers
    Socrates and Plato, the poet Homer, the physicians Galen and Hippocrates, and the
    Roman statesman, Cicero. They were esteemed for such virtues as humility, piety, pro-
    bity, integrity, temperance, and mercy. In Dante's *Inferno*, virtuous pagans are placed in
    the Limbo and are spared the pains of Hell. (Canto 4). Father Benedict's condemna-
    tion of the pagan virtues is itself a cynical denial of one of the main Christian virtues,
    charity. The Countess's remark that her "crimes are pagan" does not exonerate her
    from the deadly sin of lust.
2   According to medieval dream lore, "Friday's dreams" were not only accurate in their
    foreboding's, but ominous as well, since Friday was an unlucky day. In associating his

COUNTESS. Nor I knew superstition in the right.

BENEDICT. Madam, I must no longer hear this language.
  You do abuse my patience. I have borne,
  For your soul's health, and hoping your conversion,   50
  Opinions most deprav'd. It ill beseems
  My holy function to give countenance,
  By lending ear, to such pernicious tenets.
  The judgments hanging o'er your destin'd head
  May reach ev'n me—I see it! I am wrapt   55
  Beyond my bearing! my prophetic soul[1]
  Views the red falchion[2] of eternal justice
  Cut off your sentenc'd race—your son is dead!

COUNTESS. Father, we no prophetic dæmon bear
  Within our breast, but conscience. *That* has spoken   60
  Words more tremendous than this acted zeal,
  This poetry of fond enthusiasm
  Can conjure up. It is the still small voice
  That breathes conviction. 'Tis that voice has told me,
  'Twas my son's birth, not his mortality,   65
  Must drown my soul in woe.[3]—Those tears are shed.

BENEDICT. Unjust, uncharitable as your words,
  I pardon them. Illy of me you deem;
  I know it, lady. 'Tis humiliation:

---

dreams with the blessing of Edmund, Father Benedict conceals the portentous signifi-
cance. Walpole also might have recalled an old saying, "a Friday night's dream on the
Saturday told, is sure to come true be it never so old." See Horace G. Hutchinson,
*Dreams and their Meanings. With many accounts of experiences sent by correspondents and two
chapters contributed mainly from the journals of the Physical Research Society on telepathic and
Premonitory Dreams.* London, New York, Bombay: Longmans, Green, 1901.

1   Benedict uses Hamlet's words to his father's ghost in his reprimand to the Countess.
    (*Hamlet.* I.v.42). Walpole intended to relate the sexual crime of the Countess to the
    concupiscence of Hamlet's mother, Queen Gertrude.

2   A sword with a short curved blade.

3   Montague Summers notes that Walpole paraphrased a remark made by the Duchess de
    la Valière on the death of her son, the Comte de Vermandois. The 1781 edition of *The
    Mysterious Mother* contained a note by Walpole recounting the Duchess's remorse at
    having given birth to her son, only to bring him to disaster. Louis de Bourbon, Comte
    de Vermandois, was born on 2 October 1667. "He fell ill at The Siege of Courtai, and
    died at the early age of sixteen." (Summers, "Notes Explanatory" to *The Mysterious
    Mother*, 297).

70   As such I bow to it—yet dear I tender
        Your peace of mind. Dismiss your worthless servant:
        His pray'rs shall still be yours.
    COUNTESS.   Forgive me, father:
        Discretion does not guide my words. I meant
75   No insult on your holy character.
    BENEDICT. No, lady; chuse some other monitor,
        Whose virtues may command your estimation.
        Your useless beadsman shall behold with joy
        A worthier man mediate your peace with heav'n.
80 COUNTESS. Alás! 'till reconcil'd with my own breast
        What peace is there for me!
    BENEDICT.   In th' neighb'ring district
        There lives a holy man, whose sanctity
        Is mark'd with wond'rous gifts. Grace smiles upon him;
85   Conversion tracks his footsteps: miracles
        Spring from his touch; his sacred casuistry
        Pours balm into despair. Consult with him.
        Unfold th' impenetrable mystery,
        That sets your soul and you at endless discord.
90 COUNTESS. Consult a holy man! Inquire of him!
        —Good father, wherefore? What should I inquire?[1]
        Must I be taught of him, what guilt is woe?
        That innocence alone is happiness?
        That martyrdom itself shall leave the villain
95   The villain that it found him? Must I learn
        That minutes stamp'd with crimes are past recall?
        That joys are momentary; and remorse
        Eternal? Shall he teach me charms and spells,
        To make my sense believe against my sense?
100 Shall I think practices and penances
        Will, if he say so, give the health of virtue

---

1   The Countess refutes the suggestion of Father Benedict by quoting the response of the Roman orator Cato [Quid quæri Labiene iubes], when replying to Labienus's advice that he should consult an oracle to determine how to act virtuously. Walpole's classical source is Lucan's *Pharsalia*, IX. 565-584. In the context of the tragedy, according to Cato's reply, moral guidance for our actions should be sought within ourselves rather than from oracles.

To gnawing self-reproach?—I know they cannot.
Nor could one risen from the dead proclaim
This truth in deeper sounds to my conviction.
We want no preacher to distinguish vice   105
From virtue. At our birth the god reveal'd
All conscience needs to know. No codicil
To duty's rubric here and there was plac'd
In some saint's casual custody. Weak minds
Want their soul's fortune told by oracles   110
And holy jugglers. Me, nor oracles,
Nor prophets, Death alone can certify,
Whether, when justice's full dues exacted,
Mercy shall grant one drop to slake my torment,
—Here, father, break we off; you to your calling;   115
I to my tears and mournfull occupation.

                                                    [Exeunt.

END OF THE FIRST ACT

ACT THE SECOND

The SCENE *continues*

COUNT EDMUND, FLORIAN

EDMUND. Doubt not, my friend; Time's pencil, hardships, war,
Some taste of pleasure too, have chas'd the bloom
Of ruddy comeliness, and stamp'd this face
With harsher lineaments, that well may mock
5 The prying of a mother's eye.—a mother,
Thro' whose firm nerves tumultuous instinct's flood
Ne'er gush'd with eager eloquence, to tell her,
This is your son! your heart's own voice proclaims him.
FLORIAN. If not her love, my lord, suspect her hatred.
10 Those jarring passions spring from the same source:
Hate is distemper'd love.
EDMUND.   Why should she hate me?
For that my opening passion's swelling ardour
Prompted congenial necessary joy,
15 Was that a cause?—Nor was she then so rigid.
No sanctified dissembler had possess'd
Her scar'd imagination, teaching her,
That holiness begins where nature ends.
No, Florian, she herself was woman then;
20 A sensual woman. Nor satiety,
Sickness and age, and virtue's frowardness,
Had so obliterated pleasure's relish—
She might have pardon'd what she felt so well.
FLORIAN. Forgive me, Edmund; nay, nor think I preach,
25 If I, God wot,[1] of morals loose enough,
Seem to condemn you. You have often told me,
The night, the very night that to your arms
Gave pretty Beatrice's melting beauties,
Was the same night on which your father died.
30 EDMUND. 'Tis true—and thou, sage monitor, dost thou

---

1 God knows.

Hold love a crime so irremissible?
Wouldst thou have turned thee from a willing girl,
To sing a requiem to thy father's soul?
I thought my mother busied with her tears,
Her faintings, and her masses, while I stole   35
To Beatrice's chamber.—How my mother
Became appriz'd, I know not: but her heart,
Never too partial to me, grew estrang'd.
Estrang'd!—aversion in its fellest mood
Scowl'd from her eye, and drove me from her sight.   40
She call'd me impious, named my honest lewdness,
A prophanation of my father's ashes.
I knelt, and wept, and, like a puling boy,
For now my blood was cool, believ'd, confess'd
My father's hov'ring spirit incens'd against me.   45
This weak confession but inflam'd her wrath;
And when I would have bath'd her hand with tears,
She snatch'd it back with horror.

FLORIAN.   'Twas the trick
Of over-acted sorrow. Grief fatigues;   550
And each collateral circumstance is seiz'd
To cheat th' uneasy feeling. Sable chambers,
The winking lamp, and pomp of midnight woe,
Are but a specious theatre, on which
Th' inconstant mind with decency forgets   55
Its inward tribute. Who can doubt the love
Which to a father's shade devotes the son?   [*ironically.*

EDMUND. Still must I doubt: still deem some mystery,
Beyond a widow's pious artifice,
Lies hid beneath aversion so relentless.   60
All my inheritance, my lordships, castles,
My father's lavish love bequeath'd my mother.
Chose she some second partner of her bed,
Or did she waste her wealth on begging saints,
And rogues that act contrition, it were proof   65
Of her hypocrisy, or lust of fame
In monkish annals. But to me her hand
Is bounteous, as her heart is cold. I tell thee,

Bating enjoyment of my native soil,
70　Narbonne's revenues are as fully mine,
As if I held them by the strength of charters.

FLORIAN. Why set them on the hazard then, when she,
Who deals them, may revoke? Your absence hence
The sole condition.

75　EDMUND.　　　　　　I am weary, Florian,
Of such a vagrant life. Befits it me,
Sprung from a race of heroes, Narbonne's prince,
To lend my casual arm's approv'd valour
To quarrels, nor my country's nor my own?
80　To stain my sword with random blood!—I fought
At Buda 'gainst the Turk[1]—a holy war,
So was it deem'd—I smote the turban'd race:
Did zeal or did ambition nerve my blow?
Or matter'd it to me, on Buda's domes
85　Whether the crescent or the cross prevail'd?
Mean time on alien climes I dissipated
Wealth from my subjects wrung, the peasant's tribute,
Earn'd by his toil. Mean time in ruin laid
My mouldring castles—Yes, ye moss grown walls!
90　Ye tow'rs defenceless!—I revisit ye
Shame-stricken.—Where are all your trophies now?
Your thronged courts, the revelry, the tumult,
That spoke the grandeur of my house, the homage
Of neighb'ring barons? Thus did Thibault, Raoul,
95　Or Clodimir,[2] my brave progenitors,
Creep like a spy, and watch to thrid your gates[3]
Unnotic'd? No; with martial attributes,
With waving banners and enlivening fifes,
They bade your portal wide unfold its jaws,
100　And welcome them in triumph.

FLORIAN.　　　　　　　　　True, my lord;
They reign'd the monarchs of a score of miles;

1　Edmund has campaigned against the Ottoman Empire by fighting the Turks at Buda in
　Hungary. Buda (now Budapest) was besieged and occupied by the Turks in 1541.
2　Thibault was King of Navarre and a crusader (circa 1234); Clodimir was the eldest son
　of the Frankish king Clovis (circa 524); Raoul is obscure.
3　Penetrate or pierce the gates during a siege.

Imperial lords of ev'ry trembling cottage
With their cannon's mandate. Deadly feuds
For obsolete offences, now array'd   105
Their livery'd banditti, prompt to deal
On open vallies and unguarded herds,
On helpless virgins and unweapon'd boors,
The vengeance of their tribe. Sometimes they dar'd
To scowl defiance to the distant throne,   110
Imprison'd, canton'd inaccessibly
In their own rock-built dungeons—Are these glories
My Edmund's soul ambitions to revive?
Thus would he bless his vassals!

EDMUND.   Thy reproof,   115
My friend, is just. But had I not a cause,
A tender cause, that prompted my return?
This cruel parent, whom I blame, and mourn,
Whose harshness I resent, whose woes I pity,
Has won my love, by winning my respect.   120
Her letters! Florian; such unstudied strains
Of virtuous eloquence! She bids me, yes,
This praying Magdalen[1] enjoins my courage
To emulate my great forefather's deeds.
Tell me, that shame and guilt alone are mortal;   125
That death but bars the possibility
Of frailty, and embalms untainted honour.
Then blots and tears efface some half-told woe
Lab'ring in her full bosom. I decypher'd
In one her blessing granted, and eras'd.   130
And yet what follow'd, mark'd anxiety
For my soul's welfare. I must know this riddle.
I must, will comfort her. She cannot surely,
After such perils, wounds by her command
Encounter'd, after sixteen exil'd years,   135
Spurn me, when kneeling—Think'st thou, 'tis possible?

---

1   Edmund's reference to his "virtuous[ly] eloquent" mother as a Mary Magdalene figure
    is highly ironic since the Biblical personage is a fallen woman and a prostitute. "Mary
    called Magdalene, out of whom went seven devils" (Luke, VIII.2). In general terms, a
    Mary Magdalene is a reformed and repentant prostitute.

FLORIAN. I would not think it; but a host of priests
    Surround her. They, good men, are seldom found
    To plead the cause of pity. Self-denial,
140   Whose dissonance from nature's kindest laws
    By contradicting, wins on our perverseness,
    Is rank fanaticism's belov'd machine.
    Oh! 'twill be heroism, a sacrifice,
    To curb the torrent of maternal fondness!
145   You shall be beggar'd, that the saint your mother
    May, by cowl'd sychophants and canting jugglers,
    Be hail'd, be canoniz'd a new Teresa.[1]
    Pray be not seen here: let's again to the wars.
EDMUND. No, Florian; my dull'd soul is sick of riot:
150   Sick of the thoughtless jollity of camps,
    Where revelry subsists on desolation,
    And shouts of joy contend with dying groans.
    Our sports are fleeting; snatch'd, perhaps, not granted.
    'Tis time to bid adieu to vagrant pleasure,
155   And fix the wanderer love. Domestic bliss—
FLORIAN. Yes, your fair pensioner, young Adeliza,
    Has sober'd your inconstancy. Her smiles
    Were exquisite—to rule a family!   *[ironically.*
    So matron-like an air—She must be fruitful.
160 EDMUND. Pass we this levity—'Tis true, the maiden
    Is beauty's type renew'd. Like blooming Eve
    In nature's young simplicity, and blushing
    With wonder at creation's opening glow,
    She charms, unknowing what it is to charm.
165 FLORIAN. This is a lover's language—Is she kind?
EDMUND. Cold as the metal bars that part her from me;
    She listens, but replies not to my purpose.
FLORIAN. How gain'd you then admittance?
EDMUND.   This whole month,
170   While waiting your arrival, I have haunted

---

1 Be hail'd, be canoniz'd a new Teresa. The Carmelite nun Saint Teresa of Avila (1515–
    1582) was canonized in 1622. If the time of Walpole's drama is the mid-15th century,
    this mention of Teresa is an unintentional anachronism. Florian hints at the deceitful-
    ness and hypocrisy of the Countess's spiritual advisors. Walpole may have had in mind
    Saint Teresa's mystical ecstasy of the divine arrow of gold piercing her heart.

Her convent's parlour. 'Tis my mother's wish
To match her nobly. Hence her guardian abbess
Admits such visitors as claim her notice
By worthy bearing, and convenient splendor.
O Florian, union with that favour'd maiden   175
Might reconcile my mother—Hark! what sound—

[*A chapel bell rings.*

FLORIAN. A summons to some office of devotion.
    My lord, weigh well what you project—   [*Singing within.*
EDMUND. I hear
    Voices that seem approaching—hush! they sing.   180
    Listen!
FLORIAN. No; let us hence: you will be known.
EDMUND. They cannot know me—see!

SCENE II

FLORIAN, EDMUND, MARTIN, ORPHANS

[*A procession of children of both sexes, neatly cloathed in a white and
    blue uniform, issue from the castle, followed by friar* MARTIN, *and
    advance towards the stage-door. They stop, and the children repeat the
    following hymn,*[1] *part of which they should have sung within the castle.*

I

Throne of justice! lo! we bend,
Thither dare our hopes ascend,
Where seraphs, wrapt in light'ning rays,
Dissolve in mercy's tender blaze

II

Hear us! harmless orphans hear!   5
For her who dries our falling tear.
Hush her sorrows; calm her breast:
Give her, what she gives us, rest.

---

1   The hymn's origin is unknown. It may be Walpole's original composition.

The chorus of orphans, *The Mysterious Mother*, Act II, Scene 2.

III

Guard our spotless souls from sin!
Grant us virtue's palm to win!
Cloath the penitent with grace;
And guilt's foul spots efface! efface!

EDMUND.   I'll speak to them.
Sweet children—or thou sanctified conductor,
Give me to know what solemn pilgrimage,
What expiation of offences past,
Thus sadly ye perform? In whose behoof
To win a blessing, raise these little suppliants
Their artless hands to heav'n? Pray pardon too
A soldier's curiosity.
MARTIN.   The dew
Of grace and peace attend your steps. You seem

A stranger, or you could but know, sir knight,
That Narbonne's pious Countess dwells within:
A lady most disconsolate. Her lord, 25
Her best-beloved, by untimely fate
Was snatch'd away in lusty life's full 'vantage—
But no account made up! no absolution![1]
Hence scant the distance of a mile he fell.
His weeping relict[2] o'er his spot of doom 30
A goodly cross erected. Thither we,
At his year's mind, in sad and solemn guise,
Proceed to chant our holy dirge, and offer
Due intercession for his soul's repose.
EDMUND. 'Tis fitly done. And dar'd a voice profane 35
Join in the chorus of your holy office,
Myself would kneel for Narbonne's peace.
MARTIN.   Young sir,
It glads my soul to hear such pious breathings
From one, whose occupation rarely scans 40
The distance 'twixt enjoyment and the tomb.
Say, didst thou know the Count?
EDMUND.   I knew his son.
MARTIN. Count Edmund? Where sojourns he?
EDMUND.   In the grave. 45
MARTIN. Is Edmund dead? say, how?
EDMUND.   He fell at Buda;
And not to his dishonour.
MARTIN.   (Welcome sounds!   [aside.
I must know more of this)—proceed, my children; 50
Short of the cross I'll overtake your steps.
ORPHAN GIRL. Oh! father, but I dare not pass without you
By the church-porch. They say the Count sits there,
With clotted locks, and eyes like burning stars.
Indeed I dare not go.   55
OTHER CHILDREN.   Nor I. Nor I.

---

1 Like Hamlet's father, the Count of Narbonne died unshriven or unconfessed of his sins
   and was therefore doomed. "Cut off even in the blossoms of my sin/ Unhous'led, disappointed, unanel'd/ No reck'ning made, but sent to my account/ With all my imper-
   fections on my head" (*Hamlet*.I.v.77-80).
2 Widow.

MARTIN. My loves, he will not harm such innocents.
But wait me at the bridge. I'll strait be with ye.

[*Children go out reluctantly.*

FLORIAN. I marvel, father, gravity like yours
60   Should yield assent to tales of such complexion;
Permitting them in baby fantasy
To strike their dangerous root.
MARTIN.   I marvel not,
That levity like yours, unhallow'd boy,
65   Should spend its idle shaft on serious things.
Your comrade's bearing warrants no such licence.
FLORIAN. Think'st thou, because my friend with humble fervour
Kneels to Omnipotence, each gossip's dream,
Each village-fable domineers in turn
70   His brain's distemper'd nerves? Think'st thou a soldier
Must by his calling be an impious braggart?
Or being not, a superstitious slave?
True valour, owning no pre-eminence
In equals, dares not wag presumption's tongue
75   Against high heav'n.
MARTIN.   In us respect heav'n's servants.
FLORIAN. Monks may reach heav'n, but never came from thence.

[*Violent storm of thunder and lightning.*

MARTIN. Will this convince thee! Where's the gossip's dream?
The village-fable now? Hear heav'n's own voice
80   Condemn impiety!
FLORIAN.   Hear heav'n's own voice
Condemn imposture!
EDMUND.   Here end your dispute.
The storm comes on.
85 MARTIN.   Yes, you do well to check
Your comrade's profanation, lest swift justice
O'ertake his guilt, and stamp his doom in thunder.
FLORIAN. Father, art thou so read in languages

Thou canst interpret th' inarticulate
And quarreling elements? What says the storm? 90
Pronounces it for thee of me? Do none
Dispute within the compass of its bolt
But we? Is the same loud-voic'd oracle
Definitive for fifty various brawls?
Or but a shock of clouds to all but us? 95
What if two drunkards at this instant hour
Contend for preference of taste, one ranking
The vines of Burgundy before the juice
That dances in a foam of brilliant bubbles
From Champagne's berries, think'st thou thunder speaks 100
In favour of the white or ruby grape?
MARTIN. What mockery! I resign thee to thy fate—   [Going.

[*The* ORPHAN CHILDREN *run in terrified.*]

FIRST ORPHAN. O father, save us! save us! holy father.
MARTIN. What means this panic?
FIRST ORPHAN. Oh! a storm so dreadful! 105
  Some demon rides in th' air.
MARTIN. Undoubtedly.
  Could you distinguish aught?
FIRST ORPHAN. I fell to earth,
  And said the pray'r you taught me against spectres. 110
MARTIN. 'Twas well—but none of you, had none the courage
  To face the fiend?
SECOND ORPHAN. I wink'd, and saw the light'ning
  Burst on the monument. The shield of arms
  Shiver'd to splinters. E'er I could repeat 115
  An Ave-Mary,[1] down with hideous crash
  The cross came tumbling[2]—then I fled—

---

1 "Hail, Mary" or "Ave, Maria," the first words of a Latin version of a prayer to the Virgin Mary. The orphan mixes Latin with English.
2 Unlike the many supernatural sound effects and properties of *The Castle of Otranto*, the Gothic of *The Mysterious Mother* relies on unnatural or ominously strange events such as the child's report of the toppled crucifix. Walpole uses no castle specters or gigantic animated statues to achieve terror.

MARTIN. Retire;
This is unholy ground. Acquaint the Countess.
I will not tarry long.—[ex. *Children.*] Thou mouth accurst,

[*To* FLORIAN.

120 Repent, and tremble! Wherefore hast thou drawn
On Narbonne's plains, already visited
By long calamity, new storms of horror?
The seasons change their course; th' afflicted hind
Bewails his blasted harvest. Meteors ride
125 The troubled sky, and chase the darken'd sun.
Heav'n vindicates its altars, tongues licentious
Have scoff'd our holy rites, and hidden sins
Have forc'd the offended elements to borrow
Tremendous organs! Sixteen fatal years
130 Has Narbonne's province groan'd beneath the hand
Of desolation—for what crimes we know not!
To edge suspended vengeance art thou come?
EDMUND, *preventing* FLORIAN. My friend, reply not—Father, I
lament
This casual jarring—let us crave your pardon.
135 I feel your country's woes: I lov'd Count Edmund:
Revere his father's ashes. I will visit
The ruin'd monument—and at your leisure
Could wish some conf'rence with you.
MARTIN.   (This is well: *aside.*
140 I almost had forgotten)—Be it so.
Where is your haunt?
EDMUND.   A mile without the town;
Hard by St. Bridget's nunnery.
MARTIN. There expect me.
145 [*Aside.*] (I must to Benedict)—Heav'n's peace be with you.
[*Exeunt.*

SCENE III

COUNTESS, PORTER.

PORTER. Return, my gracious lady. Tho' the storm
    Abates his clamours, yonder angry clouds
    Are big with spouting fires—do not go forth.
COUNTESS. Wretches like me, good Peter, dread no storms.
    'Tis delicate felicity that shrinks,   5
    When rocking winds are loud, and wraps itself
    Insultingly in comfortable furs,
    Thinking how many naked objects want
    Like shelter and security.[1] Do thou
    Return; I'll seek the monument alone.   10
PORTER. No, my good lady; never be it said
    That faithful Peter his dear mistress left
    Expos'd to tempests. These thin-sprinkled hairs
    Cannot hold long. If in your service shed,
    'Twere a just debt—hark! sure I heard a groan!   15
    Pray, let us in again—
COUNTESS.   My honest servant,
    Thy fear o'er-powers thy love. I heard no groan;
    Nor could it 'scape a sense so quick as mine
    At catching misery's expressive note: 20
    'Tis my soul's proper language.—Injur'd shade!
    Shade[2] of my Narbonne! if thy scornful spirit
    Rode in yon whirlwind, and impell'd its bolt
    Implacable! indignant! 'gainst the cross
    Rais'd by thy wretched wife—behold she comes   25
    A voluntary victim! Re-assemble
    Thy light'nings, and accept her destin'd head.
PORTER. For pity! gracious dame, what words are these!
    In any mouth less holy they would seem

---

1   The Countess's speech on suffering humanity echoes King Lear's awakened sense of
   universal human misery as he roams the stormy heath in Shakespeare's (*King Lear*.
   III.iv.28-33).
2   Ghost.

30 A magic incantation. Goblins rise
 At sounds less pow'rfull. Last year's 'clipse fell out,
 Because your maidens cross'd a gypsy's palm
 To know what was become of Beatrice.[1]

COUNTESS. And didst thou dare inform them where she dwells?

35 PORTER. No, on my duty—true; they think they know;
 And so thinks Benedict, your confessor.
 He says, they could not pass the castle gates
 Without my privity—Well! I had a task
 To say him nay. The honour of my keys,
40 My office was at stake. No, father, said I,
 None pass the drawbridge without Peter's knowledge.
 How then to beat him from his point?—I had it—
 Who knows, quoth I, but sudden malady
 Took off the damsel? She might, or might not
45 Have sepulture[2] within the castle-walls—

COUNTESS. Peace, fool—and thus thy shrewd equivocation
 Has stain'd my name with murder's foul suspicion!
 —O piece of virtue! thy true votaries
 Quail not with ev'ry blast! I cloak my guilt!
50 Things foreign rise and load me with their blackness.
 Erroneous imputation must be borne;
 Lest, while unravelling the knotty web,
 I lend a clue may vibrate to my heart.
 —But who comes here?—retire we and observe.

           [They withdraw.

---

1 Beatrice is the Countess's maid with whom Edmund supposedly slept sixteen years before, unaware that his mother had substituted herself for Beatrice and was Edmund's sexual partner. The Countess's substitution of herself for her maid recalls the trickery of Helena in substituting herself for Bertram's mistress in Shakespeare's comedy *All's Well That Ends Well.* III.vii, 30–36.

2 Be buried or placed in a burial vault.

SCENE IV

FLORIAN, COUNTESS, PORTER

FLORIAN. 'Tis not far off the time the Porter will'd me
  Expect him here. My friend, indulging grief,
  Chose no companion of his pensive walk.
  Yes, I must serve thee. May my pros'prous care
  Restore thee to thy state, and aid thy love   5
  To make the blooming Adeliza thine!
COUNTESS, *apart to the* PORTER. Methought he spoke of love
      and Adeliza.
  Who may it be?
PORTER.   I never heard his name?
COUNTESS *approaching.* Stranger, did chance or purpose guide thy
      steps   10
  To this lone dwelling?

> [PORTER *makes signs to* FLORIAN *not to discover*
>   *their former interview.*

FLORIAN.   Pardon, gentle lady,
  If curious to behold the pious matron
  Whom Narbonne's plains obey, I sought this castle,
  And deem my wish indulg'd in viewing thee.   15
COUNTESS. Me! stranger. Is affliction then so rare
  It occupies the babbler Fame?—Oh! no.
  My sorrows are not new. Austerities
  And rigid penance tempt no curious eyes.
  Nor speaks your air[1] desire of searching out   20
  The house of mourning. Rather should you seek
  Some unsunn'd beauty, some unpractic'd fair one,
  Who thinks the first soft sounds she hears, are love.
  There may be such at Narbonne: none dwell here,
  But melancholy, sorrow, and contrition.   25
FLORIAN. Pleasure has charms; but so has virtue too.

---

1 Suggests your manner or bearing.

One skims the surface, like the swallow's wing,
And scuds away unnotic'd. T'other nymph,
Like spotless swans in solemn majesty,
30   Breasts the full surge, and leaves long light behind.
COUNTESS. Your courtly phrase, young knight, bespeaks a birth
  Above the vulgar. May I ask, how old
  Your residence in Narbonne? Whence your race?
FLORIAN. In Brabant[1] was I born: my father's name,
35   The Baron of St. Orme. I wait at Narbonne
  My letters of exchange, while passing homewards
  To gather my late sire's no mean succession.
COUNTESS. Dead is your father! and unwet your cheek!
  Trust me, young sir, a father's guardian arm
40   Were well worth all the treasures it withheld.
  A mother might be spar'd.
FLORIAN.   Mothers, like thee,
  Were blessings.
COUNTESS.   Curses!
45 PORTER.   Lady, 'tis the hour
  Of pray'r. Shall I ring out the chapel-bell?
COUNTESS. Stranger, I'm summon'd hence. Within these walls
  I may not speak with thee: my solemn purpose
  Admits no converse with unsteady youth.
50   But at St. Bridget's nunnery, to-morrow,
  If you can spare some moments from your pastime,
  In presence of the abbess, I would talk with thee.
FLORIAN. Madam, I shall not fail.
COUNTESS.   Good angels guard thee!

[*Exit* COUNTESS *and* PORTER.

---

1   Brabant. A provincial area or duchy between Belgium and the Netherlands.

SCENE V

FLORIAN *alone*

So, this is well, my introduction made
It follows that I move her for her son.
She seems of gentler mould than fame bespoke her.
Nor wears her eye the saucy superiority
Of bigot pride. Who knows but she may wish   5
To shake the trammels of enthusiasm off,
And reconcile herself to easier paths
Of simple goodness? Women oft wear the mask
Of piety to draw respect, or hide
The loss of it. When age dispells the train   10
That waits on beauty, then religion blows
Her trumpet, and invites another circle;
Who, full as false as the preceding crew,
Flatter her problematic mental charms:
While snuffing incense, and devoutly wanton,   15
The Pagan goddess grows a Christian saint,
And keeps her patent of divinity.
Well! Edmund, whatso'er thy mother be,
I'll put her virtue or hypocrisy
To the severest test.—Countess, expect me!   [*Exit.*   20

END OF SECOND ACT

ACT THE THIRD

SCENE I

A small garden within the castle, terminated by a long cloyster, beyond which appear some towers.

COUNTESS, *alone.*

The monument destroy'd!—Well! what of that!
Were ev'ry thunderbolt address'd to me,
Not one would miss me. Fate's unerring hand
Darts not at random. Nor, as fractious children
Are chid[1] by proxy, does it deal its wrath
On stocks and stones to frighten, not chastise us.
Omens and prodigies are but begotten
By guilt on pride. We know the doom we merit;
And self-importance makes us think all nature
Busied to warn us when that doom approaches.
Fie! fie! I blush to recollect my weakness.
My Edmund may be dead: the house of Narbonne
May perish from this earth: poor Adeliza
May taste the cup of woe that I have drug'd:
But light'nings play not to announce our fate:
Nor whirlwinds rise to prophesy to mites:[2]
Nor, like inquisitors, does heav'n dress up
In flames the victims it intends to punish;
Making a holiday for greater sinners.
—Greater! oh! impious! Were the faggots plac'd
Around me, and the fatal torch applied,
What wretch could view the dreadful apparatus,
And be a blacker criminal than I am?
—Perhaps my virtues but enhance my guilt.

---

1 Past tense of to chide, to scold or reprove.
2 Natural omens of doom or divine wrath occur for the benefit of human beings, not insects. A mite is a gnat, or small spider.

Penance attracts respect, and not reproach.   25
How dare I be esteem'd? Be known my crimes!
Let shame anticipate the woes to come!
—Ha! monster! wouldst disclose the frightful scene?
Wouldst teach the vicious world unheard-of sins,
And be a new apostle of perdition?   30
—My Edmund too! has not a mother's hand
Afflicted him enough? shall this curs'd tongue
Brand him with shame indelible, and sting
His honest bosom with his mother's scorpions?
Shall Adeliza hear the last of horrors,   35
E'er her pure breast, that sighs for sins it knows not,
Has learn'd the rudiments of human frailty?
No, hapless maid—

Enter a SERVANT

SERVANT.   Madam, young Adeliza   40
    Intreats to speak with you. The lady abbess
    Sickens to death.
COUNTESS.   Admit her.—Now, my soul,

                                        [*Exit* SERVANT.

Recall thy calm; support alone thy torments;
And envy not the peace thou ne'er must know.

SCENE II

COUNTESS, ADELIZA

COUNTESS. Approach, sweet maid. Thy melancholy mien
    Speaks thy compassionate and feeling heart.
    'Tis a grave lesson for thy blooming years,
    A scene of dissolution! But when Death
    Expands his pinions o'er a bed so holy,   5
    Sure he's a welcome guest.
ADELIZA.   Oh! do not doubt it,

The pious matron meets him like a friend
Expected long. And if a tender tear,
10   At leaving your poor ward, melts in her eye,
And downward sinks its fervent ecstacy;
Still does impatience to be gone, betray
Her inward satisfaction. Yesternight,
As weeping, praying, by her couch I knelt,
15   Behold, my Adeliza, mark, she said,
How happy the death-bed of innocence![1]
Oh! lady, how those sounds affected me!
I wish'd to die with her—and oh! forgive me,
If in that moment I forgot my patroness!
20 COUNTESS. It was a wish devout. Can that want pardon?
But to confess it, speaks thy native candour,
Thy virtuous, thy ingenuous truth disdains
To hide a thought—
ADELIZA, *falling at her feet.*   Oh! can I hear this praise,
25   And not expire in blushes at thy feet?
COUNTESS. What means this passion?
ADELIZA.   Ah! recall thy words:
Thy Adeliza merits no encomium.
COUNTESS. Thou art too modest. Praise is due to truth.
30   Thou shouldst not seek it; nor should I withhold it.
ADELIZA. For pity, spare me.—No, my honour'd mistress,
I merit not—oh! no, my guilty heart
Deserves thy frowns—I cannot speak—
COUNTESS.   Be calm:
35   Thou know'st no guilt. Unfold thy lab'ring breast.
Say, am not I thy friend? Me canst thou fear?
ADELIZA. Can I fear aught beside? Fear aught but goodness?
Has not thy lavish bounty cloath'd me, fed me?
Hast thou not taught me virtue? Whom on earth,
40   But such a benefactress, such a friend,
Can Adeliza fear? Alas! she knows

---

1 Montague Summers notes that these were the final words of Joseph Addison on his
deathbed as spoken to Lord Warwick, 17 June 1719. Adeliza's dialogue on dying with
the Countess contains both the language and sentiments of the Graveyard Poets.

No other friend! and Christian fortitude
Dreads not a foe. Methinks I would have said
That Christian innocence—but shame restrain'd
My conscious tongue—I am *not* innocent.   45
COUNTESS. Thou dearest orphan, to my bosom come,
    And vent thy little sorrows. Purity
    Like thine affrights itself with fancied guilt,
    I'll be thy confessor; and trust me, love,
    Thy penance will be light.   50
ADELIZA.   In vain you chear me.
    Say, what is guilt, but to have known a thought
    I blush'd to tell thee? To have lent mine ear,
    For three long weeks, to sounds I did not wish
    My patroness should hear! Ah! when till now   55
    Have I not hoped thy presence, thought it long,
    If two whole days detain'd thee from our mass?
    When have I wept, but when thou hast refus'd
    To let thy Adeliza call thee mother?
    I know I was not worthy of such honour,   60
    Too splendid for a child of charity.
    I now am most unworthy! I, undone,
    Have not desir'd thy presence; have not thought it
    Long, if two days thou hast declin'd our mass.
    Other discourse than thine has charm'd mine ear;   65
    Nor dare I now presume to call thee mother!
COUNTESS. My lovely innocence, restrain thy tears.
    I know thy secret; know, why beats and throbs
    Thy little heart with unaccustom'd tumult.
ADELIZA. Impossible——Oh! let me tell thee all—   70
COUNTESS. No; I will tell it thee. Thou hast convers'd
    With a young knight—
ADELIZA.   Amazement! Who inform'd thee?
    Pent in her chamber, sickness has detain'd
    Our Abbess from the parlour. There I saw him,   75
    Oft as he came alone.
COUNTESS. He talk'd of love;
    And woo'd thee for his bride.
ADELIZA. He did.

80 COUNTESS. ('Tis well: [*aside.*
    This is the stranger I beheld this morning.)
    His father dead, he hastes to take possession
    Of his paternal fortunes—is't not so?
ADELIZA. He sorrows for a father—something too
85   He utter'd of a large inheritance
    That should be his—in truth I mark'd it not.
COUNTESS. But when he spoke of love, thy very soul
    Hung on his lips. Say, canst thou not repeat
    Each word, each syllable? His accent too
90   Thou notedst: still it rings upon thine ear.
    And then his eyes—they look'd such wondrous truth;
    Art thou not sure he cannot have deceiv'd thee?
ADELIZA. Alas! my noble mistress, thou dost mock
    Poor Adeliza—what can I reply!
95 COUNTESS. The truth. Thy words have ever held its language.
    Say, dost thou love this stranger? Hast thou pledg'd
    Thy faith to him?
ADELIZA. Angels forbid! What faith have I to give?
    Can I dispose of aught without thy leave?
100 COUNTESS. Insinuating softness!—still thou turnest
    Aside my question. Thou dost love this stranger.
ADELIZA. Yes, with such love as that I feel for thee.
    His virtues I revere: his earnest words
    Sound like the precepts of a tender parent:
105   And, next to thee, methinks I could obey him.
COUNTESS. Ay, as his wife.
ADELIZA.   Oh! never. What, to lose him,
    As thou thy Narbonne!
COUNTESS.   Check not, Adeliza,
110   Thy undevelop'd passion. Should this stranger
    Prove what my wish has form'd, and what his words
    Report him, it would bless my woful days
    To see thee plac'd above the reach of want,
    And distant from his residence of sorrow.
115 ADELIZA. What! wouldst thou send me from thee! oh! for pity!
    I cannot, will not leave thee. If thy goodness
    Withdraws its bounty, at thy castle-gate

I'll wait and beg those alms thy gracious hand
To none refuses. I shall see thee pass,
And, pass'd, will kiss thy footsteps—wilt thou spurn me?   120
Well then, I'll die, and bless thee—Oh! this stranger!
'Tis he has done this; he has drawn thy anger
On thy poor ward!—I'll never see him more.
COUNTESS. Be calm, my lovely orphan; hush thy fears.
Heav'n knows how fondly, anxiously I love thee!   125
The stranger's not to blame. Myself will task him,
And know if he deserves thee. Now retire,
Nor slack thy duty to th' expiring saint.
A lover must not weigh against a friend.   [*Exit* ADELIZA
And lo! where comes the friar. 'Twere not fit   130
He knew my purpose. Benedict, I fear,
Has views on this side heav'n.

SCENE III

COUNTESS, BENEDICT.

BENEDICT.   The dew of grace
  Rest on this dwelling!
COUNTESS.   Thanks, my ghostly[1] friend.
  But sure, or I mistake, in your sad eye
  I spell affliction's signature. What woes   5
  Call for the scanty balm this hand can pour?
BENEDICT. You, lady, and you only need that balm.
COUNTESS. To tutor my unapt and ill-school'd nature
  You come then—Good, my confessor, a truce
  With doctrines and authority. If aught   10
  Can medicate a soul unsound like mine,
  Good deeds must operate the healthful change,
  And penance cleanse it to receive the blessing.
  Shall I for faith, shall I, for but believing
  What 'tis my in'trest to believe, efface   15
  The stains, which, tho' believing, I contracted?

---

1 Religious or spiritual.

BENEDICT. Lady, your subtle wit, like daring infants,
   Sports with a weight will crush it—but no more.
   It is not mine to argue, but pronounce.
20   The church, on rock of adamant establish'd,
   Now inch by inch disputes not its domain.
   Heav'n's laws promulg'd,[1] it rests obedience follow.
   And when, supreme, it taxes that obedience,
   Not at impracticable, vain perfection,
25   But rates its prodigality of blessings
   At the slight credence of its pow'r to grant them;
   Shall man with stoic pride reject the boon,
   And cry, we will do more, we will deserve it?[2]
COUNTESS. Deserve it!—oh! have all your sainted hosts,
30   Your choirs of martyrs, or your clouds of cherubim,
   Deserv'd to feel the transport but of hope?
   Away; nor tell me of this holy juggle
   'Twixt faith and conscience. Shall the latter roam,
   Wasting and spoiling with a ruffian hand,
35   While her accomplice faith, wrapt up at home
   In proud security of self-existence,
   Thinks that existence shall absolve them both?
BENEDICT. 'Twas not to war with words, so heaven's my judge,
   That your poor-rated servant sought your presence.
40   I came with charitable friendly purpose
   To sooth—but wherefore mitigate your griefs?
   You mock my friendship, and miscall my zeal.
   Since then to council, comfort, and reproof
   Obdurate—learn the measure of your woes.
45   Learn, if the mother's fortitude can brave
   The bolt the woman's arrogance defied.
COUNTESS. The mother! said'st thou?
BENEDICT.   Yes, imperious dame:
   Yes, 'twas no vision raised by dreams and fumes,

---

1   Promulgated or made known by official decree.
2   Walpole paraphrases a speech from Joseph Addison's much admired classical tragedy
   Cato (1713). In Addison's play, the republican statesman Marcus Porcius Cato makes a
   last stand for liberty against Julius Cæsar's dictatorial designs. "'Tis not in my mortals to
   command success, / but we'll do more, *Sempronius*, we'll deserve it" (*Cato*. I.iii. 44-45).

Begot 'twixt nightly fear and indigestion: 50
Nor was it artifice and pious fraud,
When but this morning I announced thy Edmund
Was number'd with the dead—
COUNTESS.   Priest, mock me not!
Nor dally with a mother's apprehension.
Lives, or lives not my son? 55
BENEDICT.   Woman, heav'n mocks thee!
On Buda's plain thy slaughter'd Edmund lies.
An unbeliever's weapon cleft his heart;
But 'twas thy unbelief that pois'd the shaft,
And sped its aim. 60
COUNTESS.   To heav'n's high will I bow me.
Oh! may its joys be open to his soul,
Tho' clos'd to mine for ever!
BENEDICT.   Then you lov'd him!
COUNTESS. Lov'd him!—oh! nature, bleeding at my heart, 65
Hearest thou this? Lov'd him!—ha!—whither!—rage,
Be dumb—Now, listen, monk, nor dare reply
Beyond my purpose. In the grave, thou sayst,
My Edmund sleeps—how didst thou learn his fate?
BENEDICT. No angel whisper'd it; no dæmon spoke it. 70
Thou, by the self-same means I learn'd, mayst learn it.
COUNTESS. Be brief.
BENEDICT.   Then—but what boots his life or death
To a poor taunted friar—Benedict,
Leave this proud mistress of the fleeting hour. 75
E'er the destroying angel's kindling brand
Smoaks in the tow'rs of Narbonne—
COUNTESS.   Hold! presumptuous!
I am thy mistress yet: nor will I brook
Such insolent reproof. Produce thy warrant, 80
Assure my Edmund's death—or dread his vengeance!
Severely shall he question ev'ry throb
His agonizing mother now endures.
BENEDICT. My warrant is at hand—

[*Goes out and returns with* EDMUND

This gentleman
       Beheld thy Edmund breathless on the ground.
COUNTESS. Hah! is this sorcery? or is't my husband?   [*Swoons.*
EDMUND. Stand off, and let me clasp her in my arms!
       The flame of filial fondness shall revive
90   The lamp of life, repay the breath she gave,
       And waken all the mother in her soul.
BENEDICT. Hah! who art thou then?
EDMUND.   Do not my fears tell thee!
       Look up! O ever dear! behold thy son!
95   It is thy Edmund's voice; blest, if thy eyes
       Awake to bless him—Soft! her pulse returns;
       She breathes—oh! speak. Dear parent, mother, hear!
       'Tis Edmund—Friar, wherefore is this horror?
       Am I then deadly to her eyes?—Dumb still!
100   Speak, tho' it be to curse me—I have kill'd her!
       My brain grows hot—
BENEDICT.   My lord, restrain your passion;
       See! she revives—
EDMUND. Oh! if these lips that quiver
105   With dread of thy disdain, have force to move thee,
       With nature's, duty's, or affection's voice,
       Feel how I print thy hand with burning zeal,
       Tho' tortur'd at this awful interval!
       Art thou, or not, a mother?
110 COUNTESS.   Hah! where am I?
       Why do you hold me? Was it not my Narbonne?
       I saw him—on my soul I did—
EDMUND.   Alas!
       She raves—recall thy wand'ring apprehension—
115   It was no phantom: at thy feet behold—
COUNTESS. Hah! whom! quick, answer—Narbonne, dost thou
          live?
       Or comest to transport me to perdition?
BENEDICT. Madam, behold your son: he kneels for pardon.
       And I, I innocent, I ignorant
120   Of what he was, implore it too—
COUNTESS.   Distraction!
       What means this complicated scene of horrors?

‘THE MYSTERIOUS MOTHER ACT 3D. SCENE 3D.

The Countess, Father Benedict, and Edmund.
The Mysterious Mother, Act III, Scene 3

Why thus assail my splitting brain?—be quick—
Art thou my husband wing'd from other orbs
To taunt my soul? What is this dubious form, 125
Impress'd with ev'ry feature I adore,
And every lineament I dread to look on!
Art thou my dead or living son?

EDMUND.   I am
Thy living Edmund. Let these scalding tears 130
Attest th'existence of thy suff'ring son.

COUNTESS. Ah! touch me not—

EDMUND.   How!—in that cruel breast
Revive then all sensations, but affection?
Why so ador'd the memory of the father, 135
And so abhorr'd the presence of the son?
But now, and to thy eyes I seem'd my father—
At least for that resemblance-sake embrace me.

COUNTESS. Horror on horror! blasted be thy tongue!
140 What sounds are these?
BENEDICT.   Lady, tho' I excuse not
     This young lord's disobedience, his contrition
     Bespeaks no rebel principle. I doubt not,
     Your blessing first obtained and gracious pardon,
145 But soon as morning streaks the ruddy East,
     He will obey your pleasure, and return
     To stranger climes—
EDMUND.   'Tis false; I will not hence.
     I have been fool'd too long, too long been patient.
150 Nor are my years so green as to endure
     The manacles of priests and nurseries.
     Am I not Narbonne's prince? who shall rule here
     But Narbonne? Have I sapp'd my country's laws,
     Or play'd the tyrant? Who shall banish me?
155 Am I a recreant knight? Has cowardice
     Disgrac'd the line of heroes I am sprung from?
     Shall I then skulk, hide my inglorious head?
     Or does it please your worship's gravity
     Dispatch me on some sleeveless pilgrimage,
160 Like other noble fools, to win you empires;
     While you at home mock our credulity,
     The masters of our wealth, our states, and wives?
COUNTESS [*Aside.* (Brave youth! there spoke his sire. How my
               soul yearns
     To own its genuine offspring!)—Edmund, hear me!
165 Thou art my son, and I will prove a mother.
     But I'm thy sovereign too. This state is mine.
     Learn to command, by learning to obey.
     Tho' frail my sex, I have a soul as masculine
     As any of thy race. This very monk,
170 Lord as thou thinkest of my ductile conscience,
     Quails—look if 'tis not true—when I command.
     Retire thee to the village. 'Tis not ripe
     As yet my purpose—Benedict, attend me.
     To-morrow, Edmund, shalt thou learn my pleasure.

                              [*Exit* COUNTESS *and* BENEDICT.

Why, this *is* majesty. Sounds of such accent   175
Ne'er struck mine ear till now. Commanding sex!
Strength, courage, all our boasted attributes,
Want estimation; ev'n the pre-eminence
We vaunt in wisdom, seems a borrow'd ray,
When virtue deigns to speak with female organs.   180
Yes, O my mother, I *will* learn t'obey:
I *will* believe, that, harsh as thy decrees,
They wear the warrant of benign intention.
Make but the blooming Adeliza mine,
And bear, of me unquestion'd, Narbonne's sceptre;   185
Till life's expiring lamp by intervals
Throws but a fainter and a fainter flash,
And then relumes its wasted oil no more.   [*Exit.*

END OF THE THIRD ACT

ACT THE FOURTH

The SCENE continues

BENEDICT, MARTIN

MARTIN. I know thy spirit well; know how it labours,
    When curb'd and driven to wear the mask of art.
    But till this hour I have not seen thy passions
    Boil o'er the bounds of prudence. So impetuous,
5   And so reserv'd!
BENEDICT.   Mistake me not, good brother:
    I want no confidence: I know thy faith.
    But can I to thy naked eye unfold,
    What I dare scarce reveal to my own bosom?
10   I would not know one half that I suspect,
    Till I have acted as if not suspecting.
MARTIN. How, brother! thou a casuist![1] and apply
    To thy own breast those damning subtleties,
    Which cowards with half-winking consciences
15   Purchase of us, when they would sin secure,
    And hope the penalty will all be ours!
BENEDICT. Brother, this moment is too big with action
    To waste on bootless curiosity.
    When I try sins upon the touchstone conscience,
20   It is for others use, not for my own.
    'Tis time enough to make up our account,
    When we confess and kneel for absolution.
MARTIN. Still does thy genius soar above mankind!
    How many fathers of our holy church
25   In Benedict I view!
BENEDICT.   No flattery, brother.
    'Tis true the church owes Benedict some thanks.

---

1   Casuistry or subtle and sometimes devious reasoning with malicious purposes is a trait
of many Gothic villains, especially Mrs. Radcliffe's Father Schedoni in *The Italian*.
Benedict himself uses the word in a conversation with the Countess (*Mysterious Mother*
II.v.86).

For her, I have forgot I am a man.
For her, each virtue from my breast I banish.
No laws I know but her prosperity; 30
No country, but her boundless acquisitions.
Who dares be true to country, king, or friend,
If enemies to Rome, are Benedict's foes.

MARTIN. Has it then gone so far? Does she speak out?
Is Edmund too infected with like errors? 35

BENEDICT. Both, brother, both are thinking heretics.
I could forgive them, did some upstart sect
With sharper rigours charm their headlong zeal.
But they, in sooth, must *reason*—curses light
On the proud talent! 'twill at last undo us. 40
When men are gorg'd with each absurdity
Their subtle wits can frame, or we adopt;
For very novelty they will fly to sense,
And we shall fall before that idol, fashion.

MARTIN. Fear not a reign so transient. Statesmen too 45
Will join to stem the torrent: or new follies
Replace the old. Each chieftain that attacks us
Must grow the pope of his own heresy.
E'en stern philosophy, if once triumphant,
Shall frame some jargon, and exact obedience 50
To metaphysic nonsense worse than ours.
The church is but a specious name for empire,
And will exist wherever fools have fears.
Rome is no city; 'tis the human heart;
And there suffice it if we plant our banners. 55
Each priest cannot command—and thence come sects.
Obdurate Zeno[1] and our great Augustine[2]
Are of one faith, and differ but for power.

---

1 Ancient Greek philosopher (circa 340-265 B.C.). He is considered the founder of the Stoic school that taught indifference to both the pleasures and pains of life.

2 There are two Saints named Augustine: Augustine the Bishop of Hippo (354-430 A.D.) and author of the *Civita Dei*, and Augustine of Canterbury (?-605 A.D.) whose mission to the English in 597 A.D. established Christianity in Britain. "Our great Augustine" probably refers to the English Augustine although Walpole might have the earlier church father in mind.

BENEDICT. So be it—therefore interest bids us crush
60   This cockatrice[1] and her egg: or we shall see
    The singing saints of Savoy's neighb'ring vale[2]
    Fly to the covert of her shadowy wings,
    And foil us at our own dexterity.
    Already to those vagrants she inclines;
65   As if the rogues, that preach reform to others,
    Like idiots, minded to reform themselves.
MARTIN. Be cautious, brother: you may lose the lady.
BENEDICT. She is already lost—or ne'er was ours.
    I cannot dupe, and therefore must destroy her;
70   Involve her house in ruin so prodigious,
    That neither she nor Edmund may survive it.
MARTIN. How may this be accomplish'd?
BENEDICT.   Ask me not.
    From hints long treasur'd up, from broken phrase
75   In frenzy dropp'd, but vibrating from truth:
    Nay, from her caution to explain away
    What the late tempest of her soul had utter'd,
    I guess her fatal secret—or, no matter—
    Say, I do not—by what she has forbidden,
80   I know what should be done—then haste thee, brother;
    Facilitate Count Edmund's interview
    With Adeliza; nourish their young passion—
    Curse them—and if you can—why—join their hands.
MARTIN. I tremble!
85 BENEDICT.   Dastard, tremble, if we fail.
    What can we fear, when we have ruin'd them?

[*A deep-toned voice is heard.*]

Forbear!
BENEDICT. Ha! whence that sound!

---

1   A serpentine mythological creature able to kill by its glance.
2   Refers to the sixteenth-century heretical sect of Waldensians. They were persecuted
    for refusing the Church of Rome. The extermination of the Waldenses heretics was
    the subject of a famous sonnet by Milton, "On the Late Massacre in Piedmont." Savoy
    is in northern Italy.

[*Voice again.*] Forbear!

BENEDICT.   Again!

    Comes it from heav'n or hell?

[*Voice again.*] Forbear!

MARTIN.   Good angels,

    Protect me!—Benedict, thy unholy purpose—

SCENE II

BENEDICT, MARTIN, ADELIZA, FRIARS

[*A procession of friars, chanting a funeral anthem, and followed by*
ADELIZA, *advance slowly from a cloyster at the end of the stage.*]

THE ANTHEM

    Forbear! forbear! forbear!
    The pious are heav'n's care.
    Lamentations ill become us,
    When the good are ravish'd from us.
    The pangs of death but smooth the way   5
    To visions of eternal day.

BENEDICT.   [*Aside to* MARTIN]

    Now, man of aspin[1] conscience! lo! the gods,

    That sentence Benedict's unholy purpose!

    Art thou a priest? Wast thou initiated

    In each fond mummery that subdues the vulgar,   10

    And standest thou appall'd at our own thunders?

MARTIN. Who trembled first? It was thy guilty conscience

    That gave th' alarm to mine.

BENEDICT.   Peace, dotard, peace!

    Nor when the lamb is nigh, must eagles wrangle.   15

    Fair saint, give us to know why flow these tears;

[*To* ADELIZA.

---

1   The stinging of the asp, a poisonous snake. Used figuratively here to mean "stinging conscience."

Why sighs that gentle bosom; and why chant ye
That heav'n-invoking, soul-dissolving dirge?
ADELIZA. Ah! holy father, art thou then to learn
20   The pious abbess is at peace? We go
To bear her parting blessing to the Countess.
BENEDICT. It must not be. Occasions of much import
Engross her faculties. By me she wills you
Restrain your steps within the cloyster's pale,
25   Nor grant access but to one stranger knight.
ADELIZA. Is't possible? Can my dear mistress bar ·
Her faithful handmaid from her gracious presence?
Shall I not pour my sorrows in her bosom,
And moisten it with grief and gratitude?
30   Two friends were all poor Adeliza's wealth.
Lo! one is gone to plead the orphan's cause.
My patroness, like Tobit's guardian spirit,[1]
Confirms my steps, and points to realms of glory.
She will not quit me in this vale of bondage;
35   She must be good, who teaches what is goodness.
BENEDICT. (Indeed! my pretty prattler!—then am I   [aside.
As sound a saint as e'er the rubric boasted.
—Ha! 'tis the Countess—now for my obedience.)
Young lady, much I marvel at these murmurs.   [To ADELIZA.
40   Just sense and sober piety still dictate
The Countess's commands. With truth I say it,
My sins diminish, as I copy her.

---

1   Refers to a story in the apocryphal *Book of Tobit* concerning the Archangel Raphael's
curing of Tobit's blindness. Montague Summers notes that a painting by Salvator Rosa
(1615-1673) depicting the miracle of restored sight was exhibited in the National
Gallery. In a note in the 1781 edition of *The Mysterious Mother*, Walpole mentions the
painting and the story of Tobit. In the same edition, Walpole's note explains the line as
"alluding to a picture of Salvator Rosa, in which the story is thus told." (Summers,
"notes explanatory" to his edition of *The Castle of Otranto* and *The Mysterious Mother*,
300). Adeliza's ignorance of her mother's incestuous crime renders her reference to
sight restored by an angel particularly ironic. When the Countess reveals her deed to
Adeliza and Edmund (or makes them see), she calls Adeliza "Thou gentle lamb, from
fell tyger sprung" (*Mysterious Mother* V.vi.30).

SCENE III

COUNTESS, ADELIZA, BENEDICT, MARTIN

COUNTESS. What voices heard I? Does my rebel son
    Attempt against my peace?—Hah! Adeliza!
    I charg'd thee guard thy convent—wherefore then
    This disobedience?

BENEDICT.   Madam, I was urging   5
    The fitness of your orders; but vain youth
    Scoff'd my importunate rebuke—

ADELIZA.   Oh! no.
    I am the thing you made me. Crush me, spurn me,
    I will not murmur. Should you bid me die,   10
    I know 'twere meant in kindness.

COUNTESS.   Bid *thee* die!
    My own detested life but lingers round thee!
    Ha! what a glance was there! It spoke resemblance
    To all I hate, adore—My child, retire: 15
    I am much discompos'd—the good old Abbess
    Claims thy attendance.

ADELIZA.   Mercy crown her soul!
    She needs no duty we can pay her now!

COUNTESS. How! art thou desolate! not a friend left   20
    To guard thy innocence?—Oh! wretched maid!
    Must thou be left to spoilers? or worse, worse,
    To the fierce onset of thy own dire passions?
    Oh! is it come to this?

ADELIZA.   My noble mistress,   25
    Can Adeliza want a minist'ring angel,
    When shelter'd by thy wing?—yet Benedict
    Says, I must shun this hospitable roof.
    Indeed I thought it hard.

COUNTESS.   Did Benedict,   30
    Did he audacious dare forbid my child,
    My little orphan to embrace her—curses
    Swell in my throat—hence—or they fall on thee.

ADELIZA. Alas! for pity! how have I offended thee?

BENEDICT. Madam, it is the pupil of your care,
Your favour'd child—
COUNTESS.   Who told thee so? Be dumb
For ever—What, art thou combin'd with Edmund,
To dash me down the precipice? Churchman, I tell thee,
I view it with impatience. I could leap
And meet the furies—but must *she* fall with me!
BENEDICT,   [*Aside.*
(Yes, and thy Edmund too.) Be patient, lady:
This fair domain, thou know'st, acknowledges
The sovereignty of the church. Thy rebel son
Dares not attempt—
COUNTESS.   Again I bid thee peace.
There is no question of Lord Edmund. Leave us;
I have to talk with her alone.
BENEDICT,   [*Aside* to MARTIN.
(Now tremble at voices supernatural; and forfeit
The spoils the tempest throws into our lap.)

Exeunt BENEDICT *and* MARTIN.

SCENE IV

COUNTESS, ADELIZA

COUNTESS. Now, Adeliza, summon all thy courage
Retrace my precepts past: nor let a tear
Profane a moment that's worth martyrdom.
Remember patience is the Christian's courage.
Stoics have bled, and demigods have died.
A Christian's task is harder—'tis to suffer.
ADELIZA. Alas! have I not learnt the bitter lesson?
Have I not borne *thy* woes? What is to come
Can tax my patience with a ruder trial?
COUNTESS. Oh! yes, thou must do more. Adversity
Has various arrows. When the soul is steel'd
By meditation to encounter sorrow,
The foe of man shifts his artillery,

And drowns in luxury and careless softness
The breast he could not storm. Canst thou bear wealth,   15
And pleasure's melting couch? Thou has known virtue
But at a scanty board. She has awak'd thee
To chilling vapours in the midnight vault,
And beckon'd thee to hardships, tears, and penance,
Wilt thou acknowledge the divine instructress,   20
When syren pleasures[1] lap thee in delights?
ADELIZA. If such the witchery that waits on guilt,
Why should I seek th' enchantress and her wiles?
The virgin veil shall guard my spotless hours,
Assure my peace, and saint me for hereafter.   25
COUNTESS. It cannot be—
To Narbonne thou must bid a last adieu!
And with the stranger knight depart a bride.
ADELIZA. Unhappy me! too sure I have o'erburthen'd
Thy charity, if thou would'st drive me from thee.   30
Restrain thy alms, dear lady. I have learnt
From our kind sister-hood the needle's art.
My needle and thy smiles will life support.
Pray let me bring my last embroidery;
'Tis all by my own hand. Indeed I meant it   35
For my kind lady's festival.
COUNTESS.   Great justice!
Does this stroke pierce not deep enough? These tears,
Wrung from my vital fondness, scald they not
Worse than the living coal that sears the limbs?   40
ADELIZA. Alas! thou hearest not! What grief o'erwhelms thee?
Why darts thy eye into my inmost soul?
Then vacant, motionless, arrests its course,
And seems not to perceive what it reads there?
My much-lov'd patroness!   45
COUNTESS.   O Adeliza,
Thy words now slake, and now augment my fever!
But oh! ere reason quits this lab'ring frame,

---

1   In Greek mythology, sirens were temptresses whose sweet song drew men to their
doom. The Countess means "alluring but fatal" pleasures.

While I dare weep these tears of anguish o'er thee,
50   Unutterable, petrifying anguish!
Hear my last breath. Avoid the scorpion pleasure.
Death lurks beneath the velvet of his lip,
And but to think him over, is perdition!
—O retrospect of horror!—To the altar!
55   Haste, Adeliza,—vow thou wilt be wretched!
ADELIZA. Dost thou then doom me to eternal sorrows?
Hast thou deceiv'd me? is not virtue, happiness?
COUNTESS. I know not that. I know that guilt is torture.
ADELIZA. Sure pestilence has flapp'd his baleful wing,
60   And shed its poison o'er thy saintlike reason!
When thou so patient, holy, so resign'd,
Doubtest of virtue's health, of virtue's peace.
—But 'tis to try me—look upon this relick:
'Twas the good abbess's bequest. 'Twill chase
65   The fiend that walks at twilight.
COUNTESS.   How she melts me!
What have I said—my lovely innocence,
Thou art my only thought—oh! wast thou form'd
The child of sin?—and dare I not embrace thee?
70   Must I with eager ecstacy gaze on thee,
Yet curse the hour that stamp'd thee with a being!
ADELIZA. Alas! was I then born the child of sin!
Who were my parents? I will pray for them.
COUNTESS. Oh! if the bolt must come, here let it strike me!

[*Flinging herself on the ground.*

75   Nature! these feelings were thy gift. Thou knowest
How ill I can resist thy forceful impulse.
If these emotions are imputed to me,
I have one sin I cannot yet repent of!
ADELIZA. Oh! raise thee from the earth. Shall I behold thee
80   Prostrate, embracing an unfriended beggar?
Or dost thou mock me still? What is my lot?
Wilt thou yet cherish me? Or do the great
Exalt us but in sport, lend us a taste,

A vision of enjoyment, and then dash us
To poverty, more poignant by comparison? 85
Sure *I* could never wanton with affliction!
COUNTESS. Ah! canst thou doubt this conflict of the soul!
Mock thee!—oh! yes, there are such savage natures,
That will deride thy woes—and thou must bear it—
With foul reproach will gall thy spotless soul, 90
And taunt thee with a crime past thy conceiving.
Oh ! 'tis to shield thee from this world of sorrows,
That thou must fly, must wed, must never view
The tow'rs of Narbonne more; must never know
The doom reserv'd for thy sad patroness! 95
ADELIZA. Who threatens thy dear life! recall thy son.
His valiant arm will stem a host of foes,
 Replace thy lord, and woo thee to be happy.
COUNTESS. Hah! little imp of darkness! dost thou wear
That angel form to gird me with upbraidings! 100
Fly, ere my rage forget distinction, nature,
And make a medley of unheard-of crimes.
Fly, ere it be too late—
ADELIZA.   For pity!
COUNTESS.   Hence! 105
Pity would bid me stab thee, while the charm
Of ignorance locks thee in its happy slumbers.
ADELIZA. Alas! she raves—I will call help.   [*Exit.*

COUNTESS, *alone.*

        [*After a long pause, in which she looks tenderly after* ADELIZA.

                                        She's gone.
—That pang, great God, was my last sacrifice! 110
Now recollect thyself, my soul! consummate
The pomp of horror, with tremendous coolness.
'Tis fit that reason punish passion's crime.
—Reason!—alas! 'tis one of my convulsions!
Now it empow'rs me past myself: now leaves me 115

Exhausted, spiritless, eyeing with despair
The heights I cannot reach. Then madness comes,
Imperial fool! and promises to waft me
Beyond the grin of scorn—but who sits there,
120   Supereminent?—'tis conscience! phrenzy shield me!
I know the foe—see! see! he points his lance!
He plunges it all flaming in my soul,
And down I sink, lost in eternal anguish!   [*runs out.*

SCENE V

BENEDICT, ADELIZA

ADELIZA. She is not here. Shall we not follow her?
    Such agonies of passion! sure some dæmon
    Assaults her. Thou shalt pray by her. Indeed
    I tremble for her life.
5 BENEDICT.   Thou know'st her not.
    Her transport is fictitious. 'Tis the coinage
    Of avarice and caprice. Dost thou not see
    Her bounty wearies? While thy babbling years
    Wore the trick of novelty, thou wast her plaything
10   The charity of the great must be amus'd.
    Mere merit surfeits it; affliction kills it.
    The sick must jest and gambol to attract
    Their pity—Come, I'll warrant, thou hast wept,
    And told her heav'n would register each ducat
15   Her piety had spar'd to cloath and feed thee.
    Go to; thou hast estrang'd her; and she means
    To drive thee hence, lest thou upbraid her change.
ADELIZA. Upbraid my patroness! I! I upbraid her,
    Who see her now the angel that she will be!
20   How knew I virtue, goodness, but from her!
    Her lessons taught me heav'n; her life reveal'd it.
    The wings of gratitude must bear me thither,
    Or I deserve not Paradise.
BENEDICT.   Thou art young.
25   Thy novice ear imbibes each silver sound,

And deems the music warbled all by truth.
Grey hairs are not fool'd thus. I know this Countess:
An errant heretic. She scoffs the church.
When did her piety adorn our altars?
What holy garments glisten with her gifts? 30
The fabric of our convent threatens ruin—
Does she repair it?—no. On lazy lepers,
On soldiers maim'd and swearing from the wars
She lavishes her wealth—but note it, young one;
Her days are number'd; and thou shalt do wisely 35
To quit her e'er the measure is complete.
ADELIZA. Alas! she bids me go. She bids me wed
The stranger knight that woo'd me at our parlour.
BENEDICT. And thou shalt take her at her word. Myself
Will join your hands—and lo! in happy hour 40
Who comes to meet her boon.

SCENE VI

EDMUND, BENEDICT, ADELIZA

EDMUND.   In tears!—that cowl
Shall not protect th' injurious tongue, that dares
Insult thy innocence—for sure, thou dear one,
Thou hast no sins to weep.
BENEDICT.   My gracious lord, 5
Yourself and virgin coyness must be chidden,
If my fair scholar wears the mien of sadness.
'Tis but a blush that melts in modest showers.
EDMUND. Unriddle, priest. My soul is too impatient
To wait th' impertinence of flowery dialect. 10
BENEDICT. Then briefly thus. The Countess wills me join
Your hand with this fair maiden's—now, my lord,
Is my poor language nauseous?
EDMUND.   Is it possible?
Dost thou consent, sweet passion of my soul? 15
May I then clasp thee to my heart?
ADELIZA.   Forbear!

It must not be—Thou shalt not wed a beggar.
EDMUND. A beggar! Thou art riches, opulence.
20 The flaming ruby and the dazzling di'mond,
Set in the world's first diadem, could not add
A ray to thy least charm—for pity, grant me
To breathe my warmth into this marble hand.
ADELIZA. Never!—This orphan, this abandon'd wanderer,
25 Taunted with poverty, with shameful origin,
Dower'd with no lot but scorn, shall ne'er bestow
That, her sole portion, on a lordly husband.
BENEDICT. My lord, the Countess is my gracious mistress:
My duty bade me to report her words.
30 It seems her charities circumscribe her wishes.
This goodly maiden has full long experienc'd
Her amplest bounty. Other piteous objects
Call for her largesse. Lovely Adeliza
Plac'd in your arms can never feel affliction.
35 This the good Countess knows—
EDMUND.   By my sire's soul
I will not thank her. Has she dar'd to scorn thee,
Thou beauteous excellence?—then from this hour
Thou art her equal. In her very presence
40 I will espouse thee. Let us seek the proud one!
—Nay, no resistance, love!
BENEDICT.   (By heav'n all's lost,   [Aside.
Should they meet now)—My lord,
A word. The maiden   [Aside to EDMUND.
45 Is tutor'd to such awe, she ne'er will yield
Consent, should but a frown dart from the Countess.
But now, and she enjoin'd your marriage. Better
Profit of that behest—
EDMUND.   I tell thee, monk,
50 My haughty soul will not—
BENEDICT.   Pray be advis'd.
Heav'n knows how dear I tender your felicity.
The chapel is few paces hence—nay, lead her
With gentle wooings, not alarm her fears.
55 Arriv'd there, I will speedily pronounce

The solemn words—
EDMUND.   Well, be it so. My fair one,
  This holy man advises well. To heaven
  We will address our vows, and ask its pleasure.
  Come, come; I will not be refus'd—   60
ADELIZA.   Yes, heav'n!
  To thee I fly; thou art my only refuge.   [*Exeunt.*

END OF THE FOURTH ACT

ACT THE FIFTH

The SCENE *continues*

Enter BENEDICT

The business is dispatch'd. Their hands are join'd.
The puling moppet[1] struggled with her wishes;
Invok'd each saint to witness her refusal:
Nor heeded, tho' I swore their golden harps
5   Were tun'd to greet her hymeneal hour.
Th' impetuous Count, fired with the impure suggestion,
As if descending clouds had spread their pillows
To meet the pressure of his eager transports,
Would have forerun the rites. The maid affrighted
10   At such tumultuous unaccustom'd onset,
Sunk lifeless on the pavement. Hastily
I mumbled o'er the spell that binds them fast,
Like an invenom'd robe, to scorch each other
With mutual ruin—Thus am I reveng'd.
15   Proud dame of Narbonne, lo! a bare-foot monk
Thus pays thy scorn, thus vindicates his altars.
Nor while this woolen frock shall wrap our order,
Shall e'en the lillied monarchs of our realm
Be plac'd so high, but a poor friar's knife[2]
20   Shall fell their tow'ring grandeur to the earth,
Oft as they scant obedience to the church.

SCENE II

BENEDICT, PORTER

Ah! woe of woes! good father, haste thee in,
And speak sweet words of comfort to our mistress,
Her brain is much disturb'd—I fear some spell,

---

1 A pitifully whimpering little girl.
2 A reference to the assassinations of two Kings of France, Henry III by a Dominican friar in 1589 and Henry IV by a religious fanatic in 1610.

Or naughty bev'rage—will you not in and pray by her?
In sooth she needs your pray'rs.   5

BENEDICT.   She scorns my pray'rs.   [*coldly.*

PORTER. Oh! no; but how she call'd for you. Pray seek her.

BENEDICT. I can administer no comfort to her.

PORTER. Yes, yes, you can. They say the soul fiend dreads
    A scholar—Tut, your holy wit can poze[1] him,   10
    Or bind him to the red waves of the ocean.[2]
    Oh! he afflicts her gentle spirit, and vomits
    Strange menaces and terrible from her mouth!
    Then he is sullen; gags her lab'ring lips,
    And she replies not—   15

BENEDICT.   Goodman exorcist,
    Thy pains are unavailing. Her sins press her.
    Guilt has unhing'd her reason.

PORTER.   Beshrew thy heart,
    Thou dost asperse her. I know those are paid   20
    For being saints that—

BENEDICT.   Stop that tongue profane:
    Thou art infected with her heresies.
    Judgments already have o'erta'en thy mistress.
    Thou at thy peril leave her to her fate.   25

PORTER. Father, belike there is a different heaven
    For learned clerks and such poor men as I am.
    Me it behoves to have such humble virtues
    As suit my simple calling. To my masters
    For raiment, food, for salary, and protection   30
    My honest heart owes gratitude. They took me
    From drudgery to guard their honour'd persons.
    Why am I called a man of worship? Why,
    As up the chancel I precede my lady,
    Do th' vassals of the castle, rang'd in rows,   35
    Bow e'en to Peter?—why? but, by the rood,[3]
    Because she plac'd this silver-garnish'd staff

---

1   Deceive or confuse.
2   Refers to the medieval belief that demons and evil spirits could be exorcized by casting
    persons possessed by them into the Red Sea.
3   Cross.

In Peter's hand. Why, but because this robe,
Floating with seemly tufts, was her gift too.
40 For honours of such note owe I not thanks?
Were my life much to sacrifice for hers?
BENEDICT. Peace with thy saucy lecture, or harangue
Thy maudling fellows o'er the hall's dull embers
With this thy gossiping morality.
45 Now answer—mentions she her son?
PORTER.   Ah me!
I had forgotten—this old brain—'tis true,
'Tis very true—she raves upon her son,
And thinks he came in vision.
50 BENEDICT.   'Twas no vision.
PORTER. How! heav'nly fathers!
BENEDICT.   He has spoken with her.
PORTER. And I not see him!—go to; it could not be.
How did he pass the gate?
55 BENEDICT.   I tell thee, Edmund,
The quondam[1] master's son, has seen his mother;
Is but few paces hence.
PORTER.   Oh! joyous sounds!
Where is my noble lord?
60 BENEDICT.   Here—and undone.

SCENE III

FLORIAN, BENEDICT, PORTER

FLORIAN. Sure the foul fogs, that hang in lazy clouds
O'er yonder moat, infect the moping air,
And steam with phrenzy's melancholy fumes.
But now and I met Edmund—with a voice
5 Appall'd and hollow like a parricide's,
He told me he was wedded. When I asked
To see his bride, he groan'd, and said his joys
Were blasted e'er accomplished. As he urg'd

---

1 Onetime or former.

His suit, the maiden's tears and shrieks had struck
On his sick fancy like his mother's cries!   10
Th' idea writhing from his brain, had won
His eye-balls, and he thought he saw his mother!
—This ague of contagious bigotry
Has gain'd almost on me. Methinks yon monk
Might fell me with a chaplet—Edmund left me   15
Abruptly—I must learn this mystery.
Health to your rev'rence—[*To* BENEDICT] Hah!
My new acquaintance!   [*To* PETER]
In tears, my good old friend! What! has the cricket
Chirp'd ominously—come, away with sorrow: 20
Joy marks this day its own.
PORTER.   A joyful day!
    The twentieth of September!—note it, sir,
    Note it for the ugliest of the calendar.
    'Twas on this day—ay, this day sixteen years   25
    The noble Count came to his death!
FLORIAN.   No matter,
    Th' arrival of a nobler younger Count
    Shall mock prognostics past, and paint the year
    With smiling white, fair fortune's favourite livery.
    But tell me, father, tell me, has the Countess   30
                                        [*To* BENEDICT.
    Pardon'd her son's return? has she receiv'd him
    With th' overflowings of a mother's joy?
    Smiles she upon his wishes—as I enter'd
    Methought I heard an hymeneal accent.
    And yet, it seems, the favour of your countenance   35
    Wears not the benediction of rejoicing.
BENEDICT. The Countess must unfold her book of fate.
    I am not skill'd to read so dark a volume.
FLORIAN. Oracular as the Delphic god![1]—good Peter,
    Thy wit and mine are more upon a level.   40
    Resolve me, has the Countess seen lord Edmund?

---

1 Refers to Apollo, whose oracle at Delphi was consulted on profound questions of religion, politics, and morality.

Say, did she frown and chide? or bathe his cheek
With tears as warm as leaping blood?
PORTER.   Ah! master,
45   You seem too good to mock our misery.
A soldier causes woe, but seldom jeers it.
Or know'st thou not—and sure t'will pity thee!
The gracious Countess, our kind lady—indeed
I trust they will return—is strangely chang'd!
50 FLORIAN. By my good sword, thou shalt unriddle, priest.
What means this tale? what mintage is at work
To coin delusion, that this fair domain
May become holy patrimony? Thus
Teach you our matrons to defraud their issue
55   By artificial fits and acted ravings?
I have beheld your juggles, heard your dreams,
Th' imposture shall be known. These sixteen years
Has my friend Edmund pin'd in banishment:
While masses, mummings, goblins and processions
60   Usurp'd his heritage, and made of Narbonne
A theatre of holy interludes[1]
And sainted frauds. But day darts on your spells.
Th' enlighten'd age eschews your vile deceits,
And truth shall do mankind and Edmund justice.
65 BENEDICT. Unhallow'd boy, I scorn thy contumely.
In camps and trenchs vent thy lewd reproaches,
Blaspheming while ye tremble. Heav'n's true soldiers,
Endu'd with more than mortal courage, defy
Hosts numerous as the Pagan chivalry
70   Pour'd forth to crush the church's rising glories.
—But this is an enlighten'd age!—behold
The triumphs of your sect! to yonder plains
Bend thy illumin'd eye! The Vaudois[2] there,

---

1   An interlude is a short scene between the acts of a play. In Renaissance dramas, interludes often featured jugglers, jesters, and trick-performing mimes. Florian accuses the
church of deceit and fraud through the "mummings" of ritual.

2   Another reference to the Waldensian heretics of the Piedmont in northern Italy and
their extermination by the Duke of Savoy in 1655. Early suppressions had occurred
throughout the 16th century. In the context of these religious massacres, Father Bene-

Writing in flames, and quiv'ring at th' approach
Of Rome's impending knife, attest the blessings 75
Conferr'd on their instructed ignorance!
FLORIAN. Monstrous! unparallel'd! Are cries and groans
Of butcher'd conscientious men the hymns
With which you chant the victories of the church?
Do you afflict and laugh? stab and huzza? 80
—But I am dallying with my own impatience—
Where is this mother? I will tent her soul;
And warn thee, if I find suggestion's whisper
Has practic'd to the detriment of my friend,
Thy caitiff[1] life shall answer to my sword, 85
Tho' shrin'd within the pillars of the Vatican.
BENEDICT. Judge heaven betwixt us!
If e'er the dews of night shall fall, thou seest not
The cup of wrath pour'd out, and triple woes
O'ertake unheard-of crimes; call me false prophet, 90
Renounce my gods and join thee to the impious!
Thou in thy turn, if truth lives on my lips,
Tremble! repent!—behold! the hour approaches!

SCENE IV

COUNTESS, FLORIAN, BENEDICT, PORTER

COUNTESS. I dare not shoot the gulf—ha! Benedict!
Thou art a priest, thy mission should be holy,
If thou beliest not heav'n,—quick, do thy work!
If there is pow'r in pray'r, teach me some sounds
To charm my senses, lest my coward flesh 5
Recoil, and win the mastery o'er my will.
—'Tis not the wound; it is the consequence!
See! see! my Narbonne stands upon the brink,
And snatches from the readiest fury there

---

dict's comment that "this is an enlighten'd age" is almost sarcastic. The Vaudois or
Waldenses were thought to practice witchcraft.
1 Cowardly. The adjective is frequent in Shakespeare's plays.

10   A blazing torch! he whirls it round my head,
      And asks where are my children!
PORTER.   Split, my heart,
      At this sad sight!
FLORIAN.   Stand off! thou'rt an accomplice—
15   Madam, it was your morning's gracious pleasure
      I should attend you. May I hope your pardon,
      If I anticipate—
COUNTESS.   Ha! who art thou?
FLORIAN. Have you forgot me, lady?
20 COUNTESS.   Memory
      Is full. A head distract as mine can hold
      Two only objects, guilt and eternity!
FLORIAN. No more of this. Time has abundant hours
      For holy meditation. Nor have years
25   Trac'd such deep admonition on your cheek,
      As call for sudden preparation—
COUNTESS   [*Wildly.*
      Prayer can do no more: its efficacy's lost—
      What must be, must be soon—He will return.
FLORIAN. He is return'd, your son—have you not seen him?
30 COUNTESS. Would I had never!
FLORIAN.   Come, this is too much.
      This villainous monk had step'd 'twixt you and nature;
      And misreported of the noblest gentleman
      That treads on Christian ground—Are you a mother?
35   Are legends dearer to you than your son?
      Think you 'tis piety to gorge these miscreants,
      And drive your child from your embrace—
COUNTESS.   Ye saints!
      This was the dæmon prompted it—avaunt!
40   He beckons me—I will not—lies my lord
      Not bleeding in the porch? I'll tear my hair
      And bathe his wounds—Where's Beatrice!—monster! monster!
      She leads the dæmon—see! they spread the couch!
      No, I will perish with my Narbonne—Oh!
45   My strength, my reason faint—darkness surrounds me!
      Tomorrow!—never will tomorrow come!
      Let me die here!   [*Sinks on a bench.*

FLORIAN.   This is too much for art.
   Chill damps sit on her brow: her pulse replies not.
BENEDICT. No; 'tis fictitious all—'twas I inspir'd   50
   The horrors she has been so kind to utter
   At my suggestion.
FLORIAN.   That insulting sneer
   Speaks more devil than if thy words were serious.
   Be her distraction counterfeit or real,   55
   Her sex demands compassion or assistance.
   But she revives!
COUNTESS.   Is death then past! my brain
   Beats not its wonted tempest—in the grave
   There is peace then.   60
FLORIAN.   Her agony abates.
   Look up and view your friends.
COUNTESS.   Alas! I fear me,
   This is life still!—am I not in my castle?
   Sure I should know this garden—good old Peter!   65
   My honest servant, thou I see wilt never
   Quit thy poor mistress!—kind old man, he weeps!
PORTER. Indeed it is for joy—how fares my lady?
COUNTESS. Exhausted, Peter, that I have not strength
   To be distracted—hah! your looks betray   70
   Tremendous innuendoes!—gracious heaven!
   Have I said aught—has wildness—trust me, sirs,
   In these sad fits my unhing'd fancy wanders
   Beyond the compass of things possible.
   Sometimes an angel of excelling brightness,   75
   I seem to whirl the orbs and launch the comet.
   Then hideous wings with forked points array me,
   And I suggest strange crimes to shuddering matrons—
   Sick fancy must be pardon'd.
BENEDICT.   (Artful woman!   [*Aside.* 80
   Thou subtle emblem of thy sex, compos'd
   Of madness and deceit—but since thy brain
   Has lost its poize, I will send those shall shake it
   Beyond recovery of its reeling bias.)   [*Exit.*

[COUNTESS *makes a sign to* PETER *to retire.*

SCENE V

COUNTESS, FLORIAN

COUNTESS. This interval is well—'tis thy last boon,
Tremendous Providence! and I will use it
As 'twere the elixir of descending mercy:
Not a drop shall be waste—accept my thanks!
5   Preserve my reason! and preserve my child!

[*To* FLORIAN.

—Stranger, thy years are green; perhaps may mock
A woman's words, a mother's woe!—but honour,
If I believe this garb, is thy profession.
Hast thou not dealt in blood?—then thou has heard
10   The dying groan, and sin's despairing accent.
Struck it not on thy soul! Recall it, sir!
What then was thy sensation, feel for me!
FLORIAN. I shudder! listen, pity, and respect thee!
COUNTESS. Resolve my anxious heart. Tho' vagrant pleasure,
15   Th' ebriety of youth, and worse than passion,
Example, lead thee to the strumpet vice;
Say, if beneath the waves of dissipation,
The germ of virtue blossoms in thy soul.
FLORIAN. A soldier's honour is his virtue. Gownmen[1]
20   Wear it for show, and barter it for gold,
And have it still. A soldier and his honour
Exist together, and together perish.
COUNTESS. I do believe thee. Thus my Narbonne thought.
Then hear me, child of honour! Canst thou cherish
25   Unblemished innocence! wilt thou protect it?
Wilt thou observe its wand'rings? call it back,
Confine it to the path that leads to happiness?
Hast thou that genuine heroism of soul
To hug the little fondling sufferer,

---

1   Priests or clergymen.

When nestling in thy bosom, drown'd in blushes,   30
    Nor cast her from thee, while a grinning world
    Reviles her with a mother's foul misdeeds?
FLORIAN. My arm is sworn to innocence distrest;
    Point out the lovely mourner.
COUNTESS.   'Tis enough.   35
    Nor suffer the ebbing moments more enquiry.
    My orphan shall be thine—nay, start not, sir,
    Your loves are known to me. Wealth past th' ambition
    Of Gallia's[1] proudest baron shall endow her.
    Within this casket is a monarch's ransom.   40
    Ten thousand ducats more are lodg'd within.
    All this is thine with Adeliza's hand.
FLORIAN. With Adeliza!
COUNTESS.   Ha! dost thou recoil?
    Dost thou not love her?   45
FLORIAN.   I love Adeliza!
    Lady, recall thy wand'ring memory.
COUNTESS. Dost thou reject her? and has hope beguil'd me
    In this sad only moment? Hast thou dar'd
    With ruffian insolence gaze on her sweetness,   50
    And mark it for an hour of wanton dalliance?
    Oh! I will guard my child, tho' gaping dæmons
    Howl with impatience!
FLORIAN.   Most rever'd of matrons,
    Tho' youth and rosy joy flush on my cheek,   55
    Tho' the licentious camp and rapine's holiday
    Have been my school; deem not so reprobate
    My morals, that my eye would note no distance
    Between the harlot's glance and my friend's bride.
COUNTESS. Thy friend! what friend!   60
FLORIAN.   Lord Edmund—
COUNTESS. What of him?
FLORIAN. Is Adeliza's lord; her wedded bridegroom.
COUNTESS. Confusion! phrenzy! blast me, all ye furies!
    Edmund and Adeliza! when! where! how!   65

---

1 France's, from Gaul, the Roman province.

Edmund wed Adeliza! quick, unsay
The monstrous tale—oh! prodigy of ruin!
Does my own son then boil with fiercer fires
Than scorch'd his impious mother's madding[1] veins?
70   Did reason reassume its shatter'd throne,
But as a spectatress of this last of horrors?
Oh! let my dagger drink my heart's black blood,
And then present my hell-born progeny
With drops of kindred sin!—*that* were a torch
75   Fit to light up such loves! and fit to quench them!
FLORIAN. What means this agony? didst thou not grant
The maiden to his wishes?
COUNTESS.   Did I not couple
Distinctions horrible! plan unnatural rites
80   To grace my funeral pile, and meet the furies
More innocent than those I leave behind me!
FLORIAN. Amazement!—I will hasten—grant, ye pow'rs!
My speed be not too late!   [*Exit.*
COUNTESS.   Globe of the world,
85   If thy frame split not with such crimes as these,
It is immortal!

SCENE VI

COUNTESS, EDMUND, ADELIZA

EDMUND *and* ADELIZA *enter at the opposite door from which*
FLORIAN *went out. They kneel to the* COUNTESS.

EDMUND. Dear parent, look on us, and bless your children!
COUNTESS. My children! horror! horror! yes, too sure
Ye are my children!—Edmund, loose that hand;
5   'Tis poison to thy soul!—hell has no venom
Like a child's touch!—oh! agonizing thought!
—Who made this marriage? whose unhallow'd breath
Pronounc'd the incestuous sounds?

---

1   Raving or frenzied.

EDMUND. Incest! Good heavens!

COUNTESS. Yes, thou devoted victim! let thy blood
   Curdle to stone! perdition circumvents thee!   10
   Lo! where this monster stands! thy mother! mistress!
   The mother of thy daughter, sister, wife!
   The pillar of accumulated horrors!
   Hear! tremble!—and then marry, if thou darest!

EDMUND. Yes, I do tremble, tho' thy words are phrenzy.   15
   So black must be the passions that inspir'd it,
   I shudder for thee! pitying duty shudders!

COUNTESS. For me!—O Edmund, I have burst the bond
   Of every tie—when thou shalt know the crimes,
   In which this fury did involve thy youth,   20
   It will seem piety to curse me, Edmund!
   Oh! impious night!—hah! is not that my lord?
   He shakes the curtains of the nuptial couch,   [*Wildly.*
   And starts to find a son there!

EDMUND.   Gracious heaven!   25
   Grant that these shocking images *be* raving!

ADELIZA. Sweet lady, be compos'd—indeed I thought
   This marriage was thy will—but we will break it—
   Benedict shall discharge us from our vows.

COUNTESS. Thou gentle lamb, from a fell tyger sprung,   30
   Unknowing half the miseries that await thee!
   —Oh! they are innocent—Almighty pow'r!—

                  [*Kneels, but rises again hastily.*

Ha! dare I pray! for others intercede!
I pray for them, the cause of all their woe!
—But for a moment give me leave, despair!   35
For a short interval lend me that reason
Thou gavest, heav'n, in vain!—it must be known
The fullness of my crime; or innocent these
May plunge them in new horrors. Not a word
Can 'scape me, but will do the work of thunder,   40
And blast these moments I regain from madness!
Ye know how fondly my luxurious fancy

Doted upon my lord. For eighteen months
An embassy detain'd him from my bed.
45 A harbinger announc'd his near return.
Love dress'd his image to my longing thoughts
In all its warmest colours—but the morn,
In which impatience grew almost to sickness,
Presented him a bloody corse before me.
50 I rav'd—the storm of disappointed passions
Assail'd my reason, fever'd all my blood—
Whether too warmly press'd, or too officious
To turn the torrent of my grief aside,
A damsel, that attended me, disclos'd
55 Thy suit, unhappy boy!

EDMUND.   What is to come!
Shield me, ye gracious pow'rs, from my own thoughts!
My dreadful apprehension!

COUNTESS.   Give it scope!
60 Thou canst not harbour a foreboding thought
More dire, than I conceiv'd, I executed.
Guilt rush'd into my soul—my fancy saw thee
Thy father's image—

EDMUND.   Swallow th' accursed sound!
65 Nor dare to say—

COUNTESS.   Yes, thou polluted son!
Grief, disappointment, opportunity,
Rais'd such a tumult in my madding blood,
I took the damsel's place; and while thy arms
70 Twin'd, to thy thinking, round another's waist,
Hear, hell, and tremble!—thou didst clasp thy mother!

EDMUND. Oh! execrable!   [ADELIZA *faints.*

COUNTESS. Be that swoon eternal!
Nor let her know the rest—she is thy daughter,
75 Fruit of that monstrous night!

EDMUND.   Infernal woman!

[*Draws his dagger.*

My dagger must repay a tale like this!

Blood so distemper'd—no—I must not strike—
I dare not punish what you dar'd commit.
COUNTESS, *seizing his dagger.* Give me the steel—my arm will not
    recoil.   80
Thus, Edmund, I revenge thee!   [*stabs herself.*
EDMUND. Help! hoa! help!
For both I tremble, dare not succour either!
COUNTESS. Peace! and conceal our shame—quick, frame some
    legend—   85
They come!

SCENE VII

CONTESS, EDMUND, ADELIZA, FLORIAN,
BENEDICT, Attendants

COUNTESS. Assist the maid—an accident—

                       [*They bear off* ADELIZA.

By my own hand—ha! Benedict!—but no!
I must not turn accuser.
BENEDICT.   Mercy! heaven! Who did this deed?
COUNTESS.   Myself.   5
BENEDICT.   What was the cause?
COUNTESS. Follow me to yon gulph, and thou wilt know.
I answer not to man.
BENEDICT.   Bethink thee, lady—
COUNTESS. Thought ebbs apace—O Edmund, could a blessing   10
Part from my lips, and not become a curse,
I would—poor Adeliza—'tis accomplish'd!   [*Dies.*
BENEDICT. My lord, explain these horrors. Wherefore fell
Your mother? and why faints your wife?
EDMUND.   My wife!   15
Thou damning priest! I have no wife—thou know'st it—
Thou gavest me indeed—no—rot my tongue
Ere the dread sound escape it!—and bear away
That hateful monk.

BENEDICT.   [*As he goes out, to* FLORIAN.
20   Who was the prophet now?
        Remember me!
EDMUND.   O Florian, we must haste,
        To where the fell war[1] assumes its ugliest form:
        I burn to rush on death!
25 FLORIAN.   I dare not ask;
        But stiffen'd with amazement I deplore—
EDMUND. O tender friend! I must not·violate
        Thy guiltless ear!—ha! 'tis my father calls!
        I dare not see him!   [*Wildly.*
30 FLORIAN.   Be compos'd, my lord,
        We are all your friends—
EDMUND. Have I no kindred here?
        They will confound all friendship! interweave
        Such monstrous union—
35 FLORIAN.   Good my lord, resume
        Your wonted reason. Let us in and comfort
        Your gentle bride—
EDMUND.   Forbid it, all ye pow'rs!
        O Florian, bear her to the holy sisters.
40   Say, 'twas my mother's will she take the veil.
        I never must behold her!—never more
        Review this theatre of monstrous guilt!
        No; to th' embattled foe I will present
        This hated form—and welcome be the sabre
45   That leaves no atom of it undefac'd!

---

1   Cruel, ferocious, and lethal war. Edmund's words recall Hamlet's dying speech, "As this
    fell sergeant, Death, is strict in his arrest" (*Hamlet*. V.ii.338-339). Edmund's determina-
    tion to die in battle ("I burn to rush on death!") would appear to be an act of Oedipal
    atonement for his mother's crimes of passion. Paul Baines calls *The Mysterious Mother* "a
    recasting of the Oedipus story ... an Oedipal drama which out-Hamlets *Hamlet* by ren-
    dering the desire for incestuous union between son and mother a conscious and con-
    summated wish." See Paul Baines, "'This Theatre of Monstrous Guilt': Horace Walpole
    and the Drama of Incest," *Studies in Eighteenth-Century Culture* 28 (1999): 287-309.

EPILOGUE

To be spoken by Mrs. Clive[1]

Our bard, whose head is fill'd with Gothic[2] fancies,
And teems with ghosts and giants and romances,
Intended to have kept your passions up,
And sent you crying out your eyes, to sup.
Would you believe it—though *mine* all the vogue,   5
He meant his nun[3] should speak the epilogue.
His nun! so pious, pliant, and demure—
Lord! you have had enough of her, I'm sure!
I storm'd—for, when my honour is at stake,
I make the pillars of the green-room[4] shake.   10
Heroes half-drest, and goddesses half-lac'd,
Avoid my wrath, and from my thunders haste.
I vow'd by all the gods of Rome and Greece,

1   Catherine "Kitty" Clive (1709-1785) was a leading comic actress on the London stage
    in Walpole's day. She lived at Little Strawberry Hill, a small house adjoining Walpole's
    estate, and frequently enjoyed Walpole's company at card games. In the light and ban-
    tering tone of the Epilogue and the choice of a leading comedienne to speak it, Wal-
    pole follows a common practice of the stage of his day by ending a tragic drama with a
    comic epilogue. Unlike *The Castle of Otranto*, no risible undertone or comic irony
    underlies the tension and suspense that Walpole maintains throughout the five acts
    themselves. "Our bard, whose head is fill'd with Gothic fancies, / And teems with
    ghosts and giants and romances" refers to *Otranto's* occasional subseriousness.
2   The adjective "Gothic" (variant spellings "Gothick" and "Gothique") is used here in
    the same sense in which Walpole used it in the subtitle of *The Castle of Otranto: A
    Gothic Story*, to mean wild and medieval characters, incidents, and architectural settings
    related to the high Gothic Age of the late eleventh, twelfth, and thirteenth centuries.
    "Gothic" has sometimes been used loosely as a synonym for "ghostly" or "supernatur-
    al," or simply "terrifying." For discussions of the various and shifting meanings of the
    adjective "Gothic" when applied to literary works of horror and terror, see Alfred
    Longueil, "The Word 'Gothic' in Eighteenth Century Criticism," *Modern Language
    Notes* 38 (1923): 453-460; Maurice Lévy, "'Gothic' and the Critical Idiom," in *Gothick
    Origins and Innovations*, eds. Allan Lloyd Smith & Victor Sage, Amsterdam & Atlanta,
    GA: Rodopi, 1994, 1-15.
3   Walpole's nun is the distraught Adeliza. Edmund has asked that she be taken to a con-
    vent. "Say, 'twas my mother's will she take the veil" (*Mysterious Mother*, V.vii.39).
4   In theatrical parlance, the actors' dressing room, often adjacent to the stage. With her
    boisterous and cheerful personality, Kitty Clive did indeed "make the pillars of the
    green-room shake."

'Twas I would finish his too doleful piece.
15 I, flush'd with comic roguery—said I,
Will make 'em laugh, more than you make 'em cry.
Bless me! said he—among the Greeks, dear Kat'rine,
Of smutty epilogues I know no pattern.
Smutty! said I—and then I stamp'd the stage
20 With all a turkey-cock's majestic rage—
When did you know in public—or in private,
Doubles entendres my strict virtue drive at?
Your muses, sir, are not more free from ill
On mount Parnassus—or on Strawb'rry hill.
25 And though with your repentance you may hum one,
I would not play your countess—to become one.
So *very* guilty, and so *very* good,
An angel, with such errant flesh and blood!
Such sinning, praying, preaching—I'll be kist,
30 If I don't think she was a methodist![1]
Saints are the produce of a vicious age:
Crimes must abound, ere sectaries can rage.
His mask no canting confessor assumes;
With acted zeal no flaming bigot fumes;
35 Till the rich harvest nods with swelling grain,
And the sharp sickle can assure his gain.
But soon shall hypocrites their flights deplore,
Nor grim enthusiasts vex Britannia more.
Virtue shall guard her daughters from their arts,
40 Shine in their eyes, and blossom in their hearts.
They need no lectures in fanatic tone:
Their lesson lives before them—on the throne.[2]

---

1 Refers to the religious fervor of the Methodists, a dissenting Protestant sect founded by John Wesley.

2 A sneering allusion to King George III (reigned 1760-1820). In 1764, Walpole's cousin, Henry Seymour Conway, had been cashiered from his post as Groom of the Royal Bedchamber and lost command of his regiment for opposing the King's proposed extensions of royal power. Walpole defended his cousin against the King's unjust treatment of Conway in a pamphlet written in June 1764. For a discussion of the Conway affair and its repercussions on Walpole's Gothicism, see Carol M. Dole, "Three Tyrants in *The Castle of Otranto*" *English Language Notes* 26 (1988): 26-35. One of the three tyrants is George III.

POSTSCRIPT

FROM the time that I first undertook the foregoing scenes, I never flattered myself that they would be proper to appear on the stage. The subject is so horrid that I thought it would shock, rather than give satisfaction to an audience. Still I found it so truly tragic in the two essential springs of terror and pity, that I could not resist the impulse of adapting it to the scene, though it should never be practicable to produce it there. I saw too that it would admit of great situations, of lofty characters, and of those sudden and unforeseen strokes, which have singular effect in operating a revolution in the passions, and in interesting the spectator. It was capable of furnishing, not only a contrast of characters, but a contrast of vice and virtue in the same character; and by laying the scene in what age and country I pleased, pictures of ancient manners might be drawn, and many allusions to historic events introduced to bring the action nearer to the imagination of the spectator. The moral resulting from the calamities attendant on an unbounded passion, even to the destruction of the criminal person's race, was obviously suited to the purpose and object of tragedy.

The subject is more truly horrid than even that of Œdipus:[1] and yet I do not doubt but a Grecian poet would have made no scruple of exhibiting it on the theatre. Revolting as it is, a son assassinating his mother, as Orestes[2] does, exceeds the guilt that appears in the foregoing scenes. As murder is the highest crime that a man can commit against his fellow beings, parricide is the deepest degree of murder. There is no age but has suffered such guilt to be represented on the stage. And yet I feel the disgust that must arise at the catastrophe of this piece; so much is our delicacy more apt to be shocked than our good nature. Nor will

---

1   In Sophocles's tragedy, *Œdipus Tyrannus*, the hero is not aware of his incestuous deed whereas the Countess is aware of her incestuous act. Consciously committed incest makes the deed, "more horrid" than the handling of the incest theme in the ancient Greek tragedy.
2   A reference to Orestes's killing of his mother Clytemnestra in revenge for his father Agamemnon's murder by her and her lover, Ægisthus, in Æschylus's trilogy *The Oresteia*.

it be an excuse that I thought the story founded on an event in real life.

I had heard, when very young, that a gentlewoman, under uncommon agonies of mind, had waited on archbishop Tillotson,[1] and besought his counsel. Many years before, a damsel that served her, acquainted her that she was importuned by the gentlewoman's son to grant him a private meeting. The mother ordered the maiden to make the assignation, when, she said, she would discover herself, and reprimand him for his criminal passion; but being hurried away by a much more criminal passion herself, she kept the assignation without discovering herself. The fruit of this horrid artifice was a daughter, whom the gentlewoman caused to be educated very privately in the country; but proving very lovely, and being accidentally met by her father-brother, who had never had the slightest suspicion of the truth, he had fallen in love with and actually married her. The wretched guilty mother learning what had happened, and distracted with the consequence of her crime, had now resorted to the archbishop to know in what manner she should act. The prelate charged her never to let her son and daughter know what had passed, as they were innocent of any criminal intention. For herself, he bade her almost despair.

Some time after I had finished the play on this ground-work, a gentleman to whom I had communicated it, accidentally discovered the origin of the tradition in the novels of the queen of Navarre, vol. II. Nov. 30; and to my great surprise I found a strange concurrence of circumstances between the story as there related, and as I had adapted it to my piece: for though I believed it to have happened in the reign of king William, I had, for a purpose mentioned below, thrown it back to the eve of the reformation; and the queen, it appears, dates the event in the reign of Louis XII. I had chosen Narbonne for the scene; the queen places it in Languedoc. The rencontres are of little importance; and perhaps curious to nobody but the author.

---

1   John Tillotson (1630-1694) was Archbishop of Canterbury. Walpole acknowledged that one of the historical sources for the Countess's plot to sleep with her son came from an account of a similar incestuous deception committed by one of Tillotson's parishioners. This anecdote is the basis for the incest plot of *The Mysterious Mother*.

In order to make use of a canvas so shocking, it was necessary as much as possible to palliate the crime, and raise the character of the criminal. To attain the former end, I imagined the moment in which she had lost a beloved husband, when grief, disappointment, and a conflict of passions might be supposed to have thrown her reason off its guard, and exposed her to the danger under which she fell. Strange as the moment may seem for vice to have seized her, still it makes her less hateful, than if she had coolly meditated so foul a crime. I have endeavoured to make her very fondness for her husband in some measure the cause of her guilt.

But as that guilt could not be lessened without destroying the subject itself, I thought that her immediate horror and consequential repentance were essential towards effectuating her being suffered on the stage. Still more was necessary; the audience must be prejudiced in her favour, or an uniform sentiment of disgust would have been raised against the whole piece. For this reason I suppressed the story till the last scene and bestowed every ornament of sense, unbigotted [sic] piety, and interesting contrition on the character that was at last to raise universal indignation; in hopes that some degree of pity would linger in the breasts of the audience; and that a whole life of virtue and penance might in some measure atone for a moment, though a most odious moment of a depraved imagination.

Some of my friends have thought that I have pushed the sublimity of sense and reason, in the character of the Countess, to too great a height, considering the dark and superstitious age in which she lived. They are of opinion that the excess of her repentance would have been more likely to have thrown her into the arms of enthusiasm. Perhaps it might—but I was willing to insinuate that virtue could and ought to leave more lasting stings in a mind conscious of having fallen; and that weak minds alone believe or feel that conscience is to be lulled asleep by the incantations of bigotry. However, to reconcile even the seeming inconsistence objected to, I have placed my fable at the dawn of the reformation; consequently the strength of mind in the Countess may be supposed to have borrowed aid from other sources, besides those she found in her own understanding.

Her character is certainly new, and the cast of the whole play unlike any other that I am acquainted with. The incidents seem to me to flow naturally from the situation; and with all the defects in the writing, of many of which I am conscious, and many more no doubt will be discovered, still I think, as a tragedy, its greatest fault is the horror which it must occasion in the audience; particularly in the fairer, more tender, and less criminal part of it.

It will be observed that, after the discovery of her son, the Countess is for some moments in every scene disordered in her understanding by the violent impression of that interview, and from the guilt that is ever uppermost in her mind. Yet she is never quite mad—still less does she talk like Belvidera of "Lutes, laurels, seas of milk, and ships of amber;"[1] which is not being mad, but light-hearted. When madness has taken possession of a person, such character ceases to be fit for the stage, or at least should appear there but for a short time; it being the business of the theatre to exhibit passions, not distempers. The finest picture ever drawn of a head discomposed by misfortune is that of King Lear.[2] His thoughts dwell on the ingratitude of his daughters, and every sentence that falls from his wildness excites reflection and pity. Had phrenzy entirely seized him, our compassion would abate; we should conclude that he no longer felt unhappiness. Shakespeare wrote as a philosopher, Otway as a poet.

The villainy of Benedict was planned to divide the indignation of the audience, and, to intercept some of it from the Countess. Nor will the blackness of his character appear extravagant, if we call to mind the crimes committed by catholic churchmen, when the reformation not only provoked their rage, but threatened them with total ruin.

I have said that terror and pity naturally arose from the subject, and that the moral is just. These are the merits of the story, not of the author. It is true also, that the rules laid down by the critics are strictly inherent in the piece—remark, I do not say, observed, for I had written above three acts before I had thought of, or set

---

1 Refers to the madly raving heroine of Thomas Otway's popular blank verse tragedy, *Venice Preserved; or, A Plot Discovered* (1682).
2 Refers to the madness of King Lear on the heath in Shakespeare's tragedy, (*King Lear*, III.iv).

myself to observe those rules; and consequently it is no vanity to say that the three unities[1] reign throughout the whole play. The time necessary is not above two or three hours longer than that of the representation; and at most does not require half of the four-and-twenty hours granted to poets by those their masters. The unity of place is but once shifted, and, that merely from the platform without the castle to the garden within it, so that a single wall is the sole infringement of the second law—and for the third, unity of action, it is so entire, that not the smallest episode intervenes. Every scene tends to bring on the catastrophe, and the story is never interrupted or diverted from its course. The return of Edmund and his marriage necessarily produce the denouement.

If the critics are pleased with this conformity to their laws, I shall be glad they have that satisfaction. For my own part, I set little value on such merit, which was accidental, and is at best mechanic, and of a subordinate kind; and more apt to produce improbable situations than to remove them.

I wish I had no more to answer for in the faults of the piece, than I have merit to boast in the mechanism. I was desirous of striking a little out of the common road, and to introduce some novelty on our stage. Our genius and cast of thinking are very different from the French; and yet our theatre, which should represent manners, depends almost entirely at present on translations and copies from our neighbours. Enslaved as they are to rules and modes, still I do not doubt, that many, both of their tragic and comic authors, would be glad they dared to use the liberties that are secured, to our stage. They are so cramped by the rigorous forms of composition, that they would think themselves greatly indemnified by an ampler latitude of thought. I have chalked out some paths that may be happily improved by better poets and men of more genius than I possess; and which may be introduced in subjects better calculated for action than the story I have chosen.

The excellence of our dramatic writers is by no means equal in number to the great men we have produced in other walks. The-

---

1 The unities of classical tragedy as discussed by Aristotle in *The Poetics* were unity of time, unity of place, and unity of action.

atric genius lay dormant after Shakespeare; waked with some bold and glorious, but irregular and often ridiculous flights in Dryden;[1] revived in Otway;[2] maintained a placid, pleasing kind of dignity in Rowe,[3] and even shone in his Jane Shore. It trod in sublime and classic fetters in Cato,[4] but void of nature, or the power of affecting the passions. In Southern[e][5] it seemed a genuine ray of nature and Shakespeare; but falling on an age still more Hottentot, was stifled in those gross and barbarous productions, tragicomedies. It turned to tuneful nonsense in the Mourning Bride;[6] grew stark mad in Lee;[7] whose cloak, a little the worse for wear, fell on Young;[8] yet in both was still a poet's cloak. It recovered its senses in Hughes[9] and Fenton,[10] who were afraid it should relapse, and, accordingly kept it down with a timid, but amiable hand—and then it languished. We have not mounted again above the two last.

---

1 The poet and playwright, John Dryden (1631-1700). Walpole probably has in mind Dryden's 1672 comedy The Assignation; or, Love in a Nunnery.

2 Thomas Otway (1652-1685) was the author of the blank verse tragedies The Orphan (1680) and Venice Preserved; or, A Plot Discovered (1682).

3 Nicholas Rowe (1674-1718) was the author of Jane Shore (1714), a tragedy based on the ill fortunes of the mistress of Edward IV.

4 Walpole refers to the tragedy Cato (1713) by Joseph Addison, a play that adhered to strict classical rules, but (in Walpole's view) lacked tragic passion. Walpole's library contained a great assortment of dramatic literature. See Allen T. Hazen, A Bibliography of Horace Walpole, New Haven: Yale UP, 1948.

5 Thomas Southerne (1659-1746) was the author of The Fatal Marriage; or, The Innocent Adultery (1694), a play containing several parallels with The Mysterious Mother.

6 Refers to the tragedy by William Congreve (1670-1729), The Mourning Bride (1697). The play contains strong Gothic moods, settings, and events, including a headless corpse.

7 The playwright Nathaniel Lee (1653-1692). He collaborated with Dryden on the tragedy, Œdipus (1679).

8 Walpole refers to the graveyard poet Edward Young (1683-1765), author of The Complaint, or Night Thoughts on Life, Death, and Immortality (1742). Walpole also has in mind Young's tragedy, The Revenge (1721).

9 Refers to the dramatist John Hughes (1677-1720), author of The Siege of Damascus (1720).

10 Elijah Fenton (1683-1730) was the author of the tragedy, Mariamne (1723), a biblical tragedy based on the Herod-Salome story. In her edition of The Mysterious Mother, Janet A. Dolan suggests that Richard Cumberland's plays, The Mysterious Husband (1783), The Carmelite (1784), The Days of Yore (1796), and Joanna of Montfaucon (1800) show the influence of The Mysterious Mother in the field of Gothic drama. See: Janet A. Dolan. "Horace Walpole's The Mysterious Mother: A Critical Edition," Dissertation Abstracts International 31 (1971): 4115A-4116A (University of Arizona).

Appendix A: Walpole's Correspondence and Strawberry Hill

1. *The Castle of Otranto* in Walpole's Letters

[A decade prior to the writing of the first Gothic novel, Walpole's imagination was already reveling in the emotional pleasures of what he calls "gloomth." In a letter to Horace Mann, Walpole comments on his attraction to the "venerable barbarism" allowed by the Gothic. Walpole's building plans for Strawberry Hill are fully evident in his intention "of imprinting the gloomth of abbeys and cathedrals on one's house," a project he carried out in full before writing the novel. The fondness for "gloomth" would be translated from architectural to literary contexts in the writing of *The Castle of Otranto*. Citations from *The Correspondence of Horace Walpole*, ed. W. S. Lewis (New Haven: Yale UP, 1937-83).]

a. To Sir Horace Mann 27 April 1753. *Horace Walpole's Correspondence*, Vol. 20: 372.

I thank you a thousand times for thinking of procuring me some Gothic remains from Rome; but I believe there is no such thing there: I scarce remember any morsel in the true taste of it in Italy. Indeed, my dear Sir, kind as you are about it, I perceive you have no idea what Gothic is; you have lived too long amidst true taste, to understand venerable barbarism. You say, 'you suppose my garden is to be Gothic too.' That can't be; Gothic is merely architecture; and as one has a satisfaction of imprinting the gloomth of abbeys and cathedrals on one's house, so one's garden on the contrary is to be nothing but riant,[1] and the gaiety of nature.... I was going to tell you that my house is so monastic that I have a little hall decked with long saints in lean arched windows and with tapered columns, which we call the Paraclete,[2] in memory of Eloisa's cloister.[3]

---

1   Cheerful or causing laughter.
2   An advocate or intercessor, especially the Holy Spirit.
3   Peter Abelard's beloved, Eloïsa, retired to a convent after the lovers' separation. Walpole has in mind the gloom of her cloister as described in the opening lines of Alexander Pope's poem, "Eloïsa to Abelard" (1717). "In these deep solitudes and awful cells, / Where heavenly-pensive contemplation dwells, / And ever-musing melancholy reigns; / What means this tumult in a vestal's veins?"

[Walpole presented his friend, the poet Thomas Gray, with a first edition of the novel. Gray's playful thank you note gratified Walpole's sense of fun at perpetrating a sham translation from a sham medieval chronicler.]

b. From Thomas Gray to Walpole 30 December 1764. *Horace Walpole's Correspondence*, Vol. 14: 137.

I have received *The Castle of Otranto*, and return you my thanks for it. It engages our attention here, makes some of us cry a little, and all in general afraid to go to bed o'nights. We take it for a translation, and should believe it to be a true story, if it were not for St. Nicholas.

[Suffering from a cold, Walpole wryly compared his appearance to the skeletal monk encountered by Frederick in the chapel, one of the moments of high horror in the novel.]

c. To George Montagu 19 February 1765. *Horace Walpole's Correspondence*, Vol. 10: 147.

I have been dying of the worst and longest cold I ever had in my days, and have been blooded and taken James's powder to no purpose. I look almost like the skeleton that Frederic found in the oratory.

[Walpole gave a copy of *The Castle of Otranto* to his friend, the Reverend William Cole, having emerged from the disguise of the two pseudonyms under which the first edition had been published. He hopes that his "little story-book" composed "in the style of former centuries" will appeal to Cole's antiquarian tastes.]

d. To the Reverend William Cole 28 February 1765. *Horace Walpole's Correspondence*, Vol. 1: 85.

But though we love the same ages, you must excuse worldly me for preferring the romantic scenes of antiquity. If you will tell me how to send it, and are partial enough to me to read a profane work in the style of former centuries, I shall convey to you a little story-book, which I published some time ago, though not boldly with my own name; but it has succeeded so well, that I do not any longer entirely keep the secret: does the title, *The Castle of Otranto*, tempt you?

[Walpole's account of the origins of the novel in a partially-recollected dream experience reveals how closely interrelated the house he redecorated and the novel he wrote truly are. The walking portrait and the "gigantic hand in armour" come directly from his surroundings in the house at Strawberry Hill. The phrase "Gothic story" would become the subtitle of the second edition of *The Castle of Otranto*.]

e. To the Reverend William Cole 9 March 1765. *Horace Walpole's Correspondence*, Vol. 1: 88.

I had time to write but a short note with *The Castle of Otranto*, as your messenger called on me at four o'clock as I was going to dine abroad. Your partiality to me and Strawberry have I hope inclined you to excuse the wildness of the story. You will even have found some traits to put you in mind of this place. When you read of the picture quitting its panel, did you recollect the portrait of Lord Falkland all in white in my gallery?[1] Shall I even confess to you what was the origin of this romance? I waked one morning in the beginning of last June from a dream, of which all I could recover was, that I had thought myself in an ancient castle (a very natural dream for a head filled like mine with Gothic story) and that on the uppermost bannister of a great staircase I saw a gigantic hand in armour. In the evening I sat down and began to write, without knowing in the least what I intended to say or relate. The work grew on my hands, and I grew fond of it—add that I was very glad to think of anything rather than politics—In short I was so engrossed with my tale, which I completed in less than two months, that one evening I wrote from the time I had drunk my tea, about six o'clock, till half an hour after one in the morning, when my hand and fingers were so weary, that I could not hold the pen to finish the sentence, but left Matilda and Isabella talking, in the middle of a paragraph.

[The first readers of the novel were willing to believe that the work was a translation of a medieval manuscript, but among Walpole's friends, some saw the novel as a diversion or regression into absurdity from serious political embroilments over the dismissal of his cousin, Henry Seymour Conway, from royal favor. Scholars continue to debate the autobiographical and political subtext of *The Castle of Otranto*. George Augustus Selwyn was a celebrated parliamentary wit. George James Williams, known as "Gilly," was a friend and occasional guest at Strawberry Hill.]

---

1   The portrait that Walpole refers to as the model for the peripatetic picture of Ricardo is that of Lord Falkland (Sir Henry Cary), Lord Deputy of Ireland, by Van Somer.

f. George James Williams to George Augustus Selwyn 19 March 1765. Letter quoted in R. W. Ketton-Cremer, *Horace Walpole: A Biography*. Ithaca, NY: Cornell UP, 1964, 178. Source in J. H. Jesse, *George Selwyn and his Contemporaries* (1882).

How do you think that he [Walpole] has employed that leisure which his political frenzy[1] has allowed of? In writing a novel, entitled *The Castle of Otranto*, and such a novel, that no boarding-school miss of thirteen could get half through without yawning. It consists of ghosts and enchantments; pictures walk out of their frames, and are good company for half an hour together; helmets drop from the moon; and cover half a family. He says it was a dream, and I fancy one when he had some feverish disposition in him.

[Following the success of the deceptive first edition of the novel, Walpole emerged from behind his two pseudonyms to claim the authorship. He would not only add a second preface but openly declare the novel to be "Gothic" by attaching the adjective to the subtitle of the second edition.]

g. To the Marquess of Hertford [Francis Seymour Conway] 26 March 1765. *Horace Walpole's Correspondence*, Vol. 38: 525.

We are extremely amused with your wonderful histories of your Hyena in *Gévaudan*;[2] but our fox-hunters despise you: it is exactly the enchanted monster of old romances. If I had known its history a few months ago, I believe it would have appeared in *The Castle of Otranto*,—the success of which has, at last, brought me to own it, though the wildness of it made me terribly afraid; but it was comfortable to have it please so much, before any mortal suspected the author: indeed, it met with too much honour far, for at last it was universally believed to be Mr. Gray's. As all the first impression is sold, I am hurrying out another, with a new preface, which I will send you.

---

1   Refers to Walpole's involvement in parliamentary and royal politics. For a reading of *The Castle of Otranto* as an instance of personalized allegory surrounding the Conway affair, see John Samson, "Politics Gothicized: The Conway Incident and *The Castle of Otranto*," *Eighteenth-Century Life* 17 (1986): 145-153.

2   Walpole refers to the famous beast of Gévaudan, a region of France located in the southern province of Langue Doc (modern Lozère). The mysterious creature appeared suddenly in 1765 and gained notoriety by allegedly attacking and devouring fifty people. Walpole calls the beast a "hyena," but it was also called a "werewolf" or "loup-garou." For a full account of the sinister story see: Montague Summers, *The Werewolf*. New Hyde Park, NY: University Books, 1966. 235-236.

[Walpole repeated his account of the dream origins of the novel to William Mason and accepted his criticism that "the dialogue [was] too modern." Mason would be far more severe and far less tolerant of Walpole's "Gothic fancies" in his suggested revisions for *The Mysterious Mother*.]

h. To the Reverend William Mason 17 April 1765. *Horace Walpole's Correspondence*, Vol. 28: 6.

The unexpected and obliging favour of your letter I own gave me great satisfaction; I published *The Castle of Otranto* with the utmost diffidence and doubt of its success. Yet though it has been received much more favourably than I could flatter myself it would be, I must say your approbation is of another sort than general opinion.... Your praise is so likely to make me vain, that I oblige myself to recollect all ... the hurry in which it was composed; and its being begun without any plan at all, for though in the short course of its progress I did conceive some views, it was so far from being sketched out without any design at all, that it was actually commenced one evening, from the very imperfect recollection of a dream with which I had waked in the morning. It was begun and finished in less than two months, and then I showed it to Mr. Gray, who encouraged me to print it; this is the true history of it; and I cannot but be happy, Sir, that he and you have been pleased with it, yet it is as true, if you will give me leave to say so, that I think your friend judged rightly in pronouncing part of the dialogue too modern. I had the same idea of it, and I could, but such a trifle does not deserve it, point out other defects, besides some of which most probably I am not insensible.

[The letter in French to Marie de Vichy-Champrond, Marquise du Deffand contains Walpole's most passionate defense of his novel as he provides an artistic justification for "the spontaneous overflow of powerful feelings"[1] that stirred the composition of the first Gothic novel. By stating that he had openly broken with neoclassic standards of literary propriety and that he "had not written the book for the present age, which will endure nothing but *cold common sense*," Walpole took a defiant stance in favor of imagination over reason, insisting that "I have composed it in defiance of rules, of critics, and of philosophers."]

---

1   William Wordsworth, preface to the second edition of the *Lyrical Ballads* in *The Complete Poetical Works of William Wordsworth*, Boston: Houghton Mifflin, 1911, Vol. X, 9.

i. To Madame du Deffand 13 March 1767. *Horace Walpole's Correspondence*, Vol. 3: 260.

On a donc traduit mon *Château d'Otrante*, c'était apparement pour me donner un ridicule; à la bonne heure—tenez-vous au parti de n'en point parler; laissez aller les critiques; elles ne me fâcheront point; je ne l'ai point écrit pour ce siècle-ci, qui ne veut que de la *raison froide*. Je vous avoue, ma Petite, et vous m'en trouverez plus fol que jamais, que de tous mes ouvrages c'est l'unique où je me suis plu; j'ai laissé courir mon imagination; les visions et les passions m'échauffaient. Je l'ai fait en dépit des règles, des critiques, et des philosophes; et il me semble qu'il n'en vaille que mieux. Je suis même persuadé qu'à quelque temps d'ici, quand le goût reprendra sa place, que la philosophie occupe, mon pauvre Château trouvera des admirateurs: il en a actuellement chez nous; j'en de donner la troisième édition. Ce que je viens de dire n'est pas pour mandier votre suffrage; je vous ai constamment dit que vous ne l'aimeriez pas; vos visions sont d'un genre différent. Je ne suis pas tout à fait faché qu'on ait donné la seconde préface; cependant la prémiere réspond mieux à la fiction; j'ai voulu qu'elle passât pour ancienne, et presque tout le monde en fut la dupe. Je ne cherche pas querelle avec Voltaire, mais je dirai jusqu'à la mort, que notre Shakespeare est mille piques au-dessus. [*Translation*: So they translated my *Castle of Otranto*, apparently in order to ridicule me; wonderful!—please make it a point not to say anything about it; let critics be what they are; they will not anger me; I did not write the book for the present age, which seeks only *cold reaso*n. I confess to you, my dear (and you will think me madder than ever), that of all my works, this is the only one in which I found.pleasure; I let my imagination run free; visions and passions spurred me on. I did it in spite of the rules, the critics, and the philosophers; and the outcome seems to me to be so much the better for that very reason. I am even convinced that in the near future, when good taste returns to its proper place, which is now occupied by philosophy, my poor *Castle* will find admirers: we do have some among us at this time, for I am now publishing the third edition. I do not say this in order to rally your support: I told you from the beginning you would not like the book—your visions are of a different nature. I am not entirely displeased the translator selected the second preface. The first, however, is better fit for a work of fiction. I wanted it to have the appearance of an old text and almost everybody fell for it. I do not seek to quarrel with Voltaire, but I will say until I die that Shakespeare is a thousand leagues above him.]

[Having received from Hamilton two ornamented shields embossed with Perseus slaying the Gorgon, Medusa, Walpole joked about another inspirational dream like the giant hand in armor that had stimulated his Gothic fancies.]

j. To Sir William Hamilton 19 June 1774. *Horace Walpole's Correspondence*, Vol. 35: 420-421.

Now they are come, it will, which is very selfish, double my gratitude, for they are fine and most charming—nay, almost in too good taste, not to put my Gothic house to shame—I wish the Medusas could turn it to stone![1] ... I am going to hang them by the beautiful armour of Francis I and they will certainly make me dream of another *Castle of Otranto*.

[Walpole reacted strongly to the claim that Clara Reeve's novel, *The Old English Baron*, was an imitation of his *Castle of Otranto*. Her work contained a haunted apartment in a castle and a family ghost, but no scenes of genuine terror. The wild and monstrous supernaturalism of Walpole's novel would not be widely imitated until the Gothic fiction of the 1790s.]

k. To the Reverend William Mason 8 April 1778. *Horace Walpole's Correspondence*, Vol. 28: 381.

Have you seen *The Old English Baron*,[2] a Gothic story, professedly written in imitation of *Otranto*, but reduced to reason and probability! It is so probable, that any trial for murder at the Old Bailey would make a more interesting story. Mrs. Barbut's [sic] fragment[3] was excellent. This is a *caput mortuum* [dead head]. Adieu, I have not a quarter of a minute to say more.

---

1   Much of the "stone" of Strawberry Hill was not stone at all. Walpole kids or teases his own architectural artifices.
2   Reeve's novel was first published in 1777 under the title, *The Champion of Virtue*. In 1778, the novel reappeared as *The Old English Baron; A Gothic Story*. Reeve's novel is less an imitation of Walpole's Gothicism than a domestication, although her use of a haunted chamber is of incalculable importance to the development of the Gothic.
3   Walpole refers to Anna Laetitia Aiken Barbauld's fragmentary Gothic tale, "Sir Bertrand," published in 1773 in a collection of *Miscellaneous Pieces* (London: J. Johnson) written with her brother, Dr. John Aikin. The collection was introduced by an important essay in Gothic theory, "On the Pleasure Derived from Objects of Terror," which mentions *The Castle of Otranto* as "a very spirited modern attempt upon the same plan of mixed terror, adapted to the model of Gothic romance."

[Walpole again reacted to Clara Reeve's[1] criticism of the unrestrained supernaturalism of *The Castle of Otranto*, charging Reeve with the crime of dullness in her misuse of his Gothic narrative in *The Old English Baron*. Reeve had not so much "imitated" his novel as she had reduced his Gothicism to the insipidly didactic.]

1. To the Reverend William Cole 22 August 1778. *Horace Walpole's Correspondence*, Vol. 2: 110.

Chatterton[2] did abuse me under the title Baron of Otranto, but unluckily the picture is much more like Dr. Milles and Chatterton's own devotees than to me, who am but a recreant antiquary, and as the poor lad found by experience, did not swallow every fragment that was offered to me as antique; though that is a feature he has bestowed on me. I have seen too the criticism you mention on *The Castle of Otranto* in the preface to the *Engish Baron* [sic]. It is not at all oblique, but though mixed with high compliments, directly attacks the visionary part, which, says the author, or authoress, makes one laugh. I do assure you I have not had the smallest inclination to return that attack. It would even be ungrateful, for the work is a professed imitation of mine, only stripped of the marvellous; and so entirely stripped, except in one awkward attempt at a ghost or two, that it is the most insipid dull nothing you ever saw. It certainly does not make one laugh, for what makes one doze, seldom makes one merry.

[Even though his playwright friend, Robert Jephson, removed all of the supernatural machinery from his rescripted version of *The Castle of Otranto*, Walpole nevertheless approved of Jephson's dramatization of the novel as *The Count of Narbonne*, which was performed at Covent Garden in November 1781. Jephson's deletion of the first and final supernatural

---

1   Reeve's preface to *The Old English Baron* (1778) is devoted almost entirely to *The Castle of Otranto*. Reeve complained that because of Walpole's unrestrained use of the supernatural, the book "palls upon the mind (though it does not upon the ear); the reason is obvious, the machinery is so violent that it destroys the effect it is intended to excite." "Preface" to *The Old English Baron* in *Seven Masterpieces of Gothic Horror*, ed. Robert Donald Spector. New York: Bantam, 1963, 106.
2   Walpole refers to the poet Thomas Chatterton (1752-1770), author of "Poems Supposed to Have Been Written by Thomas Rowley," a fictitious fifteenth-century monk invented by Chatterton. He sent the poems to Walpole who was at first deceived by the forgery, then dismissive when he discovered the hoax. Walpole was later accused of being responsible for Chatterton's suicide.

events in the novel, the falling helmet and the colossal body of Alfonso exploding through the castle walls, apparently did not offend Walpole. Walpole remained indignant over Clara Reeve's purported imitation of *The Castle of Otranto, The Old English Baron*, a work unlike Jephson's play "totally void of imagination and interest."]

m. To Robert Jephson 27 January 1780. *Horace Walpole's Correspondence*, Vol. 41: 409-410.

I must again applaud your art and judgment, Sir, in having made so rational a play out of my wild tale: and where you have changed the arrangement of the incidents, you have applied them to great advantage. The characters of the mother and daughter you have rendered more natural, by giving jealousy to the mother, and more passion to the daughter. In short, you have both honoured and improved my outlines: my vanity is content, and truth enjoins me to do justice. Bishop Warburton in his additional notes to Pope's *Works* which I saw in print in his booksellers hands, though they have not yet been published, observed that the plan of *The Castle of Otranto* was regularly a drama (an intention I am sure I do not pretend to have conceived; nor indeed can I venture to affirm that I had any intention at all but to amuse myself—no, not even a plan, till some pages were written). You, Sir, have realized his idea and yet I believe the Bishop would be surprised to see how well you have succeeded. One cannot be quite ashamed of one's follies, if genius condescends to adopt, and put them to a sensible use. Miss Aickin[1] [sic] flattered me by stooping to tread in my eccentric steps. Her *Fragment*, though but a specimen, showed her talent for imprinting terror. I cannot compliment the author of *The Old English Baron*, professedly written in imitation, but as corrective of *The Castle of Otranto*. It was totally void of imagination and interest; had scarce any incidents; and though it condemned the marvellous, admitted a ghost—I suppose the author thought a tame ghost might come within the laws of probability.

[Walpole writes to Hannah More concerning what he regards as an enthusiastic misreading of his novel by Ann Cromartie Yearsley, "the Bristol Milkwoman" whose poems were signed "Lactilla" ("the milkmaid"). Yearsley named herself "Lactilla," in keeping with the poetic tradition of the century, particularly for women, of adopting a classical per-

---

1   Another reference to Anna Laetitia Aikin Barbauld and her essay "On the Pleasure Derived from Objects of Terror."

sona in one's work and within one's literary circle. Walpole's remark dismisses her right to such a persona, derived from Virgil's *Eclogues*, saying she is a *real* milk-maid and not a candidate for the upper-class group of poets who wrote pastorals. See her poem "To the Honorable H_____E W_____E, On Reading the Castle of Otranto, December 1784." With mock severity, Walpole teases Hannah More for causing in Ann Yearsley "a hurly burly in this poor woman's head."]

n. To Hannah More 13 November 1784. *Horace Walpole's Correspondence*, Vol. 31: 219.

She must remember that she is a Lactilla,[1] not a Pastora, and is to tend real cows, not Arcadian sheep. What! if I should go a step farther, dear madam, and take the liberty of reproving you for putting into this poor woman's [Ann Yearsley's] hands such a frantic thing as *The Castle of Otranto*? It was fit for nothing but the age for which it was written, an age in which much was known; that required only to be amused, nor cared whether its amusements were conformable to truth and the models of good sense; that could not be spoiled; was in no danger of being too credulous; and rather wanted to be brought back to imagination, than to be led astray by it—but you will have made a hurly-burly in this poor woman's head which it cannot develop and digest.

[From a sketch he received from Lady Craven, Walpole was pleased to discover that there was an actual Castle of Otranto, a fact that gratified his antiquarian passions.]

o. To Lady Craven 27 November 1786. *Horace Walpole's Correspondence*, Vol. 42: 176.

Well, while I was in this quandary, I received a delightful drawing[2] of The Castle of Otranto— but still provokingly without any address.... I give your Ladyship a million of thanks for the drawing, which was really a very valuable gift to me. I did not even know that there was a Castle of Otranto. When the story was finished, I looked into the map of the

---

1   The poetic persona of Ann Cromartie Yearsley, the milk lady of Bristol. For a full discussion of her reading of Walpole's novel, see: Madeleine Kahn, "'A by-stander often sees more of the game than those that play': Ann Yearsley Reads *The Castle of Otranto*," *Making History: Textuality and the Forms of Eighteenth-Century Culture* special issue of *Bucknell Review* 42.1 (1998) 59–78. ed. Greg Clingham] 42:1 (1998): 59–78.

2   Willey Reveley's drawing of the real Castle of Otranto in 1785 appeared in the sixth edition of the novel published, by Bodoni in 1791.

kingdom of Naples for a well-sounding name, and that of Otranto was very sonorous.

[Walpole tells Hamilton how he came to name his haunted castle during the writing of the novel and again reveals his pleasure at learning that there was and still is a castle by that "well-sounding" name.]

p. To Count Anthony Hamilton 17 January 1788. *Horace Walpole's Correspondence*, Vol. 35: 435–436.

In a word, a person not long ago brought me from Italy a drawing of the real Castle of Otranto and said it had actually been taken of the spot in 1785. When I wrote my fantastic tale, I did not know there existed a castle at that place, but looked into the map of Naples for a name, and adopted Otranto as well-sounding.... I do wish that you would be so kind as to inform yourself, and then me, whether there is in fact an actual castle.

2. *The Mysterious Mother* in Walpole's Letters

[Walpole's aristocratic French friend, Madame du Deffand, tactfully accepted an opportunity to read *The Mysterious Mother* for its powerful depiction of the passions, but her real attitude toward the drama of incest cannot be ascertained from her response as it is evident from her letter of 2 March 1768 that she had not yet read the play. Like several other correspondents who responded to the play in vague or general terms, she may not have wished to jeopardize a friendship she cherished by responding directly to its forbidden themes and Walpole's indulgence in passion for passion's sake. Citations from *The Correspondence of Horace Walpole*, Ed. W.S. Lewis (New Haven: Yale UP, 1937–83).]

a. From Madame du Deffand 2 March 1768. *Horace Walpole's Correspondence*, Vol. 4: 32.

Je n'ai point deviné le sujet de votre tragédie, vous me feriez plaisir de me l'apprendre; si vous vouliez en traduire quelques scènes et me les envoyer vous me feriez beaucoup de plaisir. Je n'aime point les Héloïses,[1] ni l'ancienne ni la moderne; leurs tendresses, leurs passions ne sont point

---

1   Madame du Deffand refers to the medieval lovers, Eloise and Abelard, as well as to the heroine of Jean-Jacques Rousseau's 1761 novel, *Julie ou la Nouvelle Héloïse*, characters beset by fatal sexual passion.

de mon genre. [*Translation*: I have not been able to guess what the subject of your tragedy is and I would be delighted if you could enlighten me about it. I would be thrilled if you could translate a few scenes and send them to me. I do not like Héloïse at all, whether ancient or modern (be it the ancient one or the modern one), her endearments, her passions are not my style.]

b. To Madame du Deffand 11 March 1768. *Horace Walpole's Correspondence*, Vol. 4: 40.

Mais ce que je trouve détestable c'est le langage,[1] qui est partout d'un prosaïque bas et même rampant. Ma proprie tragédie ade bien plus grands défauts, mais au moins elle ne resemble pas au ton compassé et réglé du siècle. Je n'ai pas le temps de vous en parler. Il ne vous plairit pas assurément; il n'y a pas de beaux sentiments. Il n'y que des passions sans enveloppe, des crimes, des repentirs, et des horreurs. Il y a des hardiesses qui sont à moi, et des scènes trés faibles, et trés longues qui sont à moi aussi; du gothique que ne comporterait pas votre théâtre, et des illusions qui devraient faire gran effet et qui peut-etrê n'en feraient aucun. Je crois qu'il y a beaucoup plus de mauvais que de bon, et je saissurement quidepuis le premier acte jusqu'à la denière scene l'intéret languit au lieu d'augmenter; peut-il [y] avoir un plus gran défaut? [*Translation*: But what I find detestable is the language which, throughout, is basely, even grovel-ingly, prosaic. My own tragedy has much larger flaws but at least it does not resemble this century's prim and conventional tone. I do not have time to dwell on this. You would assuredly not like it; beautiful feelings and emotions are nowhere to be found. There is nothing but unveiled passions, crimes, repentance, and horrors. One finds in it elements of boldness that are mine, very weak and very long scenes, that are also mine, a kind of Gothic which would not be found in your theater, and illusions which should result in great effects but may end up having none. I believe that there is much more bad than good, and I strongly feel that from the first act until the last scene interest languishes instead of increasing; can there be a worse flaw?]

[Despite its controversial subject matter, Walpole gave some serious con-

---

1   Walpole refers to a previous letter of Madame du Deffand of 30 January 1768 (*Corre-spondence* 40:18) in which she had praised the language of the play *L'Honnete Criminel* [*The Honest Criminal*] (1767) by Charles Georges Fenouillot de Falbaire de Quingley (1727–1800).

siGeration to the stage production of *The Mysterious Mother*. But the play
was to remain a closet drama, a play suitable for private readings rather
than public performances, throughout his lifetime. The first of such private readings at Strawberry Hill is described in the letter. A later Gothic
drama involving incest, Shelley's *The Cenci*, would undergo a similar
exclusion from the stage.]

c. To George Montagu 15 April 1768. *Horace Walpole's Correspondence*,
Vol. 19: 259.

I have finished my tragedy, but as you would not bear the subject, I will
say no more of it, but that Mr. Chute, who is not easily pleased, likes it,
and Gray, who is still more difficult, approves it. I am not yet intoxicated
enough with it, to think it would do for the stage, though I wish to see it
acted: but as Mrs. Pritchard leaves the stage next month, I know nobody
who could play the Countess; nor am I disposed to expose myself to the
impertinences of that jackanapes Garrick,[1] who lets nothing appear but
his own wretched stuff, or that of creatures still duller, who suffer him to
alter their pieces as he pleases. I have written an epilogue in character for
the Clive,[2] which she would speak admirably—but I am not so sure she
would like to speak it. Mr. Conway, Lady Ailsbury, Lady Lyttleton and
Miss Rich are to come hither the day after tomorrow, and Mr. Conway
and I are to read my play to them, for I have not strength enough to go
through the whole alone.

[Mason voluntarily submitted to Walpole a number of revisions to the
text of *The Mysterious Mother*, apparently believing that the play was unfit
for public display without an excision of the Countess's willful incest.
Mason believed that the Countess's anguish in Walpole's version of the
play could never arouse pity in the audience because her incest was lustful, selfish, and intentional. He amended the play accordingly to depict
the incest as accidental, and like the incest of Oedipus, involuntary.
Mason also substituted jealousy for sexual lust in the motivation of the
Countess. Mason attached to this letter an enclosure ("Alterations Proposed in *The Mysterious Mother*") outlining the deletions and alterations
that he thought would render the Countess a pitiful character and separate her incest from her conscious designs. In his edition of the play,

---

1 Walpole refers to the great actor-manager, David Garrick (1717-1779).
2 Refers to Catherine "Kitty" Clive, the famous comic actress who lived at "Little"
   Strawberry Hill, a small house adjoining Walpole's property.

Montague Summers observed that "Mason's alterations, although highly interesting as illustrative of his dramatic theory, are generally superfluous and sometimes distinctly for the worse. The fact that the Countess commits incest at the moment she has lost a beloved husband may seem strange but is psychologically true and one of the keenest touches in the play."[1] Mason justified his proposed substitution of jealousy for concupiscence in the headnote to his revisions.]

d. From the Reverend William Mason 8 May 1769. *Horace Walpole's Correspondence*, Vol. 28: 10.

Since I came hither I have read your tragedy three or four times over with a good deal of attention, and as the costume, the characters and many of the sentiments, etc., please me highly, I cannot help wishing that capital defect in the dénouement was amended according to the scheme I proposed to you. To prove the thing feasible, I send you a sketch of such alterations as I think necessary.... The following alterations are founded upon what I would suppose an axiom, viz.; That incest is a crime of so horrid a nature that whoever had committed it even ignorantly and by mistake, would have the same sensations of remorse, feel them in the same degree, and express their contrition in the same manner as if they had done it wilfully. If the person in question was a woman of strong natural sense, cultivated understanding, and unaffected piety, she would forget or overlook the only thing that could alleviate her despair, the thought of its being not intended, especially if ill-grounded jealousy had led her into so dreadful an error; for the consequences of the fact being full as terrible, an ingenuous and virtuous mind would still feel the sting of conscience in the severest degree. If this be allowed, it will follow that the very few alterations proposed to be made, are all that are necessary to make in the following scenes, in order to give the principal character a claim to our pity, without diminishing our terror; and to remove that disgust and indignation which she raises at the present, in spite of all the dramatic art which the author has used to prevent it.

[Walpole wrote a private response firmly rejecting the proposed change in the Countess's character and motive. Walpole's response to Mason's "Suggested Alterations" was written on the back of Mason's letter to Walpole of 8 May 1769. *Horace Walpole's Correspondence*, Vol. 28: 10]

---

1   Montague Summers, "A Note upon Mason's Critical Remarks," *The Castle of Otranto* and *The Mysterious Mother*, 277. Summers's edition also prints Mason's alterations (268–271).

e. I did not adopt these alterations because they would have totally destroyed my object, which was to exhibit a character whose sincere penitence was not degraded by superstitious bigotry. The introduction of jealousy was utterly foreign to the subject—and though in my original it is very improbable that a wife on the very night of a beloved husband's death would think of going to bed with her own son, it would be at least as improbable that she should suspect her husband would after an absence of many months think of an intrigue with his maid on the very night of his return. Jealousy would reduce the Countess to a very hacked character, instead of being one quite new on the stage.

[In a compromising tone, Walpole assured Mason of the usefulness of his alterations, and further, that he was correcting his own copy by them, but Walpole made no such emendations. Despite Mason's urging, Walpole had decided to abandon his original desire to see *The Mysterious Mother* publicly performed.]

f. To the Reverend William Mason 11 May 1769. *Horace Walpole's Correspondence*, Vol. 28: 16.

I thank you for myself, not for my play. I care little about the latter, in comparison of the satisfaction I receive from your friendship. I cannot think the play deserved the pains you have bestowed on it, but I am very willing to flatter myself that you felt some kindness for the author: and I doubt I am one of those selfish parents that love themselves better than their offspring. I cannot think of the stage—I believe from pride—and I am weary of printing and publishing—I suppose from vanity, at least I am sure I have no better reasons for not making all possible use of your alterations, with which I am so much pleased that I shall correct my own copy by them. I am astonished to see with how few lines you have been able totally to change the canvas of a whole play, a play totally defective in the plan, and I believe not much better in the conduct, which you would not exert your judgment, or rather your chemistry to prove; for I must repeat how surprised I am at the *solution* you have made with so little trouble. I own too my own want of judgment: I believe I was so pleased with what ought to have prevented my attempting the subject, which was the singularity of it. Unfrequent crimes are as little the business of tragedy, as singular characters are of comedy; it is inviting the town to correct a single person. You see Sir, I am far from being incorrigible, on the contrary, I am willing to be corrected; but as Mr. Gray could tell you, I cannot correct myself. I write I neither know how nor why, and always make worse what I try to amend. I have begged him a thousand times to no purpose to correct trifles I have written, and which I really could not improve myself. I am not unreasonable or so impudent as to ask the same favour of you, Sir; but I accept with great thankfulness what you have voluntarily been so good as to do for me; and should *The Mysterious Mother* ever be performed when I am dead, it will owe to you its presentation.

[Copies of the play circulated *sub rosa* among Walpole's friends and guests at Strawberry Hill. Having acquired a copy, George Montagu organized a sort of impromptu evening of readers' theater. Among "the boys" who read parts in this private performance was Lt. Colonel John Burgoyne.]

g. From George Montagu to Walpole 18 September 1769. *Horace Walpole's Correspondence*, Vol. 10: 295.

The boys found your tragedy of the *Mysterious Mother*, and boys as they are they had no patience till they finished it and we read the acts amongst us, for my lungs could not Pritchard it through.[1] They left off quinze, gambling and claret, and were the Florians of your play; the churchman indeed looked grave, but they threw him his Ten Commandments and a bottle of port and amused themselves without. They would have got it by heart. However, a few similes they have retained, and cap with one another some of the lines that struck them most.

[Somewhat chagrined at the unauthorized performance, Walpole implored Montagu to keep the play a secret. He fears that the contemporary low condition of the English stage would not be able to "digest" his tragedy.]

h. To George Montagu 16 October 1769. *Horace Walpole's Correspondence*, Vol. 10: 298.

I am sorry the boys got at my tragedy. I beg you would keep it under lock and key; it is not at all food for the public—at least not till *I am food for worms, good Percy*.[2] Nay, it is not an age to encourage anybody, that has the least vanity to step forth. There is a total extinction of all taste; our

---

1   A reference to the forceful acting style of the actress Hannah Pritchard (1711–1768), who had excelled on the London stage as Lady Macbeth.

2   Walpole cleverly misquotes Hotspur's dying speech which is completed by Prince Hal in Shakespeare's *Henry IV*, Part I, V. iv. 85–86:

HOTSPUR.   And food for—

PRINCE HAL.   For worms, brave Percy.

authors are vulgar, gross, illiberal; the theatre swarms with wretched translations, and ballad operas, and we have nothing new but improving abuse.

[Walpole commented on his success in maintaining tragic suspense in *The Mysterious Mother* in a letter to Robert Jephson, whose *The Count of Narbonne*, a dramatic version of *The Castle of Otranto*, would feature certain elements of Walpole's tragedy. Walpole apparently felt that he had succeeded with the tragic character of the Countess, but had not attained it with Adeliza, the child of incest.]

i. To Robert Jephson late February 1775. *Horace Walpole's Correspondence*, Vol. 41: 291, 296, 297.

Yet how many capital ingredients in that story! [Otway's *Don Carlos*] [1] Tenderness, cruelty, heroism, policy, pity and terror. Why I gave up this fruitful canvas, was merely because the passion is incestuous as is most unfortunately that of my *Mysterious Mother*, though a different point of time, and that of Carlos a pardonable and not a digusting one. If there is any merit in my play, I think it is in interrupting the spectator's fathoming the *whole* story till the last, and in making every scene tend to advance the catastrophe. These arts are mechanic, I confess; but at least they are meritorious as the scrupulous delicacy of the French. In all my tragedy, Adeliza contents me the least.

[Lady Diana Beauclerc (also spelled "Beauclerk") made seven drawings for Walpole's play. Pleased and impressed with these illustrations, Walpole placed them in a special cabinet at Strawberry Hill.]

j. From Lady Diana Beauclerc 16 December 1775. *Horace Walpole's Correspondence*, Vol. 41: 321.

I send you the drawings, but I find the bistre[2] will not take well on the old cards. The bistre I have now seems of a browner tint also. I am going to town for the night. Have you any commands?

[The Beauclerc drawings for *The Mysterious Mother* won Walpole's praise.]

---

1   Refers to Thomas Otway's sentimental tragedy in rhymed verse, *Don Carlos* (1676).
2   Brown soot pigmentation used to create a dark brown color.

k. To Lady Ossory 27 December 1775. *Horace Walpole's Correspondence*, Vol. 32: 289.

Just at present I suppose I am the vainest creature in the universe: Lady Di has drawn three scenes of the tragedy, which, if the subject were a quarter as good as the drawings, would make me a greater genius than Shakespear, as she is superior to Guido [Reni] and Salvator Rosa.[1] Such figures! such dignity! such simplicity!

[The Beauclerc Cabinet or Closet displayed all seven illustrations for *The Mysterious Mother*. Walpole was devoted to both Lady Di and to her artistic skill and often remarked on it to close friends.]

l. To the Reverend William Mason 18 February 1776. *Horace Walpole's Correspondence*, Vol. 28: 244.

Lady Di Beauclerc has made seven large drawings in soot-water (her first attempt of the kind) for scenes of my *Mysterious Mother*. Oh! such drawings! Guido's [Reni] grace, Albano's children, Poussin's expression, Salvator's [Rosa] boldness in landscape and Andrea Sacchi's[2] simplicity of composition might perhaps have equalled them had they wrought altogether very fine.

[William Mason continued to urge both his revisions of the tragedy and its preparation for the stage, but Walpole had made up his mind to keep the play from the public. He gives his reasons for retaining privacy to Mason in this letter.]

m. To the Reverend William Mason 16 March 1778. *Horace Walpole's Correspondence*, Vol. 28: 371

You accuse me very unjustly of neglecting your alteration of my tragedy. I always thought it magic, to be effected by so few words, and should have adopted it, had I ever had thoughts of its being represented; but nothing could induce me to venture it on the stage, not from superabundant modesty, but from the abusive spirit of the times. I have no notion

---

1   Guido Reni (1575-1642) and Salvator Rosa (1615-1673) were two of Walpole's favorite Italian painters.

2   More of Walpole's favorite Renaissance painters: Francesco Albano (1578-1660), Nicholas Poussin (1594-1665), and Andrea Sacchi (1599-1661).

of presenting one's self cooly to a savage mob to be torn to pieces—and you know I am as tender of my friends as of myself. I think this country at present in every light the sink of Europe, void of taste and of everything ingenuous.

[Walpole's close friend, Horace Mann, read *The Mysterious Mother* and praised it for its tragic intensity. Walpole responded with a reassertion of its unfitness for public viewing and with another expression of pride and pleasure in the Beauclerc Closet at Strawberry Hill.]

n. To Sir Horace Mann 31 October 1779. *Horace Walpole's Correspondence*, Vol. 24: 524.

Your last letter was so full of encomiums on my tragedy, that, veteran author as I am, it made me blush. But I recollected your partiality, and then I accepted the motive with pleasure, though I must decline the exaggerations. It is plain that I am sincerely modest about it, for I not only never thought of its appearing on stage, but have not published it. It has indeed received greater honour than any of its superiors, for Lady Di Beauclerc has drawn seven scenes of it, that would be full worthy of the best of Shakespeare's plays—such drawings that Salvator Rosa and Guido could not surpass their expression and beauty. I have built a closet on purpose for them here at Strawberry Hill. It is called the *Beauclerc Closet*; and whoever sees the drawings, allows that no description comes up to their merit—and then, they do not shock and disgust like the original, the tragedy.

[With two pirated editions of the play forthcoming, Walpole decided to have *The Mysterious Mother* published by the London publisher, Dodsley, an act which would give him control over the circulation of copies.]

o. To Henry Seymour Conway 28 May 1781. *Horace Walpole's Correspondence*, Vol. 39: 372.

For my own play, I was going to publish it in my own defence, as a spurious edition was advertised here, besides one in Ireland. My advertisement has overlaid the former for the present, and that tempts me to suppress mine, as I have a thorough aversion to its appearance. Still, I think I shall produce it in the dead of summer, that it may be forgotten by winter, for I could not bear having it the subject of conversation in a full town. It is printed; so I can let it steal out in the midst of the first event that engrosses the public; and it is not quite a novelty, I have no fear but it will be stillborn, if it is twin with any babe that squalls and makes much noise.

[Guests at Strawberry Hill often reported on showings of the Beauclerc Closet.]

p. From Mary Hamilton to Lady Anne Connolly 6 October 1783. *Horace Walpole's Correspondence*, Vol. 31: 18

[On 5 July 1783] I was summoned to accompany Mrs. Walsingham and Mrs. Boyle to Strawberry Hill at half-past one.... Mr. Burke, son of the famous Burke[1] was there. Mr. Walpole was so obliging as to show us pictures, busts, drawings of Lady Di Beauclerc, not to forget the house, which is all Gothic, and the little room built on purpose for Lady D.'s drawings for his play of *The Mysterious Mother*.

[Mary Hamilton was shown the Beauclerc drawings and immediately noted the affecting contrast between their interesting style and the horridness of Walpole's subject.]

q. From Mary Hamilton's Journal for 1784. *Horace Walpole's Correspondence*, Vol. 31: 216.

The whole style of this house is true Gothic, every room, boudoir, closet, gallery, etc. has painted glass windows, it is the most perfect thing of the kind in England, I believe I may say in Europe. ... Mr. Walpole was particularly attentive to me and gave himself much trouble, as he saw I enjoyed real pleasure in looking at the pictures and other curious and beautiful works of art. He was also so obliging as to show me again (for I was here last year) the beautiful drawings of Lady Di Beauclerk, which are in a closet built on purpose, and which he only opens for his most particular friends. These drawings are subjects taken from a play he wrote of *The Mysterious Mother*. A tragedy I once heard read by Mr. Tighe. The story is the most horrible to be conceived, but these drawings, though they recall to mind the horrid subject, are most affectingly interesting.

---

1   Edmund Burke (1729-1797), parliamentarian and author of a treatise on the sublime.

[Farrington's viewing of the Beauclerc Closet suggests that Walpole reserved such displays for special guests and visitors to Strawberry Hill.]

r. Joseph Farrington's Anecdotes of Walpole, 1793-1797, 21 July 1793 *Horace Walpole's Correspondence*, 15: 318.

Went on to Strawberry Hill. Lord Orford showed us the house, which we had sufficient time to view at our leisure. We saw the small room in which are Lady Di Beauclerk's designs for Lord Orford's play of *The Mysterious Mother*—also his China closet, neither of which are shown but seldom.

[Unauthorized excerpts from *The Mysterious Mother* had appeared in Woodfall's *Public Advertiser*, infuriating Walpole who moved to suppress any further publication of parts of the play.]

s. To Henry Sampson Woodfall 8 November 1783. *Horace Walpole's Correspondence*, Vol. 42: 85.

Mr. H. Walpole sends his compliments to Mr. Woodfall, and does entreat him to print no more of *The Mysterious Mother*, which it is a little hard on the author to see retailed without his consent. Mr. Walpole is willing to make Mr. Woodfall amends for any imaginary benefit he might receive from the impression, though as copies of the play have been spread, there can be little novelty in it; and at this time the public must be curious to see more interesting articles than scenes of an old tragedy on a disgusting subject, which the author thinks so little worthy of being published, that after the first small impression, he has endeavoured to suppress it as much as lies in his power, and which he assures Mr. Woodfall he would not suffer to be represented on the stage, if any manager was injudicious enough to think of it.

[Through Walker, Walpole discovered that a pirated Dublin edition of *The Mysterious Mother* had been advertised. He continued his campaign to quash all such unauthorized publications.]

t. To Joseph Cooper Walker 5 August 1789. *Horace Walpole's Correspondence*, Vol. 42: 255.

I mention these objections, Sir, as they occur to me, but with the utmost respect to the noble lady who suggested the opinion, and who I find, like you, Sir, is too favourable to my tragedy, which I did not intend should become so public, when I imprudently printed a small number of copies of it. The subject is inexcusably disgusting, and I can only prove that I am sensible of that and other faults, by suppressing it as far as is now in my power.

[Walpole received the unsolicited assistance of Lord Charlemont in stopping the Irish edition, but spurious copies were already circulating. Therefore, he asked Lord Charlemont to abandon his efforts at suppression.]

u. To Lord Charlemont 17 February 1791. *Horace Walpole's Correspondence*, Vol. 42: 308.

How can I thank your Lordship as I ought for interesting yourself, and of yourself, to save me a little mortification, which I deserve, and should deserve more, had I the vanity to imagine that my printing a few copies of my disgusting tragedy would occasion different and surreptitious editions of it. Mr. Walker has acquainted me, my Lord, that your Lordship has most kindly interposed to prevent a bookseller of Dublin from printing an edition of *The Mysterious Mother* without my consent—and with the conscious dignity of great mind, your Lordship has not even hinted to me the graciousness of that favour. How have I merited such condescending goodness, my Lord? … In truth, my Lord, it is too late now to hinder copies of my play from being spread: it has appeared here both whole and in fragments; and to prevent a spurious one, I was forced to have some printed myself; therefore, if I consent to an Irish edition, it is from no vain desire of diffusing the performance. Indeed, my good Lord, I have lived too long not to have divested myself both of vanity and affected modesty. I have not existed to pass seventy-three without having discovered the futility and triflingness of my own talents—and at the same time it would be impertinent to pretend to think that there is no merit in the execution of a tragedy, on which I have been so much flattered; though I am sincere in condemning the egregious absurdity of selecting a subject so improper for the stage, and even offensive to private readers—but I have said too much on a personal theme; and therefore, after repeating a million of thanks to your Lordship for the honour of your personal interposition, I will beg your Lordship, if you please, to signify to the bookseller that you withdraw your prohibition.

[Having failed to suppress spurious editions of *The Mysterious Mother*, Walpole finally decided to include the play in his collected works, realizing that further attempts to stop publication would only lead to the distortion and ruin of his original text.]

v. To Sylvester Douglas 15 February 1792. *Horace Walpole's Correspondence*, Vol. 42: 351.

A performance, in which I am conscious of so many faults, and the subject of which is so disgusting, it is very indulgent in any reader to excuse; nor can the favour of such able judges as you, Sir, and the Duc de Nivernois, reconcile me to my own imprudence in letting it go out of my own hands—but having fallen into that slip of vanity, it is too late now to plead modesty, and there is less affectation, I hope, in obeying you both, than in troubling you with more words about a trifle. I have therefore the honour, Sir, of offering you a correct copy, which I had printed some years ago to prevent a spurious edition, and as I succeeded, I did not publish mine. The edition printed in Ireland lately is less exact. And though I stopped it for some time, it was to no purpose.

[Somewhat bitterly, Walpole commented to Mary Berry, the editor of his *Collected Works*, on the mocking poem by John Courtenay "Letter the Seventh, Naples, April 16 1793," in *The Present State of the Manners, Arts, Politics of France and Italy; in a Series of Poetical Epistles from Paris, Rome, and Naples, in 1792 and 1793; Addressed to Robert Jephson, Esq.*]

w. To Mary Berry 17 April 1794. *Horace Walpole's Correspondence*, Vol. 12: 94.

Mr. Courtney [sic] has published some epistles in rhyme, in which he has honoured me with a dozen lines (and which are really some of the best in the whole set) in ridicule of my writings.... If I were not as careless as I am about literary fame, still this censure would be harmless indeed, for, except the exploded story of Chatterton, of which I washed myself as white as snow, Mr. Courtney [sic] falls on my *choice* of subjects (as of *Richard III* and *The Mysterious Mother*) and not on the execution, though I fear there is enough to blame in the texture of them—but this new piece of criticism, or whatever it is, made me laugh, as I am offered up on the tomb of my poor mad nephew,[1] who is celebrated for one of his last frantic acts.

---

1 Walpole refers to George Walpole, Third Earl of Orford, who suffered from periods of insanity.

3. The Little Gothic Villa at Strawberry Hill

In 1747, Walpole purchased a small house on the upper Thames above Richmond near the village of Twickenham. The house was called "Strawberry Hill" and was an absolutely ordinary and featureless rectangle, described by Walpole's biographer, R.W. Ketton-Cremer, as "a shapeless unsymmetrical building without any architectural interest."[1] By 1763, the year before the publication of *The Castle of Otranto*, Walpole had transformed this prosaic and nondescript building ("the shapeless little box") into "a little Gothic castle ... built to please my own taste, and in some degree to realize my own visions."[2] With the assistance of his skilled friends, John Chute, Richard Bentley, and Thomas Pitt, and guided by his own antiquarian capriciousness, Walpole achieved a fantasy building whose sole function was to gratify the imagination of a medieval dilettante, "a monument to a mood" and "an admirable aid to self-dramatization."[3] On the exterior, he added a long gallery with a cloister beneath it, several towers of disparate proportions, the large round tower and the slender Beauclerc tower, to create a wild irregularity of skyline to disturb and delight the approaching visitor; canvas battlements with machicolations designed to give a glowering and beetling effect; and grounds, gardens, and gates intended to impart an atmosphere of barbaric enclosure and Gothic "gloomth." In perpendicular or high Gothic, the pointed arch and flying buttress had had necessary structural functions, but Walpole favored an ornamental ideal of the Gothic meant to please and excite the passion for "gloomth" and to stir the imagination of heads like his own that were "filled with Gothic story." The sole guiding principle, aside from the criterion of self-indulgence, in the Gothic refabrication of Strawberry Hill seemed to be exuberant irregularity or "Sharawaggi" as it was called in Walpole's day by designers whose deliberate aim was asymmetry, disproportion, and disharmony of parts.

---

1   R.W. Ketton-Cremer, *Horace Walpole: A Biography*. Ithaca, NY: Cornell UP, 1964, 24. Chapter VIII, "The First Decade at Strawberry Hill (1747–57)," contains detailed accounts of the interior and exterior Gothification of the plain country house. For other excellent descriptions of the construction and content of the little Gothic villa, see: Wilmarth S. Lewis, *The Genesis of Strawberry Hill*, New York: Metropolitan Museum Studies, 1934; Sir Kenneth Clark, "Ruins and Rococo: Strawberry Hill," in *The Gothic Revival: An Essay in the History of Taste*. Harmondsworth, Middlesex, UK: Penguin, 1962, 34–52; and Walpole's own inventory, *Description of Strawberry Hill* in the *Works*.

2   Horace Walpole, *Description of Strawberry Hill, Works II*, 398.

3   Sir Kenneth Clark, "Ruins and Rococo: Strawberry Hill," 37, 45.

Strawberry Hill, Round Tower and skyline, 1997.
Photograph by F. S. Frank

The interior of Strawberry Hill was redecorated with the same asymmetrical, or Sharawaggi spirit in mind, and contained several Gothic chambers and weird relics, which would later assume a life of their own in the novel. The compartments of Strawberry Hill, like the novel, featured a "nightmare juxtaposition of unrelated objects."[1] An armoury, a Gothic staircase, medieval chapel and oratory, dim passageways, vaulted ceilings, and imposing cabinets and bookcases lining the multi-colored rooms had sufficient supernatural décor to cause one astonished visitor to exclaim of Walpole's folly, "Lord God! Jesus! what a house!," precisely the response that Walpole was after. Special spaces such as the Holbein Chamber and the closet containing Lady Diana Beauclercc's drawings for *The Mysterious Mother* were reserved for special occasions and guests. Because he had used so much artificial stone[2] in the construction of his Gothic mockup, Walpole's whimsical Gothic edifice of cardboard, plaster, and lath inspired many quips in fashionable circles. "Horrie," the

---

1   Ketton-Cremer, *Horace Walpole: A Biography*, 175.
2   Called "lithodipra" in the eighteenth century, this sham stone was manufactured and marketed in a variety of shapes for the rapid construction of artificial ruins and prefabricated medieval dilapidation.

Strawberry Hill, South Front.

Strawberry Hill, North Front, 1784.

Strawberry Hill, East Front.

joke went round, had already outlived four sets of battlements. It might be said that the first Gothic novel was being written long before Walpole set his nightmare to paper, for as Strawberry Hill evolved, the literary fantasy grew directly out of the architectural fact. But despite the obvious synergy between the house's picturesque gloom and the first Gothic novel's places and equipment of terror, modern scholarship has been oddly reluctant to follow up on Ketton-Cremer's comment about the close relationship between the castle that Walpole built and the novel that he wrote. "In hours of reverie, in solitary musings late at night, and especially in dreams," wrote Ketton-Cremer, "the flimsy materials which surrounded him—the fretted wood, the moulded plaster, the painted wallpaper—assumed the solidity of ponderous stone: and his narrow passage-ways and snug chambers began to swell into the echoing vaults and sombre galleries of Otranto.... His fantasies found concrete form; the little house called Strawberry Hill was fast assuming the splendours of the Castle of Otranto. "[1] The enormous hand in armor, the "long labyrinth of darkness" through which Isabella scurries, and even the peregrinating painting of Ricardo, Manfred's usurping ancestor, were all part of the daily scene of Strawberry Hill and readily available to Walpole's imagination when he came to write *The Castle of Otranto*.

---

1   Ketton-Cremer, *Horace Walpole: A Biography*, 163

Strawberry Hill, the Prior's Garden and North Front.

Strawberry Hill, staircase and bannister.

Strawberry Hill, the Chapel or Tribune.

Strawberry Hill, gallery.

Appendix B: Responses and Reactions

1. Three Early Reviews of *The Castle of Otranto*

[The first review of *The Castle of Otranto* accepted the work as a translation of a medieval document, but objected strongly to its absurdities and affronts to modern taste. At this point, Walpole had not disclosed his authorship. Nor had he yet appended "Gothic" to the novel's subtitle. The reviewer did not know or care whether William Marshal, the translator of Onuphrio Muralto's Italian source, was being serious or ironic, maintaining that "The publication of any work, at this time in England composed of such rotten materials, is a phenomenon we cannot account for." After summarizing the novel and condemning such preposterous supernatural events as the walking portrait and aviating helmet, the reviewer granted that "the characters are well marked, and the narrative kept up with surprising spirit and propriety." Midway through the review, the reviewer may have had some suspicions that he had been taken in as hinted at by his remark about the walking portrait: "We cannot help thinking that this circumstance is some presumption that the castle of Otranto is a modern fabrick." By "fabrick," he meant "fabrication." Most of the first paragraph of the review is a direct quotation from Walpole's "Preface" to the first edition with several quotation marks omitted and so indicated in brackets ["].]

a. *The Critical Review: or, Annals of Literature. By a Society of Gentlemen.* Vol. XIX [19] (1765): 50-51.

The ingenious translator of this *very curious* performance informs that it ["]was found in the library of an ancient catholic family in the north of England: that it was printed at Naples, in the black letter, in the year 1529; and that the stile is of the purest Italian["]: he also conjectures, that ["]the story was written near the time when it is supposed to have happened, it must have been between 1095, the æra of the first crusade, and 1245, the date of the last, or not long afterwards.["] "There is,["] continues he, ["]no other circumstance in the work, that can lead us to guess at the period in which the scene is laid: the names of the actors are evidently fictitious, and probably disguised on purpose: yet the Spanish names of the domestics seem to indicate that this work was not composed, until the establishment of the Arragonian kings in Naples had made Spanish appelations familiar in that country. The beauty of the diction, and the zeal of the author [moderated, however by singular judgment] concur to make me think that the date of the composition was little antecedent to that of the impression. Letters were then in their most flourishing state in Italy, and contributed to dispel the empire of superstition, at that time so forcibly attacked by the Reformers. It is not unlikely that an artful priest might endeavour to turn their own arms on the innovators; and might avail himself of his abilities as an author to confirm the populace in their ancient errors and superstitions. If this was his view, he has certainly acted with single address. Such a work as the following would enslave a hundred vulgar minds beyond half the books of controversy that have been written from the days of Luther to the present hour.["]

Such is the character of this work given us by its judicious translator; but whether he speaks seriously or ironically, we neither know nor care. The publication of any work, at this time, in England composed of such rotten materials, is a phœnomenon we cannot account for. That our readers may form some idea of the absurdity of its contents, we are to inform them that Manfred, prince of Otranto, had only one son, a youth about fifteen years of age, who on the day appointed for his marriage was "dashed to pieces, and almost buried under an enormous helmet, an hundred times more large than any casque made for human being, and shaded with a proportionable quantity of black feathers." This helmet, it seems, resembled that upon a statue of Alfonso the Good, one of the former princes of Otranto, whose dominions Manfred usurped; and therefore the helmet, or the resemblance of it, by way of poetical justice, dashed out his son's brains.

The above wonder is amongst the least of the wonderful things in the story. A picture comes out of its pannel, and stalks through the room, to dissuade Manfred from marrying the princess who had been betrothed to his son. It even utters deep sighs, and heaves its breasts [sic]. We cannot help thinking that this circumstance is some presumption that the castle of Otranto is a modern fabrick; for we doubt much whether pictures were fixed in pannels before the year 1243. We shall not affront our readers' understanding so much as to describe the other monstrosities of this story; but, excepting those absurdities, the characters are well marked, and the narrative kept up with surprising spirit and propriety. The catastrophe is most wretched. Manfred stabs his own daughter inadvertently, and she dies. The true heir of Alfonso's throne is discovered, whose name is Theodore. Manfred relents and repents, and at last the whole moral of the story turns out to be, "That the *sins* of fathers are visited on their children to the third and fourth generation."

[In a second review of the first edition, the reviewer suspected that the translation was a fraud and found the novel morally deficient and useless, but praised the presentation of the passions and the dramatic energy of the characters. The reviewer may have been the first critic to use the term "Gothic fiction." The review is erroneously dated 1764. Volume 32 of the journal had been incorrectly assigned to another issue by the printer, R. Griffiths. The correct date for Volume 32 is 1765 but is shown as 1764. Like the previous review, much of the opening paragraphs are a direct quoting of Walpole "Preface" to the first edition. The reviewer does little or no reviewing until the concluding paragraph and is careful to append a footnote concerning his reservations over the authenticity of the "translation."]

b. *The Monthly Review; or, Literary Journal: By Several Hands*, Vol. XXXII [32] (1764) [1765]: 97-99.

Those who can digest the absurdities of Gothic fiction, and bear with the machinery of ghosts and goblins, may hope, at least, for considerable entertainment from the performance before us: for it is written with no common pen; the language is accurate and elegant; the characters are highly finished; and the disquisitions into human manners, passions, and pursuits, indicate the keenest penetration, and the most perfect knowledge of mankind. The Translator, in his Preface, informs us that the original "was found in the library of an ancient catholic family in the North of England. It was printed at Naples, in the black letter, in the year 1529. How much sooner it was written does not appear. The principal incidents are such as were believed in the darkest ages of Christianity; but the language and conduct have nothing that savours of barbarism. The stile [sic] is the purest Italian. If the story was written near the time when it is supposed to have happened, it must have been between 1095, the æra of the first crusade, and 1245, the date of the last, or not long afterwards. There is no other circumstance in the work, that can lead us to guess at the period in which the scene is laid: the names of the actors are evidently fictitious, and probably disguised on purpose: yet the Spanish names of the domestics seem to indicate that this work was not composed, until the establishment of the Arragonian kings in Naples had made Spanish appelations familiar in that country. The beauty of the diction, and the zeal of the author [moderated, however by singular judgment] concur to make me think that the date of the composition was little antecedent to that of the impression. Letters were then in their most flourishing state in Italy, and contributed to dispel the empire of superstition, at that time so forcibly attacked by the reformers. It is not unlikely that an artful priest might endeavour to turn their own arms on the innovators; and might avail himself of his abilities as an author to confirm the populace in their ancient errors and superstitions. If this was his view, he has certainly acted with single address. Such a work as the following would enslave a hundred vulgar minds beyond half the books of controversy that have been written from the days of Luther to the present hour.["]

"This solution of the author's motives is however offered as a mere conjecture. Whatever his views were, of whatever effects the execution of them might have, his work can only be laid before the publick at present as a matter of entertainment. Even as such, some apology for it is necessary. Miracles, visions, necromancy, dreams, and other preternatural events, are exploded now even from romances. That was not the case when our author wrote; much less when the story itself is supposed to have happened. Belief in every kind of prodigy was so established in those dark ages, that an author would not be faithful to the manners of the times, who should omit all mention of them. He is not bound to believe them himself, but must represent his actors as believing them.["]

"If this air of the miraculous is excused, the reader will find nothing else unworthy of his perusal. Allow the possibility of the facts, and all the actors comport themselves as persons would do in their situation. There is no bombast, no similes, flowers, digressions, or unnecessary descriptions. Every thing [sic] tends directly to the catastrophe. Never is the reader's attention relaxed. The rules of the drama are almost observed throughout the conduct of the piece. The characters are well drawn, and still better maintained. Terror, the author's principal engine, prevents the story from ever languishing ; and it is so often contrasted by pity, that the mind is kept up in a constant vicissitude of interesting passions."

The natural prejudice which a translator[1] entertains in favour of his original, has not carried this gentleman beyond the bounds of truth; and his criticisms on his Author bear equal marks of taste and candour. The principal defect of this performance does not remain unnoticed. That unchristian doctrine of visiting the sins of the fathers upon the children, is certainly, under our present system, not only a very useless, but a very insupportable moral, and yet it is almost the only one deducible from this story. Nor is it at all rendered more tolerable through the insinuation that such evils might be diverted by devotion to St. Nicholas; for there the good canon was evidently preaching in favour of his own household. However, as a work of genius, evincing great dramatic powers, and

---

1   This is said on the supposition that the work really is a translation, as pretended. [Reviewer's note]

exhibiting fine views of nature, the *Castle of Otranto* may still be read with pleasure. To give the Reader an analysis of the story, would be to introduce him to a company of skeletons; to refer him to the book will be to recommend him to an assemblage of beautiful pictures.

[Reassured by its enthusiastic public acceptance, Walpole announced his authorship and added "A Gothic Story" to the novel's title for the second edition of *The Castle of Otranto*. The reviewer, no doubt resentful at being taken in by the fraudulent translation, uses the review as an occasion to retract all of his former praise and charges Walpole with a betrayal of his own genius and debasement of taste in his reversion to barbarism and the promotion of a "Gothic devilism" perpetrated against both public morals and aesthetic decorum. Walpole was the first, but not the last Gothic novelist to be accused of spreading satanism and encouraging moral evil by his Gothic writing. Because of errors in the dating of previous volume numbers, this issue of *The Monthly Review* is misdated 1764 and is corrected to 1765 in the citation below.]

c. *The Monthly Review; or Literary Journal: by Several Hands* XXXII [32] (1764) [1765]: 394.

When this book was published as a translation from an old Italian romance, we had the pleasure of distinguishing in it the marks of genius, and many beautiful characteristic paintings; we were dubious, however, concerning the antiquity of the work upon considerations, but being willing to find some excuse for the absurd and monstrous fictions it contained, we wished to acquiesce in the declaration of the title-page, that it was really a translation from an ancient writer. While we considered it as such, we could readily excuse its preposterous phenomena, and consider them as sacrifices to a gross and unenlightened age.— But when, as in this edition, *The Castle of Otranto* is declared to be a modern performance, that indulgence we afforded to the foibles of a supposed antiquity, we can by no means extend to the singularity of a false taste in a cultivated period of learning. It is, indeed, more than strange, that an Author,[1] of a refined and polished genius, should be an advocate for re-establishing the barbarous superstitions of Gothic devilism! *Incredulus odi*[2]

---

1 From the initials, H.W. in this edition, and the beauty of the impression, there is no room to doubt that it is the production of Strawberry-Hill. [Reviewer's note]

2 Literally, "being skeptical, I detest it," from the Roman poet Horace. Figuratively, a skeptical state of mind.

is, or ought to be a charm against all such infatuation. Under the same banner of singularity he attempts to defend all the *trash* of Shakespeare, and what that great genius evidently threw out as a necessary sacrifice to that idol of *caecum vulgus*,[1] he would adopt in the worship of the true God of Poetry.

2. Notices of *The Mysterious Mother*

[Walpole's incest drama received two notices in *The Monthly Review*. The first review noticed Dodsley's 1781 edition of the drama and compared the play favorably to Sophocles's incest tragedy, *Œdipus Tyrannus*. The reviewer further found the play to be a powerful moral spectacle ("this tragedy has attained an excellence nearly unimpeachable") whose incest theme should not disqualify it from stage production. But the reviewer also complained of Walpole's abuse of the clergy and religion in his portrayal of Father Benedict and wrongly concluded that the Friar's malice lacked sufficient motive.]

a. *The Monthly Review; or, Literary Journal, Enlarged*, XXIII [23], new series (1797): 248-254.

The author of this far-famed tragedy, it is currently understood, was the late Earl of Orford, better known as the Hon. Horace Walpole; under which designation all his literary labours were accomplished, and all that portion of life passed which can be desirable to man.

The first edition of this drama was printed at Strawberry Hill,[2] for distribution only among the author's friends. In 1781, an impression was intended for general publication, but the greater part of it was kept back, from motives of delicacy and diffidence; and it was first legally exposed to sale only during the last year. We seize the opportunity of noticing it: for there is a pleasure in announcing one of those works of art to which genius has affixed the stamp of immortality.

The Mysterious Mother may fitly be compared with the *Oedipus Tyrannus* of Sophocles, for unity and wholeness of design in the fable, for the dexterous conduct and ascending interest of the plot, for crowded maxims of sublime instruction, and for the abominable horror of its petrifying event. The English author has indeed exchanged the trim simplicity

---

1 Literally, *caecum* is the pouch which is located at the beginning of the large intestine, but figuratively with *vulgus*, the phrase means crude or boorish stomach or appetite.
2 At the author's private press. [Reviewer's note]

of action which was habitual to the Greek stage, for the artful complexity of intrigue that is expected on our own: he has also introduced a greater variety of characters, and has given to each a consistency and an individuality that were not always attained by the Athenian. In Sophocles, the critical arrival of the messenger from Corinth is more convenient than probable: so is the extreme malice of Benedict, when he accelerates the marriage in the *Mysterious Mother*.

The scene lies before the castle of Narbonne; where resides a Countess, an elderly lady, renowned for charity, feeling, and intellect, and in religious opinions as unshackled as her contemporary the Queen of Navarre.[1] She passes her widowhood in works of piety, displaying an uneasy penitential devotion, and an industrious eleemosynary[2] profusion. She has educated the orphan Adeliza, who is now placed in a convent of nuns at Narbonne. To her son Edmund, who has hitherto followed the profession of arms, she has wholly forbidden the house of his ancestors; yet she is an attentive steward to his property, and ministers to his wants most affectionately. Her mysterious conduct has excited his curiosity: he arrives with his friend Florian at Narbonne, unannounced and unknown: they become acquainted with Adeliza, and Edmund solicits her hand. The Countess, somewhat apprized of what passes, but taught to suppose that Florian is the wooer, encourages the marriage; which Friar Benedict solemnizes. Edmund and the Countess meet—she discovers her son to be the bridegroom: wild with horror, she announces Adeliza as her daughter, and as her daughter *by incest with Edmund*. She then kills herself; Adeliza flies to the veil; and Edmund to the field of battle. The following scene between the two priests shows much of the author's spirit:[3]

We shall also introduce to the reader the Countess and Edmund:[4]

This last scene exhibits one of the most pathetic situations in the

---

1   Probably a reference to Marguerite of Navarre, sister of Francis I and Queen of Navarre from 1544 to 1549. She was the author of *Tales of the Queen of Navarre*. [*La Contes de la Reine Navarre*], and is mentioned by Walpole in his "Preface" to *The Mysterious Mother*.

2   charitable, now archaic.

3   At this point, the review quotes at length from Benedict's speech, "Ay! sift her, sift her—" to his speech "She will take none: / Offer'd, she scoffs it; and withheld, demands not." (*The Mysterious Mother*, I.iii.1-60), the scene in which Benedict reveals his schemes and discusses his emnity toward the Countess with Martin.

4   At this point the review quotes from the Countess's soliloquy, "The monument destroy'd!" to "No, hapless maid—" (*Mysterious Mother*, III.i.1-38) and the scene with the Countess, Benedict and Edmund beginning with Benedict's speech, "This gentleman beheld thy Edmund breathless on the ground" to the Countess's speech "'Tis not ripe / As yet my purpose—Benedict, attend me" (*Mysterious Mother*, III.iii.85-172).

whole compass of the drama, and in a vein of poetry not unworthy of the occasion. We cannot but think, however, that the author's aversion from that religion which he lashes has led him to ascribe an *incredible* obliquity of malice to the Friar Benedict, because it is without a motive; and that the character of the porter is ill-managed and unintelligible; he is an inconsistent oddity. In other respects, we are of opinion that this tragedy has attained an excellence nearly unimpeachable; that it will, without disparagement, bear comparison with the more regular dramas of the French stage,—with the *Mérope* or *Mahomet* of Voltaire;[1] and that it will convince the English public how very possible it is to unite all the energies of genius with all the graces of art.

Can this work be less proper for representation than Otway's *Orphan*?[2]

[Included in a review of the 1798 edition of *The Works of Horatio Walpole, Earl of Orford* was a concluding laudatory paragraph on *The Mysterious Mother*, Walpole's forbidden play. The reviewer called the play's language "more Shakespearean than that of any of his professed imitators," but held Walpole culpable of anti-clericalism in the malign character and actions of Father Benedict, the Countess's confessor, accusing Walpole of being vindicative as well as "a bitter foe to priests, without distinction." He also complained that the repulsive subject matter negated any tragic value the drama might offer. "Great force and admirable writing appear in some of its scenes; but, in perusal, it excites more disgust and horror than pathos," a criticism that Walpole had anticipated when he kept the play from being performed during his lifetime.]

b. *The Monthly Review; or, Literary Journal, Enlarged*, XXVI [26] (1798):323-327.

Of the tragedy of *The Mysterious Mother*, in this volume, the author himself thought, when he undertook to write it, "that the scenes would not be proper to appear on the stage."[3] The language of this Drama, however, is more Shaksperian [sic] than that of any of his professed imitators;

---

1   *Mohamet, or Fanaticism* (1740), a philosophical tragedy and *Mérope* (1743), a tragedy based on Racine's *Andromache*, are dramas by Voltaire.
2   Thomas Otway's popular tragedy in blank verse, *The Orphan* (1680), contains a triple suicide.
3   The reviewer misquotes Walpole's remark in his "Postscript" to the 1781 edition of the play: Walpole wrote: "From the time that I first undertook the foregoing scenes, I never flattered myself that they would be proper to appear on the stage."

and so are the sentiments.—except that Shakspeare [sic] was always a friend to religion, and treated its ministers with respect: but Mr. Walpole was a bitter foe to priests, without distinction, and seems to have had no great reverence for sacred mysteries, or the doctrinal parts of the Christian system. The hero of the piece is an amiable libertine, and a determined *philosophe*; and the heroine, though a conscientious and repentent sinner, is ever at war with the counsel and admonitions of the priesthood. As we lately gave an account of this drama, we shall only here add that great force, and admirable writing, appear in some of its scenes: but, in perusal, it excites more disgust and horror than pathos.—The noble author himself has given a critique on this Tragedy, under the title of a *Postscript*, which will perhaps sufficiently apologize for some of the most objectionable parts. For the rest, the intrinsic merit of the work itself seems not only to preclude cavil, but to extort applause.

3. Two Poems

[Walpole's friend, Hannah More (the "Stella" of Yearsley's poem), had presented a copy of *The Castle of Otranto* to Ann Yearsley, known in literary circles as the "Bristol Milkwoman Poet" and also by her poetic persona, "Lactilla." In a letter to Hannah More dated 13 November 1784, Walpole lightheartedly scolded Hannah More for filling "Lactilla's" head with Gothic stuff that her untutored mind could not control. "She must remember," Walpole chided," "that she is a Lactilla, not a Pastora, and is to tend real cows, not Arcadian sheep.... you will have made a hurly-burly in this poor woman's head which it cannot develop and digest."[1] Yearsley's poetic tribute to Walpole's Gothic genius is not entirely encomiastic. Using Walpole's character, Bianca, Isabella's maid in *The Castle of Otranto*, as her persona and narrator, Yearsley criticizes Walpole's underdevelopment of the female characters in the novel ("HYPOLITA! fond, passive to excess,/ Her low submission suits not souls like mine; ... Nor ISABELLA's equal powers reveal") (373-374). But much of her poem is an unqualified admiration of Walpole's art, an approbation that Walpole regarded as the overreaction of a silly and impressionable reader. For the additional influence of Walpole's Gothic on Yearsley's fiction, see: Terence M. Brunk, "'A Hurly-Burly in This Poor Women's Head': The Gothic Character in Ann Yearsley's Authorial Identity," *English Language*

---

1 For opposite viewpoints on Yearsley's work expressed by Hannah More and others, see: Donna Landry, *The Muses of Resistance: Laboring-Class Women's Poetry in Britain, 1739-1796*. Cambridge: Cambridge University Press, 1990.

Notes 37:4 (2000): 29-52. Yearsley's own Gothic novel, *The Royal Captives; A Fragment of Secret History, Copied from an Old Manuscript* (1795) "evinces a transformative power that *The Castle of Otranto*, for all of its grotesque flights of fancy, cannot emulate" (37).]

a. To the Honourable H——E W——E, on Reading THE CASTLE OF OTRANTO December, 1784. By Ann [Cromartie] Yearsley (1752-1806), *Poems on Several Occasions*, London: Cadell, 1785.[1]

> To praise thee, WALPOLE, asks a pen divine,
> And common sense to me is hardly given,
> BIANCA's pen now owns the daring line,
> And who expects *her* muse should drop from Heaven.
>
> My fluttering tongue, light, ever veering round,
> On Wisdom's narrow point has never fix'd;
> I dearly love to hear the ceaseless sound,
> Where Noise and Nonesense [sic] are completely mix'd.
>
> The empty tattle, true to female rules,
> In which thy happier talents ne'er appear,
> Is mine, nor mine alone, for mimic fools,
> Who boast *thy* sex, BIANCA's foibles wear.
>
> Supreme in prate shall woman ever sit,
> While Wisdom smiles to hear the senseless squall;
> Nature, who gave me tongue, deny'd me wit,
> Folly I worship, and she claims me all.
>
> The drowsy eye, half-closing to the lid,
> Stares on OTRANTO's walls; grim terrors rise,
> The horrid helmet strikes my soul unbid,
> And with thy CONRAD, lo! BIANCA dies.
>
> Funereal plumes now wave; ALPHONSO's ghost
> Frowns o'er my shoulder; silence aids the scene,

---

1 The text of Yearsley's poem is available as an appendix to the article by Madeline Kahn, "'a bystander often sees more of the game than those that play'": Ann Yearsley reads *The Castle of Otranto* in *Making History: Textuality and the Forms of Eighteenth-Century Culture*, ed. Greg Clingham. Lewisburg, PA: Bucknell University Press, 1998: 75-78.

The taper's flame, in fancy'd blueness lost,
    Pale spectres shews, to MANFRED only seen.

25   Ah! MANFRED! thine are bitter draughts of woe,
    Strong gusts of passion hurl thee on thy fate;
Tho' eager to elude, thou meet'st the blow,
    And for RICARDO MANFRED weeps in state.

By all the joys which treasur'd virtues yield,
30   I feel thy agonies in WALPOLE's line;
Love, pride, revenge, by turns maintain the field,
    And hourly tortures rend my heart for thine.

Hail, magic pen, that strongly paint'st the soul,
    Where fell Ambition holds his wildest roar,
35   The whirlwind rages to the distant pole,
    And Virtue, stranded, pleads her cause no more.

Where's MANFRED's refuge? WALPOLE, tell me where?
    Thy pen to great St. NICHOLAS points the eye,
E'en MANFRED calls to guard ALPHONSO's heir,
40   Tho' conscious shame oft gives his tongue the lie.

MATILDA! ah, how soft thy yielding mind,
    When hard obedience cleaves thy timid heart!
How nobly strong, when love and virtue join'd
    To melt thy soul and take a lover's part!

45   Ah, rigid duties, which two souls divide!
    Whose iron talons rend the panting breast!
Pluck the dear image from the widow'd side,
    Where Love had lull'd its every care to rest.

HYPOLITA! [sic] fond, passive to excess,
50   Her low submission suits not souls like mine;
BIANCA might have lov'd her MANFRED less,
    Nor offer'd less at great Religion's shrine.

Implicit faith, all hail! Imperial man
    Exacts submission; reason we resign;

Against our senses we adopt the plan 55
    Which Reverence, Fear, and Folly think divine.

But be it so, BIANCA ne'er shall prate,
    Nor ISABELLA's equal powers reveal;
Your MANFRED's boast your power, and prize your state;
    We ladies our omnipotence conceal. 60

But, Oh! then strange-inventing WALPOLE guide,
    Ah! guide me through thy subterranean isles,
Ope the trap-door where all thy powers reside,
    And mimic Fancy real woe beguiles.

The kind inventress dries the streaming tear, 65
    The deep-resounding groan shall faintly die,
The sigh shall sicken ere it meets the air,
    And Sorrow's dismal troop affrighted fly.

Thy jawless skeleton of JOPPA's wood
    Stares in my face, and frights my mental eye; 70
Not stiffen'd worse the love-sick FREDERIC stood,
    When the dim spectre shriek'd the dismal cry.

But whilst the Hermit does my soul affright,
    Love dies—Lo! in yon corner down he kneels;
I shudder, see the taper sinks in night, 75
    He rises, and his fleshless form reveals.

Hide me, thou parent Earth! see low I fall,
    My sins now meet me in the fainting hour;
Say, do thy Manes[1] for Heaven's vengeance call,
    Or can I free thee from an angry power? 80

STELLA! if WALPOLE's spectres thus can scare,
    Then near that great Magician's walls ne'er tread.
He'll surely conjure many a spirit there,
    Till, fear-struck, thou art number'd with the dead.

---

1   The souls of dead ancestors.

85   Oh! with this noble Sorcerer ne'er converse,
           Fly, STELLA, quickly from the magic storm;
      Or, soon he'll close thee in some high-plum'd hearse,
           Then raise another Angel in thy form.

      Trust not his art, for should he stop thy breath,
90   And good ALPHONSO's ghost unbidden rise;
      He'd vanish, leave thee in the jaws of death,
           And quite forget to close thy aching eyes.

      But is BIANCA safe in this slow vale?
           For should his Goblins stretch their dusky wing,
95   Would they not bruise me for the saucy tale,
           Would they not pinch me for the truths I sing?

      Yet whisper not I've call'd him names, I fear
           His ARIEL would my hapless sprite torment,
      He'd cramp my bones, and all my sinews tear,
100   Should STELLA blab the secret I'd prevent.

      But hush, ye winds, ye crickets chirp no more,
           I'll shrink to bed, nor these sad omens hear,
      An hideous rustling shakes the lattic'd door,
           His spirits hover in the sightless air.

105   Now, MORPHEUS, shut each entrance of my mind,
           Sink, sink, OTRANTO, in this vacant hour;
      To thee, Oh, balmy GOD! I'm all resign'd,
           To thee e'en WALPOLE's wand resigns its power.

[John Courtenay's verse epistle gave a satiric summary of the high points of Walpole's social and literary careers and mildly sneered at the absurd collection of relics in Walpole's "trim gothick cage," his house at Strawberry Hill. See Walpole's letter to Mary Berry of 17 April 1794 in which Walpole dismisses Courtenay's harmless ridicule.]

b. "Letter the Seventh, Naples, April 16 1793," *The Present State of the Manners, Arts, Politics of France and Italy; in a Series of Poetical Epistles from Paris, Rome, and Naples, in 1792 and 1793; Addressed to Robert Jephson, Esq.* by John Courtenay (1741-1816).

> Not the curious Otranto who brilliantly
>> sings
> Of Harry's old slippers, and Queen Bess's
>> rings;
> Who to love tunes his note with the fire of
>> old age,   5
> And chirps the trim lay, in a trim gothick
>> cage;
> That patron of letters, sprung out of a
>> Beau,
> Who Chatterton fed, and protected   10
>> Rousseau.
> Could Rousseau's keen sensations to him be
>> a jest,
> When Genius and Want found a home in
>> his breast?   15
> Who the virtues of Richard can only
>> display,
> And divert us by incest in scenes of
>> a play!
> Whose talents can shine on points not   20
>> worth a rush,
> On scribblers ennobled, and *daubs* of the
>> brush.

4. Comments on *The Castle of Otranto* and *The Mysterious Mother* by Early Readers

[William Warburton in a footnote to his edition of Alexander Pope's Verse. William Warburton (1698-1779) was Bishop of Gloucester and had a reputation as something of a literary scavenger and bully. In his edition of Alexander Pope's poetry, he reacted favorably to the dramatic qualities of Walpole's novel, a rather surprising compliment which Walpole did not expect. The comment on *The Castle of Otranto* is in the form of a footnote to line 146 of Alexander Pope's poem *First Epistle to the Second Book of Horace Imitated*.[1]]

a. Yet amidst all this nonsense, when things were at their worst, we have lately been entertained with what I will venture to call, a masterpiece, in the *fable*; and of a new species likewise. The piece I mean, is, *The Castle of Otranto*. The scene is laid in *Gothic chivalry*, where a beautiful imagination, supported by strength of judgment, has enabled the author to go beyond his subject, and effect the full purpose of the *ancient tragedy*, that is, *to purge the passions by pity and terror*, in colouring as great and harmonious as in any of the best dramatic writers.]

[Fanny Burney (Frances, Madame D'Arblay) (1752-1840) was a novelist, diarist, and lady-in-waiting at the court of Queen Charlotte. She knew Walpole casually and had visited Strawberry Hill. Her diary entry expresses moral outrage and "indignant aversion" over the incestuous subject matter, but beneath this official disdain can be heard a curious fascination with the forbidden subject.]

b. Fanny Burney in her Diary for Tuesday 28 November 1786.

The Queen, in looking over some books while I was in waiting one morning, met with *The Mysterious Mother*, Mr. Walpole's tragedy, which he printed at Strawberry Hill, and gave to a few friends but has never suffered to be published. I expressed, by looks, I suppose, my wishes, for she most graciously offered to lend it me. I had long desired to read it, from so well knowing and so much liking the author; and he had promised me, if I would come a second time to Strawberry Hill, that I

---

1   William Warburton, ed. *The Poetical Works of Alexander Pope, with his past corrections, additions, and improvements, from the text of Dr. Warburton. With the Life of the Author*. London: J. Bell, 1787-88, III, 168.

should have it.... The opening of the play contains a description of superstitious fear, extremely well, and feelingly, and naturally depicted: it begins, too, in an uncommon style, promising of interest and novelty: but my praise will soon be ended, swallowed up all in the heaviest censure. Dreadful was the whole! truly dreadful! a story of so much horror, from atrocious and voluntary guilt, never did I hear!... For myself, I felt a sort of indignant aversion rise fast and warm in my mind, against the wilful author of a story so horrible: all of the entertainment and pleasure I had received from Mr. Walpole seemed extinguished by this lecture, which almost made me regard him as the patron of the vices he had been pleased to record.... [I]t was a lasting disgrace to Mr. Walpole to have chosen such a subject, and [I] thought him deserving even of punishment for such a painting of human wickedness; and the more as the story throughout was forced and improbable. But the whole of all that could be said on this subject was summed up in one sentence by Mr. Turbulent,[1] which, for its masterly strength and justice, brought to my mind my ever-revered Dr. Johnson. "Mr. Walpole," cried he, "has chosen a plan of which nothing can equal the abomination but the absurdity!"

[Hester Lynch Thrale (1741-1821) was a prominent socialite and friend of Dr. Samuel Johnson. She enjoyed correcting Walpole's claim in his Preface to *The Mysterious Mother* that his source was an anecdote from Archbishop Tillotson.]

c. Mrs. Hester Lynch Thrale [Piozzi], Diary for 18 February 1794.

The *Mysterious Mother* is said by Lord Orford (then Horace Walpole) in his Preface, to be taken from Tillotson, who received a confession of such crimes, and bid the woman almost despair. It is not so; the story is in [Bishop Joseph] Hall's [*Diverse Practical*] *Cases of Conscience*, [*in Continual Use Amongst Men*] out of which the Bishop related it to friends delighting more in anecdote than in truth, and they told it as having happened to him.

---

1   Mr. Timothy Turbulent is a character in the anonymous Restoration comedy *Mr. Turbulent; or, the Melanchollicks* first acted by the Duke's Company in January, 1682. Fanny Burney probably has in mind a speech by Mr. Turbulent denouncing immorality in theatrical productions. See *The London Stage 1660-1800. A Calendar of Plays, Entertainments, and Afterpieces Together with Casts, Box-Receipts and Contemporary Comment*, eds. William Van Lennep, Emmett L. Avery, Arthur H. Scouten. Carbondale and Edwardsville, IL: Southern Illinois University Press, 1979: *Part I: 1660-1700*, 304.

[George Gordon, Lord Byron (1788-1824) wrote a dramatic poem, *Manfred* (1817), a Gothic drama, whose protagonist has both the name and traits of Walpole's hero-villain in *The Castle of Otranto*. His tribute to Walpole's novel and play reflects Byron's own Romantic values.]

d. Lord Byron, from Preface to *Marino Faliero, Doge of Venice. An Historical Tragedy in Five Acts.*

It is the fashion to underrate Horace Walpole; firstly, because he was a nobleman, and secondly, because he was a gentleman; but, to say nothing of the composition of his incomparable letters, and of the "Castle of Otranto," he is the "Ultimus Romanorum," the author of the "Mysterious Mother," a tragedy of the highest order, and not a puling love-play. He is the father of the first romance and of the last tragedy in our language, and is surely worthy of a higher place than any living writer, be he who he may.

[Like other nineteenth-century readers, the essayist William Hazlitt (1778-1830) found the supernatural gadgetry of *The Castle of Otranto* to be less amusing than offensive to good taste. His charge that the Gothic devices "shock the senses and have no purchase upon the imagination" would be repeated by other readers who were inimical to Gothic Romanticism.]

e. William Hazlitt, "On the English Novelists" in *Lectures on the English Comic Writers and Fugitive Writings* (1819).

The Castle of Otranto is, to my notion, dry, meager, and without effect. It is done upon false principles of taste. The great hand and arm which are thrust into the courtyard, and remain there all day long, are the pasteboard machinery of a pantomime; they shock the senses, and have no purchase upon the imagination. They are a matter-of-fact impossibility; a fixture, and no longer a phantom.

[In almost *ad hominem* fashion, Samuel Taylor Coleridge (1772-1834) attacked both the play's incest theme and the masculinity of its author. Just as he had denounced M. G. Lewis's *The Monk* as a morally dangerous book, so he pronounced Walpole's *Mysterious Mother* "disgusting, vile, detestable," the depraved product of an unmanly man.]

f. Samuel Taylor Coleridge in *The Table Talk*, 20 March 1834.

Lord Byron, as quoted by Lord Dover, says that the *Mysterious Mother* raises Horace Walpole above every author living in his, Lord Byron's, time.... *The Mysterious Mother* is the most disgusting, vile, detestable composition that ever came from the hand of man. No one with a spark of true manliness, of which Horace Walpole had none, could have written it. As to the blank verse, it is indeed better than [Nicholas] Rowe's [1674-1718] and [James] Thomson's [1700-1748], which was execrably bad: any approach, therefore, to the manner of the old dramatists was of course an improvement; but the loosest lines in [the plays of James Shirley (1596-1666)] are superior to Walpole's best.

[The historian and liberal politician Thomas Babington Macaulay (1800-1859) enjoyed *The Castle of Otranto* even though he was loath to admit his idle reading pleasures. Like other secretly hedonistic readers of Gothic fiction, he was entertained by the absurd vigor of Walpole's novel.]

g. Thomas Babington Macaulay, in *Critical and Historical Essays, Contributed to the Edinburgh Review* (1843).

The coarser morsels of antiquarian learning [Walpole] abandons to others, and sets out an entertainment worthy of a Roman epicure, an entertainment consisting of nothing but delicacies, the brains of singing birds, the roe of mullets, the sunny halves of peaches. This, we think, is the great merit of his romance. There is little skill in the delineation of the characters. Manfred is as commonplace a tyrant, Jerome as commonplace a confessor, Theodore as commonplace a young gentleman, Isabella and Matilda as commonplace a pair of young ladies, as are to be found in any of the thousand Italian castles in which *condottierri* have revelled or in which imprisoned duchesses have pined. We cannot say that we much admire the big man whose sword is dug up in one quarter of the globe, whose helmet drops from the clouds in another, and who, after clattering and rustling for some days, ends by kicking the house down. But the story, whatever its value may be, never flags for a single moment. There are no digressions, or unseasonable descriptions, or long speeches. Every sentence carries the action forward. The excitement is constantly renewed. Absurd as is the machinery, insipid as are the human actors, no reader probably ever thought the book dull.

Appendix C: Aesthetic and Intellectual Backgrounds

1. The Graveyard Poets

[The aesthetics of death, decay, ruin, pain, and fear and wonder in the face of unknown power—later to become the core emotions of Gothic fiction—filled the lines of the Graveyard Poets[1] in the four decades (1720-1760) before Walpole's *Castle of Otranto*. Its moods, scenery, and vocabulary of "gloomth" would deeply influence the style and form of Gothic fiction. Walpole and the Gothic novelists who followed would dramatize the contemplative horrors commemorated in Graveyard verse by adding violent action to these macabre materials. The prototypical Graveyard Poem was marked by a psychological appreciation of the supernatural amidst mortuarial surroundings. By brooding grandiloquently on death in the shadow of ruined tombs and moss-grown churchyards, the poets of the Graveyard School rediscovered the paradoxical connection between horror and ecstasy that empowers the Gothic aesthetic. Reason, order, and common sense gave way to an almost religious fixation with the dark sublime when ungodly shapes from the other side that had long been denied their very existence by rationality advanced to meet the rationalist. The narrators in Graveyard Poetry are almost always alone, lost, but deeply curious about the dark places they are about to enter, and, like Gothic victims later, their journey often takes the form of a descent to a cave, crypt, vault, or mausoleum reached only by dark passageways where supernatural shades beckon and glide along the walls. By the mid-eighteenth century, the poetry of "gloomth," as it might be called to link it with Walpole's art, had become a favorite artistic pastime of the antiquarian. When Walpole yielded to the appeal of its supernatural excitement and "graveyard horrifics"[2] in the writing of a first Gothic novel, he was following the lead of his friend Thomas Gray, whose melancholic narrator in the "Elegy Written in a Country Churchyard" "leaves the world to darkness and to me."

---

1 Two recent anthologies of eighteenth-century verse contain major selections from the work of the Graveyard Poets. See: *The New Oxford Book of Eighteenth Century Verse*, ed. Roger Lonsdale, Oxford & New York: Oxford UP, 1989, and *Eighteenth Century English Verse*, ed. Dennis Davison, London & New York: Penguin, 1973.

2 Eleanor Sickels, "'King Death'" In *The Gloomy Egoist: Moods and Themes of Melancholy from Gray to Keats*, New York: Columbia UP, 1932, 158-170. For another study of the strong impact of Graveyard verse, see Patricia Meyer Spacks, *The Insistence of Horror: Aspects of the Supernatural in Eighteenth Century Poetry*, Cambridge: Harvard UP, 1962.

Even Alexander Pope, one of the major voices of neoclassic balance and self-control, yielded to the Gothic impulse in his medieval poem, "Eloïsa to Abelard."[1] The monastic lovers imprisoned beneath "moss-grown domes" and "awful arches," and the Gothic phantom of "Black melancholy" creating deadly silence by her stare make a figure group worthy of the Gothic novel.]

a. From Alexander Pope, "Eloïsa to Abelard" (1717).

> In these lone walls (their days eternal bound)   141
> These moss-grown domes with spiry turrets crowned,
> Where awful arches make a noonday night,
> And the dim windows shed a solemn light;
> ....
> No more these scenes my meditation aid,   161
> Or lull to rest the visionary maid.
> But o'er the twilight groves and dusky caves,
> Long-sounding aisles, and intermingled graves,
> Black melancholy sits, and round her throws   165
> A death-like silence, and a dead repose:
> Her gloomy presence saddens all the scene,
> Shades every flower, and darkens every green,
> Deepens the murmur of the falling floods,
> And breathes a browner horror on the woods.

[From within the stately gloom of his palatial ossuary, King Death himself speaks from his kingdom of bones in Parnell's eschatological tour-de-force.]

b. From Thomas Parnell, "Night-Piece on Death" (1726).

> The marble tombs that rise on high,   39
> Whose dead in vaulted arches lie,
> Whose pillars swell with sculptured stones,
> Arms, angels, epitaphs, and bones,
> These, all poor remains of state,
> Adorn the rich, or praise the great,
> Who while on earth in fame they live,   45
> Are senseless of the fame they give.

---

1   Pope's own villa at Twickenham, not far from Strawberry Hill, offered such Gothic theatrics as a subterranean tunnel or grotto connecting to the garden.

Hah! while I gaze, pale Cynthia fades;
And bursting earth unveils the shades!
All slow, and wan, and wrapped with shrouds,
50   They rise in visionary crowds,
And all with sober accent cry,
"Think, mortal, what it is to die!"
Now from yon black and funeral yew,
That bathes the charnel-house with dew,
55   Methinks I hear a voice begin;
(Ye ravens, cease your croaking din!
Ye tolling clocks, no time resound
O'er the long lake and midnight ground!)
It sends a peal of hollow groans,
60   Thus speaking from among the bones:
"When men my scythe and darts supply
How great a King of Fears am I!"

[For the Gothic imagination, the ruined mansion or castle symbolized "the triumph of chaos over order"[1] Such an inversion of the classical ideal elevated the mouldering building (or pile) into a strangely lovely object made beautiful because of its fallen state. Walpole made annual pleasure trips in search of such ruins and delighted in these grim spectacles of former greatness now become "the raven's bleak abode" and "the apartment of the toad."]

c. From John Dyer, *Grongar Hill* (1727).

77   'Tis now the raven's bleak abode;
'Tis now the apartment of the toad;
And there the fox securely feeds;
80   And there the poisonous adder breeds,
Concealed in ruins, moss, and weeds,
While, ever and anon, there falls
Huge heaps of hoary mouldered walls.

[Amidst a gruesome conglomerate of skulls, bones, toppled arches, and obliterated tombs, the "ghastful" figure of ruin sits, a Gothic figure in a Gothic deathscape in Mallet's elegiac celebration of the triumph of chaos over order and darkness over light.]

---

1   Michael Sadleir, *The Northanger Novels: A Footnote to Jane Austen*, Oxford: English Association Pamphlet No. 68, 7.

d. From David Mallet, *Excursion* (1728).

> Behind me rises huge an awful Pile,   26
> Sole, on this heath, a place of Tombs,
> Waste, desolate, where ruin dreary dwells,
> Brooding o'er sightless sculls [*sic*], and crumbling Bones.
> Ghastful He sits, and eyes with Stedfast Glare   30
> The Column gray with Moss, the falling Bust,
> The Time-shook Arch, the monumental Stone,
> Impaired, effac'd, and hastening into Dust,
> Unfaithful to their charge of flattering fame.

[The bliss of entombment and post-mortem consciousness within the grave were powerful Gothic motifs in the verse of Edward Young, together with other "night thoughts" of "apparitions and empty shades" and the sinister excitement of the vault.]

e. From Edward Young, "Night One," in "The Complaint, or Night Thoughts on Life, Death, and Immortality" (1742).

> How populous, how vital is the grave!   115
> This is creation's melancholy vault,
> The vale funereal, the sad cypress gloom;
> The land of apparitions, empty shades!
> All, all on earth is shadow, all beyond
> Is substance; the reverse is Folly's creed: 120
> How solid all, where change shall be no more!
> His sad, sure, sudden and eternal tomb.

[The sinister acoustics of the Gothic, wild shrieks, midnight bells, grinding door hinges, and lurid lighting effects were all to be found in Blair's verse. Devoted to the glories of the tomb, "The Grave" furnished Gothic novelists with a finished array of phantasmagoric audiovisual effects.]

f. From Robert Blair, "The Grave" (1743).

> Ah! how dark   11
> Thy long-extended realms and rueful wastes,
> Where naught but silence reigns, and night, dark night,
> Dark as was chaos ere the infant sun
> Was rolled together, or had tried his beams   15

Athwart the gloom profound! The sickly taper
By glimmering through thy low-browed misty vaults
(Furred round with mouldy damps and ropy slime)
Lets fall a supernumerary horror,
20   And only serves to make thy night more irksome.
Well do I know thee by thy trusty yew,
Cheerless, unsocial plant! that loves to dwell
Midst skulls and coffins, epitaphs and worms;
Where light-heeled ghosts and visionary shades,
25   Beneath the wan cold moon (as fame reports),
Embodied thick, perform their mystic rounds.
....
32   The wind is up—hark! how it howls! methinks
Till now I never heard a sound so dreary.
Doors creak, and windows clap, and the night's foul bird,
35   Rooked in the spire, screams loud. The gloomy aisles,
Black-plastered, and hung round with shreds of 'scutcheons
And tattered coats of arms, send back the sound
Laden with heavier airs, from the low vaults,
The mansions of the dead. Roused from their slumbers,
40   In grim array the grisly spectres rise,
Grin horrible, and obstinately sullen
Pass and repass, hushed as the foot of night.
Again the screech-owl shrieks—ungracious sound!
I'll hear no more; it makes one's blood run chill.
....
50   Strange things, the neighbours say, have happened here;
Wild shrieks have issued from the hollow tombs;
Dead men have come again, and walked about;
And the great bell has tolled, unrung, untouched.

[Dreadful pleasures awaited the imagination stirred by fear of darkness and supernatural danger, the sort of ecstatic astonishment that resulted when a well-wrought Gothic tale unfolded. Akenside gives an almost perfect description of the Gothic reader's motives and desires, "with grateful terrors quelled ... mus[ing] at last amid the ghostly gloom / Of graves, and hoary vaults, and cloistered cells" and "walk[ing] with spectres through the midnight shade."]

g. From Mark Akenside, "Pleasures of the Imagination" (1744).

> Hence, finally, by night   255
> The village matron, round the blazing hearth,
> Suspends the infant audience with her tales,
> Breathing astonishment! of witching rhymes
> And evil spirits; of the death-bed call
> Of him who robbed the widow and devoured   260
> The orphan's portion; of unquiet souls
> Risen from the grave to ease the heavy guilt
> Of deeds in life concealed; of shapes that walk
> At dead of night, and clank their chains, and wave
> The torch of hell around the murderer's bed.   265
> At every solemn pause the crowd recoil
> Gazing each other speechless, and congealed
> With shivering sighs: until eager for the event,
> Around the beldame all arrect[1] they hang,
> Each trembling heart with grateful terrors quelled.   270
> ....
> And leave the wretched pilgrims all forlorn,   395
> To muse at last amid the ghostly gloom
> Of graves, and hoary vaults, and cloistered cells;
> To walk with spectres through the midnight shade,
> And to the screaming owl's accursed song
> Attune the dreadful workings of his heart.   400

[The adoration of fear for fear's sake forms the subject of Collins's allegorical ode. Attended by vengeance with demonic "red arm, exposed and bare," and a ghastly entourage of fiends, fear is no abstraction for Collins, but a Gothic presence.]

h. From William Collins, "Ode to Fear" (1746).

> Thou to whom the world unknown,
> With all its shadowy shapes, is shown;
> Who seest appalled the unreal scene,
> While Fancy lifts the veil between—
>   Ah Fear! ah frantic Fear!   5
>   I see, I see thee near!

---

1 Erect or figuratively on edge with excitement.

I know thy hurried step, thy haggard eye!
Like thee I start, like thee disordered fly,
For, lo, what monsters in thy train appear!
10   Danger, whose limbs of giant mold
What mortal eye can fixed behold?
Who stalks his round, an hideous form,
Howling amidst the midnight storm;
Or throws him on the ridgy steep
15   Of some loose-hanging rock to sleep;
And with him thousand phantoms joined,
Who prompt to deeds accursed the mind;
And those, the fiends, who near allied,
O'er Nature's wounds and wrecks preside;
20   Whilst vengeance in the lurid air
Lifts her red arm, exposed and bare;
On whom that ravening brood of Fate,
Who lap the blood of sorrow, wait;
Who, Fear, this ghastly train can see,
25   And look not madly wild, like thee?

[By the late 1740s, the Graveyard Poets were using the adjective "Gothic" to connote gloom, awe and a sublime feeling of "religious horror."
Crossing the threshold of the Gothic world, Warton's wandering narrator
sounds precisely like a Gothic victim on the verge of a subterranean
ordeal or confinement that he both dreads and desires. "Gothic" is used
to denote the architecture of the medieval church, but to connote the
"dread repose" experienced by the wanderer.]

i. From Thomas Warton the Younger, "The Pleasures of Melancholy"
(1747).

43   As on I tread, religious horror wraps
My soul in dread repose. But when the world
745   Is clad in Midnight's raven-coloured robe,
In hollow charnel let me watch the flame
Of taper dim, while airy voices talk
Along the glimmering walls, or ghostly shape
At distance seen, invites with beckoning hand
50   My lonesome steps through the far-winding vaults.
....
201   The tapered choir, at the late hour of prayer,

Oft let me tread, while to the according voice
The many-sounding organ peals on high,
In full-voiced chorus through the embowered roof;
Till all my soul is bathed in ecstasies,   205
And lapped in Paradise. Or let me sit
Far in some distant aisle of the deep dome,
There lonesome listen to the solemn sounds,
Which, as they lengthen through the Gothic vaults,
In hollow murmurs reach my ravish'd ear.   210

["Gothic" is also used to convey the savage energy of those forbidden feelings condemned by reason and censured by common sense. When the Gothic mood is lost, when "Sudden, the sombrous imagery is fled, / Which late my visionary rapture fed: / Thy powerful hand has broke the Gothic chain, And brought my bosom back to truth again."]

j. From Thomas Warton, "Verses on Sir Joshua Reynolds's Painted Window at New College, Oxford" (1782).

For long, enamoured of a barbarous age,   7
A faithless truant to the classic page,
Long have I lov'd to catch the simple chime
Of minstrel-harps, and spell the fabling rime;   10
To view the festive rites, the knightly play,
That decked heroic Albion's elder day;
To mark the mouldering halls of barons bold,
And the rough castle, cast in giant mould;
With Gothic manners Gothic arts explore,   15
And muse on the magnificence of yore.

        ....

To suit the genius of the mystic pile: 29
Whilst as around the far-retiring aisle,
And fretted shrines with hoary trophies hung,
Her dark illumination while she flung,
With new solemnity, the nooks profound,
The caves of death, and the dim arches frowned.
From bliss long felt unwillingly we part: 35
Ah, spare the weakness of a lover's heart!
Chase not the phantoms of my fairy dream,
Phantoms that shrink at Reason's painful gleam!

        ....

61 Sudden, the sombrous imagery is fled,
 Which late my visionary rapture fed:
 Thy powerful hand has broke the Gothic chain,
 And brought my bosom back to truth again;
65 To truth, by no peculiar taste confined,
 Whose universal pattern strikes mankind;
 To truth, whose bold and unresisted aim
 Checks frail caprice, and fashion's fickle claim;
 To truth, whose charms deception's magic quell,
70 And bind coy Fancy in a stronger spell.

[Walpole's close friend, Thomas Gray, wrote one of the noblest pieces of Graveyard verse. Much admired by Walpole, Gray's "Elegy" was one of the first books published by Walpole's press at Strawberry Hill. The somber beauty of the opening lines of the "Elegy" quiver with Gothic suspense.]

k. From Thomas Gray, "Elegy Written in a Country Churchyard" (1751).

1 The curfew tolls the knell of parting day.
  The lowing herd winds slowly o'er the lea,
 The ploughman homeward plods his weary way,
  And leaves the world to darkness and to me.

5 Now fades the glimmering landscape on the sight,
  And all the air a solemn stillness holds,
 Save where the beetle wheels his droning flight,
  And drowsy tinklings lull the distant folds;

 Save that from yonder ivy-mantled tower
10 The moping owl does to the moon complain
 Of such as, wandering near her secret bower,
  Molest her ancient solitary reign.

2. James Hervey's *Meditations Among the Tombs* (1745)

[The passion for exploring Gothic ruins and the love of dilapidation were stimulated by a thanatopsisian series of grandly gloomy meditations by James Hervey (1714-1758). His *Meditations Among the Tombs*[1] was extremely popular and did much to stimulate the Gothic moods of delight in charnel objects, pleasing pathos and ardent melancholy, and the dreadful pleasure inspired by gazing at fallen monuments and moul-dering tombs.

Both the Graveyard Poets and the Gothic novelists enjoyed what might be called the funereal ramble, a pensive excursion in quest of what Walpole called "the gloomth of abbeys and cathedrals." Prior to the writ-ing of his Gothic novel, Walpole made many such antiquarian tours with his friends Gray and Chute. The emotional compensation for such meanderings amidst burial grounds and ancient ruins or "piles" were moments of sheer Gothic ecstasy during which a delectable dread engulfed the wanderer. Hervey's description of this moment finds a close parallel in *The Castle of Otranto* in Walpole's first description of the cas-tle's "subterraneous regions" throughout which "an awful silence reigned." Like the "darkness visible" of Milton's Hell and of numerous later scenes in the Gothic depths, Hervey's powerful oxymoronic descriptions of a silence almost audible would be used by Walpole and later Gothic novelists to generate moods of terror and religious dread.]

a. From "Occasion of the Meditations, A Solitary Walk in a Church"(7).

It was an ancient pile; reared by hands, that, ages ago, were mouldered into dust.—Situate in the centre of a large burial ground; remote from all the noise and hurry of tumultuous life.—The body spacious; the struc-ture lofty; the whole magnificently plain. A row of regular pillars extended themselves through the midst; supporting the roof with sim-plicity, and with dignity.— The light, that passed through the windows, seemed to shed a kind of luminous obscurity, which gave every object a grave and venerable air.— The deep silence, added to the gloomy aspect, and both heightened by the loneliness of the place, greatly increased the solemnity of the scene.— A sort of religious dread stole insensibly on my

---

1   There is no modern edition of Hervey's work. Passages are cited from James Hervey. *Meditations Among the Tombs, Tending to Reform the Vices of the Age, and to Promote Evan-gelical Holiness.* New York: Printed by J. Rivington, and sold by Mr. H. Knox, Boston, 1774.

mind, while I advanced, all pensive and thoughtful, along the inmost aisle. Such a dread, as hushed every ruder passion, and dissipated all the gay images of an alluring world.

[Hervey's description of the descent of the wanderer to a place "of perpetual darkness, and night even at noonday," there to revel in images of death and mortuarial solitude, can stand as a prelude to this same descent in the first Gothic novel and many more to follow. A similar crossover from the upper to the lower world in *The Castle of Otranto* brings the fleeing maiden to "a vault totally dark." The pleasing terror engendered by the descent to a place of ultimate and permanent blackness produced emotions that were akin to religious awe in the face of some divine force totally opposite in character to divinity itself in its dreadful omnipotence.]

b. From "The Vault; Its Awful Aspect" (33–34).

Yonder entrance leads, I suppose, to the vault. Let me turn aside, and take one view of the habitation, and its tenants.— The sullen door grates upon its hinges; not used to receive many visitants, it admits me with reluctance and murmurs.— What meaneth this sudden trepidation, while I descend the steps, and am visiting the pale nations of the dead? ... Good heavens! What a solemn scene!— How dismal the gloom! Here is perpetual darkness, and night even at noon-day.— How doleful the solitude! Not one trace of cheerful society; but sorrow and terror seem to have made this their dreaded abode.— Hark! How the hollow dome resounds at every tread. The echoes, that long have slept, are awakened; and lament and sigh, along the walls. A beam, or two, finds its way through the grates; and reflects a feebler glimmer from the nails of the coffins. So many of those sad spectacles, half concealed in shades; half seen dimly by the baleful twilight; and a deep horror to these gloomy mansions.... My apprehensions recover from their surprise. I find here there are no phantoms, but such as fear raises.— However, it still amazes me to observe the wonders of this nether world. Those, who received their vast revenues, and called whole lordships their own; are here reduced to half a dozen feet of earth, or confined in a few sheets of lead.

3. Bishop Richard Hurd's *Letters on Chivalry and Romance* (1762)

[Bishop Richard Hurd (1720-1808) was chaplain to the Prince of Wales, Archdeacon of Gloucester, and Bishop of Lichfield, Coventry, and Worcester. He was well acquainted with several poets of the Graveyard School, Joseph and Thomas Warton, William Mason, and Walpole's close friend, Thomas Gray. Hurd's purpose in the *Letters on Chivalry and Romance* was to defend the romance and Gothic or medieval elements in the works of Shakespeare, Tasso, Milton, and Spenser as absolutely necessary to the evocation of the highest sublime. The wild, savage, feudal, and medieval aspects of their work were aesthetically positive features of Gothic romance as were the profusions of the nightmarish, the fantastic, and the malign supernatural. Hurd was perhaps the first aesthetic theorist to use such phrases as "Gothic Romance" and "Gothic machinery" in a critically acceptable sense that Walpole and other Gothic novelists would find conducive to their goals of awe, wonder, and sublime fear. The twelve letters are addressed to an imaginary, unnamed correspondent. Selections below are taken from *Letters on Chivalry and Romance*, ed. & intro. Hoyt Trowbridge, The Augustan Reprint Society Publication 101-102, Los Angeles: William Andrews Clark Memorial Library, University of California, Los Angeles, 1963. See also A. L. Smith, "Richard Hurd's *Letters on Chivalry and Romance*," *English Literary History* 5 (1939): 58-81 and Edith J. Morley, *Hurd's Letters on Chivalry and Romance*, London: Henry Frowde, 1911.

The opening letter reflects the movement away from Augustan attitudes of contempt for all things Gothic, i.e. the crude, barbaric, undisciplined, and ill-formed. Hurd's use of the term "Gothic romance" indicates the shift in aesthetic attitudes and perspectives that Walpole's first Gothic novel would exploit. Hurd usually capitalizes the adjective "Gothic" throughout the *Letters* to emphasize its new standing in contrast to the culturally negative and artistically derogatory connotations of lower case "gothic."]

a. From Letter I (4).

Or, May there not be something in Gothic romance peculiarly suited to the views of a genius, and to the ends of poetry? And may not the philosophic moderns have gone too far, in their perpetual ridicule and contempt of it? ... The circumstances in the Gothic fiction and manners, which are proper to the ends of poetry (if such there be) must be pointed out. Reasons for the decline and rejection of the Gothic taste in later times must be given.... You have in these particulars, both the SUBJECT and the PLAN of the following letters.

[The gigantic figure of Alfonso inhabiting the castle's superstructure was prefigured in Hurd's description of "the very castle of a Gothic giant."]

b. From Letter IV (27).

But some few circumstances of agreement between the *heroic* and *gothic* manners, such as are most obvious and occur to my memory, while I am writing, may be worth putting down, by way of specimen only of what may be expected from a professed inquiry into this curious subject ... These giants were oppressive feudal lords, and every lord was to be met with, like the Giant, in his stronghold or castle. Their dependants of a lower form, who imitated the violence of their superiors, and had not their castles, but their lurking-places, were the Savages of Romance. The greater Lord was called a Giant, for his power; the less, a Savage, for his brutality.... All this is shadowed out in the gothic tales, and sometimes expressed in plain words. Nay, could the very castle of a Gothic giant be better described than in the words of Homer, "High walls and battlements the courts inclose,/And the strong gates defy a host of foes."[1]

[Just as "Gothic language and ideas helped [Milton] to work up his tempest with such terror in *Paradise Regained*," so the Gothic mood and tone would serve Walpole's ends in *The Castle of Otranto*. For Hurd, the Gothic style is enhancing, not debilitating, making the subject matter "more poetical for being Gothic."]

c. From Letter VI (52).

And I can't but think that, when Milton wanted to paint the horrors of that night (one of noblest parts in his *Paradise Regained*) which the Devil himself is feigned to conjure up in the wilderness, the Gothic language and ideas helped him to work up his tempest with such terror. You will judge from these lines: "Nor staid the terror there;/Infernal ghosts and hellish furies round environ'd/Some howl'd, some yell'd, some shriek'd,/Some bent at thee their fiery darts" ... We are upon enchanted ground, my friend; and you are to think yourself well used that I detain you no longer in this fearful circle. The glimpse you have had of it, will

---

1   Homer, *The Odyssey*, XII. 318 (Alexander Pope's translation).

help your imagination to conceive the rest. And without more words you will readily apprehend that the fancies of our modern bards are not only more gallant, but, on a change of the scene, more sublime, more terrible, more alarming, than those of the classic fablers. In a word you will find that the *manners* they paint, and the *superstitions* they adopt, are the more poetical for being Gothic.

[Hurd calls Spenser's *Faerie Queene* a "Gothic, not a classical poem," asserts that Milton "delighted with the Gothic romances," and attributes Shakespeare's sublimest designs to his use of Gothic machinery. The Gothic has the power to elevate, to deepen, and to enchant, and to produce sublimity to a degree that eludes classical forms.]

d. From Letter VII (56).

Spenser, tho' he had been long nourished with the spirit and substance of Homer and Virgil, chose the times of chivalry for his theme, and faery land for the scene of his fictions.... He might have trimmed between the Gothic and Classic, as his contemporary Tasso did, but the charms of faery prevailed.... Under this idea then of a Gothic, not classical poem, the *Faery Queene* is to be read and criticized.... Milton it is true preferred the classic model to the Gothic.... Yet we see thro' all his poetry, where his enthusiasm flames out most, a certain predilection for the legends of chivalry before the fables of Greece.... This circumstance, you know, has given offence to the austerer and more mechanical critics. They are ready to censure his judgment, as juvenile and unformed, when they see him so delighted, on all occasions, with the Gothic romances.... Yet one thing is clear, that even he [Shakespeare] is greater when he uses Gothic manners and machinery, than when he employs classical: which brings us again to the same point, that the former [the Gothic romances] have, by their nature and genius, the advantage of the latter [the classics] in producing the *sublime*.

[Letter VIII on the "Gothic composition and method" of Spenser's *Faerie Queene* is a central document in the semantic history of the term "Gothic" and contains several ideas that Walpole found particularly appealing in his creation of the first Gothic novel. Like Gothic architecture, Gothic writing possessed its own rules and standards of unity and could not nor should not be judged by classical standards of taste and design. If the classic ideal was founded on order, so the Gothic ideal was founded on disorder. Where the classical model stressed the regularized beauty of the whole over its parts, the Gothic model stressed the irregular beauty of the parts over any whole. The disunity, deformity, and unregulated passion fostered by the Gothic allowed the artist "to ally two things, in nature incompatible," and in so doing reach new heights of sublimity.]

e. From Letter VIII (61).

When an architect examines a Gothic structure by Grecian rules, he finds nothing but deformity. But the Gothic architecture has its own rules, by which when it comes to be examined, it is seen to have its merit, as well as the Grecian. The question is not, which of the two is conducted in the simplest or truest taste: but, whether there be not sense and design in both, when scrutinized by the laws on which each is projected.... The truth was, the violence of classic prejudices force the poet to affect this appearance of unity, tho' in contradiction to his Gothic system.... and, at least with regard to the historical fable, which we are now considering, was only one of the expedients by which he would conceal the disorder of his Gothic plan.... Their purpose [i.e. Spenser's and Shakespeare's] was to ally two things, in nature incompatible, the Gothic, and the classic unity; the effect of which misalliance was to discover and expose the nakedness of the Gothic.

[In the final "Letter," Hurd attributes the decline and fall of Gothic fancy to the "dawning" of reason and laments this loss. What is too factual and too sensible cannot also be fabulous and sublime. In restoring the Gothic aesthetic to prominence in both his architectural fantasies and his first Gothic novel, Walpole would address the loss of "a world of fine fabling," echoing Hurd's complaint in his statement in the Preface to the second edition of *The Castle of Otranto* that "the great resources of fancy have been dammed up by a strict adherence to common life." Hurd's phrase, "the portentous spectres of the imagination," forecasts the eruption of the Gothic spirit too long "dammed up" by reason and common sense.]

f. From Letter XII (117).

With these helps the new Spirit of chivalry made a shift to support itself for a time, when reason was but dawning, as we may say, and just about to gain the ascendant over the portentous spectres of the imagination. Its growing splendour, in the end, put them all to flight, and allowed them no quarter even amongst the poets.... Henceforth, the taste of wit and poetry took a new turn; and *fancy*, that had wantoned it so long in the world of fiction, was now constrained, against her will, to ally herself with strict truth, if she would gain admittance into reasonable company. What we have gotten by this revolution, you will say, is a great deal of good sense. What we have lost, is a world of fine fabling.

4. Edmund Burke, *A Philosophical Enquiry into the Origin of Our Ideas of the Sublime and Beautiful* (1757)

[Seven years before the publication of *The Castle of Otranto*, Edmund Burke's treatise, *A Philosophical Enquiry into the Origin of our Ideas of the Sublime and Beautiful*,[1] postulated and analyzed the components of a Gothic aesthetic that linked anti-classical notions of the beautiful with awe, darkness, solitude, vastness, terror, and "the great power of the sublime that ... anticipates our reasonings and hurries us on by an irresistible force" (57). In contrast to the Burkean or Gothic sublime, classic notions of sublimity stressed the nobility, impressiveness, and grandeur inherent in order and form. The graceful circularity of the Roman arch (e.g., in the Colosseum in Rome) and the majestic straightness of line of the Greek column (e.g., in the Parthenon in Athens) are architectural expressions of the classical ideals of civilized balance and graceful proportion. But sublime beauty as defined in Burke's treatise was to be felt in the grand gloom inspired by natural scenery and the pleasing terror aroused by disorderly or violent natural events. To be awesome, the object or event must also be awful. His treatise on the sublime argues for an aesthetic ideal entirely opposite from the "sweetness and light"[2] of the classical sublime, replacing these values with the ugliness and darkness of the Gothic Sublime.

Without using the adjective "Gothic," Burke identified the pleasure principle inherent in the Gothic experience as well as the paradox at the core of both Graveyard poetry and Gothic fiction. Optimal pleasure arises when ideas of pain, fear, and supernatural danger displace or dismantle

---

1   Cited here in an excellent modern edition edited and introduced by James T. Boulton. Notre Dame, IN: University of Notre Dame Press, 1968.

2   The phrase "sweetness and light" was first used by Jonathan Swift in "The Battle of the Books" (1704) to describe the superiority of the classical ideals of the ancients over the moderns. See Jonathan Swift, "The Battle of the Books" in *Gullliver's Travels and Other Writings*, ed. Ricardo Quintana. (New York: Modern Library, 1958), 378. The phrase was again used by Matthew Arnold in *Culture and Anarchy* (1869) to denote the preference for order over chaos and civilization over barbarism. See Matthew Arnold, "Sweetness and Light" [Chapter I of *Culture and Anarchy*] in *The Norton Anthology of English Literature*, vol. 2. (New York: W.W. Norton, 1968), 1087-1089.

reason. Such terrible moments are enjoyable and even elating because "the mind is so entirely filled with its object that it cannot entertain any other, nor by consequence reason on that object which employs it" (57). Other emotional compensations included the evocation of a high astonishment which produced in turn an elevation of the soul "in which all its motions are suspended with some degree of horror" (57). According to these Burkean propositions, the fear and menace caused by terrible objects "operate in a manner analogous to terror" and become "sources of the Sublime" that "is productive of the strongest emotion which the mind is capable of feeling" (39). Such feelings of rapturous stupefaction were the psychological equivalent of the "religious horror that wraps / My soul in dread repose" transfixing the observer in a manner similar to a mystical moment of enlightenment. Just as the Graveyard Poets had anticipated Burke's psychology of the sublime, so Walpole and his successors in the art of Gothic fiction would apply and dramatize Burkean theory by conducting both characters and readers through "vault[s] totally dark."[2] In the aftermath of Burke's *Enquiry*, it fell to the Gothic novelists to invent those terrible objects and awesome phenomena that could propel the imagination to sublime summits of pleasure arising out of contact with the unknown, the unknowable, and the ineffably gruesome.

Burke's characterization of death as the "king of terrors" reverts back to Thomas Parnell's personification of death as "King of fears" in "The Night-Piece on Death." The intense emotion brought on by fear of death resembled the wonder and awe of a deep religious experience. For Burke, as for the Gothic novelists, this type of sublimity involved an "overflow of powerful feelings"[3] that could not be processed or categorized by reasoning.

a. From *An Enquiry*, Part One, Section VII, 39.

Whatever is fitted in any sort to excite the ideas of pain, and danger, that is to say, whatever is in any sort terrible, or is conversant about terrible objects, or operates in a manner analogous to terror, is a source of the *sublime*; that is, it is productive of the strongest emotion which the mind

---

1 Thomas Warton, "The Pleasures of Melancholy," line 44. Like Burke's oxymoronic "delightful terror," "dread repose" shows how strong Gothic feelings of pain/pleasure were made up of contradictory sentiments.

2 Walpole's simple phrase in *The Castle of Otranto* inspired thousands of future Gothic titles.

3 William Wordsworth's famous definition of Romantic poetry in the "Preface" to *The Lyrical Ballads* (1798).

is capable of feeling.... But as pain is stronger in its operation than pleasure, so death is in general a much more affecting idea than pain; because there are very few pains, however exquisite, which are not preferred to death; nay, what generally makes pain itself, if I may say so, more painful, is, that it is considered an emissary of this king of terrors.

[Some of Burke's conclusions anticipate the flight-and-pursuit pattern of action of most successful Gothic novels. The "great power of the sublime ... that hurries us on by an irresistible force" suggests the positions of the maiden and the villain in the Gothic spaces beneath the castle. Burke will also argue that "Terror is a passion which always produces delight when it does not press too close."]

b. From *An Enquiry*, Part Two, Section I, 57.

The passion caused by the great and sublime in *nature*, when those causes operate most powerfully, is Astonishment; and astonishment is that state of the soul, in which all its motions are suspended, with some degree of horror. In this case the mind is so entirely filled with its object, that it cannot entertain any other, nor by consequence reason on that object which employs it. Hence arises the great power of the sublime, that far from being produced by them, it anticipates our reasonings, and hurries us on by an irresistible force.

[The distinction between terror and horror is for Burke a matter of degree on the continuum of the sublime. Sublime terror is what is apprehended or expected in the face of vastness, obscurity, and gloom. Thoughts of pain or death "resemble actual pain" and intensify the sublimity to peaks of anguish and horror. Terror (something mental) mounting to horror (something physical) originates in the neutralization of reason in situations of supernatural crisis facing the entrapped characters of Gothic fiction.]

c. From *An Enquiry*, Part Two, Section II, 57.

No passion so effectively robs the mind of all its powers of acting and reasoning as fear. For fear being an apprehension of pain or death, it operates in a manner that resembles actual pain. Whatever therefore is terrible, with regard to sight, is sublime too, whether this cause of terror, be endued with greatness of dimension or not; for it is impossible to look on any thing as trifling, or contemptible, that may be dangerous.

[One of Burke's finest examples of Gothic sublimity is drawn from Milton's *Paradise Lost*.[1] The horrifying, but majestic, figure of King Death, utterly shapeless but "terrible as hell," is "sublime to the last degree" as well as a model for the "gloomy pomp" of future Gothic specters.]

d. From *An Enquiry*, Part Two, Section III, 59.

No person seems better to have understood the secret of heightening, or of setting terrible things, if I may use the expression, in their strongest light by the force of a judicious obscurity, than Milton. His description of Death in the second book [of *Paradise Lost*] is admirably studied; it is astonishing with what a gloomy pomp, with what a significant and expressive uncertainty of strokes and colouring he has finished the portrait of the king of terrors.

> The other shape,
> If shape it might be called that shape had none
> Distinguishable, in member, joint, or limb;
> Or substance might be called that shadow seemed,
> For each seemed either; black he stood as night;
> Fierce as ten furies; terrible as hell;
> And shook a deadly dart. What seemed his head
> The likeness of a kingly crown had on.

In this description, all is dark, uncertain, confused, terrible, and sublime to the last degree.

[Burke studies the relationship of sublimity to power, later to be seen in Gothic fiction in the form of the demonic energy or gigantic force exerted by buildings or the remains of buildings. Incarceration, entrapment, the threat of implosion or collapse, and the general power exerted by the haunted castle over its occupants is a demonstration of the power that evokes "strength, violence, pain and terror."]

---

1 John Milton, *Paradise Lost*, Book II, 666-673. Burke might have continued the quotation which depicts the materialization of Satan: "*Satan* was now at hand, and from his seat / The Monster moving onward came as fast, / With horrid strides, Hell trembled as he strode."

e. From *An Enquiry*, Part Two, Section V, 64–65.

I know of nothing sublime which is not some modification of power.
And this branch rises as naturally as the other two branches, from terror,
the common stock of every thing that is sublime.... But pain is always
inflicted by a power in some way superior, because we never submit to
pain willingly. So that strength, violence, pain and terror, are ideas that
rush in upon the mind together.

[Vastness of scale, particularly in vertical and towering form, functions as
an "engine"[1] of terror while the atmospherics of "Darkness, Solitude, and
Silence" are identified by Burke as sources of Gothic suspense and fear.
By his statement that "height is less grand than depth," he provides the
chief Gothic dynamic for *The Castle of Otranto*'s "lower part[s]," caverns,
and cloisters. As elsewhere, size as well as indeterminate or irregular
shape, are necessary properties of the terror-producing sublimity of verti-
cality.]

f. From *An Enquiry*, Part Two, Section VII, 72.

All *general* privations are great, because they are terrible; Vacuity, Darkness, Solitude, and Silence.... Greatness of dimension, is a powerful cause
of the sublime.... Extension is either in length, height, or depth. Of
these the length strikes least; an hundred yards of even ground will never
work such an effect as a tower an hundred yards high, or a rock or
mountain of that altitude. I am apt to imagine likewise, that height is less
grand than depth; and that we are more struck at looking down from a
precipice, than at looking up at an object of equal height. A perpendicular has more force in forming the sublime, than an inclined plane; and
the effects of a rugged and broken surface seem stronger than where it is
smooth and polished.

[The emotional distress of being caught in an endless maze is prefigured
in Burke's discussion of the power of infinity to fill the mind with
"delightful horror." Burke's conception of terrible infinity also applies to
perilous duration as well as to the close spaces in Gothic fiction. All of

---

1 Reflecting Burke's theory of the power of supernatural objects and the excitement and
   astonishment of terrible power, Walpole wrote in the "Preface" to the first edition of
   The Castle of Otranto, "Terror, the author's principal engine, prevents the story from ever
   languishing."

the acoustics of the Gothic, moans, shrieks, laughs, and sighs emanating from an uncertain source, can intensify sublime feelings. "Uncertain sounds, when the necessary dispositions occur, [are] more alarming than total silence" is a nearly perfect description of the acoustics of the typical Gothic novel formulated on Walpole's plan.]

g. From *An Enquiry*, Part Two, Section XIX, 73, 83–84.

Another source of the sublime is *infinity*; infinity has a tendency to fill the mind with that sort of delightful horror, which is the most genuine effect, and the truest test of the sublime.... A low, tremulous, intermitting sound is productive of the sublime. It is worth while to examine this a little. The fact itself must be determined by every man's own experience, and reflection. I have already observed, that night increases our terror more perhaps than any thing else; it is our nature, that, when we do not know what may happen to us, to fear the worst that can happen to us; and hence it is, that uncertainty is so terrible, that we often seek to be rid of it, at the hazard of a certain mischief. Now some low, confused, uncertain sounds, leave us in the same fearful anxiety concerning their causes, that no light, or an uncertain light does concerning the objects that surround us.... But a light now appearing, and now leaving us, and so off and on, is even more terrible than total darkness; and a sort of uncertain sounds are, when the necessary dispositions concur, more alarming than total silence.

[To succeed, the Gothic must excite prospects of anguish, death, and anxiety over possible extinction. At its finest extremes, Gothic sublimity threatens self-security and generates acute anxiety over self-preservation. The "emotion of distress" arises when characters in Gothic fiction, as well as those readers who vicariously share their predicaments, feel helplessly doomed. One of the major sublime thrills of the Gothic occurs when characters confront in the form of supernatural objects the forceful equivalents of divine power minus any of the benign or salvational attributes of divinity. Such forces in Gothic fiction are godlike, but godless.]

h. From *An Enquiry*, Part Two, Section XXII, 86.

Having thus run through the causes of the sublime with reference to all the senses, my observation will be found very nearly true; that the sublime is an idea belonging to self-preservation. That it is therefore one of the most affecting we have. That its strongest emotion is an emotion of distress, and that no pleasure from a positive cause belongs to it.

[Burke's version of sublimity had a direct and immediate impact on the first Gothic novel. The pain and fear that were provoked by an unmanageable supernatural world, as well as unnatural nature, and the astonishing animation of architecture coupled with "an unnatural tension of the nerves" produced the delightful terrors of *The Castle of Otranto*. Burke's sublimity and Walpole's Gothicism are parallel reactions to the deistic and mechanical constructs of the self and universe in their recognition of powers greater than the conscious self or the Deists' supreme being. The route to a full realization of that beautiful conception is terror.]

i. From *An Enquiry*, Part Four, Section III, 131–132.

I have before observed, that whatever is qualified to cause terror, is a foundation capable of the sublime; to which I add, that not only these, but many things from which we cannot probably apprehend any danger have a similar effect, because they operate in a similar manner.... Fear or terror, which is an apprehension of pain or death, exhibits exactly the same effects, approaching in violence to those just mentioned in proportion to the nearness of the cause, and the weakness of the subject.... That pain and fear consist in an unnatural tension of the nerves; that this is sometimes accompanied with an unnatural strength, which sometimes suddenly changes into an extraordinary weakness; that these effects often come on alternately, and are sometimes mixed with each other. This is the nature of all convulsive agitations, especially in weaker subjects, which are the most liable to the severest impressions of pain and fear. The only difference between pain and terror, is, that things which cause pain operate on the mind, by the intervention of the body; whereas things that cause terror generally affect the bodily organs by the operation of the mind suggesting the danger; but both agreeing, either primarily, or secondarily, in producing a tension, contraction, or violent emotion of the nerves, they agree likewise in every thing else.]

Appendix D: Sir Walter's Scott's Introduction to the 1811 Edition of The Castle of Otranto

[In his introduction to his edition of Walpole's novel, Scott praised Walpole for his revival of "the Gothic style, a term which he contributed to rescue from the bad fame into which it had fallen." Scott's admiration is rooted in his respect for Walpole's antiquarian spirit: "He brings with him the torch of genius, to illuminate the ruins through which he loves to wander." Scott also commented on Walpole's success in directing "the appeal to that secret and reserved feeling of love for the marvellous and supernatural, which occupies a hidden corner in almost everyone's bosom." Placing a high value on Walpole's use of "supernatural machinery," Scott nevertheless felt "that the character of the supernatural machinery in *The Castle of Otranto* is liable to objections. Its action and interference is rather too frequent ... to the hazard of diminishing the elasticity of the spring upon which it should operate." Scott's edition was prepared before he had published his first novel, *Waverley* (1814). In his "Preface" to *Waverley*, Scott acknowledged the influence of Walpole's novel on his own novelistic aims: "I had nourished the ambitious desire of composing a tale of chivalry, which was to be in the style of *The Castle of Otranto*, with plenty of Border characters and supernatural incident."]

The Castle of Otranto is remarkable not only for the wild interest of the story, but as the first modern attempt to found a tale of amusing fiction upon the basis of the ancient romances of chivalry. The neglect and discredit of these venerable legends had commenced so early as the reign of Queen Elizabeth, when, as we learn from the criticism of the times, Spenser's fairy web [in the *Faerie Queene*] was rather approved on account of the mystic and allegorical interpretation, than the plain and obvious meaning of his chivalrous pageant. The drama, which shortly afterwards rose into splendour, and versions from the innumerable novelists of Italy, supplied to the higher class the amusement which their fathers received from the legends of Don Belianis and *The Mirrour of Knighthood*;[1] and the huge volumes which were once the pastime of

---

1   Scott refers to a sixteenth-century courtesy book in Spanish by Diego Ortúnez de Calahorra, *Espejo de Principes y Cavalleros* [Mirror of Princes and Knights]. The work was translated into English with the title *The Mirror of Princely Deeds and Knighthood: Wherein is shewed the worthiness of the Knight of the Sunne, and his brother Rosicleer, sonnes to the great Emperour Trebetio: With the strange love of the beautiful and excellent princesse Briana,*

nobles and princes, shorn of their ornaments, and shrunk into abridgements, where banished to the kitchen and nursery, or, at best, to the hall-window of the old fashioned country manor-house. Under Charles II the-prevailing taste for French literature dictated the introduction of the dullest of dull folios, the romances of Calprenède and Scudéry,[1] works which hover between the ancient tale of chivalry and the modern novel. The alliance was so ill conceived, that they retained all the insufferable length and breadth of the prose volumes of chivalry, the same detailed account of reiterated and unvaried combats, the same unnatural and extravagant turn of incident, without the rich and sublime strokes of genius, and vigour of imagination, which often distinguished the early romance; while they exhibited all the sentimental languor and flat love-intrigue of the novel, without being enlivened by its variety of character, just traits of feeling, or acute views of life.[2] Such an ill-imagined species of composition retained its ground longer than might have been expected, only because these romances were called works of entertainment, and there was nothing better to supply their room. Even in the days of the *Spectator*, Clelia, Cleopatra, and the Grand Cyrus[3] (as that precious folio is christened by its butcherly translator), were the favorite closet companions of the fair sex. But this unnatural taste began to give way early in the eighteenth century; and, about the middle of it, was entirely superseded by the works of Le Sage, Richardson, Fielding, and Smollett;[4] so

---

and the valiant actes of other noble princes and knightes. Now newly translated out of Spanish into our vulgar English tongue, by M.T. London: Thomas East, 1578.

1   Two French romance writers. Gauthier de Costas de La Calprenède's (1614-1663) *Cléopâtre* (1647-56) was popular in England. Madeleine de Scudéry (1607-1701) scored a great success with her heroic romance *Artamène, ou le Grand Cyrus* (1649-53).

2   For the distinction between a romance and a novel see Nathaniel Hawthorne's discussion of the matter in the "Preface" to his novel, *The House of the Seven Gables* (1851). According to Hawthorne, the novel is a literary form that deals in probabilities; the romance is a literary form that deals in possibilities. The novel "aim[s] at a very minute fidelity ... to the probable and ordinary course of man's experience," whereas the romance permits the writer "a certain latitude both as to its fashion and material" thus allowing the imagination greater freedom in introducing marvellous possibilities and "connect[ing] a bygone time with the very present that is flitting away from us." Nathaniel Hawthorne, "Preface" to *The House of the Seven Gables* in *The Complete Novels and Selected Tales of Nathaniel Hawthorne*, ed. Norman Holmes Pearson. (New York: The Modern Library, 1937), 243.

3   Heroes and heroines from the romances of La Calprenède and Scudéry.

4   Scott alludes to four realistic novelists, the French novelist Alain René Le Sage (1668-1747), author of *Gil Blas* (1715-35); the English novelists Samuel Richardson (1689-1761), author of *Pamela; or, Virtue Rewarded* (1740) and *Clarissa: The History of a Young Lady* (1747-48); Henry Fielding (1707-1754), author of *Joseph Andrews* (1742) and *Tom Jones* (1749); Tobias Smollett (1721-1771), author of *Roderick Random* (1748) and *Humphry Clinker* (1771).

that even the very name of romance, now so venerable in the ear of anti-quaries and book-collectors, was almost forgotten at the time *The Castle of Otranto* made its first appearance.

The peculiar situation of Horace Walpole, the ingenious author of this work, was such as gave him a decided predilection for what may be called the Gothic style, a term which he contributed not a little to rescue from the bad fame into which it had fallen, being currently used before his time to express whatever was in pointed and diametrical opposition to the rules of true taste.

Mr. Walpole, it is needless to remind the reader, was son of that cele-brated minister, who held the reins of government under two successive monarchs, with a grasp so firm and uncontrolled, that his power seemed entwined with the rights of the Brunswick family.[1] In such a situation, his sons had necessarily their full share of that court which is usually paid to the near connections of those who have the patronage of the state at their disposal. To the feeling of importance inseparable from the object of such attention, was added the early habit of connecting and associating the interest of Sir Robert Walpole, and even the domestic affairs of this family, with the parties of the Royal Family of England, and with the changes in the public affairs of Europe. It is not therefore wonderful, that the turn of Horace Walpole's mind, which was naturally tinged with love of pedigree, and a value for family honours, should have been strength-ened in that bias by circumstances which seemed, as it were, to bind and implicate the fate of his own house with that of princes, and to give the shields of the Walpoles, Shorters, and Robsarts from whom he descend-ed, an added dignity unknown to their original owners. If Mr. Walpole ever founded hopes of raising himself to political eminence, and turning his family importance to advantage in his career, the termination of his father's power, and the personal change with which he felt it attended, disgusted him with active life, and early consigned him to literary retire-ment. He had, indeed, a seat in parliament for many years; but, unless upon one occasion, when he vindicated the memory of his father with great dignity and eloquence, he took no share in the debates of the house, and not much in the parties which maintained them. The subjects of his study were, in great measure, dictated by his habits of thinking and feeling operating upon an animated imagination, and a mind acute, active, penetrating, and fraught with a great variety of miscellaneous knowledge. Traveling had formed his taste for the fine arts; but his early

---

1 Walpole's somewhat derogatory name for the Royal family of the House of Hanover. See Walpole's letter to William Mason of 18 July 1778: "Will the House of Brunswick listen again to the flatters of prerogative?" (*Horace Walpole's Correspondence* 28: 417).

predilicton in favour of birth and rank connected even these branches of study with that of Gothic history and antiquities. His *Anecdotes of Painting and Engraving* evince many marks of his favourite pursuits; but his *Catalogue of Royal and Noble Authors*, and his *Historical Doubts*, we owe entirely to the antiquary and the genealogist. The former work evinces, in a particular degree, Mr. Walpole's respect for birth and rank; yet may, perhaps, be ill calculated to gain much sympathy for either. It would be difficult, by any process, to select a list of as many plebeian authors, containing so very few whose genius was worthy of commemoration. The *Historical Doubts* are an acute and curious example how minute antiquarian research may shake our faith in the facts most pointedly averred by general history. It is remarkable also to observe how, in defending a system which was probably at first adopted as a mere literary exercise, Mr. Walpole's doubts acquired, in his eyes, the respectablity of certainties, in which he could not brook controversy.

Mr. Walpole's domestic occupations, as well as his studies, bore evidence of a taste for English antiquities, which was then uncommon. He loved, as a satirist has expressed it, "to gaze on Gothic toys through Gothic glass"; and the villa at Strawberry-Hill, which he chose for his abode, gradually swelled into a feudal castle, by the addition of turrets, towers, galleries, and corridors, whose fretted roofs, carved panels, and illuminated windows were garnished with the appropriate furniture of scutcheons, armorial-bearings, shields, tilting lances, and all the panoply of chivalry. The Gothic order of architecture is now so generally, and, indeed, indiscriminately used, that we are rather surprised if the country-house of a tradesman retired from business does not exhibit lanceolated windows, divided by stone shafts, and garnished by painted glass, a cupboard in the form of a cathedral-stall, and a pig-house with the front borrowed from the façade of an ancient chapel. But, in the middle of the eighteenth century, when Mr. Walpole began to exhibit specimens of the Gothic style, and to show how patterns collected from cathedrals and monuments, might be applied to chimney-pieces, ceilings, windows, and balustrades, he did not comply with the dictates of a prevailing fashion, but pleased his own taste, and realised his own visions, in the romantic cast of the mansion which he erected.[1]

---

1   It is well known that Mr. Walpole composed his beautiful and lively fable of the Entail upon being asked, whether he did not mean to settle Strawberry-Hill, when he had completed its architecture and ornaments, upon his family? [Scott's note] "The Entail, a fable" is a poem by Walpole written upon being asked whether or not he intended to "entail" his little castle at Strawberry Hill on his family. In his poetic answer, Walpole quipped: "None but his heirs must own the spot, / begotten, or to be Begot."

Mr. Walpole's lighter studies were conducted upon the same principle which influenced his historical researches, and his taste in architecture. His extensive acquaintance with foreign literature, on which he justly prided himself, was subordinate to his pursuits as an English antiquary and genealogist, in which he gleaned subjects for poetry and for romantic fiction, as well as for historical controversy. These are studies, indeed, proverbially dull; but it is only when they are pursued by those whose fancies nothing can enliven. A Horace Walpole or a Thomas Warton, is not a mere collector of dry and minute facts, which the general historian passes over with disdain. He brings with him the torch of genius, to illuminate the ruins through which he loves to wander; nor does the classic scholar derive more inspiration from the pages of Virgil, than such an antiquary from the glowing, rich, and powerful feudal painting of Froissart. His mind being thus stored with information, accumulated by researches into the antiquities of the middle ages, and inspired, as he himself informs us, by the romantic cast of his own habitation, Mr. Walpole resolved to give the public a specimen of the Gothic style adapted to modern literature, as he had already exhibited its application to modern architecture.

As, in his model of a Gothic modern mansion, our author had studiously endeavoured to fit to the purposes of modern convenience, or luxury, the rich, varied, and complicated tracery and carving of the ancient cathedral, so, in *The Castle of Otranto*, it was his object to unite the marvellous turn of incident, and imposing tone of chivalry, exhibited in the ancient romance, with that accurate exhibition of human character, and contrast of feelings and passions, which is, or ought to be, delineated in the modern novel. But Mr. Walpole, being uncertain of the reception which a work upon so new a plan might experience from the world, and not caring, perhaps, to encounter the ridicule which would have attended its failure, *The Castle of Otranto* was ushered into the world as a translation from the Italian. It does not seem that the authenticity of the narrative was suspected. Mr. Gray writes to Mr. Walpole, on 30th December, 1764: "I have received *The Castle of Otranto*, and return you my thanks for it. It engages our attention here [at Cambridge], makes some of us cry a little; and all, in general, afraid to go to bed o' nights. We take it for a translation; and should believe it to be a true story, if it were not for St. Nicholas." The friends of the author were probably soon permitted to peep beneath the veil he had thought proper to assume; and, in the second edition, it was altogether withdrawn by a preface, in which the tendency and nature of the work are shortly commented upon and explained. From the following passage, translated from a letter by the author to Madame Deffand, it would seem that he repented of having laid aside his incognito; and, sensitive to criticism, like most dilettante authors, was rather more hurt by the raillery of those who liked not his tale of chivalry, than gratified by the applause of his admirers. "So they have translated my *Castle of Otranto*, probably in ridicule of the author. So be it—however, I beg you will let their raillery pass in silence. Let the critics have their own way; they give me no uneasiness. I have not written the book for the present age, which will endure nothing but *cold common sense*. I confess to you, my dear friend, (and you will think me madder than ever), that this is the only one of my works with which I am myself pleased; I have given reins to my imagination until I became on fire with visions and feelings which it excited. I have composed it in defiance of rules, of critics, and of philosophers; and it seems to me so much the better for that very reason. I am even persuaded, that some time hereafter, when taste shall resume the place which philosophy now occupies, my poor *Castle* will find admirers: we have actually a few among us already, for I am just publishing the third edition. I do not say this in order to mendicate your approbation.[1] I told you from the beginning you would not like the book—your visions are all in a different style. I am not sorry that the translator has given the second preface; the first, however, accords best with the style of the fiction. I wished it to be believed ancient, and almost everybody was imposed upon." If the public applause, however, was sufficiently qualified by the voice of censure to alarm the feelings of the author, the continued demand for various editions of *The Castle of Otranto* showed how high the work really stood in popular estimation, and probably eventually reconciled Mr. Walpole to the taste of his own age. This Romance has been justly considered not only as the original and model of a peculiar species of composition, but as one of the standard works of our lighter literature. A few remarks both on the book itself, and on the class to which it belongs, have been judged an apposite introduction to an edition of *The Castle of Otranto*, which the publishers have endeavoured to execute in a style of elegance corresponding to the estimation in which they hold the work, and the genius of the author.

It is doing injustice to Mr. Walpole's memory to allege, that all which he aimed at in *The Castle of Otranto* was "the art of exciting surprise and horror"; or, in other words, the appeal to that secret and reserved feeling

---

1   Madame Deffand had mentioned having read *The Castle of Otranto* twice over; but she did not add a word of approbation. She blamed the translator for giving the second preface, chiefly because she thought it might commit Walpole with Voltaire. [Scott's note] Letter To Madame du Deffand, 13 March 1767. *Horace Walpole's Correspondence*, III: 260.

of love for the marvellous and supernatural, which occupies a hidden corner in almost every one's bosom. Were this all which he had attempted, the means by which he sought to attain his purpose might, with justice, be termed both clumsy and puerile. But Mr. Walpole's purpose was both more difficult of attainment, and more important when attained. It was his object to draw such a picture of domestic life and manners, during the feudal times, as might actually have existed, and to paint it chequered and agitated by the action of supernatural machinery, such as the superstition of the period received as matter of devout credulity. The natural parts of the narrative are so contrived, that they associate themselves with the marvellous occurrences; and, by the force of that association, render those *speciosa miracula*[1] striking and impressive, though our cooler reason admits their impossibility. Indeed to produce, in a well-cultivated mind, any portion of that surprise and fear which is founded on supernatural events, the frame and tenor of the whole story must be adjusted in perfect harmony with this mainspring of the interest. He who, in early youth, has happened to pass a solitary night in one of the few ancient mansions which the fashion of more modern times has left undespoiled of their original furniture, has probably experienced, that the gigantic and preposterous figures dimly visible in the defaced tapestry, the remote clang of the distant doors which divide him from living society, the deep darkness which involves the high and fretted roof of the apartment, the dimly-seen pictures of ancient knights, renowned for their valour, and perhaps for their crimes, the varied and indistinct sounds which disturb the silent desolation of a half-deserted mansion; and, to crown all, the feeling that carries us back to ages of feudal power and papal superstition, join together to excite a corresponding sensation of supernatural awe, if not of terror. It is in such situations, when superstition becomes contagious, that we listen with respect, and even with dread, to the legends which are our sport in the garish light of sun-shine, and amid the dissipating sights and sounds of every-day life. Now it seems to have been Walpole's object to attain, by the minute accuracy of a fable, sketched with singular attention to the costume of the period in which the scene was laid, that same association which might prepare his reader's mind for the reception of prodigies congenial to the creed and feelings of the actors. His feudal tyrant, his distressed damsel, his resigned, yet dignified, churchman—the Castle itself, with its feudal arrangement of dungeons, trap-doors, oratories, and galleries, the incidents of the trial, the chivalrous procession, and the combat—in short, the scene, the performers, and action, so far as it is natural, form the accompaniments of his

---

1 Specious miracles.

spectres and miracles, and have the same effect on the mind of the reader that the appearance and drapery of such a chamber as we have described may produce upon that of a temporary inmate. This was a task which required no little learning, no ordinary degree of fancy, no common portion of genius, to execute. The association of which we have spoken is of a nature peculiarly delicate, and subject to be broken and disarranged. It is, for instance, almost impossible to build such a modern Gothic structure as shall impress us with the feelings we have endeavoured to describe. It may be grand, or it may be gloomy; it may excite magnificent or melancholy ideas; but it must fail in bringing forth the sensation of supernatural awe, connected with halls that have echoed to the sounds of remote generations, and have been pressed by the footsteps of those who have long since passed away. Yet Horace Walpole has attained in composition, what, as an architect, he must have felt beyond the power of his art. The remote and superstitious period in which his scene is laid, the art with which he has furnished forth its Gothic decorations, the sustained, and, in general, the dignified tone of feudal manners, prepare us gradually for the favourable reception of prodigies which, though they could not really have happened at any period, were consistent with the belief of all mankind at that in which the action is placed. It was, therefore, the author's object not merely to excite surprise and terror, by the introduction of supernatural agency, but to wind up the feelings of his reader till they became for a moment identified with those of a ruder age, which held each strange tale devoutly true.

The difficulty of attaining this nice accuracy of delineation may be best estimated by comparing *The Castle of Otranto* with the less successful efforts of later writers; where, amid all their attempts to assume the tone of antique chivalry, something occurs in every chapter so decidedly incongruous, as at once reminds us of an ill-sustained masquerade, in which ghosts, knights-errant, magicians, and damsels gent, are all equipped in hired dresses from the same warehouse in Tavistock-street.[1]

There is a remarkable particular in which Mr. Walpole's steps have been departed from by the most distinguished of his followers.

Romantic narrative is of two kinds—that which, being in itself possible, may be matter of belief at any period; and that which, though held impossible by more enlightened ages, was yet consonant with the faith of earlier times. The subject of *The Castle of Otranto* is of the latter class.

---

1 Street in London where were located various shops and warehouses in the 1790s that supplied costumes, props, and scenery to the theaters. See *The London Stage 1660-1800*, eds. Emmett L. Avery, Arthur H. Scouten, William Van Lennep. Carbondale and Edwardsville: Southern Illinois University Press, 1979, 828 and passim.

Mrs. Radcliffe,[1] a name not to be mentioned without the respect due to genius, has endeavoured to effect a compromise between those different styles of narrative, by referring her prodigies to an explanation, founded on natural causes, in the latter chapters of her romances. To this improvement upon the Gothic romance there are so many objections, that we own ourselves inclined to prefer, as more simple and impressive, the narrative of Walpole, which details supernatural incidents as they would have been readily believed and received in the eleventh or twelfth centuries. In the first place, the reader feels indignant at discovering he has been cheated into a sympathy with terrors which are finally explained as having proceeded from some very simple cause; and the interest of a second reading is entirely destroyed by his having been admitted behind the scenes at the conclusion of the first. Secondly, the precaution of relieving our spirits from the influence of supposed supernatural terror, seems as unnecessary in a work of professed fiction, as that of the prudent Bottom, who proposed that the human face of the representative of his lion should appear from under his masque[2] and acquaint the audience plainly that he was a man as other men, and nothing more than Snug the joiner. Lastly, these substitutes for supernatural agency are frequently to the full as improbable as the machinery which they are introduced to explain away and to supplant. The reader, who is required to admit the belief of supernatural interference, understands precisely what is demanded of him; and, if he be a gentle reader, throws his mind into the attitude best adapted to humour the deceit which is presented for his entertainment, and grants, for the time of perusal, the premises on which the fable depends.[3] But if the author voluntarily binds himself to account for all

---

1   The Gothic novelist, Ann Radcliffe (1764-1823) rose to prominence with her romances *The Mysteries of Udolpho* (1794) and *The Italian* (1797). Scott admired her work.

2   Honest Bottom's device [in Shakespeare's *A Midsummer Night's Dream*] seems to have been stolen by Mr. John Wiseman, schoolmaster of Linlithgow, who performed a Lion in a pageant presented before Charles I, but vindicated his identity in the following verses put into his mouth by Drummond of Hawthornden:

> Thrice royal sir, here do I thee beseech,
> Who art a lion, to hear a lion's speech:
> A miracle! for, since the days of Aesop,
> No lion till those times his voice did raise up
> To such a majesty: Then, King of Men,
> The King of beasts speaks to thee from his den,
> Who, though he now be inclosed in plaster,
> When he was free, was Lithgow's wise schoolmaster. [Scott's note]

3   There are instances to the contrary however. For example, that stern votary of severe truth, who cast aside *Gulliver's Travels* as containing a parcel of improbable fictions. [Scott's note]

the wondrous occurrences which he introduces, we are entitled to exact that the explanation shall be natural, easy, ingenious, and complete. Every reader of such works must remember instances in which the explanation of mysterious occurrences in the narrative has proved equally, nay, even more incredible, than if they had been accounted for by the agency of supernatural beings. For the most incredulous must allow, that the interference of such agency is more possible than that an effect resembling it should be produced by an inadequate cause. But it is unnecessary to enlarge further on a part of the subject, which we have only mentioned to exculpate our author from the charge of using machinery more clumsy than his tale from its nature required. The bold assertion of the actual existence of phantoms and apparitions seems to us to harmonise much more naturally with the manners of feudal times, and to produce a more powerful effect upon the reader's mind, than any attempt to reconcile the superstitious credulity of feudal ages with the philosophic skepticism of our own, by referring those prodigies to the operation of fulminating powder, combined mirrors, magic lanthorns, trap-doors, speaking trumpets, and like apparatus of German phantasmagoria.

It cannot, however, be denied, that the character of the supernatural machinery in *The Castle of Otranto* is liable to objections. Its action and interference is rather too frequent, and presses too hard and constantly upon the same feelings in the reader's mind, to the hazard of diminishing the elasticity of the spring upon which it should operate. The fund of fearful sympathy which can be afforded by a modern reader to a tale of wonder, is much diminished by the present habits of life and mode of education. Our ancestors could wonder and thrill through all the mazes of any interminable metrical romance of fairy land, and of enchantment, the work perhaps of some

> Prevailing poet, whose undoubting mind
> Believed the magic wonders which he sung.[1]

But our habits and feelings and beliefs are different, and a transient, though vivid, impression is all that can be excited by a tale of wonder even in the most fanciful mind of the present day. By the too frequent recurrence of his prodigies, Mr. Walpole ran, perhaps, his greatest risks of awakening *la raison froide*,[2] that cold common sense, which he justly

---

1 Lines 199-200 of William Collins's "Ode on the Popular Superstitions of the Highlands of Scotland Considered as the Subject of Poetry" (1749) in *The New Oxford Book of Eighteenth-Century Verse*, ed. Roger Lonsdale (New York: Oxford University Press, 1984), 384.
2 Cold reason.

deemed the greatest enemy of the effect which he hoped to produce. It may be added also, that the supernatural occurrences of *The Castle of Otranto* are brought forward into too-strong daylight, and marked by an over degree of distinctness and accuracy of outline. A mysterious obscurity seems congenial at least, if not essential, to our ideas of disembodied spirits, and the gigantic limbs of the ghost of Alphonso, as described by the terrified domestics, are somewhat too distinct and corporeal to produce the feelings which their appearance is intended to excite. This fault, however, if it be one, is more than compensated by the high merit of many of the marvellous incidents in the romance. The descent of the picture of Manfred's ancestor, although it borders on extravagance, is finely introduced, and interrupts an increasing dialogue with striking effect. We have heard it observed, that the animated figure should rather have been a statue than a picture. We greatly doubt the justice of the criticism. The advantage of the colouring induces us decidedly to prefer Mr. Walpole's fiction to the proposed substitute. There are few who have not felt, at some period of their childhood, a sort of terror from the manner in which the eye of an ancient portrait appears to fix that of the spectator from every point of view. It is, perhaps, hypercritical to remark (what, however, Walpole of all authors might have been expected to attend to), that the time assigned to the action, being about the eleventh century, is rather too early for the introduction of a full-length portrait. The apparition of the skeleton hermit to the prince of Vicenza was long accounted a master-piece of the horrible; but of late the valley of Jehosophat could hardly supply the dry bones necessary for the exhibition of similar spectres, so that injudicious and repeated imitation has, in some degree, injured the effect of its original model. What is most striking in *The Castle of Otranto*, is the manner in which the various prodigious appearances, bearing each upon the other, and all upon the accomplishment of the ancient prophecy, denouncing the ruin of the house of Manfred, gradually prepare us for the grand catastrophe. The moon-light vision of Alphonso dilated to immense magnitude, the astonished group of spectators in the front, and the shattered ruins of the castle in the back-ground, is briefly and sublimely described. We know no passage of similar merit, unless it be the apparition of Fadzean in the ancient Scottish poem.[1]

That part of the romance which depends upon human feelings and agency, is conducted with the dramatic talent which afterwards was so conspicuous in *The Mysterious Mother*. The persons are indeed rather

---

1   This spectre, the ghost of a follower whom he had slain upon suspicion of treachery, appeared to no less a person than Wallace, the champion of Scotland, in the ancient castle of Gask-hall.—see Ellis's *Specimens*, vol. I. [Scott's note]

generic than individual, but this was in a degree necessary to a plan calculated rather to exhibit a general view of society and manners during the times which the author's imagination loved to contemplate, than the more minute shades and discriminating points of particular characters. But the actors in the romance are strikingly drawn, with bold outlines becoming the age and nature of the story. Feudal tyranny was, perhaps, never better exemplified, than in the character of Manfred. He has the courage, the art, the duplicity, the ambition of a barbarous chieftain of the dark ages, yet touches of remorse and natural feeling, which preserve some sympathy for him when his pride is quelled, and his race extinguished. The pious monk, and the patient Hippolita, are well contrasted with this selfish and tyrannical prince. Theodore is the juvenile hero of a romantic tale, and Matilda has more interesting sweetness than usually belongs to its heroine. As the character of Isabella is studiously kept down, in order to relieve that of the daughter of Manfred, few readers are pleased with the concluding insinuation, that she became at length the bride of Theodore. This is in some degree a departure from the rules of chivalry; and however natural an occurrence in common life, rather injures the magic illusions of romance. In other respects, making allowance for the extraordinary incidents of a dark and tempestuous age, the story, so far as within the course of natural events, is happily detailed, its progress is uniform, its events interesting and well combined, and the conclusion grand, tragical, and affecting.

The style of *The Castle of Otranto* is pure and correct English of the earlier and more classical standard. Mr. Walpole rejected, upon taste and principle, those heavy though powerful auxiliaries which Dr. Johnson imported from the Latin language, and which have since proved to many a luckless wight, who has essayed to use them, as unmanageable as the gauntlets of Eryx.

> ─────────et pondus et ipsa
> Huc illuc vinclorum immensa volumina versat.[1]

Neither does the purity of Mr. Walpole's language, and the simplicity of his narrative, admit that luxuriant, florid, and high-varnished landscape painting with which Mrs. Radcliffe often adorned, and not unfrequently encumbered, her kindred romances. Description, for its own sake, is scarcely once attempted in *The Castle of Otranto*, and if authors

---

1   "And he turns the weight and the very great bulk of its enormous chains this way and that." "The gauntlets of Eryx" is a mythological reference to the boxing gloves of Eryx, son of Poseidon, who was slain by Heracles.

would consider how very much this restriction tends to realise narrative, they might be tempted to abridge at least the showy and wordy exuberance of a style fitter for poetry than prose. It is for the dialogue that Walpole reserves his strength; and it is remarkable how, while conducting his mortal agents with all the art of a modern dramatist, he adheres to the sustained tone of chivalry, which marks the period of the action. This not attained by patching his narrative or dialogue with glossarial terms, or antique phraseology, but by taking care to exclude all that can awaken modern associations. In the one case, his romance would have resembled a modern dress, preposterously decorated with antique ornaments; in its present shape, he has retained the form of the ancient armour, but not its rust and cobwebs. In illustration of what is above stated, we refer the reader to the first interview of Manfred with the prince of Vicenza, where the manners and language of chivalry are finely painted, as well as the perturbation of conscious guilt confusing itself in attempted exculpation, even before a mute accuser. The characters of the inferior domestics have been considered as not bearing a proportion sufficiently dignified to the rest of the story. But this is a point on which the author has pleaded his own cause fully in the original prefaces.

We have only to add, in conclusion to these desultory remarks, that if Horace Walpole, who led the way in this new species of literary composition, has been surpassed by some of his followers in diffuse brilliancy of description, and perhaps in the art of detaining the mind of the reader in a state of feverish and anxious suspense, through a protracted and complicated narrative, more will yet remain with him than the single merit of originality and invention. The applause due to chastity and precision of style, to a happy combination of supernatural agency with human interest, to a tone of feudal manners and language, sustained by characters strongly drawn and well discriminated, and to unity of action producing scenes alternately of interest and of grandeur—the applause, in fine, which cannot be denied to him who can excite the passions of fear and pity, must be awarded to the author of *The Castle of Otranto*.

Glossary

Other useful glossaries and surveys of terms may be found under "Gothic Specialisms" in *The Handbook to Gothic Literature*, ed. Marie Mulvey-Roberts, New York: New York UP, 1998. Some terms collected here also appeared in the "Glossary of Gothic Terms" in *The First Gothics: A Critical Guide to the English Gothic Novel*, New York: Garland Publishing, 1987. Where relevant, the terms in the glossary are linked to *The Castle of Otranto* and *The Mysterious Mother*.

Algolagnia. The distorted attitude that love is enjoyable only when it is preceded or accompanied by pain or the threat of pain. Male Gothic algolagniacs such as Manfred in *The Castle of Otranto* ruthlessly pursue their victims in subterranean settings and are bent on rape or something worse. Female algolagniacs secretly desire the thing they fear most and express that fear by flight through the enclosing darkness.

Anti-Catholicism. In many Gothic novels, the Catholic Church functions as a cultural metaphor for social, political, and sexual repression. Abbeys and convents presided over by monastic tyrants or twisted authority figures are never sanctuaries but are instead houses of horror and are as frequent as haunted castles or mansions in post-Walpolean Gothic fiction. The Catholic churchman was synonymous with foreign mystery, clandestine power, evil intrigue, and monstrous lust. Anti-Catholicism reflects Protestant fears and prejudices as well as historical memories of Italy and Spain as traditional enemies and decadent cultures. Although Father Jerome, the ineffectual priest in *The Castle of Otranto*, has not yet attained wicked stature, Father Benedict, the Countess's malicious and scheming confessor in *The Mysterious Mother*, is an early and memorable portrait of the Gothic's monastic villain.

Bluebook Gothics. Identified by their garish blue covers or wrappers, Gothic bluebooks were cheaply manufactured condensations of Gothic novels. These primitive paperbacks were meant to be thrown away after being literally "read to pieces." Walpole's plot as well as his cast of characters, especially the skeletal monk who startles Frederic in the oratory, recur frequently in the bluebooks. Bluebooks multiplied in their hundreds in the two decades from 1790 to 1810.

Burgverliess Gothic. The German term "Burgverliess" (Burg or "castle"; Verliess or "dungeon") was first applied by Eino Railo in *The*

Haunted Castle: A Study of the Elements of English Romanticism (1927) to designate a hideous confining space or place, usually subterranean, "from which there was not the remotest possibility of escape, a place without an exit." Many Gothics after Walpole would strive for the Burgverliess effect or horrible sensation of being permanently imprisoned or entombed.

Chapbook Gothics. Cheaply made and mass-marketed short Gothic fiction frequently illustrated with crude woodcuts and almost always pla-giaristically based on the Gothic novels of Walpole, Ann Radcliffe, and Monk Lewis. Chapbooks typically ran from 36 to 72 pages and were typically sold at a shilling or less, hence the low priced name of "shilling shocker." As with the bluebooks, chapbook authors often pilfered from· Walpole's plots, people, and places in *The Castle of Otranto* to meet their page quotas and satisfy their readership's need for formulaic horror. The heyday of the Gothic chapbook was the period 1790 to 1810, later merg-ing into crime-and-dime fiction and Victorian bloods and "penny dreadfuls."

Cryptamnesia. Term used by E.F. Bleiler in his introduction to an edi-tion of *The Castle of Otranto* to describe acts of repressive memory dur-ing which the Gothic writer subconsciously introduces recollections of real sites of fear, wonder, and alarm into the architectural textures of the tale. Places of real dread, terror, and supernatural excitement are "remembered" and reused in the cryptic imagery of the narrative. An example of how cryptamnesia operates is to be found in Walpole's description of the great courtyard of the Castle of Otranto. He told Madame du Deffand in a letter of 27 January 1775, some ten years after the publication of the novel, about a return visit he had made to Trinity College, Cambridge. Entering the courtyard of one of the colleges, he suddenly realized where he had obtained the description for the court-yard of Otranto. "En entrant dans un des collèges que j'avais entièrement oublié, je me trouvais précisément dans la cour de mon château.... Enfin l'idée de ce collège m'était restée dans la tête sans y penser, et je m'en etais servi pour le plan de mon château sans m'en apercevoir"; [*Transla-tion*: Upon entering one of the colleges that I had entirely forgotten, I found myself in the very courtyard of my castle. Thus, the idea of this college had remained hidden in my mind and, unaware, I had used it for the plans of my castle.

Cryptonomy. Literally, the practice of secret naming. Applied to Goth-ic fiction, the term refers to signs, symbols, and semiotic values associated with crypts, enclosures, recesses, and subterranean chambers.

Doppelgänger. From the German "Doppel" meaning "double" or "duplicate." Refers to a second self or second personality sometimes, but not always, a physical twin. In demonic/Gothic form, the Doppelgänger can be a lower, bestial, or Satanic self in competition with the higher or civilized self for control of the character's thoughts and deeds. The most extensive Gothic presentation of the Doppelgänger figure occurs in James Hogg's novel of the demonic double, *The Private Memoirs and Confessions of a Justified Sinner* (1824).

Female Gothic. Term first used by the critic Ellen Moers to categorize and describe that type of Gothic fiction that focuses on the distresses, perils, and victimization of women. Walpole's Isabella and Matilda in *The Castle of Otranto*, and to a much greater extent, the Countess of Narbonne in *The Mysterious Mother*, are early versions of the female Gothic.

Frénétique. From the French, meaning "frantic" or "raving."

Frisson. From the French, meaning "chilling," "shivering," or "shuddering." Terror (anticipation) is perhaps a stronger stimulus than horror (realization) of *frisson* in Gothic characters, since *frisson* relies to a greater extent on suspense.

G dài ti. The term "Gothic" in Chinese.

Ghost, Specter, Apparition, Phantom. Supernatural beings sometimes visible, sometimes seen as ectoplasmic manifestations, and sometimes as departed spirits returned in material form. Gothic ghosts are typically attached to specific locales within the haunted castle. Phantoms are phantoms "of the cloister," or specters are specters "of the turret." Walpole's ghosts in *The Castle of Otranto*, the immense body of Alfonso the Good, the walking specter of Ricardo, and the animated skeletal monk of Isabella's oratory, are all "specters of the castle."

Gigantism. The theme of enormity or hugeness or "immense magnitude," to use Walpole's phrase. Common in romance, colossal characters can be comic illusions such as Spenser's Orgoglio in Book One of *The Faerie Queene* or titanic figures such as Walpole's vindicator giant, Alfonso the Good, in *The Castle of Otranto*.

Gothic. Throughout the eighteenth century, the word retains its architectural (medieval building styles) and anthropological (Gothic tribes) associations, but with the rise of the Gothic novel, it connotes some new meanings and requires almost constant redefinition as its value shifts from a term of denigration to approbation. When Walpole appended the adjective to the title of the second edition of *The Castle of Otranto*, he sought to focus attention on the medieval, mysterious, and arcane nature of the narrative. Later Gothic writers employ the adjective as a synonym for horrific, terrifying, shocking, ghastly, and ghostly, with less reference to its architectural or cultural connections. The etymology of "Gothic" is further skewed by loose application to anything darkly bizarre or fearsome including clothes, music, cars, and hair styles. By formalist definition in a literary context the adjective refers to a narrative of supernatural fear and danger in diminishing or confining space.

Gothic Aesthetic. Ecstasy in horror, pleasure in terror, delight in the sinister, and gratification drawn from the ghastly and gruesome. Baudelaire's famous phrase "esthetique du mal" ("beauty of evil") states the paradox of Gothic pleasure. The awesome, the ugly, the misshapen, and the decayed and other repulsive characteristics are endowed with a peculiar beauty and attractiveness through the Gothic aesthetic.

Gothic Fragment. An unfinished or aborted Gothic novel, novella, or short story. See the exemplary Gothic fragment by Anna Laetitia Aikin Barbauld, *Sir Bertrand: A Fragment* (1792).

Gothic Heroine. Perennial sufferer and victim in Gothic fiction, the Gothic heroine is always virtuous, sometimes hysterical, and usually secretly attracted to the villain who menaces and pursues her through "a vault totally dark" (to use Walpole's phrase). Walpole's Isabella (and to some extent, Matilda) are important prototypes, soon to become stereotypes as the Gothic novel evolves.

Gothic Novel. In simplest terms, a tale of terror and/or horror whose action is restricted to a haunted, unsafe, or dreadful building. The atmosphere is mysterious and foreboding, character behavior is inexplicable or darkly motivated, and the supernatural must be present either physically (real specters) or psychologically (imagined demons). In Walpole's first Gothic novel, potent, superhuman forces control the human world and disrupt natural law. Subterranean shocks and surprises occur regularly. Evil is stronger than good, or at the very least, must seem so to the victimized characters. Based on Walpole's model, early twentieth-century critics have tended to define the Gothic novel by enumerating its generic parts, e. g. a haunted castle, a terrifying underground, and various supernatural props or contraptions such as animated statuary and peregrinating portraits. Later contemporary criticism defines the Gothic novel from a trans-generic perspective, with a concentration on intent and reader response rather than a fixed nomenclature of parts. Whether defined by its content or intent, the true Gothic novel must have the following seven imperative features: 1) Claustrophobic containment or some form of circumscription or enclosure, either physical or psychological; 2) Subterraneous pursuit; 3) Inorganic sentience, i.e. buildings have eyes or throats, pictures have moving eyes, statues have nosebleeds; 4) "Extraordinary positions," and lethal predicaments. Death by lightning, by the crushing impact of a falling helmet, by being hurled from some great height, or live burial by collapsing structures are prominent examples of the Gothic's "extraordinary positions," a phrase first used by Walpole in his Preface to the first edition of *The Castle of Otranto*; 5) Abeyance of rationality. Beginning with Walpole, high Gothic fiction creates an overriding sense of irrational helplessness and defenselessness against the superiority of dark forces; characters cannot reason their way out of the labyrinth; 6) Ubiquity of evil. Gothic fiction attains apexes of horror and terror when both characters and readers come to feel the possibility of evil's triumph over good, a dreadful awareness of "virtue unrewarded." Even in the most didactic forms of Gothic fiction, the ubiquity of evil must be present as a counterforce; 7) "A Constant vicissitude of interesting passions." Walpole's phrase from the "Preface" to the first edition of *The Castle of Otranto* delineates the acute emotional extremes that drive Gothic characters. Powerful emotions, many of these sexual or psychopathic in nature, are not limited to the human characters but motivate the demonic and spectral personalities as well. Constantly fluctuating emotions produce interesting, if irregular, passions such as those to be seen in the behavior of the Countess of Narbonne in Walpole's *The Mysterious Mother*.

Gothic Revival. A movement in the arts both preceding and concurrent with the rise of the Gothic novel in the final decades of the eighteenth century. The attitudes of the Gothic revival were a reaction against the symmetry and regularity of Palladian and classical styles of architecture. Gothic revivalists, such as Walpole at Strawberry Hill and John Wyatt in his design for the Houses of Parliament, thought of their buildings as romantic reproductions of the edifices of the high middle ages, such as cathedrals, castles, and Gothic fortresses. The Gothic revival reaches its extremes in the construction of ruins and other kinds of counterfeit devastation. See Sir Kenneth Clark, *The Gothic Revival: An Essay in the History of Taste* (1928).

Gothic Villain. The main perpetrator of evil and violence in the Gothic novel, he is a mixed character, a tormented tormentor or lacerated being who apprehends goodness but prefers its opposite. These contradictions are to be found in Manfred, the proto-Gothic villain whose character "was naturally humane; and his virtues were always ready to operate, when his passions did not obscure his reason" (*Otranto*, 87).

Gothified History. A type of Gothic novel evolving in part from Walpole's counterfeit translation of episodes in medieval history. Gothified history presents an imaginary middle ages or invented past to startle and excite the audience. Thomas Leland's *Longsword, Earl of Salisbury* (1762) is an early example of Gothified history. An atmosphere of terror, danger, suffering, and gloom is joined to a complex plot usually involving a mystery of royal or noble genealogy. The nobility of the peasant Theodore in Walpole's cast is a typical element of Gothified history. Gothified history or the historical Gothic novel would be carried to a fine art in the work of Sir Walter Scott who comments on his preference for the form in the "Preface" to his edition of *The Castle of Otranto*.

Gothique. The term "Gothic" in French.

The Goths. Barbarian tribes and peoples inhabiting northern Europe in the first, second, third, and fourth centuries. The Goths are first mentioned by the Roman historian Tacitus in *Germania* (circa 98 A.D.). Under their king, Alaric, the Goths attacked and sacked the city of Rome in 410 A.D. Thus, the Goths came to be seen as annihilators of classical culture, disseminators of barbarism over civilization. Shakespeare depicted the Goths as bestial, cruel, and crude in his blood tragedy, *Titus Andronicus*. In the eighteenth century, Graveyard poetry, antiquarian enthusiasm, and the arrival of the Gothic novel rendered the Goths objects of dark fascination, as the culture of the sublime eagerly converted the noun into the adjective. Out of the history of the Goths came the term Gothic, a protean epithet for savage, medieval, mysterious, and horrible, but alluring.

Goticeskijstil. The term "Gothic" in Russian.

Gótico. The term "Gothic" in Italian, Portuguese, and Spanish.

Gotisch. The term "Gothic" in German.

Graveyard Poetry. Poems celebrating the morbid grandeur of death and extolling the glories of the grave. Their settings, their point of view and their lost characters are examples of pure Gothic before the fact. See Appendix C:1.

Grotesque. The word derives from the Italian "grottesca," referring to Roman grottos or caves and their exotic decorations. Grotesque has come to signify a strange or distorted mixture of incompatibles such as human and animal qualities in one object. In the larger sense, grotesque means any unnatural arrangement emphasizing the ugly, the bizarre, and the fantastic. Grotesque objects, characters, and settings in Gothic fiction often display a merger of the loathsome and the ludicrous.

Grotto Gothic. A Gothic in which the main action is restricted to a cavernous or subterranean setting.

Grottophilia. A preference on the part of some characters to seek out an adventure within a contractive enclosure located somewhere inside the dark building. Such a compulsion suggests a psychological return to the darkness of the womb, an attempt to descend into primal identity, or a fall into another order of being.

Horror. Although it is sometimes used interchangeably with the word terror, it must be defined as the final stage or degree of terror, when the terrible or terrifying is touched, seen, or swallowed, thus becoming horrible or horrorific to an ineffable degree. Horror is both a response and an effect in Gothic fiction, provoking disgust, shock, panic, uncontrollable fear, and speechlessness. In its crudest physical forms, it is less cathartic than simply emetic, a sickening or benumbing assault on the senses. "The difference between Terror and Horror is the difference between awful apprehension and sickening realization: between the smell of death and stumbling against a corpse" (Devendra P. Varma, *The Gothic Flame*, 1957). See Terror.

Inset Tale. A common feature of Gothic narrative, especially in longer Gothic fiction. The inset or tale within the larger tale often recounts the adventures of a dead or missing relative of the heroine and relates in some mysterious or ingenious way to the riddle of her paternity or identity.

Märchen. German fairytale containing fantastic, grotesque, and supernatural elements.

Monastic Shocker. Term introduced by William Whyte Watt (*Shilling Shockers of the Gothic School*, 1932) to describe a special subspecies of Gothic fiction "whose principal background was a monastery or convent." The monastic shocker featured a nefarious abbot or abbess, a menaced heroine under coercion to take the veil but actually under sexual intimidation, and harassed by apparitions in ecclesiastic garb. The monastic shocker has a beginning in the scene in Isabella's chapel when Frederic of Vicenza is confronted by the skeletal monk.

Qiah uiyah. The term "Gothic" in Arabic.

Räuberroman. Literally, "robber romance." Brigands and bandits filled the role of Gothic villain in the robber romances.

Ritterroman. *Ritter* is the German for "knight" or "chevalier." A Ritterroman is a romance of chivalry. Feudal tyranny, Catholic treachery, supernatural incident, and the dark journey are typical elements.

Romance of the Ruin. Category of Gothic novel that locates its main action in, around, and beneath an ancient devastated building. Passion for the ruin was part of the aesthetic climate of both the Gothic revival and the Gothic novel.

Roman Noir. Literally meaning "dark romance," the term is used for the French Gothic novel and is often simply translated as such. The *roman noir* was present on the literary scene at least as early as Walpole's *Castle of Otranto* in such dark works as *Les Amants malheureux; ou, les comte de comminge* (The Unfortunate Lovers; or, The Count of Comminge) by Thomas Marie de Baculard d'Arnaud, published in 1764.

Roman Terrifiant. The term "terrifying romance" is often applied to Mrs. Radcliffe's imitators in French Gothic fiction.

Satan. The devil appears both as himself and in the form of Satanic personalities in the pages of Gothic fiction. The traits of the Gothic hero-villain are rooted in the Satanic archetype. Generally speaking, Gothic Satans are modeled on the suavity, dark handsomeness, and fallen goodness of the Miltonic Satan rather than drawn from the ghastly creatured Satans of medieval iconography. Walpole's Father Benedict in *The Mysterious Mother* is an early instance of the Satanic personality, a man who is driven to invade the secret lives of others and inflict pain through power.

Schauerroman. Literally, a "shudder" novel, dependent for its effects on Gothic horror rather than Gothic terror. The term is sometimes reserved to characterize a special variety of German Gothicism which causes quivers, chills, and similar numbing effects through its extreme horrors and unchecked supernatural gore.

Shilling Shocker. Short Gothic fiction consisting of 36 to 72 roughly stitched pages and given the form of a primitive paperback. Walpole's plot, paraphernalia, and characters furnished the grist for thousands of these little Gothics.

Souterrain. The French for the "underground."

Terror. Not horror's opposite, but horror's complement on a scale of responses. Terror is caused by what is dreaded and anticipated and relies heavily on suspense. It also has an apprehensive and suggestive dimension that can evoke feelings of the sublime that the directness and intensity of horror lacks. Terror, then, is preliminary fear accompanied by a certain delight in the awful anticipation that terror brings. Pleasure ceases when terror proceeds to horror. One of the first to differentiate between terror and horror in Gothic fiction was Mrs. Radcliffe, who wrote in her 1826 essay "On the Supernatural in Poetry" that "Terror and horror are so far opposite, that the first expands the soul, and awakens the faculties to a high degree of life; the other contracts, freezes, and nearly annihilates them."[1] When Walpole refers to "terror" as his "principal engine," he indicates his attitude toward terror as both a sublime and aesthetically positive value.

Unheimlich. Usually translated as "uncanny," the word also connotes "unhomely" or "alien to the home" in the sense of inducing uneasiness

---

1   Ann Radcliffe, "On the Supernatural in Poetry," *New Monthly Magazine* vol. 16 (1826):
    145-52. Reprinted with an introduction in *Gothic Readings: The First Wave, 1764-1840*,
    ed. Rictor Norton. (London and New York: Leicester Univ. Press, 2000), 311-316.

or uncomfortable feelings. The primary meaning in the Gothic context relates uncanniness to the sinister, the weird, the gloomy, the dismal, and the ominous. See Freud's famous 1919 essay, "The Uncanny."

Wraith. The ghost of a living person.

Zerrissenheit. A condition of disunion or inner strife often seen in the psychomachic character laceration of the Gothic hero-villain. In Gothic fiction, laceration of the self appears in the divided condition of Manfred, whose nature is both heroic and villainous. He is described by Walpole as both "a man of many sorrows" and a tyrant of "exquisite villainy." His "temper ... was naturally humane and his virtues were always ready to operate when his passions did not obscure his reason" (*Otranto*, 87).

Bibliography

Primary and Secondary Sources

Frank, Frederick S. "Horace Walpole," in *Guide to the Gothic: An Annotated Bibliography of Criticism* and *Guide to the Gothic II: An Annotated
Bibliography of Criticism, 1983-1993*. Lanham, MD: UPA/Scarecrow P,
1984. 40-48; 1995: 86-93.

Hazen, Allen T. *A Bibliography of Horace Walpole*. New Haven, CT: Yale
UP, 1948.

——. *A Catalogue of Horace Walpole's Library*. 3 vols. New Haven, CT:
Yale UP, 1969.

McNutt, Dan J. "Horace Walpole, 4th Earl of Orford (1717-1797)," In
*The Eighteenth-Century Gothic Novel: An Annotated Bibliography of
Criticism and Selected Texts*. New York & London: Garland P, 1975.
136-165.

Spector, Robert D. "The Beginnings: Horace Walpole and Clara Reeve"
In *The English Gothic: A Bibliographic Guide to Writers from Horace
Walpole to Mary Shelley*. Westport, CT: Greenwood P, 1984: 83-98.

Articles and Essays on *The Castle of Otranto* and *The Mysterious Mother*

Ames, Diane S. "Strawberry Hill: Architecture of the 'as if.'" *Studies in
Eighteenth-Century Culture* 8 (1979): 353-363.

Baines, Paul. "'This Theatre of Monstrous Guilt': Horace Walpole and
the Drama of Incest." *Studies in Eighteenth-Century Culture* 28 (1999):
287-309.

Bedford, Kristina. "'This Castle Hath a Pleasant Seat': Shakespearean
Allusion in *The Castle of Otranto*." *English Studies in Canada* 14
(1988): 415-435.

Bentman, Raymond. "Horace Walpole's Forbidden Passion," in *Queer
Representations; Reading Lives, Reading Cultures*. Ed. & intro. Martin
Duberman. New York: New York UP, 1997: 276-289.

Brandenberg, Alice S. "The Theme of *The Mysterious Mother*." *Modern
Language Quarterly* 10 (1949): 464-474.

Campbell, Jill. "'I Am No Giant': Horace Walpole, Heterosexual Incest,
and Love among Men." *The Eighteenth Century: Theory and Interpretation* 39 (1998): 238-260.

Clery, E.J. "Against Gothic," in *Gothick Origins and Innovations*. Eds. Allan Lloyd Smith and Victor Sage. Amsterdam & Atlanta, GA: Rodopi; Costerus New Series 91, 1994: 34-43.

Conant, Kenneth J. "Horace Walpole and the Gothic Revival." *Old Wedgwood* 12 (1945): 62-69.

Conger, Syndy M. "Faith and Doubt in *The Castle of Otranto*." *Gothic: The Review of Supernatural Horror Fiction* 1 (1979): 51-59.

Crook, J.M. "Walpole's 'little Gothic castle': The Ups and Downs of Strawberry Hill, and its Future." *Times Literary Supplement* 28 February 1997: 15.

Dole, Carol M. "Three Tyrants in *The Castle of Otranto*." *English Language Notes* 26 (1988): 26-35.

Ehlers, Leigh A. "The Gothic World as Stage: Providence and Character in *The Castle of Otranto*." *Wascana Review* 14:2 (1980): 17-30.

Frank, Frederick S. "Proto-Gothicism: The Infernal Iconography of Walpole's *Castle of Otranto*." *Orbis Litterarum* 41 (1986): 199-212.

Haggerty, George. "Literature and Homosexuality in the Late Eighteenth Century: Walpole, Beckford, and Lewis," in *Homosexual Themes in Literary Studies*. Eds. Wayne R. Dynes, Stephen Donaldson. New York: Garland P, 1992: 167-178. Essay reprinted from *Studies in the Novel* 18 (1986): 341-352.

Hirai, Masako. "Burke's Sublime and *The Castle of Otranto*: The Gothic Image and the Novel." *Kobe College Studies* 40:3 (1994): 1-12.

Hogle, Jerrold E. "The Ghost of the Counterfeit in the Genesis of the Gothic," in *Gothick Origins and Innovations*. Eds. Allan Lloyd Smith and Victor Sage. Amsterdam & Atlanta, GA: Rodopi; Costerus New Series 91, 1994: 23-33.

Holzknecht, Karl J. "Horace Walpole as Dramatist." *South Atlantic Quarterly* 28 (1929): 174-189.

Johnson, Anthony. "Gaps and Gothic Sensibility: Walpole, Lewis, Mary Shelley, and Maturin," in *Exhibited by Candlelight: Sources and Developments in the Gothic Tradition*. Eds. Valeria Tinkler Viviani, Peter Davidson, Jane Stevenson. Amsterdam: Rodopi, 1995: 7-24.

Kahn, Madeleine. "'A By-Stander Often Sees More of the Game Than Those That Play': Ann Yearsley Reads *The Castle of Otranto*." *Bucknell Review* 42 (1998): 59-78.

Kallich, Martin. "Houghton Hall: The House of the Walpoles." *Papers on Language and Literature* 4 (1968): 360-369.

Lewis, Paul. "*The Atheist's Tragedy* and *The Castle of Otranto*: Expressions of the Gothic Vision." *Notes & Queries* 25 (1978): 52-54.

Lewis, Wilmarth S. "The Genesis of Strawberry Hill." *Metropolitan Museum Studies*, 5:1 (1934): 57-92.

——. "Horace Walpole Reread." *Atlantic Monthly*, July 1945: 48-51.

Magnier, Mireille. "Sir Horace Walpole: *Le Château d'Otrante*, ébauche d'un retour au moyen âge des merveilles." *Mythes, Croyances, et Religions dans le Monde Anglo-Saxon* 2 (1984): 55-65. [*The Castle of Otranto*, Rough Draft of a Return to the Marvellous Middle Ages].

"March 2nd, 1797: Death of Horace Walpole, 'Gothick' Man of Letters." *History Today* 47: 3 (1997): 33.

McKinney, David. "'The Castle of my Ancestors': Horace Walpole and Strawberry Hill." *British Journal for Eighteenth-Century Studies* 13 (1990): 199-214.

McWhir, Anne. "The Gothic Transgression of Disbelief: Walpole, Radcliffe, and Lewis," in *Gothic Fictions: Prohibition / Transgression.* Ed. Kenneth W. Graham. New York: AMS Press, 1989: 29-47.

Miller, Norbert. *Strawberry Hill, Horace Walpole und die ästhetik der schönen unregelmässikeit.* Munchen: Hanser, 1986. [Strawberry Hill, Horace Walpole and the Aesthetik of the Beautiful Irregularity.]

Morrissey, Lee. "'To Invent in Art and Folly': Postmodernism and Walpole's *Castle of Otranto*." *Bucknell Review* 41 (1998): 86-99.

Perkinson, Richard H. "Walpole and a Dublin Pirate." *Philological Quarterly* 15 (1936): 391-400.

Quennell, Peter. "The Moon Stood Still on Strawberry Hill." *Horizon Magazine* 11 (1969): 113-119.

Riely, John. "*The Castle of Otranto* Revisited." *Yale University Library Gazette* 53 (1978): 1-17.

Rose, Edward J. "'The Queenly Personality': Walpole, Melville, and Mother." *Literature and Psychology* 15 (1965): 216-229.

Rutherford, S. "*The Castle of Otranto*." *The Teaching of English* 3 (1993): 38-44.

Samson, John. "Politics Gothicized: The Conway Incident and *The Castle of Otranto*." *Eighteenth-Century Life* 17 (1986): 145-153.

Smith, Warren Hunting. "Strawberry Hill and *Otranto*." *Times Literary Supplement* 23 May 1936: 440.

Solomon, Stanley J. "Subverting Propriety as a Pattern of Irony in Three Eighteenth-Century Novels: *The Castle of Otranto, Vathek*, and *Fanny Hill*." *Erasmus Review* 1 (1971): 107- 116.

Stevenson, John Allen. "*The Castle of Otranto*: Political Supernaturalism," in *The British Novel, Defoe to Austen: A Critical History*. Boston: Twayne/G.K. Hall, 1990: 90-109.

Summers, Montague. "Strawberry Hill Castle." *Everybody's Weekly* 4 September 1943: 11-12.

Svilpis, J.E. "Coupling and Transgression in *The Castle of Otranto* and *The Monk*." *Transactions of the Samuel Johnson Society of the Northwest* 16 (1985): 101-106.

Thacker, Christopher. "That Long Labyrinth of Darkness," in *The Wildness Pleases: The Origins of Romanticism*. London: Croom Helm; New York: St. Martin's P, 1983: 111-128.

W., C. "Origin of '*The Mysterious Mother*,'" *New Monthly Magazine and Universal Register* 1:10 (September, 1818): 109.

Watt, Ian. "Time and the Family in the Gothic Novel: *The Castle of Otranto*." *Eighteenth-Century Life* 10 (1986): 159-171.

Wein, Toni. "Tangled Webs: Horace Walpole and the Practice of History in *The Castle of Otranto*." *English Language Notes* 35 (1998): 12-22.

Whyte, S. "On the Plot of Lord Orford's *Mysterious Mother*." *Monthly Mirror* 11 (1801): 187-191.

Books, Book Chapters, Doctoral Dissertations and Sections in Books and Essay Collections on *The Castle of Otranto* and *The Mysterious Mother*

Auffret-Boucé, Hélène. "Contraintes et libertés du désir dans *The Castle of Otranto* (1765) d'Horace Walpole" [Constraints and Liberties of Desire in *The Castle of Otranto*] In *Contraintes et libertés dans le Grand-Bretagne du XVIIIᵉ siècle*. Ed. Paul-Gabriel Boucé. Paris: Pubs. de la Sorbonne, 1988: 109-124.

Bentman, Raymond. "Horace Walpole's Forbidden Passion," in *Queer Representations; Reading Lives, Reading Cultures*. Ed. & Intro. Martin Duberman. New York: New York UP, 1997: 276-289.

Botting, Fred. "Gothic Forms: *The Castle of Otranto*," in *Gothic*. London & New York: Routledge, 1996: 48-54.

Brantlinger, Patrick. "Gothic Toxins: *The Castle of Otranto*, *The Monk*, and *Caleb Williams*," In *The Reading Lesson: The Threat of Mass Literacy in Nineteenth-Century British Fiction*. Bloomington: Indiana UP, 1998: 46-68.

Clark, Sir Kenneth. "Ruins and Rococo: Strawberry Hill," in *The Gothic Revival: An Essay in the History of Taste*. London: Constable, 1928; Rpt. Harmondsworth: Penguin, 1964: 34-52.

Clemens, Valdine. "Sexual Violence and Woman's Place: *The Castle of Otranto*," in *The Return of the Repressed: Gothic Horror from The Castle of Otranto to Alien*. Albany, NY: SUNY Albany P, 1999: 29-40.

Clery, Emma. "Against Gothic," in *Gothick Origins and Innovations*. Eds. Allan Lloyd Smith, Victor Sage. Amsterdam & Atlanta, GA: Rodopi; Costerus New Series 91, 1994: 34-43.

Davenport-Hines, Richard. "'The Dead Have Exhausted Their Power of Deceiving': *The Castle of Otranto*," in *Gothic: 400 Years of Excess, Horror, Evil, and Ruin*. London: Fourth Estate, 1998: 135-150.

Ellis, Markman. "Reading gothic histories: Walpole's *The Castle of Otranto*," in *The History of Gothic Fiction*. Edinburgh: Edinburgh UP, 2000: 27-37.

English, Sarah Warder. "The Hunger of the Imagination: A Study of the Prose Style of Four Gothic Novels." *Dissertation Abstracts International* 39 (1979): 6773A-6774A (University of North Carolina).

Evans, Bertrand. "The First Gothic Plays: *The Mysterious Mother*," in *Gothic Drama from Walpole to Shelley*. Berkeley & Los Angeles: U of California P, 1947: 31-48.

Frank, Frederick S. "Horace Walpole's *The Castle of Otranto: A Gothic Story*," in *Survey of Modern Fantasy Literature*. Ed. Keith Neilson. Englewood Cliffs, NJ: Salem P, 1983: 211-216.

Gardner, Elizabeth. *The Gothic Novel: Horace Walpole, The Castle of Otranto, Jane Austen, Northanger Abbey, Henry James, The Turn of the Screw*. Willoughby, New South Wales: Deed P, 1993.

Gray, Jennie. *Horace Walpole and William Beckford: Pioneers of the Gothic Revival*. Chislehurst, UK: The Gothic Society. Monograph Series 1, 1994.

Harfst, Betsy Perteit. *Horace Walpole and the Unconscious: An Experiment in Freudian Analysis*. New York: Arno P, 1980.

Havens, Munson A. *Horace Walpole and the Strawberry Hill Press*. Canton, PA: Kirgate P, 1901.

Hogan, Charles Beecher. *Horace Walpole: Writer, Politician, and Connoisseur. Essays on the 250th Anniversary of Walpole's Birth*. Ed. Warren Hunting Smith. New Haven, CT: Yale UP, 1967. 227-240.

Jacobs, Edward H. "Horace Walpole and the Culture of Triviality," in *Accidental Migrations: An Archeology of Gothic Discourse*. Lewisburg, PA & London: Bucknell UP & Associated University Presses, 2000: 123-156.

Kallich, Martin. *Horace Walpole*. New York: Twayne, 1971.

Lévy, Maurice. "Lectures plurielles du *Château d'Otrante*," in *La Mort, le fantastique, le surnaturel du XVIᵉ siècle a l'epoque romantique*. Lille: Université de Lille, Centre de Recherches sur Angleterre des Tudors à la Regence, 1980: 149-153. [Plural Reading of *The Castle of Otranto*].

Norton, Rictor. "The *Castle of Otranto*, Horace Walpole," in *Gothic Readings, The First Wave, 1764-1840*. London & New York: Leicester UP, 2000: 2-7.

Sabor, Peter. *Horace Walpole: The Critical Heritage*. London & New York: Routledge & Kegan Paul, 1987.

——. "'An old tragedy on a disgusting subject': Horace Walpole and *The Mysterious Mother*," in *Writing and Censorship in Britain*. Ed. Paul Hyland and Neil Sammells. London & New York: Routledge, 1992: 92-106.

Van Luchene, Stephen R. "Essays in Gothic Fiction: From Horace Walpole to Mary Shelley." *Dissertation Abstracts International* 34 (1974): 4220A-4221A (Notre Dame University). Republished under the same title by Arno Press, 1980.

Varma, Devendra "Horace Walpole," in *Supernatural Fiction Writers*. Vol I. Ed. E.F. Bleiler. New York: Charles Scribner's, 1985: 131-137.

Watt, James. "Origins: Horace Walpole and *The Castle of Otranto*," in *Contesting the Gothic: Fiction, Genre, and Cultural Conflict, 1764-1832*. Cambridge, UK: Cambridge UP, 1999: 12-41.

Welcher, Jeanne K. "The Literary Opinions of Horace Walpole." Doctoral Dissertation, Fordham University, 1954.

Introductions to Previous Editions of *The Castle of Otranto* and *The Mysterious Mother*

Bleiler, E.F. "Introduction" to *Three Gothic Novels: The Castle of Otranto, Vathek, The Vampyre*. New York: Dover, 1966: vii-xviii.

Clery, E.J. "Introduction" to *The Castle of Otranto: A Gothic Story*. Oxford & New York: Oxford UP, 1996: vii-xxxiii.

Dolan, Janet A. "Introduction," "Horace Walpole's *The Mysterious Mother*: A Critical Edition," *Dissertation Abstracts International* 31 (1971): 4115A-4116A (University of Arizona): x- lxiv.

Doughty, Oswald. "Introduction" and "Notes" to *The Castle of Otranto*. London: Scholartis, 1929: iv-xvii.

Lewis, W.[ilmarth] S. "Introduction" and "Explanatory Notes and a Note on the Text" of *The Castle of Otranto* by Joseph W. Reed, Jr. London: Oxford UP, 1969.

Mack, Robert. "Introduction" to *The Castle of Otranto and Hieroglyphic Tales*. London: Everyman / J.M. Dent, 1993; Rutland, VT: Charles E. Tuttle, n.d: xi-xxvii.

Praz, Mario. "Introductory Essay" in *Three Gothic Novels*: *Walpole/The Castle of Otranto*, *Beckford/Vathek*, *Mary Shelley/Frankenstein*. Baltimore: Penguin, 1973: 7-34.

Sabor, Peter, ed. *The Works of Horatio Walpole, Earl of Orford, 1798*. From the 1798 edition. London: Pickering & Chatto, 1998.

Spector, Robert D. "Introduction" to *Seven Masterpieces of Gothic Horror*. New York: Bantam, 1963: 1-11. The first "masterpiece" is *The Castle of Otranto*.

Summers, Montague. "Introduction" to *The Castle of Otranto* and *The Mysterious Mother*. London: Houghton Mifflin & Constable, 1925: xi-lvii.

Wright, Andrew. "Introduction" to *The Castle of Otranto*, *The Mysteries of Udolpho*, and *Northanger Abbey*. New York: Holt, Rinehart, Winston, 1963: vii-xxi.

Websites and Internet Resources

Gothic Literature. <http://www2.gasou.edu/facstaff/dougt/gothic.html>. Maintained by Douglass H. Thomson.

The Gothic Literature Page. <http://members.aol.com/iamudolpho/basic.html>. Maintained by Franz Potter.

The International Gothic Association. <http://www-sul.stanford.edu/mirrors/romnet/iga/>.

Lewis Walpole Library, Yale University. <http://www.library.yale.edu/Walpole/index.htm>

The Literary Gothic. <http://www.Litgothic.com/>. Maintained by Jack G. Voller.

Materials for Gothic Studies. <http://www.engl.virginia.edu/~enec981/Group/Title.html>. Maintained by The University of Virginia.

The Sickly Taper. Current Walpole Bibliography. <http://www.toolcity.net/~ffrank/Index.html>. Maintained by Fred Frank.

Walpole Online. <http://www.cottagesoft.com/~felis/library/otranto/otranto.html>

Using 896 lb. of Rolland Enviro100 Print instead
of virgin fibres paper reduces your ecological footprint of:

Trees: 8
Solid waste: 484lb
Water: 4,568gal
Suspended particles in the water: 3.1lb
Air emissions: 1,063lb
Natural gas: 1,107ft³